THE FALL OF THE DAGGER

"A sorcerous artefact concocted by Va-forsaken heathens and you *dare* to bring it here, into my palace?"

His reaction caught Lord Juster by surprise. She saw the flicker of amazement cross his face, followed immediately by a rueful recognition of how much he had erred. He went back down on one knee.

"If I have offended, sire, it is out of a desire to please you. It is but a toy—"

"You would give your king a toy?" Masterton asked, enraged. "As if he is a child to be humoured?"

"I thought to give my liege a work of art!"

"It's a work of Pashali heathens. A corruption that defiles our sight," the king roared. "You have brought an abomination into our company!"

She winced. She had not thought Edwayn had the strength left in him to express himself with such volume and with such passionate vituperation. Juster was in dire trouble.

"Masterton?"

"Yes, sire?"

"Why did you bother me with all this?" In the blink of an eye, rage was replaced by the petulance of a child. He sank back against the chair, just a wizened old man again.

She hoped he'd forgotten his anger, but his next words gave the lie to that thought and her hopes plunged still further. "Seize Dornbeck's ships and property and behead him in the morning. And now will someone help me to my bed?"

By Glenda Larke

The Mirage Makers
Heart of the Mirage
The Shadow of Tyr
Song of the Shiver Barrens

The Stormlord trilogy
The Last Stormlord
Stormlord Rising
Stormlord's Exile

The Forsaken Lands
The Lascar's Dagger
The Dagger's Path
The Fall of the Dagger

The Fall of the Dagger

GLENDA LARKE

www.orbitbooks.net

ORBIT

First published in Great Britain in 2016 by Orbit

Copyright © 2016 by Glenda Larke

Maps copyright © 2013 by Perdita Phillips

Excerpt from *The Falcon Throne* by Karen Miller
Copyright © 2014 by Karen Miller

The moral right of the author has been asserted.

A CIP catalogue record for this book is available from the British Library.

ISBN 978-0-356-50271-7

Typeset in Minion by Palimpsest Book Production Limited,
Falkirk, Stirlingshire
Printed and bound in Great Britain by CPI Group (UK) Ltd,
Croydon, CR0 4YY

Papers used by Orbit are from well-managed
forests and other responsible sources.

 MIX
Paper from
responsible sources
FSC
www.fsc.org FSC® C104740

Orbit
An imprint of
Little, Brown Book Group
Carmelite House
50 Victoria Embankment
London EC4Y 0DZ

An Hachette UK Company
www.hachette.co.uk

www.orbitbooks.net

*For all my Malaysian family who made
me welcome when I came to live among
them, especially my Malaysian sister,
Norsham, with love.*

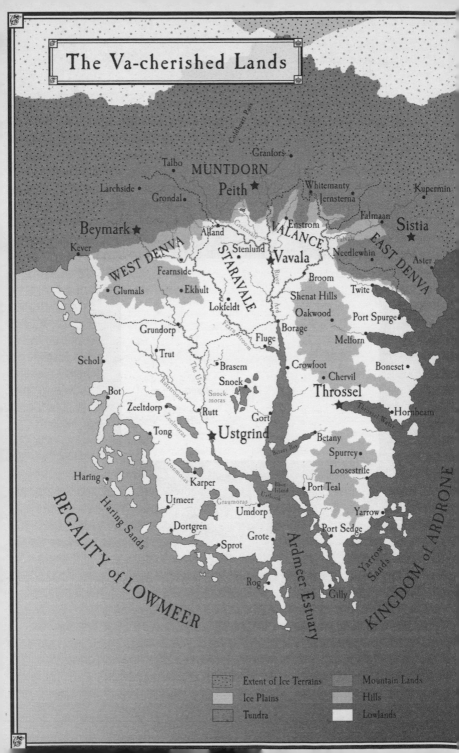

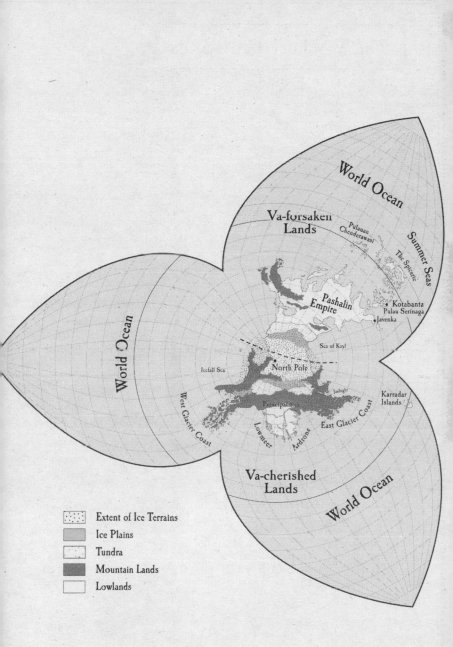

World Ocean

Va-forsaken
Lands

Summer Seas

Pulauan
Chenderawasi

The Spicerie

Pashalin
Empire

Kotabanta
Pulau Serinaga

Javenka

Sea of Kzyl

Icefall Sea

North Pole

West Glacier Coast

Jaihght

East Glacier Coast

Karradar
Islands

World Ocean

Principalities

Loenneer

Ardrone

Va-cherished
Lands

World Ocean

Extent of Ice Terrains
Ice Plains
Tundra
Mountain Lands
Lowlands

1

The Fall of Vavala

Pontifect Fritillary Reedling stood on the terrace overlooking the white-walled city of Vavala, her gaze fixed on the most distant roofs. When a breeze stirred the strands of her grey hair straying from the confines of her coif, she brushed them away from her face in irritation. Next to her, Barden, her private secretary, leaned against the balustrade for support, his breathing as noisy as the huffing of bellows. Waiting behind them were the only two remaining members of her guard, Hawthorn and his aide, Vetch, neither of them quite young enough, or fit enough, to provide her with any protection other than the wisdom of advice.

A cerulean sky was almost cloudless. Spiralling up into the blue, a songbird poured a joyous melody into the spring air to entice his mate and threaten his rivals.

A perfect day, a day to feel good about being alive.

Except it held no promise that any of them would live long enough to see another sunrise.

A puff of smoke rose above the distant buildings, silent and silky white, followed a moment later by an explosion that overwhelmed the birdsong and tore the air apart. The foundations below their feet quivered. A distant cloud of dust and debris lifted into the air, blossomed outwards with the beauty of an unfolding flower, then rained down on the city with an ugly roar. Fritillary winced and looked away.

"Cannon," Vetch said unnecessarily.

"It was only a matter of time," said Hawthorn. "The sole unanswered question is where they got them." Cannon were rare in the Va-cherished lands.

"Raided the gun decks of one of the king's galleons?" Vetch suggested.

1

"Imported by mastodon across the ice from Pashalin, more likely," Fritillary said. "With the gunpowder to fire them."

"Va-less curs." Another unnecessary mutter from Vetch.

Silence returned.

Below, the streets were eerily empty, the houses shuttered, the chimneys cold, the doors closed. The only living thing within her sight was a cat, which a moment ago had been sunning itself on a doorstep with undisturbed aplomb. Now it was scrabbling up a wall in fright. In the distance to the north, another rumble of cannon fire was followed by a brief silence as the world held its breath, then a second jarring, heart-wrenching impact that shattered her soul.

Her city. Her failure.

She had long since given the order for civilians to evacuate, to flee across the river to Staravale, leaving only those prepared to fight alongside the city guard and the soldiers of the Pontificate. *Her* soldiers.

In truth, she had asked them to die so that others could escape. So far, they had held the walls, but that wouldn't last.

Another cannonball shot, another hit, another puff of dust and smoke, more birds rising with startled cries into the sky. By the sound of it, the besiegers only had several light cannon, but pound away at the northern gate for long enough, and it would eventually splinter. Lob explosive-filled balls over the wall and defenders would die.

We've lost.

So where are you, Va? Are we the Forsaken Lands now? She sighed. There she was, blaming Va. How ridiculous was that?

The minutes dragged by. More cannon fire, more sounds of a city falling, brick by brick, tile by tile. Man by man.

"Your Reverence, it's time." Hawthorn, nagging as usual. Unable to fight because of his failing eyesight, but still desperate to protect her.

"Not yet."

"He's right," Barden said.

"Soon." She couldn't leave, not until she was sure all was lost. *My city. My resplendent city.*

In the street below, a horse swung into the main palace thorough-fare bearing a man in the uniform of her palace guard. They all watched in silence as he rode at a gallop into the forecourt through the open gate, halted his mount at the foot of the stairs to the terrace, then flung himself off to take the steps three at a time. A makeshift bandage on one of his arms partially covered a tattered sleeve drenched in blood.

He was young. Seventeen? Eighteen? Too young to have endured all he must have seen and done that day.

"Reporting from Captain Marsh," he said when he reached them, the words pitched too high, just short of panic.

"What's the latest?" She tried to sound calm, but rage and fear had tightened her throat until it ached.

His voice wavered as he answered. "The wall is breached to the north. The men are still fighting, street by street, but – it's just a matter of time."

"I can smell the burning." Wood, and worse. They could see it now, too; a plume of smoke carrying showers of sparks upwards. Why would they burn the city? Didn't he want to rule it, that sorcerous horror Fox? Valerian Fox. What good was a city to him if it was burned to the ground? "The shrine?" she asked. The lad would have passed it on his way to the palace. The city of Vavala had been built to encompass a spring that fed the River Ard and the Great Oak that grew there, the oldest and most sacred place in the whole Va-cherished Hemisphere, where the Way of the Flow and the Way of the Oak combined.

"Gone," he whispered. He was choking, forcing the words out as he struggled to control his emotion. "There's no sign of the oak."

She nodded. It was the answer she'd expected. "Have faith. It will return when times are safe." She patted his arm, despising herself for the futile pretension of both words and action, but she didn't know what else to do. How could you comfort someone who had indeed put their faith in Va, and in their Pontifect, only to be let down so badly?

He looked at her, appalled, and she was pierced to the bone by his horror. He could not conceive of a world where the oak was not a constant, a place to turn to in troubled times.

By earth and oak, what have you done to him and others like him, Fritillary?

3

"The evacuation?" she asked, and wondered at the blandness of her tone.

"Th – those who wanted to leave have gone. The captain says you must go now. He doesn't know how much longer he can hold against the Grey Lancers. The smutch—" He choked back a sob. "It makes men despair when they should be fighting. I saw—" He swallowed. "I saw grown men drop their swords and sink to their knees, weeping."

"You've felt the smutch?"

"We all have." He wiped tears from his begrimed face. "If Your Reverence had not sent the oak leaves, we would all have succumbed."

She had ordered every guard to place a leaf against his chest; she'd had sacred acorns distributed, hoping that would grant them courage, but, dear Va, Prime Valerian Fox was at the gates and he had grown in power. She shuddered to think how. Lord Herelt Deremer of the Dire Sweepers had told her that Valerian gained his greatest strength by draining his own ill-begotten sons. Possibly Herelt was right. She'd certainly believed him earlier, when he'd told her Fox sucked the life from children in order to add to his own life force, leaving them to sicken and die of the Horned Plague.

She took a deep breath. "Tell the captain I am leaving now. Tell him there are no further orders; he is to do what he thinks is best. Tell him Va is with us all in the end, and every man who fights here today will be remembered for all time."

But, oh, Va! Why have you not shown us how to combat this evil? What have we done that we are left so helpless?

Deceived by words, confused by the power of coercion and entice-ment that Prime Fox's numerous sons possessed, men and boys had flocked to the Prime's banner, like hens after a strutting rooster. Ordinary men made into willing, mindless automatons by sorcery. Even unseen guardians and shrine keepers, who were able to resist the coercion themselves, had been unable to combat the spreading evil. She had drained the coffers of the Pontificate in an effort to recruit and train the faithful, but there was only so much an ordinary man or woman could do when faced with sorcery. In desperation, she had swallowed her revulsion of all Lord Herelt Deremer stood for, and allied herself to him – but most of his resources and his men were in Lowmeer, not in the Principalities or the kingdom of Ardrone.

When the young guardsman had gone, she could not rid herself of the notion that she had sent him to his death. Bitterly, she accepted the truth of that thought, and turned to Hawthorn. "Sergeant, you and Vetch bring our packs to the postern door. Barden and I will meet you both there."

As she and her secretary headed through the palace halls, their footsteps and the tap of his wooden staff echoing in the emptiness, she muttered, "I was not born for this. I am no warrior."

"No one is born for war."

For once, he was moving fast alongside her, even with his bent back. His liver-spotted hand clasped the head of his walking stick, using it with a driving purpose. She blinked, surprised at his turn of speed.

"All it would have taken was a word from you," he said, and she heard condemnation in his tone. "You could have ordered those clerics blessed with witcheries to use them—"

"They would have lost their witcheries. Or died! Not now, Barden, not now." They'd had this argument a hundred times over the past year. Was it moral to use a Va-given witchery to kill? All she'd been taught, all she'd believed in, had told her witcheries were to be used for good, that to use one to kill was not only wrong, but would result in the loss of the perpetrator's witchery. While she would not have had the slightest compunction to do so to kill Fox or one of his tainted sons, the idea of using a witchery to slaughter farm boys and artisans tricked or twisted by sorcery into the Grey Lancer army was so repugnant that she had sent out her order: a witchery could be used to hide, or to escape, or to confuse, or to deceive the enemy. But not to kill or maim.

And they had *lost*.

"Men are dying today," Barden said, limping beside her. "Good men who might have lived if those with witcheries had felt free to use them to fight."

"Va is not in the business of slaughter and warfare."

"Va is not in the business of making it easy for evil to rule the world!"

Her stomach heaved. Obedience to her orders had led to defeat. *Sweet Va, please tell me I am not wrong. I cannot have been wrong.* The thought that her mistake might have killed her men, emptied the city and destroyed the Pontificate – no, it was unthinkable. Va would have told her if there was a better way, surely?

"Am I going too fast for you?" she asked coldly, even though he wasn't having any difficulty keeping up with her. Given his decrepit body and his advanced age, that didn't make sense, but she had no energy or will to think about it.

"No," he said as they descended the winding stair to the lowest level. Around them the stillness of the building was disconcerting; she had grown used to being surrounded by clerics and guards and civil servants and palace staff, all working to keep the Pontificate operating smoothly, but they had all gone now, some to fight, others to seek safety elsewhere.

I will not give up.

They were leaving nothing behind that would be of use to Fox. He might win a battle, but he wouldn't win the war. How could he? *Va . . .*

But Va was silent, leaving a bitter coldness in her heart.

She wasn't sure she believed her own words. *I don't know if Va is really with us. So what kind of Pontifect am I?* She fingered the acorn and the dried oak leaves in her pocket, and for one precious moment felt a surge of hope, of comfort.

Barden reached the postern door in the outer wall before her. His stride was confident, even though his back was still hunched over his walking stick.

Stride? He doesn't stride! He hobbles!

"What herbs have you been taking, old friend?" she asked as they waited there for Hawthorn and Vetch with their packs. "You are as frisky as a pup today." When he didn't answer, she added, "That's not your usual walking stick. Where did you get it?"

"I went to the Great Oak to pray yesterday. The shrine tree ate the old one, and gave me this staff in its place."

She stared in astonishment. "Are you jesting?"

He turned to look at her. "When have you ever known me to jest?"

"But . . ."

"I leaned my walking stick against the root of the oak. When I finished my prayers the root had grown around it, holding it tight. That's when the tree offered me a branch to break off." He held it up. "This. It's a staff, not a walking stick. With a smooth knob at the top to hold, and a rough heel at the bottom so it won't slip in the wet. You're the Pontifect. You explain it."

She couldn't think of anything to say.

"I have given the whole of my working life to the Pontificate," he said slowly, "and my heart has always been Shenat, though no Shenat blood flows there. I longed for a witchery, always knowing I would never have one. I never asked for a reward for my faithfulness, nor expected one, but I was granted it, nonetheless, on my last shrine visit. My back may still be crooked, my hands and knees still knobbled, but for the first time in years, I feel no pain and my tread is sure, my grip is strong."

She tried to hide her shock. "Did you speak to Shrine Keeper Akorna about this?"

"I did. She said a witchery is to be accepted without reservation."

"A *witchery*?"

"Her words." He raised his gaze to meet hers, and tears welled in his eyes. "In an unexpected form perhaps, but a witchery nonetheless. You are a stubborn woman, Fritillary Reedling. War is indeed an evil thing, but confronted with an even greater evil, you must make judicious use of *all* your resources. In this, you have made a mistake. You have hobbled your greatest advantage: your shrine keepers and all those with witcheries."

His words hit her in the gut like a fist, depriving her of words. Her witchery ability to hear honesty and to recognise a lie told her every word he spoke was true, at least to the best of his belief. She felt her life spin out of her control, disintegrating around her.

When Hawthorn and Vetch hurried up with their packs, Barden turned to slip back the three iron bolts on the door and lift the heavy wooden bar. Barden, who ordinarily could not keep up with her normal walking pace, or lift anything heavier than an inkwell or a clutch of papers.

It wasn't the time to continue the conversation. Instead, she slipped off her Pontifect's robe and her coif and dropped them on the paving. Underneath she was wearing the clothes of a working townswoman – ankle-length skirt, over-tunic and coat, all slightly grubby and well-worn. She tied a plain square of linen over her head as a scarf, took the key out of the door and nodded to Hawthorn. "Let's go."

Outside, the smell of burning was an assault. Hawthorn, who had picked up her robe and coif, shut the door behind them. She locked it and slipped the key into her purse, knowing the gesture was ridiculous; a locked door would stop no one for long. She said to Hawthorn, "This is where we part company, Sergeant." Her best chance at disappearing was to do so alone, not accompanied by uniformed guards. She gestured at the clothing he held. "I don't need that any more."

He halted a salute midway, and nodded instead.

"Go with Va," she said. "Both of you. Try . . . try to live to fight another day."

Barden was already swinging his way down the street supported by his staff, heading for the docks.

When she took one last glance behind as she strode after him, it was to see Vetch donning her robe and coif. She halted and called to him, but he just smiled and hurried away, the robe flapping around his feet.

Dear oak, she didn't deserve their sacrifice.

Before Va, I will win this fight. I swear it. But the thought echoed in her head like the growl of a toothless dog.

Hurrying after Barden as he disappeared around a corner ahead, she heard nothing to warn her anything was amiss until she turned into the side street that headed towards the riverside docks. She was confronted by the sight of Barden raising his staff in a gesture of defiance before two attackers. A doomed gesture, because the two men he faced were dressed in dirty grey uniforms and armed with lances.

She halted, paralysed, unable to think of how she could help, yet equally unable to flee, deserting him. This was Barden, who had been at her side in all her years as Pontifect, her guide, her mentor, her friend.

The taller of the lancers, a gauntly thin man, poked his lance at

Barden almost as if he was bored. "You can kill this one," he said to his younger, shorter companion.

Barden swung his staff at the stock of the older man's lance. His clout was weak, ineffectual. The lancer casually moved to deflect the thwack, even as his younger companion moved in to deliver a killing stab with his lance blade.

The staff flew out of Barden's hand, spinning so fast it was just a blur. It slammed into the younger man's face with a crack. He dropped where he stood, his lance tumbling from his hand. Half of his face was a bloodied mess of bone and skin, with teeth poking through his cheek. For a moment the older man stood, blinking in surprise, then he raised his lance with an angry cry, jabbing it at Barden with all his body weight behind what should have been a killing blow.

Barden, a frantic look of horror on his face, threw himself backwards to avoid the jab. His staff picked itself up off the cobbles and slammed against the knee of the older lancer to knock him off his feet. He landed with a bone-crunching thud.

Fritillary ran forward to help Barden up. The staff moved – by itself – lifting from the pavement into Barden's hand. With a look of heartfelt gratitude, he leaned on it. The older lancer, wailing as he clutched his thigh, rocked to and fro, his lower·leg at a strange angle. Blood seeped through the cloth of his trousers.

Barden looked down at the staff and ran a loving hand over its smoothed wood. "This," he said, "is my witchery." Looking up, he smiled at Fritillary. "I think we are done here. Neither of these fellows will fight again, methinks."

She took a deep breath, but said nothing. No words would come. Picking up her pack from where she'd dropped it, she followed Barden as he scuttled away from the wounded men like a three-legged spider.

Va help them, she'd been wrong. Horribly, disastrously wrong. Barden's walking stick, crafted from the wood of the living oak of the hemisphere's greatest shrine by an unseen guardian, told her that much. The knowledge was an indigestible lump of grief – and hope – in her insides.

As they approached the waiting barge a few minutes later, Barden's nose wrinkled with distaste. "Curdle me sour, what is it carrying?"

"Salted fish, I believe," she said. "It seemed an unlikely cargo for a barge bearing the Pontifect."

He glanced at her, puzzled. "You asked for a barge full of smelly sprats? But aren't we just crossing the Ard to Staravale?"

"That's what I wanted everyone to think. In fact, we are going to the last place anyone would think to look for the Pontifect, and the best place to be to get anything done."

He waited for her to explain, but she didn't oblige. At this stage, the fewer people who knew, the better. Instead, she said, "We have a war to win."

"No holds barred?"

She took a deep breath. "No holds barred. Va help us all."

2

The Eagle and the Oak

"Something's wrong."

The words, uttered by Saker Rampion, were said softly, but the chill of them iced the back of Ardhi's neck.

"Something is *definitely* wrong."

Ardhi looked upwards. Yes, there was the sea eagle, drifting effortlessly above, scarcely moving a wingtip. It had followed them all the way from Chenderawasi to the coast of Ardrone, often perched on one of the yardarms, sometimes fed fish by the sailors after Saker had assured them it was a bird of good omen.

A bird of the Summer Seas, irrevocably connected now to a man of Ardrone, by Chenderawasi *sakti*. Va-forsaken magic, these people called it, in their ignorance. Everything the bird saw and felt, Saker saw and felt too, though he often struggled to interpret it.

Even so, when Saker said something was wrong, not one of those standing on the weather deck of *Golden Petrel* was prepared to ridicule his assertion. His increased perception had proved invaluable on their journey home. He even had the ability to twin himself with the bird, to have his consciousness fly with the eagle and guide it. It meant leaving his body inert and unthinking and vulnerable, not something to be done lightly, especially as there was no guarantee he would or could return to it. Those times were the hardest, and they left Saker exhausted. Bird and man, they'd hated one another in the beginning as they'd fought the link, both wanting to be free and yet both incapable of breaking the tie the *sakti* had forged.

Ardhi had watched unhappily as the conflict gradually changed from a battle, to acceptance, to respect, but never to affection. It had been difficult for Saker to acknowledge that this wasn't supposed to be a punishment or a penance, but rather an added weapon in a magical arsenal, all part of the *sakti* protecting a Summer Seas archipelago from the rapine of invasion.

He looked back at Saker, worry niggling him. The man had paid a high price for that avian connection. The strain was etched into his face, visible in the troubled depths of his gaze as he laboured to maintain his humanity and his sanity. The only time Ardhi saw something of the man Saker had once been was when he played with Piper. Then his sorrow was banished and his eyes would soften with tenderness.

Sighing, he turned his gaze to the shoreline slipping past. Borne on a following breeze, *Golden Petrel* was making good time towards the royal city of Throssel, already visible in the distance. The larger buildings caught the afternoon sun, walls and towers aglow, glassed windows burnished. The royal standard flew from the palace's highest point, indicating the king was in residence.

"Over two years," Lord Juster Dornbeck muttered from where he stood behind the helmsman. "Anything could have happened in that time." The last news they'd had, in Karradar from a newly arrived Ardronese trader, had been four months old even then. The ship's merchant-captain had spoken of marauding bands of religious zealots called the Grey Lancers, and an argument between the king and his heir, Prince Ryce, which had left the king well-nigh blind. Pressed for details, the man had been vague. "We're from Port Sedge down south," he'd said. "What do we know of snotty nobles and sodding clerics up in Throssel?"

Now, looking at Saker gripping the bulwarks with both hands as if his life depended on his hold, Ardhi wondered if it hadn't been a mistake to come straight to the Ardronese capital. He couldn't help but think they should have stopped for news instead of bypassing the port of Hornbeam.

It would have been easy enough. Hornbeam was not far from the estuary's entrance to the open ocean, and Lord Juster had ordered his prizes, the two Lowmian ships they'd commandeered, to divert there while *Golden Petrel* sailed on to the royal city. Both of the captured vessels, ravaged by ship's worm, wallowed like pregnant sows even with the pumps constantly manned. Juster had deemed that the sometimes choppy tidal flows of the Throssel Water might prove the final fatal blow to their seaworthiness and had ordered them in for repairs.

"Saker," Juster said in answer to his remark about something being amiss, "cryptic utterances about things looking 'wrong' are not overly helpful. Could we have a comment, an elucidation of some sort, possibly a scintilla more . . . specific? You know, like perhaps that fobbing feathered spy of yours can see cannon aimed in our direction?"

"No, it's not that. It's the coastline – it's altered." Saker had appeared more puzzled than alarmed, but now his bewilderment changed to the shock of realisation. "The oak," he said. "The King's Oak. It's *gone*."

The words meant nothing to Ardhi, but all those within earshot on the weather deck blanched.

Juster glowered. "What do you mean? Shrine-oaks don't disappear!" When a reply was not forthcoming, he snapped out a stream of commands, sending seamen aloft with instructions to report anything out of the ordinary, then ordering the ship's boy, Banstel, to fetch the telescope from his cabin. "Saker, position that heap of feathers above the palace and tell me what it sees."

"What do you expect? It doesn't talk to me, you know. All I get is a picture."

Juster hesitated, obviously wanting Saker to twin with the bird, but when no offer to do so was forthcoming, he said instead, "A picture which you can interpret."

Saker sent an eloquent glance Juster's way, but a moment later the eagle tilted its wings and slid across the sky towards the palace, still several miles ahead of them.

When the telescope was produced, Lord Juster scanned the coast-line where the King's Oak shrine should have been. "That is . . . uncanny," he admitted. "I can't spot the oak, it's true. But I also can't discern signs that there's been a tree cut down. Or burned. It's just—"

"Not there," Saker finished. "All I could see was a kind of blur."

"A local ground mist?"

"No."

"Rattling pox, a fobbing great tree can't just *vanish*."

"This one has."

"Could it be the work of A'va?"

"How am I supposed to know?"

"You're the Shenat witan! You tell me!"

"I would have thought it impossible to wipe a shrine-oak from the surface of the earth, but that's what it looks like."

Ardhi edged away into the shadow of the mizzen mast, where he could unsheathe his kris and glance at the blade without them noticing. As always, when his hand closed over the bone of the hilt – Raja Wiramulia's bone, cleaned and carved by Rani Marsyanda, washed with her tears – he felt the anguish of his memories. And now gold flecks of the Raja's regalia gleamed fiery red in the blade, always a sign that trouble was close.

"What do you see?" The whisper came from behind him, making him jump. Sorrel, glamoured, had been standing there all along, blended into the mast. In spite of the *sakti* which allowed him to see through her witchery, he had not noticed her there. Simply dressed in a sailor's culottes and shirt, she was barefoot because she had been up on the rigging and, like him, preferred the firmer grip of unshod feet. As he watched, she changed the glamour that had blended her into the mast to her own appearance – except this time she clad herself in the illusion of a demure gown.

He smiled, amused at her successful deception travelling the length of the ship aloft without anyone spotting her. "*Si-nakal!* You imp! You know the captain hates you using your witchery on board." Juster Dornbeck didn't particularly like her clad as a sailor either, so it was just as well he'd have no idea that the glamoured dress she was apparently now wearing was all a sham.

"Fig on him! He's ready enough to make use of it when it suits him. What's the blade telling you?"

"It's unhappy," he said. "Nothing more than that." They were using the Chenderawasi language, as they often did when alone. She'd asked to learn it and now, speaking with an accent he thought charming, her grasp of the nuances of his island tongue never failed to delight him.

"Not good, then." She pulled a face.

"No. But did we expect anything different?"

She shook her head. "I'm frightened. I was scared even before I knew a shrine-oak could disappear . . ." Her gaze remained steady, but her words were poignant in their honesty.

His breath caught in his throat. "All – all we can do is our best."

"We can't afford to fail."

"No. But the Rani implied that our unity – our ternion – is a strength."

Her hand touched the small pendant at her neck. It was made of stoppered bambu and hung on a gold chain he had bought for her on one of the Spicerie islands. Inside the hollow were three tiny pieces of the old Raja's tail feathers, each imbued with his Avian *sakti*. Saker had two more pieces, but no one knew exactly how best to use that magic.

"Piper," she whispered, and the name summed up all her worries in one word. Her gaze slid away to where the child was playing on the deck with a rope doll made for her by one of the sailors. The dark curls of her hair flopped over her forehead. The prettiest of two-year-olds, she never would keep her bonnet on for more than a few minutes at a time. She looked up just then, saw Sorrel and waved the doll in her direction. "Look, Mama!"

Sorrel waved back.

If they failed . . . If they didn't use the *sakti* wisely . . .

He swallowed hard at the thought of what would happen. If the Chenderawasi circlet Piper wore around her neck failed to control the sorcerous blood she had inherited, she could follow in the footsteps of her father, Valerian Fox. Possibly even worse was the knowledge that – if they failed to contain the rampant greed of the Va-cherished Hemisphere – then the islands of the Summer Seas, his own included, would be devastated by the guns of Lowmian and Ardronese merchants. His people would lose their freedom.

"Our failures are all in the past," he said, striving to sound confident. "Yours, mine, Saker's – they were monumental, they delivered their lessons, but they are in the past. Now we are three, a ternion, united to succeed. The Rani said the ternion was our hope. We will rid *your* hemisphere of its sorcerers and we will persuade your leaders to treat *my* hemisphere with respect."

She could so easily have mocked his certainty; instead she arched an eyebrow and asked, "What do you know about my failures?"

"I know you married the wrong man. And I know you'll never do *that* again."

He grinned at her, and she punched him on the arm. "Only you could ever make me smile about that!" She shook her head at him and glanced over to where Lord Juster and Saker were still arguing. "They are being snippety with one another again."

"They enjoy it."

"Tell me, please," Captain Juster Dornbeck was saying, "what that flapping bundle of fluff and quills is telling you about the palace."

"It has a roof. Oh, and chimney pots."

"*Saker*—"

"Oak 'n' galls, my lord, what do you expect? The bird can't *tell* me anything! All I get is a picture of what it sees, and even then it is not interested in what interests *me*. All it ever wants to do is hunt, eat, preen and find a female it can mate with. Yes, I can order it here and there, and force it to do certain things, but I can't change its nature. Nor would I want to."

"You could do more. I've *seen* you do more."

"Yes, and you've seen what twinning with it does to me, too. I have to give up all of myself and be a bird . . . And I would beg you to consider this: I am never sure if I will be able to return. Every time it is a struggle to come back. Don't ask it of me, my lord, unless it is a matter of life or death."

They were gazing at each other, the captain rigid as he glared, Saker expressionless. Ardhi did not quite understand the subtleties of why Saker was sometimes formal with Juster Dornbeck and sometimes not; he suspected it was a game only the two men involved fully understood.

"One of the oldest oaks in Ardrone has vanished," Saker continued. "Which means that whatever has happened since we left here has been disastrous. We should take heed."

Juster gave a perfunctory nod and turned to the helmsman, Forrest. "We won't try for a berth tonight. Instead, let's anchor leeside of Beggar's Island. Just in case."

Ardhi raised a questioning eyebrow at Sorrel.

"That's the one anchorage close to the city that's safe from the palace cannon," she explained. Seeing his surprise at her knowledge, she added, "I was the Lady Mathilda's spy, remember? I learned a lot from eavesdropping."

"Best I keep to the middle of the waterway, mayhap, cap'n?" Helmsman Forrest asked. Even Ardhi knew that normally they would have run up close to the town, advertising their return.

"That would be judicious, I think." Juster glanced upwards to the sprinkling of seamen now on the top yards, but no one had reported anything amiss yet. Even so, he was scowling.

Later, as they slipped past the city in the last of the evening sunlight to anchor behind Beggar's Island, the lack of activity onshore was troubling. Ardhi knew from his time working dockside in Ustgrind that the return of a merchant vessel from Karradar or Pashalin was a matter for hubbub and bustle and rejoicing. Families would flock to see if their relatives among the ship's crew had returned safely. Brokers and bankers and city merchants would gather dockside to find out what was in the cargo. Carpenters and chandlers, sail makers, rope makers and coopers – they all thronged there too, hoping for business or employment. The return of a privateer after more than two years, especially one owned by a buccaneer as notorious as Juster Dornbeck, would normally have been celebrated throughout the city.

Yet, when they took turns viewing the docks and shoreline through the ship's spyglass, the people gathering dockside appeared subdued. Worse still, the usual flotilla of small boats seeking news from an arriving vessel was absent. No one approached *Golden Petrel*.

"Where the Va-less hells is my agent?" Juster asked half under his breath, his tone sharp.

No one had an answer to that.

Eight bells of the dog watch sounded just as they finished dinner. It had been a hurried meal, eaten in silence. Saker knew Juster well enough to know he'd been using the time to plan and he wasn't surprised when the captain asked Surgeon Barklee, Ardhi, Sorrel and himself to stay after the plates had been cleared. Grig Cranald might ordinarily have been asked to join them, but Grig was the officer on watch. Moreover, although their present anchorage was sheltered, tucked away behind the heaped boulders of the uninhabited Beggar's

Island, Juster was edgy anyway and had told Grig to inform the crew that no one was to sleep below that night.

Reeky hells, I don't blame him.

King's Oak had disappeared. Vanished as if it had never existed. Perhaps not as important as the Great Oak of the Pontifect's city of Vavala, King's Oak was nonetheless revered as one of the oldest of Shenat shrines. Because it served Throssel, the Ardronese capital, it had additional significance.

Something was deeply awry in Ardrone, and they were not well-positioned to deal with any threats. *Golden Petrel* was sorely under-manned. Splitting the ship's company up in order to sail three ships all the way home had meant the first mate, Finch Aspen, was no longer on board; he was in command of the captured prizes now in Hornbeam, along with a number of other members of the crew.

"What are you planning?" he asked Juster. "Because I'm blistering sure you aren't going to sit here and wait for the dawn."

"Of course not. I'm going to bend my knee to the king. But first I need more information. Barklee, you have a brother living in the docklands, right?"

"Aye, cap'n. He's an advocate for some of the merchants. My wife and bairns live with him and his wife while I'm gone." Barklee had married late in life and was itching to get back to his much younger spouse and their young children.

"Then I'll talk to him first." Juster looked across at Sorrel. "Tomorrow, I want that ev—" He stopped to glance at Barklee, then said, "I want Piper off this ship. It's no place for a child."

Sorrel stiffened at his words.

That evil man's bastard. That's what the captain had been going to say. He'd caught himself when he remembered Barklee had no idea of Piper's possible parentage.

She stood up, saying, "I still have every intention of taking her to the Pontifect, as soon as I can be on my way." When he didn't reply she added, "Right now, I had better check that Banstel has managed to get her to sleep."

However, before she could leave the wardroom, Grig Cranald appeared in the doorway to interrupt. "Cap'n, sir, a sailboat just approached the starboard bow. It looked like Master Rotherby's wherry, so I didn't sound the alarm, but it veered away at the last moment. Someone lobbed this on to our weather deck as it passed." He held out an oilskin packet.

Juster rose to take it from him with a nod. "Did you see Rotherby?"

"No, cap'n. I don't think he was on board. And the wherry headed back to Throssel, as far as I could tell. No lights. Reckon it didn't want anyone on shore to know it came here."

Juster opened the packet and took out the folded paper it contained. Face blank, he read the contents, then returned to the beginning and read it again as if he was having trouble believing what was written there. "It *is* from Rotherby, my agent, I'm sure of that, although he hasn't signed it. But—" He shook his head. "It's unimaginable. The news, I mean."

He glanced around the table, his expression a warning that none of them would like what he was about to say. "He writes that Prince Ryce has been removed from the line of succession in favour of his son, Prince Garred, who has been declared a ward of the Crown. However, Ryce refused to surrender Garred to the king's men, and fled to his northern seat, a keep near Twite, with his wife, Princess Bealina of Staravale, and their son. They are now under siege there. A place called Gromwell Holdfast. I was there once, with his highness. Rotherby also says the king has dismissed his advisory Council."

"So who's in char—" Saker began, then stopped. "Fox. Of course."

Juster nodded, his expression of distaste saying more than any words would. "Rotherby mentions, very politely, that Prime Valerian Fox is now Pontifect Fox. Pontifect Fritillary Reedling was killed when Vavala was taken by marauding Primordials about six months ago, and he was then unanimously elected to the post by the synod. So Fox, with the aid of his clerics, rules Va-faith throughout the Va-cherished Hemisphere. He's also governing Ardrone through his position as Lord Chancellor to King Edwayn."

A hammer blow of shock thudded into the centre of Saker's breast. "Fritillary *died*?"

"The letter does not mention exactly how," Juster said, sympathy softening his tone. He looked up from the letter. "I'm sorry. We both know that the post of Pontifect is for life, and they wouldn't have held another election unless she was dead."

Fritillary. He swayed, heart pounding. *Sweet Va.* "When did this happen?"

"He's not precise about how long Prince Ryce has been holed up in Gromwell, but the fall of Vavala was six months ago."

Saker gave a derisive snort. "One thing I can tell you, it wasn't marauding Primordials. They couldn't organise themselves long enough to agree on what to throw into a stew pot, let alone bring down a city. And I won't be convinced Fritillary's dead until I find someone who saw her corpse."

"There is a warning at the bottom of the letter. Rotherby says to watch out for armed men called Grey Lancers. There's more that concerns us too," Juster continued. "All spice cargoes have been declared the king's property. All ocean-going merchant vessels are now annexed for the use of the Royal Merchant Navy."

It was Cranald who broke the stunned silence that followed this news. "*Golden Petrel* included?"

"So it seems." Juster's grated reply left no doubt of how he felt.

"Well, fuck that for a possibility!" Cranald took a deep breath. "Not while there's a single one of us sailors left alive, cap'n."

"I appreciate the sentiment, Grig, but Edwayn is our king, so guard your tongue before you end up dancing from a gibbet." Saker was used to Juster's ability to separate his friendship for Grig Cranald, lover, from his captain's attitude to Grig Cranald, ship's mate, but even he found that remark harsh.

"And Lowmeer?" Sorrel asked, breaking the startled silence in the cabin. "What of Lowmeer?"

"Not mentioned." Juster took a deep breath. "Cranald, ready the pinnace, will you? I'm going ashore."

Grig continued to look appalled, but his reply was disciplined. "Aye, aye, sir."

"After I've left, move the ship further west of Curlew Cape. No lights. If we're lucky, no one will see you shift anchorage. It's a cloudy night."

"Aye, aye, sir. Will you be going ashore alone?"

It was obvious that Cranald would have given much to go with his captain, but as the senior officer on a ship that was short on crew, there was no way that could happen.

"I'll go with you," Saker said.

Juster snorted. "Don't be ridiculous! You were nulled. You were supposed to die, or at the very least be exiled, remember? You can just imagine what King Edwayn would say if you turned up at his gate. Fox, on the other hand, would be ecstatic at your crass stupidity. Anyway, I have something else I want you to do come sun-up. Your beaked and taloned messenger boy has to carry a letter to Port Hornbeam because I want Finch to sell the spice cargoes on our two prizes immediately. In Hornbeam, for whatever price he can get in his pocket."

Cranald gave a strangled sound of protest. "In *Hornbeam*? What kind of a price will you get in a tinpot port like Hornbeam?"

"More than I'll get in Throssel, it seems! Here the king will have it all, and apparently my ship as well. Or more likely Fox will, I wouldn't mind wagering. In fact, Mate Cranald, your orders are to make sure no one gets their hands on the nutmeg in our hold, either. You sail without me if it looks like any of the king's ships come near. Take the *Golden Petrel* to Twite. That's where we'll sell the nutmeg. I'll join you there overland, if you have to leave me behind. Understand? I'll give you my seal of authority, just in case – although I have every intention of returning to the ship before tomorrow morning."

Cranald flushed, probably with shock at being trusted with not only the ship, but with Dornbeck's seal. Saker guessed this was Juster's way of indicating he was not truly irritated with the man, and his previous annoyance had been to indicate the need to be circumspect when it came to matters of treason.

"Surely the king wouldn't take all your cargo," Sorrel said. "It makes no sense! You'd never make another voyage."

"But my *Petrel* would. My beautiful lady would sail without me." His voice filled with rage. "I'd sink her first."

"Is it wise to go to the king, then? If he's mad, and wanting to steal your ship—" she began.

"King Edwayn is my liege lord, and I must know that there is no way I can help him before I act against him."

Saker almost groaned. "If what your agent says is true, you're doomed, probably even before you reach the king. Fox wouldn't let you near King Edwayn. Believe me, you don't want to taste Prime Fox's brand of justice, nor lie in one of the cells in the king's keep."

"Nonetheless, Edwayn is my king. This is something I must do." His smile was more ironic than amused. "I may be a buccaneer, but I still have a sense of honour."

Saker did groan this time. "Now? Of all times?"

"Don't worry, witan. You'll get your money, I promise."

He had no idea what Juster meant and raised an eyebrow in question.

"You've forgotten? You won a wager, remember? Ten per cent of the cargo profits . . ."

"Sweet cankers! You weren't serious, surely." He'd beaten Lord Juster in a race to the top of the mainmast, a contest that had seemed asinine even at the time.

"I *never* jest about money. Or my honour – or my ship if it comes to that. But let's turn our minds to tonight . . ."

"I'll go with you, Lord Juster," Sorrel said. "I know the palace better than you, I feel sure. At night, by candlelight, my glamour is doubly undetectable. Should you find yourself in trouble, I'd be in a position to aid you."

Saker was appalled. "Don't be ridiculous, Sorrel!"

She arched an eyebrow in interrogation. "Oh? Would you like to explain why my offer is to be ridiculed? I seem to remember a time when you were happy enough to have it."

Oh, rot it! She was remembering him naked on the moor, he could tell. "If there is someone with a witchery, they will see the glow of your glamour."

"All the time that I was sneaking about the palace with a glamour," she said, "I was never detected because there was no one with a witchery at court. King Edwayn would never have agreed to your appointment if you'd had a witchery back then!"

"That's true," Juster said before he could think of a suitably sharp reply. "Your offer is accepted, Mistress Sorrel. Your knowledge and your witchery will be very useful. You, however, Saker, are definitely staying behind." He turned to Cranald. "Ask someone to bring up that gilded salt cellar from the orlop would you?"

The mate was flummoxed. "You're taking a *salt cellar*?"

"One does not visit the king after a long voyage without an expensive, ornate gift."

"I hardly think—" Saker began.

"Do not presume to advise me on how to conduct my relationship with my liege lord, Saker. My family has a long history of service and loyalty, and I will not shatter that until I am certain I have justice and right on my side." He turned to Surgeon Barklee, who had been silent throughout the exchange. "I'd like you to come with me to your brother's house. I need as much information as I can get before going to the palace, and I am loath to involve Agent Rotherby at this point. He obviously does not want to draw further attention to our business arrangements."

"Of course."

"If all is well in your household, would your wife welcome another child into your home?" Juster asked.

Barklee shot an uncomfortable look at Sorrel, who appeared stunned. "You mean Piper?" he asked. "Mariet would be delighted. Nothing she likes better than surrounding herself with bairns to love—"

"Don't think to dispose of Piper like an unwanted piece of jetsam, my lord," Saker interrupted. "Not without consulting Sorrel. Or me. That is beyond—"

She touched his arm to silence him. "No. Wait. Go on, my lord."

"It's true I've never wanted her on board after I knew more of her . . . antecedents. But that has nothing to do with my suggestion now." He stood and went to look out the aft window of the wardroom, even though there was little to see in the darkness. "I fear what might happen to my ship tomorrow. Possibly there will be a fire fight. We passed three royal sloops-of-war anchored back there near the Throssel docks. They might be small, but they are fully armed and they're very manoeuvrable in waters like these, compared to us." He turned back to look at Sorrel. "You have experienced cannon fire, mistress."

Her silent regard was sombre.

"Piper would be safer with Barklee's family ashore," he continued. "He will stay with her. We can send Banstel as well. She adores that lad. If all is well, she can come back on board when we do, until more permanent arrangements are made. It's just a temporary measure."

She gave a reluctant nod. "If that is acceptable to Surgeon Barklee and his family."

The surgeon was quick to agree, and Saker, overruled, subsided. There was good sense in the idea, but he still didn't like it.

Juster turned to Cranald again. "You have your orders."

"Aye, aye, sir. Perhaps Master Ardhi and Surgeon Barklee would assist me with the salt cellar, seeing as we are short-handed?"

"And I'll change my gown while you do that," Sorrel said, and followed them out. Saker watched her go, worried. She was wearing her favourite blue dress, the one with the disturbingly low-cut bodice. As usual, she'd attempted to cover the tantalising plunge of her cleavage with the kerchief he had once given her, and, also as usual, he found the endeavour even more of a distraction. Worse, it made him feel uncomfortable, simply because it was Sorrel. Pickles 'n' hay, how long had it been since he'd bedded a woman? Far too long apparently . . .

His thoughts strayed to Gerelda, until he dragged them back to the present. "*Three* men to carry a salt cellar?" he asked, incredulous, after the others had disappeared below.

"It *is* heavy. A gilded automaton, with clockwork insides and a set of bellows that plays a miniature organ when you pick up the salt spoon. Utterly delightful Pashali workmanship. Shaped like a ship with blown glass rigging and sails—"

"Right. A gift fit for a king. But my lord, about Sorrel—"

"Don't say it, my friend," Juster said. "We're all in this together. You know that. You can't protect her. We work together or not at all."

"My head knows that, but sometimes—" He sighed. "And Piper? Piper's a child, my lord."

"She's a *sorcerer's* child. A devil-kin. Our hemisphere would be better off if both the twins died, and you know it. Now, tell me, will you be able to get that message to Finch in Hornbeam?"

"It's a long way, but I'll do my best." His stomach cramped. He'd have to twin with the sea eagle and he had no idea how often he could do that before his humanity was subsumed by the mind of a bird. A raptor, with a killer's instinct.

As he headed for the door, Juster said, "And the next time you start calling me 'my lord this' and 'my lord that' when you're peeved with me, I'm likely to duck you headfirst in a water butt."

Fob it, Saker. How do you manage to make everyone annoyed with you in the space of a few minutes? He took a deep breath and followed Juster up to the weather deck.

The night was dark, with a half-moon just a dim glow where it skulked behind thick cloud. Seamen cursed – albeit softly – as they winched one of the ship's boats down into water they could scarcely see.

A good night for sneaking around a town, Saker thought as he leaned against the bulwarks around the weather deck. He waited quietly, fingering the hilt of his sword. When Sorrel came up from below, the blue dress was gone, but even in the dark, he could identify her. By the standards of the Va-cherished Hemisphere, dressed as a man like this she was a hoyden, but he was reminded of a cat, graceful and limber. She spent a lot of time up in the rigging, and Ardhi had been teaching her to fight as they did in Chenderawasi. Both activities had developed muscles a woman wasn't supposed to have and he was appreciative.

She came to stand beside him, not speaking. Piper, warmly wrapped, was sound asleep against her shoulder.

"You're doing the right thing," he said quietly. "I do know that. I just find it hard to stay behind and wait, knowing you could be in danger."

"I know. That's what friends are for – to worry about us. To care."

"And to help, surely."

"Sometimes. But my glamour is my strength, and it is just as powerful as your sword arm, or your connection to birds. It serves me well."

"I know that, too, and I do understand why Juster feels he has to do this, but I suspect it's not going to end well. Expect the worst."

"I will. I do. If things go wrong, I have the pieces of the Chenderawasi tail feather."

The trouble was that none of them knew quite what to do with them. "Only to be used in the direst emergency," he said, and added wryly, "Accidentally swallowing one is not something I'd recommend." That had changed him, and he would not have wished the result on anyone.

Juster came out on the deck from his cabin, clad – as far as Saker could tell in the dark – in his best suit of clothes, complete with rings, brooches and an earring, and with his sword at his side. A moment later, Ardhi and Barklee emerged from below, lugging a wooden box between them.

"Good," Juster said. "I'll hire a couple of dock lumpers onshore to carry it to the palace for me. Get it loaded on the pinnace."

"He's daft," Saker muttered to Sorrel.

She gave a low laugh in amused agreement.

Several minutes later the pinnace pulled away, rowed by several sailors, with Surgeon Barklee, Banstel the ship's boy, Sorrel, Piper and Juster on board.

Ardhi came to stand beside Saker. "The sailors are going to wait for them at the docks until dawn," he remarked. "If they haven't returned by then, the men are under orders to leave for *Golden Petrel* anyway."

"And Grig will up anchor and head for Twite."

"Those are Juster's orders," Ardhi agreed neutrally.

"Hmm."

"What do you think?"

"Same as you, I suspect."

Cranald came to lean on the bulwarks next to Saker and Ardhi. "I can't leave the ship," he said. "And that fobbing bastard knows I won't."

"You do realise, don't you," Saker said softly, "that I don't have to be on the ship to persuade that bird of mine to go to Hornbeam. I can do that from the docks . . . the town . . . anywhere. Although I do have to wait for dawn, because it won't fly at night."

"I thought that might be the case." Grig paused and they all fell silent until the pinnace was well and truly swallowed by the dark. Then he added, "I think I'll order the men to launch the dinghy and leave it tied up to the pilot ladder. Just in case it's needed . . ."

Saker gave a shrug that fooled no one. "Excellent notion."

"This ship needs its captain." Grig's voice was unusually husky.

"I agree."

"I'm sure I can rely on you to do what's best."

As Cranald walked away, Ardhi grinned broadly. "Juster is going to be *very* angry with us."

"So you're coming with me?"

"Try and stop me!"

3

Loyalty and Royalty

"Are you there?" Juster asked softly.

Sorrel glanced back over her shoulder to make sure the two dock lumpers he'd employed to carry the salt cellar in its wooden box were not close enough to hear her reply. The hired torchbearer had already pulled further ahead so the taint of burning pitch no longer assailed Juster's nostrils.

"Right at your shoulder," she whispered.

He jumped. "Sweet nonce and hell's tomorrows! Do you have to curdle the blood in my veins?"

"Well, you asked."

He stared right through her and lowered his voice. "I can't see you."

"You're not supposed to. I'm very good at what I do."

"So I see. Or rather, don't see."

Afraid that the king would soon be abed if they tarried, she and Juster had not stayed long in the Barklee house. Her heart tight with fear for Piper, she took comfort from Mistress Barklee's apparent delight at having another child around. If the woman had been astonished to have her husband arrive back with a child and the ship's boy in tow, she hadn't let it show.

Information garnered from the surgeon's brother-in-law was mostly the same as that given in Agent Rotherby's letter, all of it more rumoured than confirmed. The man did blame the current troubles on Grey Lancers rather than Primordials, but could offer little information about exactly who they were.

"You see grey coats and lances?" he'd warned. "You don't linger. And you don't complain. Ever."

When Juster asked who led them, the man spoke of "black-clad gaunt men with doomed eyes", which the nobleman put down to scaremongering exaggeration rather than accurate description. Clearly, no one could predict the nature of his reception at the palace.

Few people were in the streets at that time of night. No one approached them, not when Juster thrust his cloak back to reveal his hand on the hilt of his sword. Together with the lanky torchbearer, who carried a cudgel as well as the burning brand, and the two burly dock lumpers, they were more than enough to discourage any cut-throat, but still she did not feel safe. The king had wanted her dead once and, as Fox was a sorcerer, it was possible he'd see through her witchery. Saker said even the Pontifect had been unable to use her witchery against the Prime.

Barklee's brother-in-law was an advocate, a lawyer, not a nobleman or a courtier privy to the comings and goings of the notables, but he had heard the Prime now lived mainly in Vavala as that was the seat of the Pontifect. She prayed his information was correct.

At the gates, the guards admitted Lord Juster through the small portal, and closed it after him before she or the hired men with the box could enter. She waited, alert, to one side, until a minute or two later two soldiers came out with Juster. He paid off all three hired men and asked the guards to carry the box inside. Sorrel sidled in behind them.

Within the archway of the gate tower, a pair of hanging candle lanterns battled to dispel the gloom. The balding watch commander, lips pursed, regarded Juster and the box unhappily.

"My lord," he said, "I'm sure His Majesty would be glad to see you come morn, but it's nigh near ten of the clock, and with his blighted sight, he retires early nowadays."

"His orders were for me to report the moment I returned," Juster said calmly. "Best that you leave the decision to His Majesty, or to his chamberlain." He smiled pleasantly. "You know me well, I think. Peebolt, is it not?"

"Yes, my lord. Tomat Peebolt. My uncle was a gamekeeper on your estate."

"I remember. Well, I'm sure you know I present no threat to His Majesty. If he has no wish to see me tonight, then I will ask for a bed and present myself to the king tomorrow."

The commander capitulated, and ordered two of the younger guards to accompany Lord Juster to the chamberlain's room in the king's solar, adding, "They can carry your gift."

They set off, the guards in the lead. Sorrel touched Juster's arm to tell him she was still with him. He nodded in acknowledgement, but didn't glance her way. She dropped a step or two behind, careful to keep her pace steady and perfectly blended to the background.

The solar was on the second floor, up two broad sweeping flights of stairs. She had only been into the inner chambers once – a night she preferred to forget – but she was familiar with the entrance room, which served as a reception chamber where people waited to be admitted to the king. It led into a much more impressive audience room with a line of tall windows down one side, dressed with velvet curtains.

At the entrance to the solar, there were two guards on duty, and here Juster halted, while one of these guardsmen checked to see if the king would see him. She chose to flatten herself against the wall because the uneven linenfold moulding of the wooden panels helped to disguise her outline.

Shortly afterwards, Conrid Masterton came bustling out of the solar. She knew him well enough by sight. When she'd been Lady Mathilda's handmaiden, he'd been the palace's resident prelate. She was appalled to see that now, although still clad in clerical robes, he was also wearing the elaborate chain of the king's chamberlain. The elderly, pragmatic man who had held that post previously had been replaced by a cleric who owed much to Prime Valerian Fox. Almost as bad, it was a deviation from the usual separation of Va-faith from political dominion.

"My lord." Masterton inclined his head towards Lord Juster in barely polite acknowledgement. "Welcome. The king expected you earlier this afternoon when he was told your vessel had been sighted . . ."

Frowning slightly, Juster stared at the chain, then, with deliberate disregard of its relevance, said airily, "Prelate Masterton. I had to make sure that my ship was well anchored. A captain's duty, you know."

"I believe the harbourmaster expected you to berth at the wharf."

"Oh? I was unaware of that. I would have done so if my agent had arranged it. But alas, there has been no sign of the fellow. Thus I fear this is a late hour to pay my respects to His Majesty. Is he perhaps already abed?"

"No. He awaits you." Masterton held open the door to the solar apartments and gestured for Juster to enter.

Juster, however, lingered to divert his attention in order to give Sorrel a chance to precede him. "My gift . . ." he said, and pointed to the box.

Hugging the wall, she slipped inside the reception room and glanced around. Besides several distant relatives of the king, there were a couple of young clerics she didn't recognise, and several men whom she guessed to be wealthy merchants, if the expensive foreign cloth and cut of their suits was any indication. Three or four servants were attending to their needs, bringing wine and food.

Still in the doorway, Juster beckoned to the guards. "Bring that box inside and unpack it, will you?" He waved them in without waiting for permission, even as he smiled pleasantly at Masterton. "A token of my esteem for His Majesty. Can't visit the king without a suitable gift from my travels, can I? Tell me, what happened to Chamberlain Brockhart? Passed away in my absence?"

"I'm afraid so," Masterton replied with a tight-lipped smile.

"Sorry to hear that. He was my mother's cousin, you know. Used to dandle me on his knee when I was a nipper. Delightful man, if a little pedantic. Can't be easy for you to be both chamberlain and prelate . . . surely you are overworked, Masterton! I shall have a word to say about that to my old friend, Prime Fox. Is he here tonight?"

"I'm afraid not. He's a busy man and had matters to attend to in the north. And it's Pontifect Fox now."

"Indeed? Yet I've heard he's been advising His Majesty in the capacity of Chancellor! Well, doubtless that will be just a temporary affair. We need our clerics to guard our spiritual well-being, not our temporal concerns, as you doubtless agree, Master Conrid. It must be *such* an imposition for you to be tasked with matters so mundane as civil administration when your talents are needed in matters spiritual!"

Sorrel almost laughed. Justified or not, nobles were experts at making their underlings squirm, even as a veneer of impeccable manners never wavered. Still, she wondered if Juster's words were wise. As he prattled on, each apparently artless, offhand comment as pointed as a sharpened dagger, he interspersed his remarks with greetings to the noblemen, requests for introductions to the merchants and exhortations to the guards to be careful not to break the glass of the gift. Masterton, barely able to insert a word in edgeways, looked increasingly irrelevant. All eyes were on Juster, and no one as much as glanced her way.

The guards lifted the salt cellar from the box and two of the servants, wide-eyed, bustled forward with a large silver serving tray to place it on. It was her first glimpse of the gift, and she was just as astonished as everyone else. *That* was a mere salt cellar?

It was a model of a three-masted sailing ship, as long as a man's arm from shoulder to fingertip. Mounted on a gold-plated base, the opened shell of a huge clam formed the hull. The deck, of exquisitely carved wood, supported an array of carved onyx cannons. The sails and rigging, crafted out of Javenka glass, glistened and shone. The crow's nest was studded with pearls, and flags of hammered silver topped each of the masts of polished horn.

For a moment even Masterton was dazzled into speechless admiration, but then he glared at Juster, saying, "The king awaits."

Juster flicked his hand at the prelate. "Then lead on, man. Lead on." Glancing back at the servants holding the tray, he beckoned them to follow. With all eyes on him and the magnificent present, Sorrel slipped ahead into the audience room, still unobserved. Even the king's personal bodyguard, standing by the door, did not look her way. She knew him. What was his name?

Brace, that's right. Willas Brace.

She'd never expected to return to the palace, never thought to come face to face with King Edwayn again. As she looked around, the cold of unwelcome memories turned her insides into a quivering mess. The last time she'd been here was the morning Mathilda accused Saker of ravishing her, and life had changed for all of them.

Blending herself against more of the solid oak linenfold panels, she stared at the king. Somehow she'd expected him to be standing;

instead he was huddled into a winged chair, more shrivelled than she remembered, not just older, but shrunken and frail. His right eye socket was empty and puckered, but his left eye, hardly more than a faded pearl nestling in a sunken hollow, could still focus if its glare in Juster's direction was any indication.

Not blind then, but not far from it either.

To her alarm, the room was ablaze with light, perhaps in an attempt to compensate for the king's poor eyesight. Every candle in the huge central chandelier was lit, as was every taper in the wall sconces. Mirrors had been erected on the walls where once there had been royal portraits. Aghast, she caught sight of her reflection in the one opposite where she stood, every detail of her appearance as clear as day. Fortunately, she was the only person looking at a mirror; everyone else had their gaze riveted on Juster. No one appeared to notice her entry into the room.

Don't be a goose, she thought, pulling herself together. *Of course you can see yourself in the mirror. But no one else can.* At least, she hoped that was right. Just to be sure and to remain unobtrusive, she slipped stealthily into one of the window embrasures and concealed herself behind the thick velvet of the drapes, adjusting them so she was peeping through the smallest of gaps between the two halves. There wasn't much space separating the curtains in front of her and the diamond panes of the leadlight window behind her. Her back was flat to the glass. If there was anyone in the gardens below who bothered to look up . . .

Don't be silly. If someone glanced up, they wouldn't know she was an intruder.

She concentrated on the scene before her. Tonias Pedding, Prime Fox's secretary, thinner and paler than she remembered, had been standing at King Edwayn's left, but was now elbowed aside by Masterton, who bent low to whisper something in the king's ear. A manservant hovered to the right of the king's chair. The Earl of Fremont, the man who had been the chief judge at Saker's trial, also more frail than she remembered, stood nearby, leaning on the back of an armchair occupied by one of Edwayn's second cousins, Lady Nerill. The grey-headed flat-chested woman standing next to her was her lady attendant, whose name Sorrel couldn't remember. Another two male clerics, strangers to her, stood side by side watching from the other end of the room. Ten people for her to keep an eye on . . . no, twelve. The two servants carrying the salt cellar had just entered. Brace, the bodyguard, closed the door behind them.

All eyes were on Juster, but no one greeted him. Brace did murmur something, and by way of answer Juster unbuckled his sword belt and handed it over, blade and all. That was new: no nobleman had been obliged to disarm in the king's presence in the past.

Juster marched across the room, and knelt on one knee before the king. He briefly bowed his head, then looked up straight at Edwayn as he spoke. "Your Majesty, greetings to my liege. I have returned with a cargo of spices for the health and prosperity of your kingdom. For Your Majesty, I bring a gift from far-off lands, worthy of a great monarch. I am also the purveyor of intelligence concerning the other side of the world and, alas, I have grievous tidings of the perfidy of sailors flying Lowmian colours."

"Your ship is forfeit," the king replied as if he'd heard nothing Juster had said. "All seagoing traders now sail under the flag of my house. You will berth *Golden Petrel* in the city docks. Your spices will be unloaded and sold by my agents. The proceeds will go into the royal coffers as taxes. Our land fights the Primordials and the heretics that assail us and our brave soldiers and the clerics who lead them need to be paid!"

Before Juster could marshal a coherent answer, Masterton intervened, his words smoothly suave. "Of course, my lord, you would still be captain of the vessel, but you will sail it under the king's orders, and be paid a fee from the king's coffers for your services. The land has need of sailors and merchants."

The king gave him a slightly puzzled look, but did not contradict him.

"Sire," Juster said, "*Golden Petrel* is my ship. Have I offended in some way that you should take her from me?"

"You supported my son! He has rebelled against my wishes. Ryce is a traitor to the Crown!"

"Sire, I know nothing of any of this. I have been away and heard naught of any disagreement between Your Majesty and Prince Ryce—"

"Do you think I did not see you two in collusion? Do you think

I did not hear how you and that – that – that traitorous spawn of my loins cooperated to wrench our naval forces out of my control?"

"But, sire, it was on your command that I aided Prince R—"

King Edwayn half rose from his seat, levering himself up, spluttering with rage. Spittle dribbled down his chin but he didn't appear to notice. "You dare to contradict your liege lord?"

Juster, still kneeling, did not move. "Never, sire," he said quietly, breaking a silence just before it evolved from a mere pause to an act of unpardonable rudeness. He bowed his head. "Whatever you order, this humble servant shall obey, as is my duty."

Sorrel almost snorted. She knew Juster better than that.

Edwayn fell back into the chair. Masterton once again bent forward to whisper in his ear. She wished she was close enough to hear, but there was no way she could risk moving, not in the bright candlelight, not when she couldn't be positive she would not be reflected in half a dozen mirrors.

The king's gaze switched from Juster to the salt cellar, still on its tray. The two servants holding it stood ramrod straight, faces expressionless.

"Bring that thing here," Edwayn ordered.

They crossed the room until they were level with Juster.

"Get up, get up, and explain this contraption to me," the king ordered, waving an agitated hand.

The buccaneer stood, more sober and restrained than Sorrel had ever seen him. "It is an exceptional example of Javenka glasswork, carving and gilding," he began. "A salt cellar I deemed precious enough to grace the table of the king of Ardrone. The salt is placed in the little mother-of-pearl dish, here, where it poses as the ship's longboat suspended above the deck." He pointed amidships. "The spoon for the salt is the oar, here. There's a delightful whimsy in this, sire. When someone picks up the salt spoon, it sets off a music box within the bowels of the ship, and also starts the automaton within, like this."

He raised the spoon from the miniature boat and the tinkling sound of a music box started up. Sorrel didn't know the tune, but it was unmistakably of Pashalin origin. At the same time, without Juster doing anything further, the silver flags – pulled, she guessed, on strings threaded through the hollow masts – dipped halfway down and then scooted up to the mast-tops again. The figure on the foredeck, clad in Pashalin costume and wearing a captain's ceremonial headgear, gazed ahead and raised an arm in salute. In the crow's nest, a sailor put his spyglass to his eye. Simultaneously, one of the cannon on the foredeck – no longer than a man's thumb – rumbled and gave off a puff of smoke.

The servants holding the tray nearly dropped it in shock. Lady Nerill gave a squeal that sounded more scared than amused, which made her lady companion produce a bottle of smelling salts to wave under her mistress's nose. The king pursed his lips and glowered.

Oh, fob it. He's working himself up into a rage.

"A Pashali monstrosity!" he cried. "A sorcerous artefact concocted by Va-forsaken heathens and you *dare* to bring it here, into my palace?"

His reaction caught Lord Juster by surprise. She saw the flicker of amazement cross his face, followed immediately by a rueful recognition of how much he had erred. He went back down on one knee.

"If I have offended, sire, it is out of a desire to please you. It is but a toy—"

"You would give your king a toy?" Masterton asked, enraged. "As if he is a child to be humoured?"

"I thought to give my liege a work of art!"

"It's a work of Pashali heathens. A corruption that defiles our sight," the king roared. "You have brought an abomination into our company!"

She winced. She had not thought Edwayn had the strength left in him to express himself with such volume and with such passionate vituperation. Juster was in dire trouble.

"Masterton?"

"Yes, sire?"

"Why did you bother me with all this?" In the blink of an eye, rage was replaced by the petulance of a child. He sank back against the chair, just a wizened old man again.

She hoped he'd forgotten his anger, but his next words gave the lie to that thought and her hopes plunged still further. "Seize Dornbeck's ships and property and behead him in the morning. And now will someone help me to my bed?"

"Sire, a trial will be necessary—" the Earl of Fremont said in appalled protest.

"Then try him! And execute him afterwards. I do not wish to be bothered with this . . . this tedium. Fetch the queen. Where's my queen?"

As far as Sorrel knew, his only queen had died in childbirth when Mathilda was a toddler. Could he have married again? No. If he had, Barklee's brother-in-law would surely have mentioned it. This was just another indication that the king was losing his wits to the creep of old age. Or to sorcery, perhaps?

"And the – er – salt cellar?" Masterton asked.

"You fellows there," King Edwayn said, addressing the two young clerics, "destroy the abomination! Take it away and smash it to pieces. And show them to me afterwards. I don't trust you black-clad mewlers with your weasel snouts . . ."

He looked around vaguely for a moment as if he'd lost track of what he was saying, then heaved himself upright. He grabbed for the staff propped against his chair and scrambled to his feet as his manservant hastened to steady him. "Seize Lord Juster and remove him from my sight," he said to Willas Brace, who was still standing by the door. "Yes. Seize him."

Oh, rattling pox, what do I do now?

There was a tapping behind her, as if a branch was knocking against the window glass. She thrust away that stray thought. *Concentrate. You have to do something to save Juster, that's why you came . . .*

Everything was happening at once. Willas Brace, still clutching Juster's sword belt, hurried across to obey the king. Fremont drew his formidable black eyebrows together in a thunderous straight line, even as he flapped an ineffectual hand in apparent protest at the king's orders. Lady Nerill burst into tears as she rose to her feet, clutching at her lady attendant's arm. The two clerics bustled forward to take the salt cellar from the servants, who thrust the tray at them with relieved expressions and headed for the door that led back to the reception room.

Sorrel laid a hand to one side of the velvet drapes to draw it back enough for her to slip through, but paused because the tapping behind had become so insistent. She glanced over her shoulder. Something stared at her through the distortion of the imperfections of the glass: a face with two weird eyes and a long, lank black beard growing around the rim of a chin – yet with no nose and no mouth in between, and no neck or body below.

In shock, she let out a squeal. She plunged through the curtains in fright and emerged into the room unglamoured. When she snapped to her senses again and glamoured herself back into obscurity, she expected everyone to be looking at her.

No one was.

The room was in chaos, her cry lost in the noise, her flick into sight, and then out again, unremarked. No one had been looking her way. The king was bellowing and beating off his manservant with his staff, Masterton was shouting orders that were lost in the general hubbub, and the Earl was clinging to Masterton, protesting. Lady Nerill was hysterical and flung up an arm just as her attendant, attempting to calm her, waved a bottle of spirits of hartshorn under her nose. The salts solution sprayed over the two women and a strong smell of ammonia began to pervade the air, causing them and those closest to them to gasp.

In the middle of it all, all his meekness vanished, Juster snatched his sword back from Brace and hit him under the chin with its hilt. Brace, taken completely by surprise, crashed into one of the two servants who had been heading for the door, and fell to the floor, half-stunned.

The grin on Juster's face was grim as he placed himself in front of the door, blocking the servants from leaving. They edged cautiously away.

"Sorrel?" he bawled. "Are you there?"

A leak on you, Juster. She pushed away the weird memory of what she'd seen at the window and ran across the room towards the clerics and the salt cellar, still holding on to her glamour as best she could, a vague plan forming in her head. *A diversion. He needs a diversion.*

"This is all your fault, you wretched man!" she told him, knowing her disembodied voice would just add to the consternation of those in the room.

She grabbed the salt cellar from the tray, and headed for the door.

The weight of the gift made her stagger and she came within a whisker of dropping it. She hoped her reeling across the floor added authenticity to the impression of a ship gliding through the air all on its own, apparently impelled by invisible winds filling its glorious sails of glass.

As she lurched along, her arms aching and her form fully lit by the brightness of the mirrored candles, her glamour laboured to disguise her presence by blending her into her surroundings – and failed.

4

Through a Palace Window

Ardhi leaned against the back wall of the livery stables near the palace, a hand on the hilt of his kris, and watched as a sentry marched past on his rounds. He and Saker, deep in the shadow, remained unseen.

"About twenty minutes before he'll be back again," he said. His grasp of the language of the Va-cherished lands was now both fluent and colloquial, but as a precaution against being overheard, they'd chatted in Pashali ever since they'd left the ship. "Do you know, until I went to Javenka when I was fifteen, I had no idea anyone broke time up into small units. We'd just say things like, 'I'll be back before noon.' We don't have a word for 'minute' in Chenderawasi." He pulled the kris out of its sheath and began to pare his nails.

"Isn't using that on your fingernails being sacrilegious? Or at the very least, disrespectful?"

"We islanders are very practical folk."

"A practical man would wait until daylight to make sure he didn't chop off a fingertip or two. Is it – the kris – telling you anything?" Saker asked.

"Not really. It's . . . uneasy, I suppose is the best way to describe it. No immediate danger. At least, not a danger it's aware of. Bone-headed, though, to think that it can sense all threats. If a bunch of wine guzzled guards were ambling towards us, with no thoughts except their beds, the kris wouldn't tell me of an approaching danger."

"Although one of them could possibly recognise me . . ."

"Exactly." Ardhi glanced towards the main palace gateway, lit by a pitch torch in a sconce. "Can we be sure Juster and Sorrel aren't already inside the palace?"

"I think so," Saker replied. "We did come a shorter way. Barklee's brother-in-law's house is over on the far side of the docks. They'll walk from there, I imagine."

"This Prince Ryce – you know him personally, don't you? What's he like?"

Saker pondered before answering. "When I knew him, he wasn't even married, let alone a father. He had a lot of growing up to do. I rather imagine he's done that in a hurry, if his father has lost his senses, disinherited him and tried to take away his son. Edwayn always was a little . . . odd. As a king, he ought to have married again and produced more heirs, but he refused. Thought the idea was disrespectful to his deceased queen. He never quite recovered from her death in childbirth. Mind you, I believe his grief didn't stop him from fathering a couple of unacknowledged bastards."

"There has to be a better way of governing yourselves than relying on the sanity – or maturity – of a hereditary ruler and his ability to produce heirs. It's ridiculous!"

"That's probably a treasonous pronouncement. If all too true." Saker sighed. "It's unlikely to change any time soon, unfortunately."

"And yet you call yourselves the Va-cherished. Your god doesn't give you good advice, does it?"

"Now *that* sounds like blasphemy. I think, as a cleric, I'm now supposed to tell you that Va grants the freedom of choice and what we do with it is up to us."

"Which conveniently excuses your god of any blame for the mistakes of believers."

"That's one way of putting it, I suppose. Va only knows!"

Ardhi gave a soft laugh.

"Anyway," Saker said, "didn't you recently tell me that until you messed things up, you were the heir to your grandfather – who rules part of the Pulauan Chenderawasi?"

"I was his heir presumptive, as the Pashali call it."

"They have a word for everything, don't they?!"

"Especially ones to do with administration," he agreed, remembering his university days. "In practical terms, the Chenderawasi heir to someone in my grandfather's position has to be accepted by a Council before he inherits, and the same Council can order his unseating if he makes a mess of things."

"And who makes up the Council? Nobles?"

"Not in the way you understand the word. Every large village in an administrative area elects a representative. In theory, anyone is eligible, man or woman. In practice, only those who are wealthier can spare the time away from their fishing or farming or caring for their children."

"I don't think that would work in Ardrone. Prince Ryce may not be the wisest of men, but he expects to be king one day, no matter what. And he expects to be able to choose his own advisers."

"And you'd support him in that?"

Saker shrugged. "A stable monarchy has its advantages. All I know for sure now is that my belief in Shenat teachings doesn't waver. Ever."

"No more than my belief in the way of Chenderawasi *sakti*. I believe that's why I am here, with the kris, and why the Rani gave you what you wear around your neck. Our *sakti* is reaching out to help your Shenat guardians and Shenat ways, because ultimately Chenderawasi safety and independence relies on the behaviour of Lowmian and Ardronese traders. And your unseen guardians need our help because of the sorcery that's now apparently rampant here."

"Kindred, eh? Your *sakti* and our witchery; our Shenat unseen guardians and your Avian Chenderawasi. There's a nice symmetry to it."

"A purpose, too." The kris stirred in its sheath. "Ah, is that someone coming?" He withdrew the blade, but the gold flecks within did not glow red. "All's well. It's probably them." Balancing it across his palm, he waited. A moment later it swung around, pointing at Saker. "Splinter it, it's finding the *sakti* around your neck because you're closer than Sorrel."

"I think it's time to fix the rope anyway."

Keeping to the shadows, he left Saker and crossed over to the wall encircling the palace complex, the climbing rope slung over his shoulder. At the base, he lingered for a moment to make sure those on guard at the main gate further along had not noticed him. When there was no reaction from that direction, he began his climb.

For him, it was easy. His fingertips and the underside of his bare toes felt the cracks and roughness of the wall, and his skin softened and moulded to give him traction on the stonework. In less than a minute, he was sitting astride one of the crenels, fitting the loop at one end of the rope over a merlon. He let the other end snake down the wall for Saker to climb up.

Last time I broke into Throssel Palace, it was to find Saker.

Grinning at the irony, he lay flat on top of the wall and gave a soft whistle. Nothing stirred where Saker was hidden. A moment later, he realised why: a torch flared near the gate, followed by voices, then the creak of a gate opening. He edged out his kris, and the flecks of gold within it glowed as the dagger responded to the presence of more *sakti*. Sorrel must have arrived.

He peered down into the palace grounds. The wall enclosed not just the main palace building with its royal apartments and administration offices, but many other structures, including stables, coach houses, kennels, a dairy, a bakery, a guardhouse and the lesser servants' quarters. These were all separated from the main palace building by gardens and lawns, which extended down towards the river where the keep and the royal docks bordered Throssel Water. All seemed quiet. He hunkered down to wait.

After the voices stopped, he heard the main gate creak again as it was closed. A moment later, Saker emerged from the shadows and ran to the wall. He climbed the knotted rope with ease, hauled the end up behind him, then flipped it down into the garden.

"You first," Ardhi whispered.

Saker shimmied down to the ground. Ardhi pulled the loop free of the merlon and dropped the whole length of rope into the garden. By the time he'd reached the ground, Saker had it coiled over his shoulder, ready to leave.

"Was it them at the gate?" Ardhi asked.

"Yes. With that damned salt cellar thing. I'll lead now."

Saker's first guess on where Juster would be taken, the Great Hall on the ground floor, proved to be incorrect. No light gleamed behind the stained glass windows to indicate the hall was in use. Finding his next guess, the audience room in the king's solar on the second floor, involved a fraught circuit through the gardens. Several times they had to scurry between the cover of hedges and bushes to dodge sentries.

Many of the drapes at upper floor windows were not fully drawn, and light blazed within. The tip of the kris blade obligingly pointed up to the second storey.

"It's indicating the audience room," Saker said.

Ardhi studied the configuration of windows and balconies. Saker had told him all the entries to the building would be either locked or guarded, so he already knew his climbing skills would be called upon.

"Unfortunately, it has no balcony," Saker said. "Nothing to attach a rope to."

"There's the balcony a floor above. I can tie the rope there and dangle it past one of the audience room windows below."

"Right. Do you know the whistle of the nightjar?" Saker whistled softly.

He imitated the call. "Like that?"

"That's it. One whistle if you need me to come up the rope after you; two if you need a flock of birds as a distraction."

"Where are you going to get birds at this time of night?"

"The king's dovecote. It's huge: four hundred nests in one brick building, just behind the stables. Did you know the argumentative little bastards hardly sleep? I can hear them now inside my head, quarrelling non-stop."

He repressed a shudder at the thought. "Rather you than me."

"Believe me, there are a great many times when I wish I had any other witchery but this one."

"I hope we don't need birds. And maybe we'd better say three nightjar whistles means get the pox out of here as blistering fast as you can." He grinned at Saker through the darkness.

"Understood. Get going. If they are meeting the king, they'll probably be up there in that room by now. Good luck, and don't intervene until – and if – you're sure they need you."

He took the rope from Saker and hoisted it over his shoulder. "Don't worry, I'd prefer to make it back to the ship without Juster knowing we'd ever left it."

Saker gave a low laugh. "You reckon no one on board will let him know?"

"I'm sure they won't. We swabbies stick together." He grinned again, and set off up the wall. The age of the stonework made it an easy climb with lots of crannies into which he could insert his fingers and toes. When he stopped halfway and looked back down into the garden, Saker had disappeared into the shrubbery to wait. Silently he resumed the climb, avoiding the windows of both the first floor and the audience room above.

Once he'd scrambled up to straddle the balustrade, he tied the rope securely to a stanchion, then dropped the free end down to the ground in such a way that it ran past one of the windows below. The casement was closed and the rope dangled about an arm's length from the glass. He slid down it until he was directly opposite. Twisting one leg into the rope, and steadying himself by clutching the brick-work at the side of the window with one hand, he was comfortable – more so than in the rigging of a ship above a heaving sea.

The trouble was he couldn't see anything.

The drapes were not completely drawn and he'd assumed he would be able to see through the gap into the room; instead his view was blocked by someone standing with their back to the window.

Someone hiding, obviously.

Sorrel?

He couldn't be sure. Whoever it was, they were standing in the dark, no more than a shape to him. Hauling himself up above the window, he twisted his leg into the rope, then turned himself upside down. Only the top of his head and his eyes now dipped below the top level of the frame. If the person who had their back to the window turned around, they wouldn't see him unless they also looked upwards.

Relaxing a little, he studied the audience chamber. At least now he could peek through the gap in the drapes.

He'd never seen King Edwyn, but everyone's attention was directed towards an old man huddled into a chair. His jewellery was certainly the most impressive in the room, rivalled only by Lord Juster's.

Juster was there, still safe, pointing out to the old man some of the features of an ornamental ship. Ardhi puzzled over that, until he realised it must be the salt cellar and that the buccaneer's flamboyance evidently extended to his gift-giving.

He was unable to view the entire room, but if Juster had arrived at the stage of presenting his gift to the king in front of members of the court, then perhaps all was well. He turned his attention to whoever was hiding behind the curtains.

Sorrel. It had to be, even though all he could see now was the top of her head, most of that shadowed. When he concentrated, he could see the vague glow about her that was the working of her witchery. So, at this point all was well. She was undiscovered and Juster was talking to the king.

Ardhi settled down to wait.

Just after he'd made himself comfortable, there was a sudden change inside the room. First there was a popping sound, followed by a puff of smoke. Someone squealed. Voices were raised and several people moved, gesticulating. With his narrow view of the room and the distortions of improperly made glass, it was difficult to know who was shouting, let alone why. Nor was it possible for him to hear exactly what was being said, but it was clear Juster was in trouble.

For a moment, he hesitated. When the king scrambled to his feet, his expression furious, Ardhi decided the best thing he could do would be to let Sorrel know that he was there, and to show her the rope.

Holding on to the top ledge of the window, still upside down, he tapped on the glass behind her head. She didn't look around. When the disturbance in the room ratcheted up a notch, he tried again. This time he knocked louder.

Just as his headband fell to the ground and his hair streamed free, she turned to look at him. Her mouth dropped open and she gave him a fleeting look of bafflement and alarm. Before he could show her the rope, she squealed and turned away leaving the window embrasure through the curtains.

Aghast, he saw her glamour slip and thought for a moment she'd given herself away, but no one appeared to notice. When she moved out from the embrasure, she left the curtains open wider and he had a better view of the room. No one was looking her way. Everyone was on their feet and Juster was using his sword to fend off a uniformed guard. A middle-aged cleric had hold of the king on one side, while a man in servant's livery helped to hold him upright on the other. Edwayn's face was twisted with rage and he appeared to be trying to throw himself at Juster.

Horrified, Ardhi could only watch as Sorrel launched herself across the room and grabbed the salt cellar ship. What the beggary was she doing? If anyone knew about glamours they might guess how the salt cellar was being moved.

Oh, of course. She's creating a distraction.

One of the women fainted, several people screamed and everyone scattered. Even the black-clad cleric and the servant reeled away, leaving the king standing precariously, leaning on his staff. Given the ruckus, Ardhi half-expected other people to flood into the room, until he realised Juster was guarding the closed door. In fact, he had jammed a chair under the doorknob in case someone tried to enter from the outside.

Splinter you, cap'n. There's no way you can extricate yourself without our help.

He gave the nightjar whistle, twice. Without waiting for an acknowledgement, he let go of the ledge and pushed himself away from the building as hard as he could. Swinging outwards on the rope, he raised his legs and aimed the soles of his feet for the centre of the casement, where the triangles of leaded glass would be weakest.

5

On the Run

In the gardens below, hidden from the window by overhanging foliage, Saker heard the two whistles. For a moment he hoped it was the actual call of a nightjar, but failed to convince himself. The call of a real bird would have meant something to him. This was an empty imitation and not a particularly good one either. Worse, it was followed by the sound of glass smashing and the patter of broken pieces falling on the garden. He peered upwards, aghast. There was a huge hole in one of the audience room windows and light and sound flooded out.

What the hells had happened? There was no sign of Ardhi.

Focus. Call up the birds.

He turned his mind to enticing the pigeons in the dovecote to fly out, even though he had no idea of how they were needed. The building was familiar to him from his time as a palace resident: a beehive-shaped structure four times the height of a man, a tower of cooing noise and pungent smells, its floor slick and slimy with droppings. A circular hole under a cupola in the centre of the corbelled roof was the entry and exit for the free-flying pigeons. The curving walls of the interior were dotted with gaps in the brickwork, hundreds of them, where the birds roosted and nested and lost their squabs or eggs to the harvesting, again and again.

Stirring the pigeons into wakefulness was easy; persuading them to venture out into the dark through the cupola ran counter to their instincts and was much more difficult. He closed his eyes and dismissed all thought of what had gone wrong in the audience room.

The birds rustled and fussed, anxious, alert. One by one they started to leave their roosts and spiral upwards out of the hole in the roof. Most of them, confronted by the darkness, promptly landed on the sloping top of the dovecote and murmured their unease to one another. He pulled at their will, enticed and cajoled. One broke free of its fear and flew towards him through the darkness. As soon as it was overhead, he sent it up to the shattered window to look inside. As the others straggled up to where he stood, he allowed them to land on the lawn, where he soothed them with comforting thoughts, telling them there was nothing to fear.

Soon he was surrounded by a raft of pigeons, all of them facing him, pressing close. He opened his mind to the bird now perched on the ledge of the broken window, one eye angled to stare inside.

Gradually a picture formed in his head, but it was a pigeon's-eye view, not his. The bird focused on movement and little else, and its interest leaped from one vignette of motion to the next. A single image captured his appalled attention: a bejewelled hand – Juster's, because he recognised the rings – holding a naked blade.

Cankers 'n' galls, he's gibbet-bait. No one pulled a sword in the king's presence unless it was to defend him, and he didn't think that was what was happening.

Juster, not even that salt cellar can help you now.

Everyone in the audience room froze when the window shattered, turning their heads in time to see Ardhi hurtle through the broken gap in a shower of splintering glass and snapped pieces of lead framing. He landed on his feet, skidded on the polished oak floorboards and came to a halt with his dagger already in his hand.

Sorrel's thoughts were mired in her disbelief. *Ardhi? What the pox—?*

Lady Nerill, who had been revived, now fainted again, crashing to the floor in an inelegant heap. Her companion lady fell to her knees beside her, but she was shaking so hard she was incapable of helping anyone.

"Exquisitely well-timed, sailor," Juster said with a grim smile. While everyone else was still too shocked to react, he coolly removed the chair under the knob of the reception room door and pushed a heavy walnut side table to take its place. "But Ardhi, have you any idea of how we can effect a tactical retreat?"

Masterton, who had a moment before been shouting at the clerics to destroy the moving salt cellar, was the next to move. Bravely, he stepped between Ardhi and the king, holding out his arms wide as if that could stop an armed man.

"Grab him!" he yelled at Brace.

Brace dithered, apparently uncertain whether to abandon his attempt to disarm Juster in order to pursue the intruder. He looked towards the king for orders.

Sorrel was just as confused about what to do as anyone. Still carrying the salt cellar, her arms sagging under the weight, she'd been heading for the second door in the room, guessing it led into the king's more private chambers. She'd hoped to lead the clerics and servants there, deposit her burden and double back to help Juster. Now she quickly jettisoned that plan and raised an eyebrow at Ardhi in question instead, knowing he could see it through her glamour.

Someone started to knock at the barricaded door, politely at first, then hammering with more resolution.

"Rope, outside the window," Ardhi said to her in his own tongue. "You go first. *Now.*" When Juster glanced at him, not understanding the language, he said, "Backstay to the deck on your portside, cap'n."

Oh, clever Ardhi.

Wilting under the weight of the salt cellar, she thought of lowering it gently to the floor, but no sooner had she made that decision than the king pushed past Masterton, waving his staff. "Blasphemy! Abomination!"

For a moment she thought he was addressing her, but his words were for the salt cellar. He still had no idea she was there. Straightening up, he took a deep breath, reversed his staff and swung its polished head parallel to the floor in a sweeping two-handed blow. She bent away in shock, utterly unprepared, but still gripping the clam shell hull tightly. The brass knob smashed into the carved figurehead on the prow, and was deflected upwards. Its destructive path plunged on through the superstructure of the ship, splintering the masts into glass slivers, crumpling the silver flags, disintegrating the delicate curve of the sails into multi-hued snowflake shards that caught the candlelight and danced with colour as they fell. Pearls dropped to the floor and bounced like fresh-fallen hail.

Shocked, Sorrel dropped the remains of the hull.

The clockwork within the clam shell, jarred by the fall into one final task, created a spark which set fire to the residue of gunpowder within. The explosion lifted the deck from the hull and hurtled the fifteen onyx cannon and their carved gun carriages in all directions, peppering the room with pieces of stone and wood.

Sorrel lost her balance and her hold on her witchery, and thumped down on her backside amid the wreckage. Before she could gather her wits, she found herself face to face with King Edwayn, who was also now sitting on the floor, legs inelegantly sprawled. He wiped a trickle of blood from his face and looked at it on his hand with a puzzled expression. Then his gaze met hers, and he snarled, "Devil-kin!"

Or that was what she thought he said. Her ears were ringing and her head ached. Her eyes were gritty, and when she touched her face, her hand came away blackened with gunpowder.

Then Ardhi was there, hauling her to her feet, whispering something into her ear.

"I can't hear you," she said. She looked around to find everyone except Juster was staring at her, their expressions a mix of fear and disbelief.

Oh, pox. Everyone could see her.

She reached for her witchery.

From somewhere she dragged the power, but her thoughts and skills were in disarray as Ardhi tugged her across the room towards the window. Her glamoured self flickered in and out of sight, arms and legs fading into the background and reappearing, her clothes and body just ragged bits and pieces.

"Well, that would give *me* nightmares, certainly," Ardhi said, as they reached the window. He thrust away some of the broken glass edges to make it easier for her to climb out.

She glanced back. Lord Juster Dornbeck had sent Brace sprawling and was now using his swordpoint to winkle the bodyguard's weapon out of his grip. It skidded under a chair. Masterton and the manservant were helping the king to his feet. The earl knelt at Lady Nerill's side with her attendant lady. Pedding was jumping from foot to foot, flapping his hands like a demented hen. One of the clerics had a long splinter of glass in his eye and was squawking in pain while the other lay flat on his back, unconscious. The two servants had run to the door, where the pounding and cries on the other side grew more insistent by the moment, and together they were pushing the table aside.

Juster strode across towards her, saying calmly, "Let's remove ourselves from this madhouse."

Clambering out on to the window ledge, she saw the rope dangling just a stretch away. Her hands were gritty with splinters of glass, so she gingerly brushed them together to dislodge the larger pieces.

Rot it.

She reached out and grasped the rope. Pain jabbed into her palms as she stepped into space, holding tight. The rope spun around and she had one last view of the room. She saw past Ardhi, crouched on the window ledge, to where Lord Juster Dornbeck stood, gazing back at his king.

His voice carried into the night, full of grief even as his words resonated with rage and repugnance. "Sire," he said, "you destroyed something of great beauty here tonight, an artefact crafted with love and artistry. That was unforgivable. But your real crime was to destroy the loyalty and fealty given to you by one honour-bound."

Hugging the rope to her body, she began to slide.

Saker was waiting for her at the foot of the rope, surrounded by a flock of restless birds.

"You weren't supposed to be here," she said in an annoyed whisper, stepping over a pigeon.

"Just as well we came, by the look of it."

"We would have managed," she snapped.

"Really?"

"Probably."

Well, possibly.

She looked down at her bloodied hands, wincing. Juster joined them then, saying, "Ardhi's untying the rope. He said he'd meet us at the wall – and to use the birds as necessary. It seems my third mate is giving the orders tonight." He glared at Saker. "Certainly it appears that *my* orders have been universally disobeyed!"

They followed Saker at a run, while he used his hold over the pigeons to obfuscate any attempt by guards to find them. The birds flapped and blundered around the garden in the dark, their noise and movement drawing attention away both from their escape and from Ardhi's climb down the side of the palace with the rope over his shoulder. While they waited for him at the wall, Sorrel did her best to extract the splinters of glass from her hands, dreading another climb – *up* the rope this time. Her palms were slick with blood and she couldn't see what she was doing, but throbbing pain told her she had to extract all that glass before clutching a rope again.

She had a sudden vision of Ardhi in the reception room, barefoot, unflinching as he crossed the glass-littered floor towards her . . .

"The dinghy is nearby," Saker told Juster. "We left it tied up near the palace wharf, right near the wall to the keep. You and Ardhi and Sorrel can go straight back to the ship and get her prepared for sailing. If you tell me where the pinnace and our sailors are, I can tell them we all have to return to the ship in a hurry."

Sweet oak.

Piper.

No . . . !

"No," Juster said, and then added, in tones that boded ill for them all, "We'll all go in the dinghy. In this breeze we can sail around to where we left the pinnace. It won't take as long as a man on foot."

"You – you intend to sail from Throssel tonight?" she asked him, feeling the leaden weight of despair even before he answered.

"If we don't get blown out of the water first. And some time or another when we all have a spare moment, I'm going to have a discussion about shipboard discipline and exactly who commands my vessel."

Ardhi reached them then, saying, "We've got to be quick. It's a hornets' nest back there. Armed guards pouring into the gardens." He was already climbing before he finished speaking.

Sorrel grabbed Saker by the arm, forgetting her own pain. "Piper . . ."

"I know."

"I'm the only mother she's ever known!"

"*Golden Petrel* might be blown out of the water before sunset tomorrow. She's safer where she is."

"Then I'll stay onshore too."

He said nothing to that idea, asking instead, "What did Barklee's brother-in-law say about Fritillary Reedling?"

"He thinks she's dead too."

Ardhi whistled softly from the top of the wall, and Juster grabbed the rope to climb up. In the garden behind them, the blaze of torches danced and flickered as men searched.

"We've got to get out of here now," Saker said. "And I doubt she's dead."

She fingered the bambu locket around her neck. "I can't leave Piper. I want to stay behind."

"Sorrel, the ternion, remember?" His voice broke. "We need you to defeat Fox and his sorcery. There has to be the three of us."

"No! You can't ask this of me . . ."

To lose another daughter. Another Heather . . . "I won't. I can't . . . We don't know when we'll ever be back!"

"Quick, your turn. Climb the wall."

She climbed, heartbroken, her hands feeling nothing of the cuts or the grit of glass jabbing at the flesh of her palms. Ardhi hauled her up on to a crenel. Juster was already at the base on the other side. She could see guards beginning to exit the main gate further along the wall.

Ardhi grabbed her wrists. "I'll lower you over the edge. The rest of the way, you jump."

He gave her no time to think. He swung her over the side and for a moment she was suspended there, safe in the strength of his hold.

Then he let go and she fell.

6

The Prince Besieged

The debris from the yawl bobbed on the water, mostly planks from the hull, although there was also rope tangled up in what could have been part of the mast. That was all that was left of the small sailboat and the men who'd crewed her. A cannonball filled with gunpowder had ploughed through the stern and then exploded.

Yesterday, they'd been alive, fishermen at home with their families perhaps, doing all the normal things normal people did. Perhaps they'd even laughed about sneaking in to the cliff-side landing stage in the dark, ridiculing the inability of the larger ship, the naval sloop which patrolled the coast, to prevent the smuggling of supplies to Gromwell Holdfast. They'd done it so many times before, successfully. The rocks that guarded the coastline were Gromwell's most stoic sentries, armed with jagged edges and barnacled ledges to fend off the sloop with its deeper keel.

Prince Ryce had seen the yawl's demise. A break in the clouds at the crucial moment, an alert sentry on the king's sloop-of-war spotting the tiny boat in the moonlight as it threaded its way through the rocks, a lucky shot. Hideously unlucky for those in the yawl.

He wrenched his gaze away from all that remained of their vessel, visible now in dawn's light. "I hated this place as a child," he remarked. "I swore I would never live here."

His words were addressed to the only other person on the open roof of the seaward tower of Gromwell Holdfast: his wife Bealina, princess of Staravale, now seventeen years old. He still found it hard to believe how much she'd come to mean to him when he'd once found her childish and dull.

She didn't know about the yawl, and he wasn't about to tell her. In fact, he hadn't wanted her to climb up the staircase at all that

55

morning, but it had become a daily ritual for them. A way to begin the day, to stand looking down on the Twite River estuary as the sun rose . . . She would have known something was wrong if he'd refused.

"Why didn't you like it?" she asked. "Wasn't Gromwell always the inheritance of the Ardronese heir apparent?"

"Oh, yes. That's why the king made me come here every couple of years." Even so, he'd never dreamed he would one day need to huddle in such a fortress, under attack by forces nominally under his father's command.

Heartsick, he turned away from the sea to regard the interior of the castle. The inner ward, with the Landward Tower at the far end, was divided into two baileys by the wall they called The Belt, and each bailey was already alive with the bustle of men and women going about their daily chores. The holdfast was a grim edifice nonetheless, a castle born of a time when cross-border raiders from East Denva made life miserable for the people of northern Ardrone with their constant plundering. Built on a promontory jutting into deep estuarine waters, Gromwell's walls on three sides joined seamlessly with the cliff that plunged into the sea. When he'd leaned over the parapet of the Seaward Tower that morning, he'd gazed directly down at the waves beating against the granite at the foot, their foam frothing on the rocks.

"It's not such a very drear place." Bealina laced her dainty fingers into his callused ones.

"It's a bleak place for milady. I would I could offer you more." He smiled down at her. He was a good head taller than she was, and her small stature and sweet smile had once reminded him of one of those cloyingly sentimental porcelain figurines of shepherdesses that had become popular in Throssel: sweet and fragile. The resemblance was ridiculous, he knew that now. Bealina was about as breakable as forged steel. And since the birth of their son, her figure had blossomed. Right then, when the wind teased her tippet back to display the full swell of her breasts above her tight-laced bodice, he felt his cock respond, pushing uncomfortably against his breeks.

"The view is pleasant," she continued, blithely unaware of his lascivious thoughts. She'd discarded her coif so her hair could blow free and now she laughed as it tangled in the gusting wind.

Va, but that was exactly the kind of behaviour that had irritated the old biddies back in Throssel. She was braver than he was . . .

"See how the estuary sparkles in the sun," she said, pointing, "and how the gulls twist and weave over the waves? I even saw a sea-hawk fishing yesterday morning."

"Pleasant?" Abruptly brought back to reality, he gave a bitter laugh. "Well, I suppose if we disregard all those grey-clad ensorcelled haggards besieging us below the landward wall, it might be considered pleasant enough. Or if we refuse to see that armed sloop out there, patrolling to make sure we don't leave." He waved a hand at the only ship of any size in view. Fortunately the holdfast was too high up for any ship's cannon to be a threat, but the sloop's presence had just proven itself to be a menace to those bringing them food and fodder. The yawl was the second casualty in the past month.

She looked hurt, so he added, "Ah, forgive my megrims, my sweet. My spirits are low, I fear."

"Do you hate this place so very much?" she asked, her hand holding tight to his.

"I'd never hate any place where you were," he said gallantly. "But I do fear what will become of us all."

"You must never lose faith, my lord prince. Va will shield us."

He wished he could believe that. Sometimes he found her faith touching; at other times, like right now, it irritated him. Although a well supplied them with as much water as they could possibly need, food was another matter. How much longer would their supporters outside the walls remain loyal if some of their number were regularly blown to pieces, especially when the monetary reserves he used to pay them were dwindling? His father had already cut off the tax revenue from his southern estates.

He squeezed her hand in an attempt to reassure, although he wasn't sure she needed it. She never dwelled on anything she could not change. Upon learning that they had to leave the luxuries of Throssel Palace and flee into exile with their son, she could have bemoaned her fate and cried; instead she organised the packing with a minimum of fuss. Once they'd arrived at Gromwell, instead of complaining about the lack of elegant furnishing or glassed windows, she had turned the bleakness of the holdfast into an efficient, well-run household. Still later, when King Edwayn's madness had deepened and he'd ordered them besieged because they would not surrender Prince Garred to him, she had taken charge of ensuring all those within the castle were fed. The inner baileys were given over to pigpens and goats, roosters and hens; vegetables were grown on the flat roofs; grain and hay were laboriously hauled up the cliff from the estuary on particularly dark or misty nights.

"Have faith, not just in Va," she said, "but in those who came with us into exile. You have good friends in Lord Anthon Seaforth and Cousin Beargold, and good men in your own guards, like Sergeant Horntail – not to mention all those armsmen who chose to leave the King's Company to follow you."

"More motivated by their hatred of Grey Lancers than any particular desire to place me on the throne," he pointed out, not for the first time.

Father, how could you ally yourself with Fox and those madmen?

He sighed, knowing the answer to that one. Sorcery. The Pontifect had told him enough about Fox to make that clear. The Prime even sucked the life out of his own sons to extend his longevity, or to give him added power.

"It's not your fault, Ryce," she said gently, as if she knew what he was thinking. "Fox can make people believe – and see – things that aren't real, that's what the Regala Mathilda wrote. That's what the Pontifect told you. How could you stop it from happening when your father did nothing?"

Just thinking about the future made him feel ill. *Saker, I wish you were here.*

A stupid thought. Va only knew where that wretched cleric was now, and besides, he was banned from the kingdom anyway.

"I must go downstairs before I'm blown away," Bealina said and turned to leave. "Ah, here is Horntail come to talk to you, anyway. I shall depart so you may both discuss affairs of much more moment than mine." She smiled at Horntail, who gave her a stiff military bow as she passed him on her way down.

"A word, if I might, Your Highness?" he asked.

"Of course." His heart sank. There was something in the set of the man's jaw that told him there were ill tidings.

"The sentry on the spyglass spotted a military force up on the northern road from Broom. Looks like another contingent of the grey bastards."

Curse them to beggary. Was there no *end* to the men who would join the fobbing lancers with their penchant for torture and other horrors he didn't even want to think about?

"And that's not the worst of the news, Your Highness. They have cannons."

The cold fingers of fear that never left him nowadays dug a little deeper into his bowels.

"How many?" At least he could pride himself on being good at hiding his dread. His spoken words were firm and calm.

"Four. Gun carriages drawn by oxen."

"Ah." He tried to sound as if he was pondering what to do, but in truth he was thinking that he never used to be so scared. But then, back in the days before his marriage, he'd only had to worry about himself. Now there was his son and Bealina, and all the men and women in the holdfast. Not to mention that Gromwell, with its complement of soldiers and servants, was all that stood in the way of a sorcerer and a ruthless contingent of men who killed anyone, anywhere, without compunction.

Dear Va, where was everyone else? Where were the unseen guardians? Where was the Pontifect and her clerics? He'd heard that Vavala had fallen, and Fox had taken her place . . .

Fob it, I wish I'd never been born a prince.

He asked, "The cannon, how large?"

"Too far away to say as yet. Might be twelve pounders."

Twelve pounds referred to the weight of the cannonball, not the cannon itself, he'd learned that much. It could have been worse, he supposed.

"They could be local made," Horntail added, trying valiantly for optimism. Cannon cast locally had a poor reputation for reliability. Pashali-made ones rarely blew up, but they weren't common except on ships.

"Any other encouraging remarks, sergeant? I could do with such."

"Well, gunpowder is usually in short supply. Oh, and their gun carriages are a bit bogged down at the moment," Horntail added.

"Ah." They exchanged grim smiles. Heavy rain and the besieging army had churned up the road into a quagmire – and a cannon on a gun carriage could weigh two thousand pounds.

"I don't think they'll get them here before nightfall," Horntail continued. "We could try a raiding party tonight. Blow them up before they arrive."

They'd raided the besiegers before, with some limited success. It meant lowering men and their small rowboat to the foot of the cliffs in the middle of the night, after which they had to row – unseen by the enemy's sloop – to a beach further north, then backtrack overland. In the end, they'd ceased these forays because too many had died.

"I don't like sending men to their deaths," he said.

"If the cannon get to where they can bring the walls down, we all die," Horntail pointed out. "Repeated pounding with cannon shot will make blighted rubble of the outer wall eventually, probably at its weakest point – the gate. In fact, just lobbing cannonballs over the wall would be right proper messy, given what we've got out in the open in the baileys."

He meant their livestock and the vegetable gardens. He was right, of course. Horntail usually was. "All right. We'll call for volunteers," he said. "Where's Lord Seaforth?"

"He and Sir Beargold are over on Landward Tower. They are taking a look through the spyglass."

"I'll join them." He tried to sound calm, but his feet felt leaden as he clattered down the stones of the spiral stairway.

For some odd reason, it was Mathilda who came to his mind. Mathilda, who had always said she'd make a better prince than he would. He'd certainly made a mess of this. He ought to have spent more of his income buying cannon for the holdfast. But how could he have foretold this war? Apart from the odd skirmish at sea between Ardrone and Lowmeer, the Va-cherished lands had been mostly at peace for generations. The union of the Ways under Va had achieved that much.

Too late now to change his past. He had to think of the future.

He stayed atop Landward Tower most of the night with Seaforth, Beargold, Horntail and Gromwell's commander, Rossworth. They weren't the only ones who kept watch. Many of the other defenders, even those not on sentry duty, arrayed themselves along the parapet walls. Who could sleep anyway? Not when you knew what was happening out there, and certainly not once you'd heard the screams.

The night rang with their cries, those men who'd left by sea after dusk hoping to render the cannons unusable. Instead, they'd been captured and brought close to the walls so that their agony would be heard as they were tortured to death.

"Consign the grey maggots to a Va-less hell," Ryce muttered, the words heartfelt as he stared out into the darkness. The lack of moonlight and clouded sky that had offered his men cover were now providing their torturers with the same protection. A couple of candles lit by the lancers failed to illuminate the details for those on the wall. He had to clear his throat before he could speak again. "Horntail, I want unlit torches, four or five of them, and a glowing coal. The best archers, and some men with strong arms. Right *now*."

It was one thing to give the orders; it was another to listen to brave men scream while you waited out the minutes of their agony as those orders were carried out.

"Your Highness," Rossworth asked, "what are you intending?"

"First, we light the torches and throw them out there so we can see what's happening."

"You think they've made themselves vulnerable by coming so close? It's possible. But more likely the whoresons have dragged their wicker hurdles with them, for protection. And they'll be gone by sun-up."

"Oh, I'm sure you're right," he replied. "Nonetheless, I want everyone except the archers and the strong-armed fellows off the wall."

"Your Highness, are you s—"

"Do it, Rossworth! Now!

"Yes, my liege."

Ryce didn't say anything more until the men he'd asked for had assembled. His commands to them, given coldly and precisely, left no doubt what he intended. There was a sharp intake of breath as he finished. "This is on my head," he said. "You are absolved."

The men selected for their strength lit the pitch of the torches and flung them out as far as they could.

The scene revealed was unbearable. Yet it had to be borne, by

him, with stoicism, because he was the prince. Four young men
stripped naked and tied spreadeagled between upright wooden stakes,
easily visible to anyone on the walls several hundred paces away.
Being flayed alive, their skin removed, one small strip at a time, by
two men. Other Grey Lancers remained out of sight, protected by
portable wicker hurdles.

The archers stepped forward and loosed their arrows.

When they were done, there were six dead men, and four of them
were Gromwell's own.

"May Va grant them peace in the Way," someone muttered.

"'Ware!" Horntail yelled. "Arquebus!"

Everyone ducked down as a few balls peppered the parapet. After
the firing stopped, there was silence beyond the walls. Their thrown
torches flickered and died, one by one, returning the horror to the
darkness.

The next morning dawned bleak and cloudy, leaden skies to match
leaden hearts. The four men still hung on the stakes, their wrists and
ankles tied. Each had two arrows in their chest. The two who had
tortured them lay sprawled on the ground at their feet. The rest of
those responsible had retreated out of arrow range, leaving their dead
behind.

"They were *skinning* them," said Horntail, his voice gritty with
grief.

"Intended to keep them alive as long as they could," Seaforth
added. "What manner of men are these?"

King Edwayn's men, Ryce thought bitterly. *We blame Fox, but it's
my father who allowed the rot to start.* Those bodies would stay there,
on display for them all to grieve over, for however long they remained
besieged.

"They are our arrows, aren't they?"

Ryce whirled around to see Bealina behind him.

Shocked, he said, "My lady, you should not be here! This is not
a sight for women to have to bear."

"Oh, tush," she said, wrapping her shawl tighter around her body
and tucking her hair more securely under her coif as the wind whipped
around her. "I will never understand why men have this strange idea

that we women don't know about pain and blood and death and loss. Do you think that keeping us blind to sights like this –" she waved her hand at the dead men "– shields us from enduring the agony of losing those we care about? What we don't see, we imagine." She rubbed the back of her hand across her eyes to dash away the tears. "They died to keep us safe, and we should all bear witness to how much they suffered for us, and how much distress those who ended their suffering must feel."

Seaforth and Beargold exchanged glances with Horntail and Rossworth, then all four filed away down the steps, pretending they hadn't heard.

Ryce, embarrassed, was still hunting for words to say when she added, "Are those the cannon there, the ones these men were trying to destroy last night?" She was looking at the top of the rise in front of them.

He nodded.

"So our men didn't succeed."

"No." He swallowed, but the bitterness stayed in his mouth. He'd asked for volunteers. Thank goodness the boat only held four men other than the boatman, who had waited for them. When they didn't come, he'd brought the boat back.

"When will the cannon be ready to use?"

He shrugged, trying to look as if he wasn't afraid. "Tomorrow perhaps. They will need to construct some kind of timber shutters to protect those who light the fuses. We heard at least two arquebus last night too."

"What – what will happen?"

"Once they have the cannon working . . . it depends on how much ammunition they have. Bealina, we might be able to hold them off for a few weeks. Maybe even months. But you and Garred must leave. Soon."

She stared at him in horror.

"By boat. It will be dangerous, but it will be worse if you stay. You have to see Garred safe. You must go to your father. You're still a Staravale princess; they'll welcome you home."

"No."

"Bealina, please, let's have no argument."

"Indeed, no argument would be agreeable. Let us go below and discuss this over breakfast. The table is laid in our room, awaiting us."

He stifled a sigh, knowing she would not capitulate without a lengthy fight.

It was hard to look at food with the memory of the night's horror fresh in his mind, but he ate to please Bealina.

"Let's consider this now," she said. She sat with her hands demurely folded in her lap, but he wasn't fooled. There was never anything demure about her when she'd made up her mind to get her own way. "You want me to be dropped down the cliff, in the middle of the night, with Garred, into a boat. A rope broke once, I seem to remember. A man fell into the sea, and he drowned because he couldn't swim. Neither can I. And certainly Garred can't. Then there's that sloop out there. But worst of all, think of all the other things that can go wrong on my way back to Staravale! From what little we hear, there are Grey Lancers everywhere."

"You would not be alone. I would send the best of my men with you—"

"Now that's another reason why this is a bad idea. You can't spare anyone, not now. Ryce, you know in your heart that sending me away is not without danger to me and to your son. Will you at least admit that much?"

Pox on't, why was she always so *logical*? "Well, of course there is a risk. What we have to do is weigh up which is the greater peril, and I believe that it is here, in this castle. We don't have cannon. They do. Once they start firing them, people are going to die."

"Oh, I agree. But I won't be one of them, and neither will Garred. If there is one thing we know, it is this: King Edwayn wants his grandson. He's made that quite clear. Moreover, he's quite fond of me, and I do not think that he would part me from my son."

"We can't be certain of that! He has lost his wits. We don't know what he might do. Moreover, it's not the king who controls those monsters beyond our walls; it's Fox. Oh, he might not be here, but it is his commands these men obey."

"True. And Fox is in full command of his senses."

"He's also a sorcerer." Mathilda had written to tell him that long before the siege had started. So had the Pontifect, before she'd died.

She tore at a piece of bread, but didn't eat it. "An ambitious sorcerer who can never *be* a king needs to *control* a king. What better way than to kill you and seize Garred while he is still a babe? Fox has already had himself elected Pontifect by the senior clerics, he still maintains his position as Prime of Ardrone, and he acts as King Edwayn's chancellor. His next step is to have Garred under his care. He doesn't want our son dead. He wants to be Regent for a child when Edwayn dies. We both know that." She waved her hand at the narrow arrow slit of a window. "Those men out there with their cannon will never fire it at anything other than the gate, not while Garred is inside. If they did, Prime Fox would have their livers for breakfast. I suspect they will even offer me and Garred free passage before they start the bombardment."

He was incredulous. "You'd want to accept it?"

"No, of course not. I want to appear on the battlements with our son in my arms, confirming we are still here. Just in case there's any doubt of that. And then I refuse their offer. After that, everything will continue as before."

Agitated, he stood up so suddenly that he knocked a plate and sent a round of cheese rolling across the floor. "And what next? Do we stay here all our lives? *I have to get out of here.* We have to *fight* Fox, not live behind a barricade."

She was silent.

"I – forget I said that." He bent to pick up the cheese, changed his mind and ended up kneeling beside her chair, anguished. "I don't know what we should do, and nobody can agree on a solution." He laid a hand on her knee. "True, you may not be in much danger if you stay in Seaward Tower, but the gate will collapse and they'll enter the castle. Oh, we can fall back to the other bailey, and finally to Seaward Tower. But in the end, we'll have to surrender. Bealina, love, you are my weakness."

For a moment their gaze locked and his heart turned over at the hurt in her eyes. He looked away and picked up the cheese and replaced it on the plate.

"It's true, what you say," he acknowledged, standing up. "Neither Fox nor the king wants anything at all to happen to Garred, but with you both here, they have the lever they need to make me do anything they want anyway, and sooner or later they will. They'll threaten you, and make me believe they mean it, and I'll stride out the main gate to their tune, bringing all my men with me to die. If you leave, though, you have a chance of getting away. And so do the rest of us." True, or not? He didn't know, but he knew he had to convince her it was.

She thought long and hard, then said slowly, "Years ago, the journey to Staravale would have been easy. No Grey Lancers. Shrines along the roads . . . Now? Oh, Ryce, I'm scared. You – you wouldn't come with me?"

He was appalled. "I can't ask my soldiers to hold the castle in my stead!"

"I'm – I'm sorry. I should not have asked that. It was wrong of me."

"We will hold Gromwell as long as we can. Who knows what may happen yet? I won't give up. We may get aid from outside . . ." He had even sent to Mathilda for help months before. "But you and Garred have to leave."

7

Fugitives

Sorrel stood on the deck of *Golden Petrel*, clasping Saker's hand far too tightly. Both the pinnace and the dinghy had made it back to the ship without being detected, and Lord Juster had ordered the ship to leave immediately, retracing their route to Port Hornbeam where they had left the two prize ships.

"Blister it, Sorrel, I am so very sorry. I don't know what to say." He knew why she gripped him so hard. Piper was still ashore and there was nothing either of them could do about it.

She groped for words, wanting comfort even when she knew there was none. "When we agreed that Piper go ashore, I – I thought it was just going to be for a short while."

"I know."

Anguished, she asked in a whisper, "Is it possible to bear it?"

He didn't reply.

"I don't know *how*!" She was gutted, the emptiness inside swallowing her ability to think. A terrible calm had her clamped in its grip, keeping her still, preventing her thoughts from breaking out of their ghastly circling. She should have been running, screaming, fighting, clawing something to pieces – anything except this: standing, watching the ship preparing to leave Throssel Water in a hurry.

Leaving Piper behind. Her daughter in all ways but one.

But . . . what else could she have done?

Juster had refused to allow the dinghy into the docks again. By the time they were in sight of the wharf where they'd left the pinnace tied up under the care of the ship's tars, the entire portside was bustling with armed men carrying torches. Happily the two seamen had quietly poled the pinnace offshore in the dark, and they bumped into the dinghy without being seen by those onshore.

Juster gave the order for them all to return to the ship. When Sorrel protested, he'd simply looked at her, and said quietly, "The rest of us don't have glamour witcheries, mistress."

She'd subsided, shamed, knowing he was right. She might have been able to pass unseen on the docks, but none of the others could.

And now, back on *Golden Petrel*, all she could do was watch the crew winch up the pinnace and the dinghy, wind up the anchor and set the sails.

She endeavoured to distract herself. "Do you think it was Fox who sent the king's wits wandering?"

"I don't know. Possibly. We may never know for sure."

She looked aloft to where the sailors were tugging at the reefs to untie the canvas. Everywhere men were busy, ignoring them where they stood, the only two people who had nothing to do.

"I don't know how I will survive without her, but what's worse is how she will cope when she realises I'm not coming back. Oh, Saker, she's not even three years old!"

"Even if you could've gone back for her, it wouldn't have been right to bring her with us. We're fugitives now. There will be a price on our heads."

"I could have remained with her."

"We have to stay together, the three of us, that's what the Rani said."

She bit her lip until it hurt. "You've never told me exactly what she did say about that. If it's important, then I think I should know the precise words."

"It embarrassed us. She's a bird, and they – they see things differently."

"Tell me."

"You won't like it."

"*Tell me.*"

"All right. She said, 'You have accomplished much as a ternion. Yet two males and one breeding female rarely works when neither male is subordinate.' Then she added something that sounded like a proverb: 'Those who fly alone, die alone.' She said we should think deeply about that. It sounded like a warning."

She was speechless. A slow flush started at her neck and its warmth rose into her cheeks where it flamed in the cool night air. She was deeply grateful there were no lights anywhere near.

"Rani Marsyanda is a bird," he reiterated. "And I assure you, Ardhi and I are not fighting over anyone."

"And I'm not a prize hen for the rooster with the longest spurs." She gave a mortified laugh. "I can see why you were embarrassed."

"I – I don't think we should entirely dismiss what she said though. She thought our strength was in our unity."

"The ternion." She sighed. "So you are asking me to dismiss any idea of returning to Piper."

"I – yes. For the time being. You know I love her too. So does Ardhi. This is tough on us all, but we are also doing this for her. It's the only way we have of saving her."

"She has the feather circlet. That's supposed to keep her safe." She was trying to convince herself everything would be fine, but in her heart she had to accept she might never know. "I did tell both Barklee and Banstel that her life depended on it never being removed from around her neck, although I didn't say why."

Above them, a light breeze puffed at the sails, and the deck trembled underfoot as *Golden Petrel* stirred in the water. Lord Juster came up to them then, his face a grim mask in the dim light. "Go below," he said. "We'll be hugging the far coast, but those cannons of Throssel Castle . . ." He shrugged. "They are new and we don't know their capabilities."

As *Golden Petrel* slid past the walls of Throssel and its castle in the dark, the wind dropped and a pre-dawn mist began to wisp along the surface of the estuary. If it hadn't been for a strong outgoing tide, they would have been in trouble. As it was, the ship slipped on its way in ghostly silence. If there was a flotilla of ships looking for them, or just the three sloops, none came close.

By the time the mist lifted several hours after dawn, Throssel was far behind them and the only vessels to be seen were on the horizon.

"Sluggards," Juster said with a laugh when he joined Saker and Sorrel in the wardroom for breakfast. "Not a match for my lady of the sea."

"So what's next?" Saker asked. "Where are we going?"

"I want to see what we can salvage from our prize ships, then sell them before the king seizes them. And I hope you and I have some spice money to collect in Hornbeam, Witan Saker. I trust you sent the message."

"As soon as I could persuade the eagle to leave its perch. He wasn't happy taking off until the mist had lifted, but he's on his way now with your instructions tied to his foot." The look he gave Juster dared him to complain. Wisely, the captain said nothing. Saker relented and added, "I will join the bird when it flies into Hornbeam, just to make sure the letter is delivered."

Sorrel frowned, worried. "It will be a long way ahead of us by then. Can you twin with it from such a distance?"

"We'll find out, won't we? I think it's less dangerous for me that way than it would be to stay inside its head for too long. Juster, I think what we have to discuss now, though, is what do we do *after* Hornbeam?"

"We'll have a full complement of men then."

"Men who've been away for over two years and want to go home. And home is Throssel."

"Some, perhaps. Mostly, though, I choose men I think will regard *this* as home." He gestured with his hand to indicate the ship. "We have a war to fight. I rather think we are going to put Prince Ryce on the throne, don't you? So the first thing we must accomplish is to break the siege of Gromwell."

"Deposing a seriously ill king is all very well," Sorrel remarked later when the three of them – Saker, Ardhi and herself – were alone on a corner of the deck, "but we are one ship, a few sailors, and us, this so-called ternion. We have three witcheries between us, plus a dagger and pieces of a feather. Where do we even begin?"

"You forgot the bird," Saker said. "Don't underestimate him."

"All right. We also have a bird." She looked at him curiously. "Are you ever going to give him a name?"

"No. Never. I don't ever want him to be thought of as a sort of – of pet. He's wild and magnificent. Unfortunately for him, he's not really free. To give him a name seems to add to the – the loss of dignity he has to endure because of our link. As for where we begin?

We need to find out as much as we possibly can about the state of the kingdom. If Hornbeam is the first port of call, then that's where we'll start by asking questions. Let's hope that port is not overrun by Fox's spies."

"We have to find out some way of delivering the Rani's second circlet to the prince-regal," she said. "I gathered from Barklee's wife that his name is Karel."

"That's got to be a priority," Saker agreed. "Right now, let's start with what we have. Ardhi, do you know *anything* you haven't already told us about these wisps of feathers given to us?"

He looked unhappily at them both. "Most of what I know is legend."

"Rani Marsyanda did say you knew more. What did she mean about there often being a sting in the tail?"

"I'm not sure. That might have been Chenderawasi humour," Ardhi said, "because the pieces came from the Raja's tail and a tail feather is not as powerful as breast plumes, so sometimes things don't work out the way you think they will."

"As when I used a piece," Saker said, not trying to hide his bitterness. "With the result that I now have a permanent connection to a bird."

Ever since he'd swallowed part of the feather, there had been an expression lurking in his eyes, a look of deep-seated pain, almost of horror. Sorrel tried – and failed – to imagine what it was like to have an alien mind always edging into one's thoughts. Ardhi had told her that Saker often cried out in his sleep, begging to be left alone.

"The Rani also said that each piece could only be used once," said Saker.

"And we have no idea of how to use them," she said.

"Well, I wouldn't advise swallowing one," Saker said wryly.

"Legends are variations of the same story that goes something like this," Ardhi began. "A poor villager finds a wisp of a tail feather. He picks it up and keeps it safe, thinking it might be useful in the future. One day, something awful happens. Perhaps his prau sinks out at sea in a storm. He clasps the piece tight in his hand and calls upon its *sakti* to help him. He's expecting something miraculous. He thinks maybe an Avian will appear, seize him in its claws and fly him safely to land. Or perhaps dolphins will come to his rescue. Instead, a huge wave picks him up and carries him safely to shore. Unhappily, that same wave destroys his village and drowns his family."

"Oh, wonderful," Saker said.

"Use a piece of feather and you get what you want, but you pay too high a price."

"Avian tales to prevent people exploiting the *sakti* in any Chenderawasi feathers that they find?" Sorrel asked. "After all, birds do moult, and Avians might worry about the *sakti* in feathers being misused."

"That's a quite likely explanation," Ardhi agreed. "There are other tales, though, that might be of more use. Stories of how the sorcerers were defeated. They were difficult to ambush because of their powers. The Avians could rip them with their talons and beaks and dewclaws and spurs; our warriors could wound them, but the sorcery healed all but the most horrendous of injuries. Eventually Avian and human warriors forged weapons using a combination of Avian blood and plumes and the sky iron found in the mountains. Our finest *empu*, our blademakers, made weapons like my kris. Even that wasn't successful unless it was wielded by an Avian warrior."

"Like those we saw guarding your Raja?" she asked.

He nodded.

"We don't have an Avian warrior," Saker said. "And only three pieces of feather." They had agreed to reserve the other two just in case the children ever removed their necklets and became sorcerers. "Let's be honest here. We haven't the slightest idea of how to defeat Fox."

"Maybe there's a clue in those old stories," Ardhi said. "When the time comes to deal with your sorcerer and his power, we need to think about a combination of *sakti* and witchery. I believe that's why our ternion is important. Where is this sorcerer of yours now?"

"Barklee's brother thought he might be in Vavala," she said. "He also said he's heard Fox commands the Grey Lancers, and they're the ones who are besieging Prince Ryce's stronghold outside of Twite."

"I thought Valerian was recruiting men for his own purposes even before we left for the Summer Seas," Saker said. "He had a ledger labelled 'lances.'"

"In other words, he has an army of sorts, and we don't," Ardhi said.

"Fritillary Reedling once told me not to listen to any reports of her death," Saker said. "Which means she was already preparing for the worst back then. She's not dead."

"Let's hope you're right," Sorrel said, "because she's the one who has the best chance of getting the circlet to Princess Mathilda and persuading her to put it on her son."

"If the Pontifect didn't die, where would she be?" Ardhi asked.

"No idea," he replied. "A shrine keeper might know more. I'm intrigued by the hints you had from the Barklee family, and that Juster had from his agent, about all shrines and witchery folk disappearing at the same time as Vavala fell and Fritillary supposedly died. Marvellous coordination. Makes me think of powerful sorcery – or powerful witchery."

"Barklee's family said some people think the shrine keepers ran away and the oaks shrivelled because Va was angry with them for leaning more to Shenat ways than to Va-worship. He said there was talk of Primordials being responsible—"

Saker was indignant. "What codswallop! Primordials are as mad as hares in spring, but they would be the *last* folk to destroy a shrine!"

"Barklee thought the talk was poppycock too. He thought it more likely to be people turning on the shrines because they associate them with Primordials. Clerics in cities have been preaching against shrines, calling them hotbeds of superstition and ignorance led by elderly keepers who are all unbelievers refusing to worship Va."

"A load of lies," Saker muttered. "How could anyone believe that?"

"Sorcery?" she suggested. "And then he also said people don't know what's happening elsewhere because no one travels much now. It's too dangerous. Folk disappear on the roads. Merchant caravans employ companies of armed guards."

"The King's Oak?"

"Barklee said it's shrouded in some kind of mist. If you try to enter that mist, you encounter impenetrable brambles. When the king's men were ordered to cut through those briars, some men lost their wits and others disappeared entirely. No one tries any more."

"What about Lowmeer?" Saker asked suddenly. "Is there any help to be had there?"

"Regal Vilmar is dead, and the Regala rules for her son, Prince-regal Karel Vollendorn."

Saker's face was a picture of startled shock. Then he started to laugh.

"What's so funny?" Ardhi asked.

"Oh, you'd have to know the Lady Mathilda to understand. Let's just say I imagine she's exceptionally happy to be a widow. I'd love to know how she persuaded the Lowmians to make an Ardronese princess a Regent, though."

Sorrel thought of all the rich pastries and creamy desserts prepared for the Regal. *I just hope his death was nothing more than plying him with sweetmeats . . .*

Thrusting the thought away as mean-spirited, but not fully convinced, she dragged her thoughts back to the present. "So what can we do now? It'll be a couple of days before we arrive in Hornbeam."

"I'll use the eagle to spy. If there are shrines still around, I should be able to see them. If there's anything else amiss, I might be able to pick up on it as well."

He looked so desolate, her heart lurched in sympathy. His whole youth and adult life had been lived in harmony with Shenat and shrines, and what he was facing now must have been overwhelming. She laid a hand on his forearm, and he placed his own hand on top.

"When the eagle nears Hornbeam, I will have to join it," he said. "I rely on you to bring me back. You know, if – if I get stuck inside its head, keep talking to me, Sorrel. Don't let me get lost."

"Never."

"We will see this through," Ardhi said. "We, the ternion."

8

A Fawn and a Fox

Pickle it, but the night was dark. They had waited several days, through bombardment, for just such a dark sky, a time when clouds obscured the stars and the moon had not yet risen, when the wind was not strong enough to slam someone lowered on a rope against the rock face and yet playful enough to make sure the surface of the estuary was choppy, for that would make a small boat harder to see.

Ryce schooled his face to appear calm in the lamplight on the tower roof, but he had to clear his throat before he could speak. "Bealina," he said, "if things do go wrong, if you are caught, tell them who you are, and ask to be taken to the king. Failing that, to Fox. That will keep you safe. And always remember this: if you do fall into his hands, I will not rest until you are free." He glanced around at those gathered on the roof of the tower. "I won't be alone in that, either. There's not a man here who doesn't care about you, who wouldn't die for Garred."

His voice was steady, his smile didn't waver – but he'd never felt so sick.

In the next few minutes his wife, or his son, or both, could die. If he had been a stronger man, more far-sighted, smarter and able to outwit Fox, perhaps none of this would ever have happened. Perhaps his father was right to say he hadn't the stomach for being a ruler. Perhaps Mathilda had been right. She was the one who should have been heir.

Bealina lifted a finger to place it across his lips, and said, "Hush, my love. You've already said everything that needed to be said. Be strong, as I will be. For our son."

They had spent precious time arguing, their last hours together

75

consumed by their wrangling over how she was to travel. He'd wanted to send the boat back and forth several times, until she had a small band of his best men to accompany her, plus her handmaiden and Garred's nursemaid, but it would have delayed her departure and increased the likelihood of something going amiss. She'd said she had a better chance of reaching Staravale if she travelled as a common woman, dressed simply and accompanied only by a single reliable man.

"It won't be so difficult for me. I was used to a simpler life once," she said. "Being a Staravale princess wasn't a bit like being an Ardronese one."

"Still, you can't travel without a lady-in-waiting of some kind," he protested, shocked.

She fixed him with a cold stare. "If I can live through a siege, I can do anything. I'd rather be safe and inconspicuous than proper."

In the end, she'd prevailed, and he was sending only Horntail with her.

Pox on't, she looked so small and fragile. He wanted to wrap his arms around her and shield her from everything. He nodded, not trusting himself to say anything more.

"It's time, my liege. The boatmen have signalled they are ready."

Horntail, with Garred in his arms. Rot it, he'd miss that man too, but the sergeant was the only person he could trust to take care of those most precious to him. "Farewell, my friend," he said, and his voice was husky.

He stood there, at the top of the castle wall, and watched while his men winched Horntail over the edge, Garred asleep in his arms after being given a couple of drops of a sleeping draught. Leaning over the parapet, hand in hand, he and Bealina watched their descent. He thought his heart would stop beating when he lost sight of them in the darkness. The boat and its crew were already down there, although he couldn't see them either. It seemed an age, time enough to imagine all that might have gone wrong, before the rope wriggled and then went loose, the signal that Horntail had reached the rocky platform at the foot of the cliff with his precious burden. The slack rope was hauled up again.

She stood on tiptoe and brushed her lips against his cheek, whispered in his ear, "Carry my love in your heart." And then she was slipping on the harness, smiling at the men who were going to winch her downwards, giving one last wave of her hand. She looked up at him, holding his gaze as she was lowered until he could see her no more.

He waited there until dawn, until the sun rose and told him the sloop still patrolled the sea, and the tiny craft holding his wife and child was nowhere to be seen.

Bealina sat very still in the stern of the boat next to Horntail, who had Prince Garred in his arms. Her left hand gripped tight to the gunwale, nails digging into the wood, while her right grasped the sergeant's arm. If the boat turned turtle, she was not going to be separated from either him or her son.

Praying under her breath, she begged for Va's protection. Surely Va would care for Garred – he was the hope of the kingdom, Ardrone's future. Then, because that future now depended on the two brothers who rowed the boat and she knew from their names, Gorse and Holm Campion, that they were Shenat folk, she also prayed to the Way of the Oak to keep them safe. As an afterthought, she added a fervent prayer to the Way of the Flow, requesting smooth seas.

She wasn't certain they would all survive the night. The Campion brothers were chosen for the job because they'd both fished the coast in boats like this one in their younger days, before they had come to work for Prince Ryce in the holdfast, but the task appeared impossible to her.

Without a moon or stars, the dark was impenetrable. Waves came out of nowhere sending spray to drench them, the boat rose nose-up and then tipped into the next trough, rocks loomed up out of the dark and passed by far too close. Only Garred, tucked under a piece of sail canvas, remained dry. The brothers rarely looked over their shoulder to see what was ahead, so she couldn't understand how they knew where they were going, yet every now and then one or the other would ship an oar to allow the boat to veer this way or that.

It will be worth it, she thought.

The bombardment had already begun to take its toll on Garred. Every time the cannon had boomed, he ran to hide in her skirts,

Glenda Larke

trembling, and the night before he'd refused to go to bed and had to
be rocked to sleep in his nurse's arms.

You will love Staravale, little one.

At last, daylight began to creep into the sky as if reluctant to begin
a new day. When they finally slipped into the safety of a tiny cove
and could step out on to the sand, she was wet to the skin and shivering. As had been agreed, Gorse and Holm guided them up through
the dunes to the farm that belonged to their uncle, Sprig Campion.

Although Sprig and his wife had no idea they were coming, they
were welcomed. As they had earlier agreed among themselves, she
was introduced as the wife of one of Ryce's commanders, who'd been
willing to take the risk of leaving for the sake of her son. If they
guessed her real identity, nothing was said. They were given clothes
to wear while their own were dried in front of the kitchen fire, and
then offered a hearty meal of fresh farm produce. For the first time
in her life, she was tempted to be greedy; it had been a long while
since she'd had an actual choice about what to eat. Garred, now
wide-awake and wide-eyed at his new surroundings, chewed happily
at everything he was offered, but shyly refused to say a word.

Later, when she took him out to see the geese in the pond, and
help look for eggs, he became his normal chatty self. When they
heard the occasional low rumble of cannon in the distance, he didn't
notice. It was Bealina who shuddered. Nobody commented at the
sound.

That night, Gorse and Holm left to take the boat back to the
holdfast, and this time there was a sack of dried peas, several hams,
a bag of hazelnuts, four cheeses and two live geese as cargo. Bealina,
Horntail and Garred stayed one more night and then set off the next
morning in the farmer's cart, laden with a crop of freshly pulled
turnips and mangelworzels bound for the market in the next town.

"There's none of them grey men on the road," Sprig assured them.
"They's all yonder at the holdfast, damn them to beggary."

It was a pleasant day for a journey. If it hadn't been for the distant
rumbling that told Bealina the bombardment continued, she might
have even enjoyed it. She sat up next to Sprig, Garred in her arms.
He was constantly on the move, twisting round to look at things,
pointing at a squirrel, waving at a labourer in a field, trying to escape

her hold to scramble over the turnips behind. Finally Sprig allowed him to sit between his legs and hold the end of the reins. Thrilled, he settled down, looking at her occasionally, saying, "Me drive, Mama!"

There was no room on the cart for Horntail, so he walked. They'd agreed he was to pose as her father-in-law, bringing her back home after the death of her husband. He hid his sword under the pile of turnips. His face was unreadable, but every time the rumble of the cannon sounded, his shoulders tensed.

The road headed to the market town of Beck Crossways, after which she and Horntail would be on their own, travelling north to the border. At least they would not have any trouble paying for an inn or buying mounts in Beck Crossways. Ryce had given Horntail a pouch of coins and she had a heavy gold chain hidden in her undergarments if she needed it.

As the morning wore on, Sprig seemed restless, until Horntail asked him what was wrong. "Should be more folk on the road," he muttered. "Market day tomorra. But folk be feared. Bad times when folk stay home 'stead of taking their crop to sell." He shook his head sorrowfully. "They says when nobles quarrel, 'tis the serving lad gets beat, and I reckon there be truth in that."

Neither of them replied, although she thought Horntail tensed even more.

"How long to Beck Crossways?" she asked.

He looked up at the sun, spat in the dust, and said vaguely, "Be there by dark."

About half an hour after that, they heard the sound of hooves behind them. When they looked back, it was to see a party of horsemen raising dust as they approached at a quick canter.

"Brazen it out," Horntail said. "Draw to the side as much as you can, Sprig. Keep calm. And remember, you don't know us. You're just giving fellow travellers a ride to the market."

Bealina took a calming breath.

The black-clad man in the lead was young, but it was those who followed who sent her heart galloping and her arms reaching out to gather Garred into her lap.

Grey Lancers. Six of them, one leading an extra saddled mount.

"Quiet now," Horntail said.

The young man passed them, but once in front he swung his mount around to halt in the middle of the road, and the others drew up around him to block the way. Sprig's carthorse stopped dead. Garred, sensing her tension, half-hid his face in her chest.

"What's amiss, sirs?" Horntail asked, pulling at his forelock in a gesture of deference. He'd edged closer to the cart, near where his sword was hidden. He rested one of his hands on the turnips.

The young man did not acknowledge him, or even look his way. His gaze was on Garred, intent, yet with eyes strangely devoid of human expression, or even real interest. His skin was deathly pale, hollowed cheeks lacking all colour, and her immediate thought was that he was ill, close to death.

He's having the life sucked out of him . . .

Sorcery did that to you: that was what Pontifect Fritillary had written to Ryce.

"I've come for the prince," he said.

How does he know who we are? She did not know him; to the best of her recollection, she had never seen him before.

"What prince?" Sprig asked, astonished.

The young man's blank indifference sent chills down her spine. Her heart hammered so hard her chest ached. She knew, without the slightest understanding of how it had come about, that she walked a thin line between life and death, between integrity and compromise.

"Give me the child," he said.

"What do you want with my grandson?" Horntail asked.

The man deigned to look at Horntail then. "He's no grandson of yours. The boy is the son of Prince Ryce, and the king has demanded his return to Throssel."

"Twaddle!" Horntail said, simulating indignation. "Whatever makes you think that?"

The blood drained from her face, leaving her lightheaded.

A momentary expression of doubt flickered across the man's face. He dismounted and walked over to her side. "Show me the lad's hand," he said.

"Who are you?" she asked, her voice hardly even a whisper, and leaned away from his reach.

"Endor Fox," he said, "of Boneset." He took hold of Garred's hand.

Reacting to her fear, the boy screamed. Endor did not flinch, almost as if he didn't hear. He turned Garred's hand to look at the palm. "There," he said. "My father's mark. I knew the moment the child left Gromwell."

She rubbed Garred's back to calm him. "There's nothing there," she said, looking at his palm. It was clean and unmarked. Then she remembered the warnings sent by the Pontifect, about how Valerian Fox could mark those he wanted so they could be recognised by his minions.

"I tracked him," the young man said with the pride of an immature lad seeking approval. "He travelled by sea. Yet I have found him."

Fiddle-me-witless, he's little more than a child himself. Confused and ill, too. Part of her felt a moment's compassion, but she dismissed that out of hand. She must not underestimate him. There was a blankness behind his eyes, a lack that made him less than human. He was soulless.

She sensed rather than saw Horntail's move to seize his sword and turned to frown at him. His only chance was to keep still, not to become this man's target. "You can be on your way in a moment. These men mean me no harm, I feel sure," she told him and turned back to address Endor Fox. "What instructions were given to you?"

"The prince is to be returned to Throssel."

"And the prince's mother?" she asked, but her archness fell flat. He shrugged, the indifference even more chilling now. "Whatever you will. His Reverence said it would be easier for the child if his mother accompanied him. I brought an extra mount. A palfrey. I'm told that's best for a lady. Are you the Princess Bealina?"

"I am."

She looked over his head at his men. They waited impassively, without pity, without even apparent interest. Looking from face to face, she searched for any hint that offered her hope, but there was nothing there to see. Unlike Ryce's disciplined men, they were begrimed and slovenly, their hair lank and matted, and they smelled of more than just sweat. Their once grey coats were caked with mud, blood and grease. They were like a pack of stray dogs, unkempt and disorderly, kept in line by the power of the pack leader, but ready to rip the weak to pieces.

"I will go with you," she said, trying for a cold imperiousness. "You may address me as 'Your Highness'. Pontifect Fox would be angry if I were treated with disrespect. Your hand, sir, if you be so kind."

Obediently, he took her hand and his look of confusion told her that her composure and arrogance had dented his confidence. Her moment of success was short-lived. When he touched her, a horrible black tarry finger of wrongness rubbed across her soul, leaving her reeling.

Sorcery. She wanted to vomit, and had to swallow back the bile that burned her throat. With Garred clutched hard to her shoulder, she was forced to allow the man to help her down. Once on the ground, she grabbed up her small carryall from the cart and handed it to him, her tremble making a lie of the confidence she was trying to impart.

Horntail had thrust his hand into the turnips. She guessed he clutched the hilt of his sword, ready to pull it out of its scabbard. She made a quick gesture of negation and turned to speak to Sprig Campion. "Thank you, kind sirs, for the ride. I trust you will sell your turnips for a good price."

Turning her back on them, she walked ahead of Endor Fox towards the riderless horse. It bore a woman's side-saddle and she was thankful for that. Behind her, Fox said something to Sprig and Horntail, but she didn't catch the words.

She waited beside the horse until he came up, then said, "I'll need the aid of one of your men to mount up, and another to hold the prince."

"Give the boy to me," he said.

"Never."

He shrugged and gestured for two of his men to dismount. One took Garred from her. He started crying in terror. Aching for him, she turned away to put her foot into the other's cradled hands so he could lift her into the saddle. When she bent down to take her son back, Garred was trembling, his breath coming in sobbing gasps.

Crooning soothingly and holding him tight, she glanced back to Horntail and Sprig Campion. They did not appear to have moved and there was something odd about their stillness, but there was no time to consider it. Fox ordered a lancer to take the reins from her and she realised she was going to be led. At least she'd have both arms to attend to Garred, who was gradually calming.

I will not cry . . .

Fox turned his mount to lead them all back the way he had come. "Where are we going?" she asked, but he didn't bother to reply.

He bent down in the saddle as he passed Sprig and Horntail, saying something to them that she didn't catch. The air shimmered, and she choked, feeling she'd breathed in something foul. Garred wailed anew, and fought her, throwing himself backwards, as rigid as a board. Terrified he would fling himself out of her grasp, she battled to calm him, and by the time she had, the cart was behind them. When she looked back, it was to see Horntail and Sprigg talking, not even looking her way.

Appalled, she dragged her gaze back to Endor Fox. He was smiling at her.

It was not a nice smile.

"What did you do to them?" she asked, her voice rasping as she tried to make her throat work properly. "*What did you do?*"

"Don't play games with me," he said. "Every time you do, you will regret it."

"Your Highness? There's something you need to see."

Ryce had been looking at the reinforcements for the gate and worrying about the large hole dug in the centre of the outer bailey. Digging a pit to source soil and rock to reinforce the gate and the walls was all very well, but it was a fobbing nuisance having to walk around the hole all the time, not to mention useless now it was filled up with rainwater. He sighed. At least the geese were happy.

"Where?" he asked the young guard who had addressed him.

"Landward Tower," the guard replied. "Sir Beargold said to come immediately."

Beargold was the most phlegmatic of men; if he said "immediately", then something was wrong. Ryce hurried, running up the tower steps. Sir Beargold stepped away from the spyglass on its tripod and gestured for him to take a look, saying, "Brace yourself, cousin. This is not good."

In spite of the warning, Ryce was in no way prepared for what he saw. On the rise a few hundred paces away, Bealina stood, holding Garred's hand. The boy was tugging at her and pointing. Next to her was a man in black, his hand gripping her upper arm in a proprietary way, someone he didn't know. Behind them was an array of Grey Lancers.

His mouth went dry and his hands began to shake.

Black-clad men. Gaunt Recruiters. Pontifect Fritillary had thought they were Fox's sons.

Va . . . Oh why? Why?

The holdfast was lost.

Minutes passed. No one moved. He waited, eyes misting, expecting the Gaunt Recruiter to send a messenger demanding their surrender, yet he had no idea what he would say when the order came. The men around him, breath bated, said nothing, uttered no advice, no recriminations. Inside, he howled and wondered why there was no sound.

Bealina raised a hand in salute. He waved back. They turned away then, and disappeared with the Gaunt Recruiter over the rise back towards the besiegers' camp.

Still he did not move and nothing happened. There was no challenge. And the lack of a command was as frightening as one would have been.

He stayed there until the sun set.

"Why didn't they insist we surrender?" Anthon asked, perplexed.

"I don't know," he said.

They wouldn't kill Garred. He was sure they wouldn't kill him. They'd take him to Throssel, to the palace, to the king. Fox *needed* Garred.

He had to believe that. If he didn't, he'd just curl up and die.

9

The Eagle and Saker

The sea eagle floated in indolent circles over Hornbeam, regarding the scene below with a cold, yellow-eyed stare. An occasional tilt of its tail feathers or a raised tip of a wing kept it on its circuit of the port area, from the carcass of an ageing carrack propped on its keel in the dry dock, to the Lowmian ship tied up at the wharf nearby, to the warehouses bordering the delivery canals. The bird, indifferent to all it saw, would have preferred to be seeking a mate over a warmer coastline, but it had no choice. Another consciousness within its skull directed its trajectory and it had learned not to fight that other presence. It made life easier.

Half an hour before it had reached Hornbeam, Saker had twinned with it, only to be obliged to wait while it perched on a dead tree along the coast and demolished a freshly caught herring. The jump he'd made had been a long one, and he had an idea he'd been close to losing himself in a fog of non-existence, eternally lost between his own head and the eagle's. The thought scared him witless.

Now, at his insistence, the eagle spiralled downwards towards the moored Lowmian merchantman: Juster's prize, the spice-laden fluyt captured in the Spicerie. Saker had long since learned not to interfere with the mechanics of flying. The first time he'd found himself inside the mind of the bird in the Summer Seas, he'd been so panicked he'd almost killed both the sea eagle and himself. It wasn't something he ever wanted to risk again.

Months had gone by since then, yet he remained enchanted by the extraordinary vision he possessed when he stared out through those golden eyes. He marvelled at the clarity of every tiny detail of the ship below – every splinter in the decking, every frayed fibre of the ropes, every grizzled hair in Finch Aspen's beard. He sought the

85

minutiae, revelled in the sharpness of the definition denied him by his human eyesight. Colours were brighter and more radiant; light sometimes shone with a luminous glow that his own eyesight never saw.

He was puzzled now, though, by what was happening on board the docked fluyt. By the look of it, its spice cargo was being unloaded, which was odd, as the instructions to do so were still tied to the bird's leg. Finch Aspen, whom Juster had asked to take charge of the fluyt and the carrack, was speaking to a man – a merchant if his clothing told the truth – near the open hatches to the hold, while dock lumpers hoisted gunny sacks up from below decks.

Saker cajoled the eagle to land on the cross trees of the mainmast. The smell wafting upwards was a glorious mix of cinnamon and cloves, mace and star anise. One of the sailors saw him land and said something to Finch, who glanced upwards, then broke off his conversation and sent the merchant on his way. Once the man had gone, Finch gestured for the eagle to come down to the deck.

Interrupting the bird's ruffling of feathers and preening, Saker urged it to fly to the taffrail. Finch came across to its new perch, his back to the stream of dock lumpers, and halted a step or two away from where the bird was settling down to preen once more.

"Saker?" he whispered. The expression on his face implied that he doubted he'd receive a coherent reply. Finch had never accustomed himself to the link between man and bird, and Saker didn't blame him.

At Saker's instigation, the eagle nodded in response, a human gesture that must have appeared absurd, and held out its foot with the letter attached.

Finch, nervously eyeing the vicious curve of its beak, untied the oilskin packet and slit the stitching open with his dagger to read the letter inside.

"Rattling pox," he muttered as he read. When he'd finished, he raised his head to regard the eagle and added, "It's bad here too. Saker – there are no shrines any more. None! They've vanished and in their place there's nothing but mist and tangled brambles. If people try to cut their way in, they never seem to get anywhere. Most folk

86

with witcheries, they disappeared when the shrines did. Killed, prob-ably. There are still healers about, praise be. But the others?" He shook his head. "It's all the fault of them bastards in black."

Saker cocked the bird's head in enquiry.

"Gaunt Recruiters, people call 'em. They all look like men with lung-rot. They mostly wear black. They're the fellows who went around persuading the clay-brained to join the Grey Lancers. Some say they're sorcerers. They say the new Pontifect – Valerian Fox – is the only fellow who can save us. Others say the Grey Lancers are all his doing." He snorted. "You hear all sorts of scuttlebutt nowadays: 'Lancers defend us. No, they're the murderers. Shrine keepers are evil. No, they were murdered innocents. People with witcheries were slaugh-tered. No, they are the ones helping Primordials spread the Horned Plague.'"

Finch forgot who might have been watching and flung up his hands in exasperation before continuing. "Tell the cap'n everything's a mess here in Hornbeam. No one knows what to think. People barricade themselves in their homes mostly."

Belatedly, he glanced around to make sure no one was listening before adding, "Or they buy spices because some say cinnamon sticks will ward off evil and cloves prevent the plague, or star anise gives you powers to resist a sorcerer. Truth has run away down the gutter here in Ardrone, Saker, since we've been gone."

He made the bird nod again.

Finch took a deep breath. "You going back to the *Petrel*?"

Another nod.

"Tell the cap'n I had to sell the spice anyway, even without his say-so. What with this rumour going about that spices ward off sorcery as well as plague, there was a nasty crowd on the wharves yesterday threatening to sink us if we didn't offload our cargo. So that's what I'm doing. Got a good price, tell him. And I got a buyer interested in the carrack, even though it needs new planking on the hull." He ran a hand through the wind-blown tangle of his salt-laden hair. "Cankers 'n' galls, Saker. Things are real bad here. How can shrines have *gone*?"

Saker did his best to answer some of Finch's questions by nods or shakes of the eagle's head, and shrugs of its shoulders, but there wasn't really much he could add to what he knew Juster had already put in the letter.

"All right," Finch mumbled finally. "Tell him at the moment there are no Grey Lancers in town. The local Gaunt Recruiter died a month back. He got stabbed by someone. His bilge-crawling recruits panicked and disappeared. They'd thought he was invulnerable, you see."

He stumped away, tucking Juster's letter into his jacket.

Saker urged the bird into the air. His body felt terrifyingly far away and he longed to return to it, but he had something else he wanted to do.

He took the bird hunting for the main Hornbeam oak shrine.

Many years earlier he'd visited it while on a mission for the Pontifect, so he was able to guide the eagle in the correct general direction. For a while he just gloried in what he was seeing, the land laid out like a map below, so beautiful, so intricate, so . . . *vast*. There was the river, and the oak had been around that bend . . . Yes, that was the spot. Or rather, where it had once been. Just as with Throssel's King's Oak, he now saw a smudge of obscurity where once there had been a magnificent tree. He set the eagle to circling while he stared at it, and as the bird had eaten well that morning, it obliged him willingly enough.

Each time they passed overhead, he strove to see through that fog. He eased the bird still lower, until they were scraping the top of the blur. Even then, he saw nothing but impenetrable murk. No feeling of wrongness, just a vague . . . emptiness. The bird remained unworried, and its thoughts exuded nothing more than boredom. He found that comforting, at least, but decided to give up.

The eagle had other ideas. It spilled air out from under its wings, extended its legs – and landed.

On *nothingness*. Nothing Saker could see, anyway. And yet he felt *something* under his claws.

Va rot you, Saker, keep a hold of yourself. Not his claws. Under the eagle's claws. Something it gripped, like a tree branch. He bent down to take a look, and still could not see a thing.

Leak on it, for once he and the eagle were not sharing the same vision, that was obvious. What the sweet acorns was going on?

Sorcery? he wondered. *Aimed at humans, and not felt by other living creatures?* Yes, that had to be it. The eagle wasn't affected, but he was.

"He's been away far too long." Restless, driven by worry, Sorrel had left the cabin where Saker's body lay, unmoving, to pace the deck. He'd been gone since morning, and now the sun was setting. "If he doesn't get back soon, he'll have to spend the night inside that bird's head, perched on a tree somewhere."

Ardhi was the only person within earshot, and in spite of her pacing, she was addressing him.

"That won't hurt him," he said calmly.

"You can't possibly know that," she snapped.

"No, but I do have faith in Saker. So should you."

She sighed. "I do, I suppose. Well, maybe."

"He's not the same person who once unwisely slept with a king's daughter."

She stopped dead, gaped at him, then hurriedly looked around to make sure no one else was within earshot. "How did you know that? Surely he never told you!"

"No more than you did." He shrugged. "I guessed – before we knew she'd been fathered by your sorcerer – that Saker wondered if he was Piper's father. But I didn't know for sure until you just this moment confirmed it."

"Oh! Oh, you – you – I could wring your neck!"

He gave her one of his broad smiles.

"Very few people know that, Ardhi, and those who do risk losing their head. In two different countries, what's more."

His eyes crinkled cheerfully. "By the time we've finished, maybe everyone will want us dead, I think."

"Even Lord Juster doesn't know what Saker did, although he did guess Piper is the Regala Mathilda's child."

"Young men have a tendency to do some very muckle-headed things around women who are – what's the word I want? Gravy?"

She frowned, doubtful, then laughed. "I think you mean saucy. And Princess Mathilda would *never* consider herself so vulgar as to be saucy."

"Well, anyway, Saker is not that person any longer."

"None of us is who we were before all this started."

"Speak of the wind and it blows – here he is now. You don't need to worry any more."

She turned in time to see Saker come up from below, followed by Lord Juster, who had taken a turn keeping watch over his comatose body. "You're here!" she said in relief. "I mean, you're back. You've been so long. We were worried."

Ardhi grinned. "No, *we* weren't. *You* were."

Saker came and sat on the hatch cover next to her. "I shared part of the return flight with the bird; I felt safer that way. On the journey out, I almost lost myself. The bird was too far away." The stark horror in his voice warned her not to ask for details. He added, striving to be more light-hearted, "On the way back, I left when he wanted to go fishing again. I *hate* the taste of raw fish."

"You're a barbarian," Ardhi said. "Raw fish is a delicacy where I come from. Wrapped in seaweed, flavoured with lime and eaten with *sambal*, it is delicious. What did you find out in Hornbeam?"

He told them all he had learned from Finch Aspen, then described what had happened at the Hornbeam shrine.

"So you're saying that the shrine was still there, but you couldn't see it?" Juster asked. His face reflected his conflict: he wanted to believe, but found it hard.

"I couldn't see a thing, although I felt the branch under the eagle's feet. It even sharpened its beak on it! I did hear things though. I think. The twittering of small songbirds in the tree."

"In this tree that didn't exist," Juster said.

"So this is a *sakti*, or a sorcery, that affects people but not birds. The tree is really there, but people can't see it?" Ardhi asked.

"I'm not convinced it was sorcery. Maybe they did it deliberately. Because they were in dire danger."

"They?" Juster asked. "Who's they?"

"The unseen guardian and the shrine keeper of each oak. They feared for themselves, for the health of the tree, for those with witcheries. I suspect people with a witchery were targeted, killed by the lancers. So they used their power to hide the tree and those who sought refuge there."

Juster gave a snort of disbelief. "Do you know how ridiculous that sounds?"

"Yes, as a matter of fact, I do. So I checked on the way back here. Before I left the eagle, we dropped in at another couple of smaller village shrines. Same thing."

"You knew where to find them?" Juster asked, still dubious.

"Not really. We just flew over places until I saw something. I was looking for large, old oaks, but there weren't any, not to my eyes, anyway. But I saw the same kind of blur. Each time I asked the bird to perch and it happily did so – in a tree I couldn't even see."

Sorrel looked at him with increasing dismay. "So all the shrines have disappeared, everywhere, just as Barklee's brother said. Maybe even all on the same day, as he thought, along with folk with witcheries."

"That's preposterous." Juster threw up his hands. "I'm more likely to believe Va destroyed the shrines than to accept that people with witcheries are huddled under an oak tree in hiding. Waiting for what? Eating what? Living how? *Where?*"

"The idea that Va would allow shrines to vanish and Shenat belief to be wiped into nothingness is unthinkable," Saker snapped. "Look, healers are still around apparently. We need to speak to some of them. Perhaps they know more."

"I don't know too much about your shrines and beliefs," Ardhi said in his quiet, understated way, "but if I shared your faith, for a keeper and a guardian to hide their shrine in a time of turmoil would seem like a terrible betrayal. The very people who guard the faith and grant the witcheries deserting me when I was threatened and attacked from all sides? Hiding away, using their faith-granted talents to do so?"

They all looked at him, and Saker paled. "I can't say why they did what they did. If they hadn't, maybe everyone with a witchery would have been murdered by Grey Lancers, and all the oak shrine trees been cut and burned. If that happened, there would never be another witchery granted. That would mean the end of all healing, for a start. Which one of us has never used a healer?"

"Maybe that's why healers didn't hide," Sorrel said. "They were safe because even Grey Lancers and Fox's clerics use healers. The lancers wouldn't want them dead."

Saker nodded. "I want to talk to some of the clerics; and another witan if I can."

"What *is* the difference between a witan and a cleric?" Ardhi asked.

"Well, all witans are clerics, but not all clerics are witans. A witan is always one of Shenat background, with a close connection to the Way of the Oak or the Way of the Flow. Clerics serve in chapels; witans never do. They usually serve rural areas, not chapels."

"You were an exception, then?"

"Decidedly."

He looked from Ardhi to Sorrel and back again. "All three of us need to get inside a shrine. We need to talk to a shrine keeper."

"Right," said Juster. "Walk up and knock at an oak tree that isn't there. And someone will let you in via an entrance that doesn't exist."

"The three of us might just have the right . . . key," Saker said. "We won't know until we try. I just hope we are prepared to pay the price."

"Let's hope for fair winds tonight," Juster said, shaking his head in disbelief. "I can't wait to put your theory to the test."

10

Dire Times

"Lord Herelt Deremer to see you, Your Grace. In the library."

Regala Mathilda, who'd been discussing dreary accounting matters with her advisers and lawyers, glanced up at the chamberlain's words. "I think we are done here, gentlemen." She waved a hand at the paperwork scattered across the table in front of her. "Take action, as we have just discussed."

In fact, there had not been much discussion. She had listened carefully to their opinions and asked numerous questions, after which she made decisions. There had been a time, early in her regency, when they'd argued because they'd assumed that as a woman she was either weak or fickle, not to mention suspect because she was Ardronese. She had gradually refined differing ways of dealing with dissent, each method tailored to undermine the author of the objection. Slowly they had learned the folly of their assumptions – she was neither weak, nor fickle, nor did her loyalty to Lowmeer waver – and they'd also learned the imprudence of dispute if you wanted your career or business to prosper.

She turned back to the chamberlain. "I shall see Lord Herelt. You may bring him upstairs when these gentlemen have departed." Nodding towards her ward's-dame, Lady Friselda Drumveld, she added, "Your ladyship may also leave, as I am sure you are tired, having had to listen to several hours of tedium on financial matters."

Lady Friselda stood, wincing as if her backbone objected to the move.

Just punishment for your past, Mathilda thought uncharitably.

"The townsfolk won't like the new tax based on street frontage," Friselda remarked as the accountants and officials filed out. "And the merchants won't like the increased tax on imports."

"Of course they won't like it. Taxes are universally despised, but they expect the Basalt Throne to pay the army nonetheless. So far, we have kept the Grey Lancers at bay, but that won't last unless we have more men, more archers, more cannon, more guns, more gunpowder. Swords and lances and pikes will not win this war." Not when Fox could turn men into quivering jelly with a few spoken words and his black smutch.

"We are not at war," Lady Friselda snapped. "Unlike the rest of the Va-cherished Hemisphere appears to be!"

"Exactly so. We are not, because we have a well-paid, well-trained army, thanks to the foresight of my late dear husband." All balderdash, of course. For a start, the preparedness of the army was more her own doing than Vilmar's, but the heart of their defence had really lain with the Dire Sweepers, Sir Herelt Deremer's band of armed men, the force once taxed with eliminating the so-called devil-kin twins and the Horned Death. Because of the Sweepers, Fox had not dared to bring the lancers into Lowmeer – not yet, and she intended to keep it that way. Ardrone and the Principalities had not been so fortunate; a long period of peace meant they had not invested in arms or armies.

"Indeed," Friselda agreed. "A far-sighted man. Very well, my dear, I will leave you to deal with Lord Deremer. A tiresome fellow. Just make sure that your handmaiden remains with you. We want no gossip, now."

With that barbed remark, she sailed from the room.

"Old witch," Mathilda muttered.

"Neither 'old' nor 'witch' is an insult, my dear. Think of something else if you wish to be derisive."

The remark came from the only other person remaining in the room: Sister Genet Bitterling, her present handmaiden, and the third replacement for Sorrel Redwing that the Pontifect Fritillary Reedling had sent her. Sometimes Mathilda wondered at the idiocy of her desperation that had led her to ask Fritillary to place a contact in her royal household, but then her commonsense told her she'd had no choice. At first it was necessary because of her worry over giving birth to devil-kin twins; now it was more that she needed a direct connection to the forces fighting the Grey Lancers, and that was only possible through Fritillary's network of loyal clerics and witans.

She suppressed a desire to apologise to Genet. Drat the woman; she had a habit of saying odd things that seemed off-hand, but which had a jabbing point to them when one stopped to consider. Why the sweet oak couldn't Fritillary Reedling have sent someone younger and more personable? The first two had been older still, but even Genet was a tall, dried-up scarecrow, scrawny with age. All three were nuns, adherents of a Way of the Flow religious order called the Sisters of the Veil, known for their charity. Genet always dressed plainly in the dull grey of the order, including a grey wimple that covered her hair, forehead, neck and chin in a swathe of cloth. Only that area of her face between her upper eyelids and her bottom lip was visible. The top of the wimple jutted forward, so that her face was often shadowed, making her expression hard to read. It was the headgear decreed by her order, but Mathilda was sure the woman took delight in her inscrutability.

"Be careful, my dear, with the lawyer fellow," Genet continued. "The one from the Customs House. He might not have lied, but he's shifty, nonetheless. I doubt he told the whole truth about Kesleer's taxes. I suspect Kesleer pays him not to look too hard into what is due the Crown, if you ask me."

"I do not recall asking you, Sister Genet."

"I consider it my duty to give you my considered opinion, based on many years of dealing with duplicitous humanity. Nuns see a great deal more villainy than most people realise."

The wretched woman was indeed remarkably astute. It was galling how often these asides from her were helpful.

Biting back a retort, she went to sit in the Regal's chair, the one Vilmar had always used when he gave audiences. Sister Genet took a seat to the side in the deepest shadows of the room. "Servants and handmaidens," the irritating woman had said several times, "should be like useful items of furniture: indispensable, but seen and heard as little as possible. Rather like a commode, don't you think?"

On another occasion, she'd pointed out that she wanted to be as anonymous as possible, especially as she considered herself to be a spy.

"You think of yourself that way?" Mathilda had asked, startled.

"Of course! Was that not the service Sorrel Redwing once

performed for you? Never think of me as a mere handmaiden. I am not here to pick up your dropped reticule or to straighten your kirtle. I am here to listen and advise you, and to be your channel to Pontifect Fritillary. As the Pontifect has access to all trustworthy clerics and shrine keepers, I can also tell you what is happening elsewhere in the Va-cherished world. This channel runs in both directions."

"Even though Fritillary Reedling is no longer Pontifect? Besides, I thought the shrine keepers had all disappeared when the shrines vanished!"

"A Pontifect is still Pontifect as long as he or she is alive. Fox is the usurper. He coerced those fools of the Synod into voting for him. And never underestimate the power of the Ways, my dear." She leaned over at that point and patted Mathilda's hand. Although the gesture should have made her feel like a child, just as being addressed as "my dear" should have done, somehow Genet's confident demeanour made such actions and words comforting rather than patronising. Nonetheless, she was an irritating addition to the court.

When Lord Herelt was ushered into her presence, Mathilda watched him closely as he crossed the room towards her. Of all the Lowmians she had ever met, he was probably the most worthy of being reviled and despised for his crimes. Being in the same room with him made her nauseous – and yet in looks, he seemed so . . . so *ordinary*.

A man of substance, of course. The Deremers were a noble family with a long recorded lineage, a family of astonishing wealth and impressive influence, known for their charity and generosity towards universities and hospices and poorhouses – but none of that mitigated what she knew him to be: a murderer of babies, his actions and those of his family based on the erroneous assumption that twins were devil-kin, carriers of the Horned Plague, rather than victims of Fox family sorcerers.

As much as Sir Herelt might now have ceased that slaughter of innocent children, she could never forgive it, nor forget it, and one day she would see him punished. Fate, however, decreed that for now he had to live, because she needed him. Lowmeer needed him. It was the ultimate irony that his family and the private army he controlled were now her greatest ally against the sorcery that had prompted child slaughter.

He walked with the assurance of a wealthy, good-looking man.

He'd been handsome once, and those good looks lingered on. He could still be charming, damn him. A man used to getting his own way. Not young any more, of course: he was, what, nearing fifty? His haunted eyes were those of a man who had discovered that his entire life was based on a premise that was not only wrong, but utterly unconscionable. He knew his guilt.

"Lord Herelt," she said, "I expected a visit from you much earlier than this."

He bowed deeply. "My sincerest apologies, Your Grace. I have been fully occupied with the tasks that have been my burden since we last spoke." His gaze flicked to where Sister Genet was seated, her head bent as if she perused the missal on her lap.

"I have every confidence in the discretion of my handmaiden," Mathilda said, reading caution in his glance. "Although I will ask her to pass on anything relevant to Pontifect Fritillary."

"Your latest information confirms the Pontifect's continued health?"

"Indeed it does."

"I am glad to have it confirmed that reports of her death are inaccurate." He shot another look at Genet.

"She awaits your report with regard to the Horned Plague and infected twins, as I do. Proceed."

"We have examined all the papers found inside the Institute of Advanced Learning—"

"—that you stole before you burned the Institute to the ground, having murdered everyone inside. Let's not mince matters here, Lord Herelt." He was referring to an incident that had happened more than two years before, but she would never let him forget his past murders. Never.

He inclined his head. "As you say. It took time to trace all the twins mentioned in those documents. Those who are still alive and well will be watched closely. Before she disappeared, Pontifect Fritillary ordered local clerics and religious houses and shrine keepers to monitor them. If there is any sign of any being infected, they will be dealt with – by local agents of the Dire Sweepers – before they spread the disease."

"They will be murdered."

"I prefer to call it mercy killing. Left alone, they all die in unimaginable pain, after having passed on the infection to others. No one ever survives, as well you know, Your Grace. No healer has been able to save a single infected person. From the moment any member of the Fox family touched the life of a twin with the intention of stealing that life, they were doomed.

"However, I believe that Valerian Fox no longer bothers with the whole twin-devil-kin deception. He must be aware that we are no longer fooled by it, and feels powerful enough to take what he needs, when he needs it. I have received several recent reports of babies dying or disappearing under mysterious circumstances in the Principalities around the time Fox – or sometimes just his Grey Lancers – were in the vicinity. Tens of small children. Usually from burned-out orphanages, or slums, or areas devastated by fighting. My assessment is that Valerian has lost all sense of restraint and he grows in power as a consequence."

Mathilda shuddered. "Killing them outright?"

"Yes. At least it saves them from dying of the Horned Plague before they reach adulthood. A mercy, I suppose."

"So you think we can safely say the Horned Plague will soon run its course within the boundaries of Lowmeer?"

"I do. Those who were infected as babies will die within the next few years, and there will be no new infections as long as Valerian does not return to the Regality. We have seized all of the Fox estates within the boundaries of Lowmeer, as per your orders." He pulled some papers out from his coat pocket. "A list of every place and an estimation of the value. Local bailiffs have been appointed to run them as going concerns until sales are affected, or until you decide to keep them as the property of the Basalt Throne. We have brought a number of coffers of coin with us, which I have delivered to the treasury. I should point out that we would appreciate having some of this returned to us."

"Would you indeed? The Dire Sweepers and the Deremers *deserve* nothing but opprobrium from us, Lord Herelt."

He paused then, and she thought she glimpsed an expression of pain. Or was it exasperation? It was gone before she could be sure.

"Forgive me, Your Grace, for my presumption. What we deserve is nothing, I agree, but without money, we cannot purchase the means to defeat men who have access to sorcery. We need guns and gunpowder. With them, we might stand a chance if cannonballs and gunshot can reach further than the workings of sorcery, which I believe to be the case. In addition, the rank and file need to be fed and paid. So far, my family have – to assuage their shame – dug deep into their pockets, but maintaining a private troop to supplement Your Grace's own army does not come cheap."

She considered that, and gave an unladylike grunt of assent. "Put in a notice of your requirements to the treasury and it will be considered."

"Thank you, Your Grace." He inclined his head. Polite, but restrained.

"Tell me about what you found on the Fox estates," she said, leaning back, her hands clasping the carved basalt arms of her chair.

"Most remarkably, no adult male members of the Fox family. Servants told us that any Fox offspring over the age of twelve was ordered to leave the estate and report to Prime Fox early last year. Er, Pontifect Fox, that is." He gave another embarrassed glance towards Genet. "As far as we could determine, all living Fox children are descended from Valerian. He had relationships with a great many women whose ancestry was through the Fox line. His cousins mostly, at various degrees of remove. He was deliberately seeking to keep the sorcerous blood alive. As for his male cousins? Who knows. They seem to have died young."

There was a rushing sound inside Mathilda's ears. She wanted to ask him – she *needed* to ask him something, but her tongue wouldn't work. She opened her mouth, and closed it again.

It was Genet who leaned forward then and addressed him, her sharp eyes worried. "Are all Valerian's male children sorcerers?"

"If there were any who weren't, they were probably killed. There are whispers about him sucking the life out of them. All the so-called Gaunt Recruiters are Valerian's sons."

"How many of these sons are there?" Genet asked.

"We don't know. We have evidence for fifteen, but we believe there are a lot more."

Mathilda licked her dry lips, struggling to find her voice again. "The mothers of Valerian's offspring?" she asked. *Va forgive me. How could I have been so stupid as to ever let that man lay a finger on me?*

"Never found any. Not alive. Surprising number of them appear to have killed themselves shortly after giving birth, if the gossip of the servants on the Fox estates is to be believed. There were a few had multiple sons before their demise, but Valerian preferred them dead to interfering with the raising of his children." Noting her expression of distaste, he added, "There's no such person as a good sorcerer. We have cleaned the vermin from your stables, Your Grace. There was one Fox son I was extremely sorry not to lay my hands on. Fellow called Ruthgar. He's one of Valerian's older offspring, born in Fearnside. He appears to be one of the more intelligent, because Valerian raised him to look after some of the family finances instead of sending him off to be a Gaunt Recruiter."

"Or stealing his life in order to prolong his own," Mathilda said sourly.

"Precisely. And he was clever enough to realise when we were closing in on him. He realised his assets and disappeared. We're fairly certain he's no longer in Lowmeer. So, the problem remains: what do we do now? There are other rats and other Foxes just over the borders."

She felt so ill, she couldn't reply. Fortunately Sister Genet had plenty to say. "But the Fox has obedient underlings within Lowmeer!" she snapped. "Valerian is supposedly our Pontifect. The Grey Lancers may still be kept at bay beyond our borders, but Fox commands our clerics. Her Grace cannot denounce him. He was duly elected by the Synod of Clerics after he told them Fritillary Reedling had gone mad and died. Lowmians are *happy* to have him as Pontifect. He panders to their fear of the Ardronese Way of the Oak dominance by reminding them of his Lowmian ancestry and his commitment to the importance of chapels rather than either of the Ways."

"The disappearance of shrines and those folk with witcheries doesn't help," Deremer said. "People are angry about that. What does it mean? Where did they go?"

Mathilda raised an eyebrow. "I was hoping you might be able to tell me!"

"*I* don't have a direct line to Fritillary, wherever she's hiding." He sighed and gave Genet another pointed look. "For all I know, Her Reverence may indeed be insane. If anyone knows what happened to the shrines, Pontifect Fritillary does, and she should tell us."

"Well, she hasn't told me," Mathilda snapped. If ever she met Fritillary Reedling face to face, she would tell the impudent upstart of a farmer's daughter what she thought of her.

"May I advise then," Deremer continued smoothly, "that you inform her that we need answers? We need to know what happened to the shrines and to people with witcheries. Did sorcery destroy them? Where is Va in all this? People will lose their belief in Va-faith if something doesn't give them hope soon! She's hiding when she should be fighting. She's failing us all." He looked across at Genet once more. "You tell her that, sister. Tell her to write to me if she is unable to pay me a visit."

Mathilda heard both anger and anguish in his voice and her own optimism faltered. "Her last message was to be patient."

He rolled his gaze up at the ceiling in an extravagant gesture of exasperation. "Maybe she's out of her mind. Ardrone is as good as gone. As soon as Fox and his numerous sons have consolidated their hold on the Principalities, they will turn their attention to us. Tell me, please, just how do I protect my men from this black smutch I hear about? It confuses the brave; scares them into throwing down their weapons and makes them run like frightened mole-rats."

"If we get more arquebuses or those wheel lock pistols . . .?"

"Certainly they might be a way of killing sorcerers from a distance. But it's not so easy. We have no skills at making them. The black powder arms we have, we imported overland from Pashalin, and they are very expensive. We need the balls and the powder as well. In another year or two, we might have enough skilled workers to make our own, and we need to find out more about how to make gunpowder . . ."

"But you're not sure we have the time."

"No, I'm not. Your Grace, tell the Pontifect I need to talk to her. I need to know what the plan is, because right now, all I can see ahead is ultimate defeat. We need people with witcheries. Without them, we have nothing. Without shrines and their unseen guardians, there will never be another person granted a witchery."

"Do you think I don't know that?" Mathilda said. "What I don't understand is this: we might not have many pistols or arquebuses, but you do have *some*. Why don't you just send an assassin to kill

Valerian Fox from afar? Shoot a ball at him when he comes out into the street! Someone with an arquebus can kill without getting close enough to be coerced."

"Do you think we haven't tried that? A dozen times! More. And every time the man who volunteered turned his weapon on himself when Fox appeared. And died by his own hand. Coerced from a distance, without a word being spoken that the assassin could hear."

"You once told me coercion diminishes his power and that's why he uses his sons to do it for him," Mathilda said.

"So I believe."

"Then send more and more assassins," she cried, "until he is so weak he can be killed!"

Deremer levelled a look at her that made her shiver. "Your Grace, I grieve for every man of mine who dies thus. But still I might yet do as you suggest – but for one thing. Every time his power is diminished by such a murder, he seeks out more and more children. And those deaths sit ill on my conscience these days."

There was a long silence, during which none of them moved. Then she said quietly, "Tell me, do you know of the whereabouts of the lawyer, Gerelda Brantheld, and that lad of hers?"

"No. Why do you ask?"

"He had an interesting witchery. An ability to see the contamination of sorcery. Able both to identify a sorcerer, and to see someone besmirched by sorcery."

"Ah. I did not know that."

"I believe you have done your best, Lord Herelt, under difficult circumstances. You have, in fact, *begun* to redeem yourself and your family." Her slight emphasis was meant to remind him that his entire extended family had forfeited any rights to her consideration. If they wanted to live and prosper, they had to continue to risk everything.

She stood and extended her hand, indicating the audience was over. "Sister Genet will see that Pontifect Fritillary is informed of all that we have discussed."

"Have you ever met her, Your Grace?"

"No."

He bowed deeply over her fingers. "Your Grace." He straightened, and retreated four steps, before turning to leave the room.

She waited until he had gone and the door was closed before she spoke again. "What did you think, Sister Genet?"

The nun stepped out from the shadows to stand at her side. "A tormented man." There was both pity and sorrow in her tone.

"He *deserves* to be tormented for what he has done!"

"If a child is brought up to believe something from birth, no matter how dreadful that thing, he accepts it as the truth. Told his duty was to spend his life performing a dreadful task, he believed it necessary." She shook her head in sadness. "It was a soul-destroying thing, to be born a Deremer."

"You are more forgiving than I."

"You have reason. You are the mother of twins."

"*Never* speak of that, or I'll see you dead!"

Genet did not appear abashed. "Speak of it or not, it does not change the truth."

"If someone were to hear you . . ." She choked at the thought. What would the Lowmian court and nobility do? Condemn her for the deception? Condemn her for casting out her daughter? She didn't know, but her position as an Ardronese princess acting as a Regent was a precarious one. There were a dozen men high in the royal court who would be delighted to have her denounced as too immoral to be a Regent. There would even be those who would separate her from Prince-regal Karel. If that were to happen, she'd die of grief.

"Your Grace, his information has presented us with an interesting conundrum."

"What conundrum is that?" she asked, irritated.

"How did Prince-regal Karel gain his smutch?"

She felt all the colour drain from her face, leaving her faint.

Genet, her face expressionless, continued, "Valerian Fox has never been here, or seen your son. The whole devil-kin thing was never what we thought it was. So how was the prince contaminated?"

"I would have thought it obvious! One of his sons was the man who came and threatened me just before Karel's investiture. He coerced his way into the solar and he coerced *me*. He said he was a devil-kin and he did something to Karel."

Genet regarded her steadily from under her wimple. "Long before that, while Regal Vilmar was still alive, the Pontifect sent Agent Gerelda to look at Prince-regal Karel . . ."

"You've been misinformed! Go, you wretched woman! Send your messages to the Pontifect. Tell her the Regala wants answers – how do we win this war? Where are the shrines and the witcheries to aid us?"

She turned on her heel and left the room. Outside the door, she began to shake. Prince-regal Karel didn't have a black smutch of contamination. He *was* the contamination. She knew it for sure now. He was Valerian's son. He was a sorcerer.

And she – cankers and galls, she'd been a stupid child, allowing Valerian Fox to touch her. *No, you mustn't think like that. It was never your fault! He* coerced *you into his bed. No one can resist coercion, can they?*

Taking a deep, calming breath, she headed up to the nursery. She needed to see her son.

If only she could stop shaking . . .

When he saw her, he came running, his arms held out, calling, "Mama, Mama! Come look what me did!"

He had raised a pile of carved wooden blocks into a wobbly tower, complete with turrets and crenellations. As she duly admired his handiwork and tousled his golden hair, so silky and fine, she wondered at the pain of the love she felt. She would do anything for this child. Anything.

He looked up at her and smiled, proud of his accomplishment. Then, as she watched, he kicked the bottom block and the tower collapsed on to the wooden floor with a clatter. He laughed. "Look. All fall down! All deaded! Me killed them all." When he looked up at her, she saw Fox gazing back. His eyes, his lips.

The stab in her heart festered as her dread spread, freezing her smile into something false.

No, Karel is mine. All mine.

Then the unwanted memory of another child, Karel's twin. Her pain deepened until she almost cried out. *They did this to us. Prime Valerian Fox. Regal Vilmar Vollendorn. The Dire Sweepers. Herelt Deremer.*

She would not rest until they were all dead, every one of them.

11

The Lost Man and
the Stolen Princess

"Who are you?"

He roused himself. Feeling ill, he looked around. He was standing beside a horse cart laden with root vegetables, driven by the elderly man who'd asked the question. A man he'd never seen before.

"Pardon?" he asked.

"Who are you?"

He didn't answer. He couldn't. "Where the flubbing hells am I?"

"This here's the road to Beck Crossways. I'm taking the load from my farm to market. Did yer want a ride?" The elderly carter rubbed a hand across his forehead as if his head ached. "I think I must have nodded off . . ."

"I don't know why I'm here. I was . . ." But he couldn't remember what he'd been doing or where he'd been going. "Do I know you?"

"Never saw you before in my life. Been into the grog, have you?"

He shook his head, more a gesture of bewilderment than answer. He couldn't remember anything.

"So, d'you want a ride to Beck Crossways?"

He shrugged. "Mayhap I do."

The farmer indicated the space on the driving seat. "Hop up, then. Me name's Sprig."

"I stay overnight here," the carter told him, pointing, when they reached the outskirts of Beck Crossways. "In the common field, with the other folk who come a ways to sell their crops. Sleep under the cart, I do."

Sprig made no offer to share the space, so his passenger alighted from the cart, saying, "Thank you for the ride. Much obliged." He'd tried to extract as much information as possible from Sprig before they arrived at Beck Crossways, but questioning had confused the carter, and finally he'd sunk into a sullen silence.

As he turned to go, Sprig stopped him. "The pack," he said. "That's yourn, no?"

He looked at the battered leather bag tucked under the seat without recognition. "Oh, aye." Slinging it on to his shoulder, he nodded his thanks, and headed down the road towards the first of the houses of the market town while the farmer turned the cart, full of its turnips and mangelwurzels, on to the common.

His hand dropped to touch the hilt of his sword. There was comfort there in that touch, although he couldn't have said why. The truth was he remembered nothing of his past, not his name nor why he'd been heading towards Beck Crossways, let alone why he felt so . . . bereft.

The town had no wall. If he remembered his history, it was five hundred years since there'd been as much as a skirmish here. There, he could dredge stupid history of past kings and battles out of his addled pate, so why couldn't he think of his name? He swore, the foulest words he usually kept for someone trying to kill him.

Someone trying to kill him.

Was that a memory? Maybe.

He knew the steel in his sword was the finest Ardrone had to offer. He knew how to fight; and he was good at it. If he pulled that sword out of its scabbard, it would fit into his grasp as if it belonged in his hand. He knew that he had an important task, and that knowledge scratched at his memory as if it wanted to claw its way to the surface, but . . .

No, he couldn't remember.

He looked down at his clothes. He was dressed like a fobbing farmer, yet he wore a sword. Why did his head feel like it was stuffed with sheep shit?

Think, you dewberry! The tote. Look inside . . .

Good quality leather, he noted. Deer skin. Something told him it was not what he usually carried. His own would have been grubbier, more worn and made of heavier cowhide. It was late afternoon, and the only other person he could see was a lad with a flock of geese in the field, so he stepped off the rutted road, to sit on the grass and examine the contents of the bag.

His investigation revealed a round of hard cheese, a dagger, a woollen blanket waxed on one side to make it waterproof, a pair of well-worn gloves, an extra length of leather thong, a small tub of liniment, a spoon, a tin cookpot, and the wherewithal to sharpen his sword – oil, whetstone and file. There was also a fine leather purse. He tipped the contents of the latter into his hand, and his jaw dropped. What the sweet cankers was he doing with all that cabbage? Beggar him speechless, there was a glint of gold among the silver and the brass! Hurriedly, he rammed the more valuable coins into his fob. They'd be safer there.

Everything else felt familiar to him. When he handled the whetstone, he knew it was his. But the money? He doubted that he normally had access to that kind of coinage, yet every time he tried to think about who he was, or where he was going, or what his mission was, his brain fogged up. It was like trying to see through a window streaked with rain: nothing was clear. Thoughts disintegrated, leaving tantalising hints, but nothing more. His past was just a bad taste in his mouth and his future was an acrid smell pinching his nostrils.

Something was terribly wrong.

When he stood up and continued on his way into the town, he slung the bag across his chest. He wasn't going to risk losing it.

The public buildings of Beck Crossways gathered around the cobbled marketplace, windows watching over the bustling preparations for the next day's market. He sat on the edge of the horse trough near the pump to observe, hoping to recognise someone, or something.

It didn't happen.

Before the daylight disappeared, he ambled across to the inn, only to find that on the eve of market day every bed was taken, so he paid a few coppers to doss down in the livery stable instead. He slept with his pack in his arms.

He woke early with the same nagging feeling that there was something desperately important he ought to be doing. At the baker's, he bought a heel of stale bread and ate it with a slice of his own cheese, washing it all down with a mug of cheap beer. He had more money in his purse than he'd probably ever had, yet he couldn't bring himself to spend it.

By the time he'd finished, the town square – now packed with carts and makeshift stands – was thrumming with the commerce of the day. He noticed Sprig the turnip grower there, but didn't approach him.

His horror at his inactivity began to overwhelm him. He could feel his temper rising, like hot water bubbling under a copper lid. To subdue it, he left the square and walked the streets of the town. He had no memory of any of them. The day crawled by.

He returned to the square in the early afternoon and seated himself near the pump again, next to a knife sharpener, an elderly man with a grindstone and a lad to turn the wheel. "Your sword need an edge?" the fellow asked.

Removing it from its sheath, he ran a finger down the blade. No nicks, freshly oiled. He shook his head. "I take good care of it," he said sliding it back into its sheath, and knew that to be true.

A minute or two later, there was a stir at one end of the square. A troop of horsemen had ridden in, paying scant attention to the people already there. They made no attempt to avoid the crowd, but rode straight into it. The leader, a young, pale man wearing black, looked neither to right nor left, but set his mount straight at the livery stable opposite. The crowd peeled away from them like a wave before the prow of a boat. The others wore dirty grey coats, giving the impression of a uniform, but they were a slovenly-looking lot, with dull expressions and hard about the eyes.

The young man's darkness bit into him, sending cold shivers skittering across his skin. He leaped up from his seat, dry-mouthed, hunting within for the cause of his fear. The retreating crowd buffeted him, sweeping him along, out of the way of the horses.

He looked back over his shoulder. In the centre of the mounted troop was a woman with a child, sagging with fatigue. His initial stir of pity for her blossomed into a hard tug of emotion, paining him. She didn't see him. He doubted she was seeing much at all. She was too scared, too miserable. Her fatigue appalled him, and he knew that her tear-streaked child mattered – but he couldn't have said why.

None of them spared him a glance as they rode by to the inn.

Something of his turmoil must have shown on his face, because a large man wearing the red apron of a butcher grabbed him by the elbow to steady him. "Are you all right? Those bastards, they care for no one!"

He managed a nod. "Who are they?"

"Not come across them before? You're a lucky one, then. Grey Lancers. Protecting us from the Horned Plague and Primordial heretics, bless 'em. Trouble is, sometimes we need protecting from them too, I reckon." His tone was more resigned than resentful.

"Who's the man in black?" he asked.

"Don't rightly know."

"If they wear black and lead a troop of lancers, they're a Fox, so I've heard tell," the knife sharpener said. He shrugged. "And if you ask me, that's reason enough not to ask questions."

Fox? He'd heard that name before. The Prime of Ardrone, Valerian Fox. The name bothered him, but the memory skittered away like a timid cat from an outstretched hand. "And the woman and child?" he asked.

"How the blithering acorns am I supposed to know that?" the knife sharpener asked. "You better learn to keep your questions to yourself, my man. Them fellows have short tempers and quick reactions. Sensible men keep their chops shut and their tongues still."

He nodded, and glanced over towards the inn, wondering if he ought at least to approach the woman. As he watched, the man in black went to help her, offering to take the child as she dismounted, but the look she gave him was pure ferocity. She beckoned to the ostler and handed the lad down to him instead, then climbed from the saddle by herself, almost toppling when her feet hit the ground. She clung to the stirrup for a moment, then moved to take her young'un.

No. He wouldn't speak. Not while the Fox fellow was anywhere near.

By the time they reined in their horses in front of the inn on the market square of Beck Crossways, Bealina could barely think straight.

Her whole body ached with fatigue and her distress at Garred's misery was overwhelming. His skin was chafed and raw in patches and he hadn't been eating well.

At first, she'd believed they were bound for Throssel and King Edwayn, until the sorcerer – she thought of him as the Foxcub – told her he'd lied, and they were only retracing her steps as far as Gromwell. She guessed then that they meant to use her and Garred to force Ryce to surrender, but she was wrong.

"Valerian Fox has no interest in making a martyr of Ryce," the Foxcub said. "Better that the prince sit in his holdfast, looking like the weak peahen he is. After all, Pontifect Fox now has the pawn he really wants: your little mewler."

The whole point of the return to Gromwell was a simple cruelty: to show Ryce that her flight had been in vain. Their true destination was Vavala. She was being taken to Pontifect Valerian Fox.

She wept when she heard that.

Va, she hated that whey-faced son of a sorcerer with a searing venom. *One day*, she promised herself, *I'll kill you. And I don't care if I have to slice you up piece by piece* . . .

Finally, after a horrible night spent beside the road, they were in Beck Crossways, and she was following him into the inn, Garred in her arms, her chin held high even as her eyes blurred with tears. Inside, he paid for a room for her and another for himself. She was vaguely aware that other guests had to be moved to give them rooms, but as she mounted the stairs behind him, she didn't care.

The servants lit a fire and prepared a bath in her chamber, but the Foxcub remained with her the whole time they were about their tasks. After they'd left, she asked, "Are you going to stay in the room while I bathe?"

"I have no interest in your body," he said. His indifference was chilling rather than reassuring. "Just remember, there will be guards outside the door. You aren't going anywhere."

He left her then, and she luxuriated in the clean hot water of the tin bath, and in the joy that brought her son. After she was dressed again, she lifted him out of the water, rubbed him dry with the fire-warmed towel, and tucked him into bed. He was asleep immediately.

She opened the door and looked outside. Two guards lounged

against the opposite wall. "Ask the servants to remove the bath," she said, ignoring their open sneering.

Garred had splashed water everywhere with his enthusiastic play, so when the menservants came to take the tub, she asked them to send someone to mop the floor. While she waited, she sat on the bed, and thought of Horntail. She wanted so badly to believe that he would rescue her, but her last sight of him had appalled her. He had looked befuddled. So ensorcelled.

When the Foxcub entered, accompanied by a maid with rags and bucket, Bealina stood up. She felt safer on her feet. The sorcerer leaned against the mantelpiece at the side of the fire watching the girl as she knelt to wipe up the pool of soapy water. She was young, a grubby skivvy with lank, greasy hair, who ducked her head rather than look at either of them.

"Thank you," Bealina said when she had finished. "You may go now."

The girl bobbed a curtsey. Lugging the bucket to the door, she had to pass the Foxcub. He whispered something in her ear. She gasped, clutched at her throat and dropped to the floor.

Bealina gaped. There seemed no reason for her sudden collapse. "Are you all right?" she asked, words she knew to be absurd even as she gave them voice. The girl was far from all right.

She knelt beside her, taking up her hand. "What happened? Can you sit up?"

The skivvy tried to speak, but could not draw breath. Her eyes begged for help, and then, abruptly, filmed over. Her face still registered her terror, but her eyes – in her eyes, there was nothing. Nothing at all.

She couldn't believe it. The girl had *died*?

Still kneeling, still holding that grubby hand with its broken nails and rough skin, Bealina looked up at the Foxcub – and he smiled.

She knew then; it had been his doing.

"*Why?*" she asked. Her body started shaking and she dropped the lifeless hand. "Why would you do something so – so utterly pointless?"

"To show you I can. To remind you what your situation is. You look for ways to escape. You look for people to help you. Do you think I don't see it?"

She was shaking so hard now, she couldn't reply.

He smiled at her, but there was no humour in it. "Remember this. Remember how easy it is for me. And how little I care. I was told to keep Prince Garred alive and well – and you are a convenient instrument to do that, but you aren't essential." He sounded tired, not triumphant.

She clenched her hands into fists in an attempt to control her trembling, and noticed the bloodless white pallor of his face and the way he was still propped against the mantel.

"Every time you use your power, you are closer to dying," she said. In one of her communications before she'd disappeared, Pontifect Fritillary had told them that much. "You can feel your life slipping away, can't you? Valerian is using you up, burning you like a candle, and once the wick ends, the candle dies. He does that to all his sons. He's the flame that sucks you of all life."

For a long time she knelt there, shaking, incapable of climbing to her feet, unable even to wonder if her words would have a disastrous effect, or work to her advantage. How could she ever know what thoughts occurred in the head of a sorcerer's son?

"I'm my father's heir," he said. It was scarcely more than a whisper.

"That's what you all think," she replied. "He has many sons."

He pushed himself away from the fireplace to open the door, then spoke to one of the two guards outside. "Get rid of this body, will you?" he asked. "Fresh meat."

She wouldn't have thought the evening could get any worse, but when she saw the guard's face light up with an expectation of pleasure, she remembered a story she'd heard of a scribe, a man called Clary, who had been cooked and eaten. The meaning of the guard's anticipation filtered through to her understanding, and her gorge rose. She bent over the bucket, heaving until there was nothing left in her stomach. When she raised her head again, the guard and the girl were gone.

The Foxcub stood, his hands hanging loose by his sides. "You're a fool," he said.

"P-probably," she agreed, shivering as she sat back on her heels. "I'm not very old. Seventeen, still. I've seen little of life outside my safe little world. But I think I know not only why you never killed the farmers who helped me, but why you never asked your Grey Lancers to kill them either. You're not sure you can control them around dead bodies, are you? Each time that you have to *coerce* them into obedience takes a little more of your life." He stared at her, the hatred seeping from every pore. She could smell it.

"You need me," she said. "If I die, you'll never bring Prince Garred safely to Vavala. Your men would—" She swallowed hard before she could say the words. "What? Eat him the moment your back was turned?"

He left her then, slamming the door behind him.

She doubled over where she was, rocking her body and crying. She had no idea whether she had made things better, or worse, for herself.

12

The Different Man
and His Executioner

Peregrine Clary always thought of his father before he killed. He would remember his smile, his slow way of speaking, his red-tongued shoes . . . Then he'd remember the smell of burned flesh, the horror of knowing the Grey Lancers had eaten his father. The memory gave him permission to do the work Pontifect Fritillary had asked of him and Gerelda Brantheld: kill sorcerers. Valerian Fox's sons, the Gaunt Recruiters.

They were on the trail of their tenth sorcerer. Perie had found the first four in Valence, where they'd been leading troops of Grey Lancers. The next two had been killing Primordials and attacking shrine keepers and shrines along the Ardronese border, in the Shenat Hills.

Soon after that, all the shrines had vanished, and he and Gerelda had set off to Melforn and Boneset in the east, searching for more of the Fox progeny where the Prime's family had manor estates. There, he killed another couple where they'd been enticing farm folk into joining the Grey Lancers. They'd headed to Hornbeam then, where they'd heard the lancers were killing Shenat clerics. They'd killed the leader of the troop, another Fox son.

When they'd heard that Prince Ryce was under siege in Gromwell Holdfast, they decided to investigate whether a sorcerer was involved. Just out of Melforn, though, Perie had picked up the stench of the tenth sorcerer travelling the road north several days ahead of them, and the trail had led them to Oakwood, not Gromwell.

"We are close to him," he said to Gerelda after they'd ridden into the town and stabled their horses at a livery. "He's here somewhere."

"Just the one man?"

He nodded, then frowned. "That's odd, isn't it? But I can't smell any Grey Lancers here, none. Just him." He called it a smell, but it wasn't really. It was a smutch he could sense, but not with his nose. With his witchery. He shouldered his pack and looked up and down the street, in an attempt to trace the direction of the taint. They were still standing outside the livery, and the strong, rich odour of horse sweat and manure swamped much of his witchery perception.

"Up that way, I think," he said, and turned in that direction. "This town is a strange sort of place. I've never seen buildings like these before."

Along one side of the cobbled roadway, houses of three or four storeys were squashed up against one another, the frontage of each not much wider than the length of two horses standing head to tail. In fact, each was so narrow that the stairs had been built on the outside. On the opposite side of the road, the buildings were completely different, long and unadorned, with only one narrow door and many shutters that could be propped open to let in air and light. He thought they looked more like barns.

"Oakwood's more university than town, and you're in the heart of Shenat country," she said. "That makes a difference."

"Where's the university?" he asked as they walked on into the heart of the town.

"Everywhere. There's no single building." She pointed to the barn-like structure. "That's a student doss house, the cheapest place to stay. If you're a bit richer, then you rent a room with a family. If you're really wealthy, then you arrange to stay with one of the professors."

"So where do students go to *learn*?"

"Classes are held in the teacher's house, usually. Tutorials, they're called. Some of the poorer tutors hold a class in a tavern and charge less."

"Then the most popular teachers are the best and they charge the most?"

She grinned. "That's the theory, but as I recall, classes in a tavern were top in popularity." They had come to a cross street, so she stopped and looked at him. "Which way?"

He took a deep breath, tasting the air and that awful smear of tarry vileness that was a sorcerer's taint. "Down there," he said, pointing along the broader thoroughfare.

"Might have guessed," she said, turning that way. "This leads to the better side of town. Our sorcerer wouldn't be stopping in the run-down section."

"What would he be doing in a university town anyway?"

"I don't know. But somehow the idea scares me."

The town was a labyrinth of winding lanes, some of them noxious and drear, some opening on to wider thoroughfares, even tree-lined boulevards. And everywhere there were students, many of them wearing black gowns with coloured sleeve bands that proclaimed their allegiance to one of the five disciplines: theology, science, mathematics, law or history. Peregrine had already decided that students came in all shapes, sizes and ages. The one thing they had in common was that they all carried something – books, scrolls, slates, pen-and-ink sets or writing tablets. As both he and Gerelda were carrying their packs, they fitted right in, especially as Gerelda was keeping her sword out of sight under her cloak.

Perie touched the side of his thigh where his own weapon was hidden. He had long abandoned any attempt to master swordplay. His weapon of choice was now an assassin's blade called a spiker, a slender, tapered dagger that was easy to slip into a man's chest, or into his back, to the heart. It was light to carry, simple to conceal – and a stab from it resulted in little mess.

Nine men, dead on its blade. Number ten was within reach . . .

"They like their ale, don't they?" he asked as they passed yet another noisy tavern full of students.

"Cheaper than a meal if you don't have money," she remarked.

"Were you one of the poorer ones at your university?"

"Indeed I was. But I had good friends. I got by." And she smiled, as if remembering something pleasant. "It's important to have friends," she added.

He'd never had friends, at least not since he'd started travelling with his Da. Nine years old, he'd been then, and a boy couldn't find a friend when they were always on the move. He frowned, wondering what he'd missed. Would a friend be better than Gerelda on this quest of his – to kill as many sorcerers as he could? He doubted it.

Although . . . maybe Gerelda was a friend. He would not have liked it if she left him. Was that what having a friend was?

"How close is he, do you think?" she asked as he guided her into a wide street of handsome colonnaded homes.

"Very. Do you know this road?"

"I do, as a matter of fact. The head of the university's professorial board lives in that house on the right, the one with the tree outside. He conducts lectures in law on the ground floor. I attended them for one term."

"You told me you went to university in Lowmeer!"

"Yes, I did. My degree is from Grundorp. But a lot of students do a term or two at other universities, especially if there's a particularly good scholar giving the lectures. That's how I met Saker Rampion. He turned up in Grundorp."

"I've heard you mention that name before. Or was it Fritillary who spoke of him? Who is he?"

"Oh, never mind. This is the street where all the richest academics live. Let's walk down and see if you can work out where our sorcerer is."

They ambled along as if they weren't looking for anything in particular, and no one gave them a second glance. At the end of the street, he told her they had to retrace their steps because they'd passed their quarry.

"That's the house," he said at last, pointing. "He's in there. I'm sure of it." He nodded at an elegant mansion accessed by broad steps up to an impressive doorway. Even as he spoke, one side of the doors opened and ten or so students spilled out, laughing and chattering down the steps.

"Is he one of those?" she asked.

He shook his head.

"Let me find out who lives there," she muttered. Smiling, she waved to one of the students. "Hey, my friend, is this the house of Marmot Crake, professor of law?"

The young man halted, with several of his friends lingering as well, to wait for him. "No, he lives in that one with the tree. This is Professor Hoddison Rork's house, professor of theology. You must be visiting students?"

"That's right," she said, her smile widening. "Not long in Oakwood. Rork. I was going to take his course as well. I heard he's a fellow with a beard down to his waist, who mumbles all the time?"

"That's him. But this month, he's not giving the tutorials. He's turned over his course to someone else for a term. Arbiter Camber Fox."

"Oh!" Gerelda glanced at Perie with an expression of dismay before turning back to the student, "Should we be disappointed? I mean, we were looking forward to benefiting from Professor Rork's expertise, and to have a replacement—"

"He seems to know his stuff," the student replied. "He gave his first tutorial just now. Young fellow, but entertaining. Hard to believe he's an arbiter!"

Gerelda pursed her lips. "I didn't come all this way to be entertained! I want someone with experience, who can give me theological guidance. Tell me, does he advocate putting Shenat teachings before Va-chapel sermons?"

One of the other students, a woman, laughed. "Hardly. He's the Pontifect's nephew, for a start. Which probably explains why he's an arbiter already, when he can't be more than twenty-five, if he's a day."

"So what course is he teaching?"

"'Va-faith Renewed', he calls it. The next tutorial is at ten tomorrow morning. And he was enlightening. Made good sense to me."

The students went on their way and Perie looked across at Gerelda. She was biting her lip and frowning.

He said, "He's used sorcery on them, just a bit."

"To coerce them?"

"No. Not exactly. More to—" He thought about it. "What I sense is not evil enough for that. More to charm them, I think. Do you think he's really Valerian's nephew?"

"More likely his son. As Pontifect, Valerian can hardly admit he's sired tens of sons from one end of the hemisphere to the other."

"I suppose not."

"Think of the damage this Camber fellow could do teaching a whole term of the theology course, twisting Shenat customs and beliefs until it sounds like a perversion instead of something that protects the land and forests and rivers. He could have those students – most of whom will one day be clerics – calling for the death of witchery and shrine keepers." She drew in a heavy breath. "Tomorrow we're going to be students of his. We'd better find somewhere to stay

118

for the night." She looked down at herself. "*Not* a doss house, I think. Somewhere with a bath."

"You look worried," Perie remarked as they walked to the tutorial the next morning.

"That's because this one does worry me. It's different, and when a sorcerer is unpredictable . . ." She shrugged. "One of these days we are going to be caught."

He imitated her shrug. "Everybody runs out of luck sooner or later."

"One keeps on hoping it's going to be later." She paused, then added, "We can always stop, if you want."

He looked at her in surprise. "No, we can't! We can't stop while there is a single sorcerer alive."

"I guess what I meant is that *you* could stop. Fobbing hells, Perie, you're only fourteen, and you have—" She hesitated.

"—murdered nine sorcerers. Yes. It's what I do."

"You don't feel *anything*?" she asked in a whisper.

He was surprised. "I feel glad. Should I feel anything else?"

Her glance his way was uneasy.

"I asked *not* to feel, you know. It was the bargain I made with the unseen guardian. It's what I wanted."

She was silent. He hadn't told her that before.

"You can't do this without me," he pointed out.

He knew that was true; she had no witchery, couldn't track a sorcerer and never felt that horrible taint of sorcery in the air. He didn't know whether to pity her for her lack of acumen, or envy her because she didn't know how foul the spoor of sorcery and ensor-cellment was. Moreover, she wouldn't have been able to kill a sorcerer either, because any one of them would have read her like an open page of a book and used his magic to stop her.

But no sorcerer had recognised him as a danger. Their eyes told them he was just a lad; their sorcery told them nothing of his intentions.

"What you mean, I suppose," he said, "is that someone my age should be doing something different, like going to school, or learning a trade. Proctor, you keep thinking that I'm just a lad." When she didn't reply, he added, "I haven't been a lad since the day Da was murdered."

"What happened that day? After you left me, I mean."

"I saw what had been done to Da, then I spoke to an unseen guardian. And after that . . . I was different. The Pontifect knew that when she met me. She *knew*. Both of them, the guardian and the Pontifect, gave me a choice – and this is what I chose, to serve the Way of the Oak. I'm not a lad. I'm not even sure I'm Peregrine Clary any more."

"I'm a lawyer. I don't know what the sweet cankers you're talking about. All I see is a lad who should be enjoying life, not fighting an evil."

"If I don't, who will?" he asked, knowing she had no answer.

It was astonishingly simple to gain entrance to Professor Rork's house. They joined the dribble of students wanting to attend the tutorial. Just inside the door, someone was collecting the fees for attendance, and they were directed into a room, which to Perie's eyes was more like a chapel hall than anything he'd imagined a classroom would resemble. It had pews rather than chairs, and a raised platform for the tutor. Perie counted the number of students attending – thirty-two. He and Gerelda sat quietly at the back, each with a cheap writing tablet and graphite stick so that they both looked like students.

Camber Fox, who entered the room a few minutes later, was pale and ill-looking, not at all like Valerian, who reeked of a foul energy, powerful, vibrant, knowing, ancient. There was a softer element in Camber's features, something less assertive in his attitude, something more ambivalent in the way he held himself. Perie's senses did not scream a warning of wrongness; it was more a whisper. Up close like this, the foulness was still muted.

He settled back to listen, occasionally making a pretence of scribbling notes. The basic premise of the lecture was that the use of a witchery interfered with the natural processes of life, and was therefore antithetical to the Shenat belief in the inviolate essence of nature, and therefore called into question whether Shenat was truly Va predicated. He didn't understand much of it, except that it sounded like nonsense. Camber Fox was saying that using a fishing witchery to call fish into your nets was wrong, but he didn't appear to have a problem with using a net in the first place. Moreover, he was certainly using a mild form of coercion to persuade his audience of the rightness of all he was saying; Perie felt it pushing against him with an incessant gentleness.

When he glanced around at the rapt audience he could see them nodding in agreement. Worried, he nudged Gerelda, but she didn't react. He scribbled on his tablet the word *Coercion*, and tilted it for her to read, jabbing her with his elbow, much harder this time. She glanced at the tablet, looked at him for a long moment, then nodded and bit her lip. Hard. He saw a bead of blood form, and knew she was concentrating on the pain in the hope it would enable her to resist.

When the lecture was over and the students were filing out, chatting to one another, he asked in a whisper, "Are you all right?"

"Thanks for snapping me out of it. I spent the rest of the time reciting in my head all the forty-two laws pertaining to land taxation in Vavala and Valance." She shook her head ruefully. "The utter bastard. He's dangerous, Perie. Perhaps even more dangerous than the Gaunt Recruiters. He's recruiting our future generation of clerics and thinkers. Twisting the truth and making them believe something false. Even after you warned me, it took me a while to realise how I'd been drawn in to what he was saying."

She dropped her tablet and pencil to the floor, and knelt to scrabble around under the pew to pick them up. He guessed she'd done it in order to delay their exit.

"Do we deal with him now?" he asked in a whisper.

"No time like the present. Let's go up to him, if we can, as if to ask a question. If we get him alone . . . Worth a try. Otherwise, we'll leave it for another day."

By the time the last of the students had left, she'd retrieved her belongings and they and Camber Fox were the only ones left in the room. Fox was still standing in the middle of the platform, regarding them sombrely.

"I have a question, sir, if I may?" Gerelda said, walking towards him down the aisle between the pews. "It's about witcheries . . ."

He nodded. "Of course."

Perie walked immediately behind her, half-hidden, glancing over his shoulder to make sure they were truly alone. He reached through the slit inside his trouser pocket to grasp the hilt of the spiker where he kept it in the sheath strapped to his thigh. He didn't pull it out. Not yet.

"I was wondering about the fact that we still have healers," Gerelda said. "All other folk with witcheries disappeared. Does that mean that healers are somehow exempt from the guilt of interfering with the natural state of things? Is that why they are still with us? And if it is, I'm not sure I understand. I mean, what you said today seemed to imply that even witchery healing would be a sin."

She sounded hesitant and rubbed a hand across her forehead in a puzzled way. Perie wasn't sure if she was entirely putting on an act; he'd seen coercion muddle people's logic before this. He hoped her asking a question was just as an excuse to approach, but it was also a way to draw Camber Fox's attention to herself rather to him.

Stepping up on to the platform, she casually spread the fingers of her left hand. In the sign language the two of them had developed, it meant, *Kill him when you safely can.*

In front of him, the entry door on to the platform was closed. He checked behind once more. They were still alone. With his right hand out of sight behind Gerelda's back, he pulled the dagger free.

He breathed in a wave of foulness, and gagged, choking. *Sorcery. Coercion.*

Gerelda stopped dead, her next words dying half-spoken in her throat. She stood rigidly still, rooted. When Perie stepped up to her side, he could see the panic in her eyes, begging him to hurry up. Another time, he would never have hesitated. The sorcerer would have died before he could even switch his attention from Gerelda to the unremarkable lad who accompanied her.

This time, it was different.

He was reluctant to kill.

13

The Heart of an Executioner

"You came to kill me," Camber Fox said, addressing Perie. He spread his arms wide, to show he was unarmed.

Of course he was: sorcerers never had need of a weapon.

"Go ahead," the man said, the words gently spoken, as if he was asking for an opinion rather than daring him to do it. The coercion was as thick as ever, and Gerelda was mired in it.

Perie hesitated. He halted, his spiker held at the ready in front of him. He wasn't coerced; Camber wasn't even trying to coerce him. No, he was snagged by his own indecision and he didn't even know why.

"I knew that one day someone would come," Camber said. "Someone who would not respond to my sorcery. I just didn't realise it would be so soon, or that my . . . adversary . . . would be so young." He continued to ignore Gerelda. "We've been hearing about the other deaths. Was that you too?"

"I've killed sorcerers, yes," Perie said. "It's what I do."

"And nobody suspected you until it was too late for them. I understand now. They sent a lad who can't be coerced." He looked back at Gerelda. "I could kill you though."

Struggling with the power he was exerting over her will, she was silent.

"Speak," he ordered.

"Do you know that some of you also die because every time you use your sorcery, it sucks the life out of you?" she asked, directing a glare at Perie as she spoke.

"I know that," Camber said. "We all know that. But Pontifect Fox has promised to tell the secret to those of us who are loyal, so we too can rejuvenate ourselves."

123

She dredged up her best sneer. "And you believe him? He'll never show you. And I think I can guess why."

Camber waited, but she didn't explain, so he sighed and said, "All right. I'll ask. Why?"

"Because the moment Valerian's father told him how to do it, Valerian turned around and killed him."

"You can't possibly know that."

"We did a lot of research into your family. We think there's an excellent chance that's what happened."

Camber considered that, then replied with a question. "An extended life span – do you know how enticing that is?"

Perie shrugged. "I don't expect to make twenty," he said. "I don't think about it much."

"I do," Camber whispered. "And I want to live."

A ripple of cold moved down Perie's spine. His gaze locked on Camber's. Beside him, he could feel Gerelda struggling to free herself physically from the coercion, but still he didn't kill the man. This time, it was different. The *sorcerer* was different. "Did you believe what you were teaching them?" he asked, making a gesture at the pews where the students had been sitting. "Do you really think that about Shenat beliefs?"

He shook his head. "No, not really."

"Then why say it?"

"I'm a Fox. I'm a sorcerer. What else is there left for me? I can't fight what I am. Unseen guardians, the Ways of the Oak and the Flow – they are my antithesis. My enemy. If they are true and I am not, then kill me, lad. Just kill me."

Perie felt all the man's coercion die, the taint fade, the thick blanket of pollution dissipate. The sorcerer still stood with his arms spread away from his body, palms up, hands empty. Defenceless.

And he could not do it. He could not kill him. Even though the man had lied to the students and used coercion, Perie still could not kill him. "I can't," he whispered.

"I can," said Gerelda. And before Perie could say or do anything, her sword was swinging and her two-fisted blow slammed the blade into Camber Fox's exposed throat. Blood spurted, spattering across Perie's face and chest like wind spray from a fountain. Thick red drops trickled down his cheeks as Camber dropped on to his knees in front of him, swaying, his mouth gaping as he tried to draw air into his lungs. One hand reached out towards Perie, who stepped back smartly. Camber toppled sideways to the floor, face-down. His body convulsed once or twice, blood pumping into a widening pool, then diminishing to a trickle.

"Well." Gerelda poked him with the toe of her boot. "I guess he's dead." She glanced across at Perie. "You're a mess. Blood all over you! Blister it, Perie, how are we going to get you out of here looking like that?" She bent to wipe her sword clean on the skirt of the sorcerer's gown.

"Hardly my fault."

She handed him her cloak. "Here, put this on and let's get out of here before someone comes to see why he's still in here after the students have gone."

He did as she asked, without speaking.

For the next hour, when they returned to their student digs so he could change his clothes and they could gather their things, and while they collected their horses from the livery and rode out of Oakwood, he never said another word..

They took the road towards Beck Crossways, intending to head from there to Gromwell and the siege, as had been their original intention. That evening, they paid a farmer for a meal and permission to stable their horses and sleep in his barn. In spite of the chill of the evening air, Perie took the opportunity to wash thoroughly under the farmer's pump and rinse the blood from his dirty clothing.

When he re-entered the barn, shivering and carrying the wet clothes, Gerelda said, "I'm sorry about that. Getting blood all over you, I mean."

He shrugged as he spread his washing on the hay pile. "It doesn't matter." His voice sounded flat to his ears.

"You're acting as though it does. Perie – why didn't you kill him? I was coerced. I was in his power. He could have done anything to me. He could have asked me to kill you, and I would have done it! I couldn't have stopped myself. He could have asked me to fall on my sword, and I would have done that." She paused, groping for the right words while he pulled on his dry shirt and coat. "I have to be able to trust you. And right now, I don't."

He tried silence, but she was relentless. "What happened back there?"

"He was different," he mumbled.

"Well, yes," she conceded. "He was. Else why did he stop his coercion? I don't think he expected *me* to kill him, but inexplicably, he appeared quite happy for you to do so. But that's no reason to have let him live."

She pointed vaguely in the direction of Oakwood and waggled her finger. "Those students back there might one day have been calling for the axing of the ancient oaks."

"Coercion doesn't last for ever."

"No, probably not. But once an idea is planted, it's hard to root out. True, he coerced them to believe it. His coercion made it all sound so true, so factual, so logical, that he must have thought that even after he'd gone, the ideas would stick."

He stared at his feet, ashamed. "You're right. I should have killed him. I'm glad he's dead. It was just hard . . . hard to take the life of someone who – who knew what he was and wanted to die."

"He said he wanted to live!"

"Yes, but he didn't want to live *as a sorcerer*. It was horrible, Gerelda. I could . . ." He groped for words. "It was as if I could see into his soul."

He raised his head to stare at her miserably and she stared back. Then she did something she had never done before, not even on the day his father had died. She reached out to him and pulled him into the comfort of an embrace.

"Oh, Va help us, Perie," she whispered. "We are a pair of ninny-heads on a very hard road. You should be in school, or kicking a ball around on a village green. And I should be arguing about taxes with some weasely goat of a cleric trying to cheat his parishioners, and then at the end of a day, putting my feet up in front of a tavern fire with a mug of mulled wine in my hand. Instead we are walking this unpleasant path. I wish it wasn't so."

When she released him, she turned her back and he wondered if he'd really seen tears in her eyes.

* * *

126

"So that's Gromwell Holdfast," Perie said. "It looks like any other old castle."

From where they were standing on the crest of a hill several miles away, separated from the holdfast by a river, the walls appeared toy-like, built of blocks with symmetrical towers at either end.

"That's because it *is* an old castle." A distant puff of smoke, followed a moment later by a booming sound and then a thud, made Gerelda add, "Although perhaps not for long. What can you tell me about the people we're looking at, Perie?"

"The men surrounding it are mostly Grey Lancers." When she raised an eyebrow, he amended the assertion to fit her lawyerly love of facts. "Well, that's an assumption. Let's say, they are folk with a dirty smudge of sorcery rising from them."

"Are they led by a sorcerer?"

"There's no sorcerer there."

"Are you sure?"

"Yes. There was one a few days back, but he's gone."

"Which way?"

"North, I think."

"Ah." She frowned as she added, "We're standing up like scarecrows on a fallow field here. We need to find a place where we can hunker down while we watch what's happening there for a bit."

"Gathering information for Pontifect Fritillary?"

She nodded. She was always leaving written reports at shrines, or rather at places where shrines had once been. Luck-letterboxes, she called them, because if you were lucky, the letter found its way to the right recipient. They were actually caskets disguised as stones, always to be found next to a particular red-flowering plant. Neither he nor Gerelda was certain what happened to the reports after that, but sometimes – if she had indicated where they would be next – they would find a reply from Fritillary Reedling. Sometimes there would be letters left for other people as well.

They headed for a copse below them, off the road and closer to the walls of Gromwell. They were still on the far side of the river and all they'd have to do was keep an eye on the bridge to make sure none of the soldiers came their way. As they hid the horses among the trees, he said, "There's a war going on over there. They are lobbing cannonballs at the walls. People might be dying inside, or maybe starving."

She looked at him oddly. "So?"

"In Oakwood, and in Beck Crossways, and along the roads, everything looks normal. People take their produce to market. The farmers plant and harvest. The students go to tutorials."

"I guess that's the way with wars sometimes. Some people suffer terribly; for others it's just an inconvenience, and for still others, an opportunity. I think the oddest thing about this one is that many folk don't know who their real enemy is. They get it all wrong, and talk about fighting Primordials or Shenat, when they should be looking at their own Prime and his clerics. They say they'll fight for the king, when it's their prince who's on their side."

"Do you know Prince Ryce?"

She gave a laugh that sounded more despairing than amused. "I'm a cooper's daughter, Perie, brought up on a dusty, noisy street in the port of Gore. A cooper's daughter who dreamed high. Who wanted to be a lawyer. That girl never thought to meet a pontifect, let alone a prince."

"You met the Regala."

"*Not* the highlight of my life, I assure you."

"You know what I think the worst thing is about what's happened? It's that no one can find the shrines."

She shrugged. "Really? I can take 'em or leave 'em myself."

"A lack of shrines means it's harder to find a connection to the Way."

"So?"

"That means folk have no . . ." He thought of his father, and how much shrines had meant to him, especially after Ma had died. "Folk have naught to turn to for comfort. They'll lose heart. They feel abandoned. Might mean they'll turn to sorcerers making promises they ought never to believe."

"Could be," she admitted, albeit grudgingly.

"Unseen guardians would never abandon us. Never. People should believe that and be patient. If it's Fritillary Reedling who sent the shrines away, then she ought to bring them back right quick, or it'll get worse. Folk *need* them."

128

"Do *you*?" she asked.

He touched his breastbone. "I have oak in here already. I don't need a shrine. It is already part of me."

She stared at him. "I'm not sure I know what you mean."

"Without a heart of oak, I couldn't do this."

Her stare widened, and then she looked away uneasily. "I don't know what Fritillary did, or why," she said. "I can make a guess. Do you remember that Shrine on the Clouds? The lancers tried to cut it down, and when that didn't work, they tried to burn it."

"I remember. It wasn't much damaged."

"Because none of that lot were sorcerers. Sorcerers are out there now, though, and they *can* destroy shrines and shrine keepers and maybe folk with witcheries too. I think Fritillary has hidden them all to keep them safe."

"You don't win a war by hiding."

"No, but maybe you can by sending a couple of sorcerer-killers."

He was horrified. "Do you mean – *we* could be the only people who can make it so that the shrines can come back?"

She shrugged. "Do you know of any others tripping around the Va-cherished lands killing sorcerers?"

"Pickle me sour, Gerelda . . . ! Oh. Sorry. Proctor . . ."

"Oh, for pity's sake, lad. Considering what we do, I think we've got to the stage where you can call me Gerelda."

"Are you *sure* Pontifect Fritillary had something to do with the disappearance of the shrines?"

"She must have done. Because if she didn't, it was Valerian Fox. And that is too horrible to contemplate."

Not a comforting remark. He turned his attention back to the castle.

"That's the prince's standard still flying from the tower on the right," she said. "Which means he still holds the castle."

They found a patch of brush at the edge of the copse where they could lie down comfortably, out of sight and yet with a fine view of the holdfast's walls and main gate. It wasn't an encouraging sight. The gate, built from huge wooden beams, was so battered it was hard to say what held the remaining splinters together. Part of the walls were little more than rubble. One of the towers had been partially blown away, leaving it looking as if a winter gale would topple it entirely.

"Is it supposed to look like that?" Perie asked.

"I've passed this way before, and it wasn't half-ruined. It looks as if it's only a matter of time before Prince Ryce loses the castle."

"How long?"

"Depends on how much gunpowder the lancers have and how much food and water and arrows the besieged have."

"Can't we do anything?"

There was a long silence as she considered. "That's an army of Grey Lancers," she said at last. "We are two people. I did think that if they were using a sorcerer we might try to even it up a bit by killing him. Now we know there isn't one, it would be ridiculous for us to risk our lives. I can't see any point in dying just for the pleasure of sending a handful of lancers to their Va-less death. No, we push on to the north."

He knew she was right, but her words settled into his stomach like a greasy meal.

14

Caged Dove

"Come to gloat?" Bealina asked.

She'd been standing at the window of her tower room – her prison – looking out over the city of Vavala, and she'd seen in the glass the reflection of the man who entered behind her. Even with that distorted image, she recognised him. Prime Valerian Fox, now wearing the robes of a Pontifect, living in the Pontifect's palace in Vavala, playing the part he had no rights to usurp, for all that he said he'd been fairly elected even though no Shenat cleric or shrine keeper would have supported his candidature, not even Lowmian ones.

Well, she would never give him the title.

She turned in time to see him doff his hat and bow.

"I regret I was not here to greet you on your arrival this afternoon," he said. "I trust that my son Ruthgar acquitted himself well, looking after you."

She shuddered and said nothing. Ruthgar Fox, dead-eyed and cold, had met her on her arrival, telling her that he was acting on behalf of the Pontifect. She'd found him even more frightening than his father, if that was possible.

"Anyway, I am here now, to welcome you to my palace."

"Not rightly yours, I believe. It belongs to the true Pontifect."

"Do not aggravate me, Princess. It is not wise. I wish you well and I hope your journey was pleasant."

"I'm alive. One must be grateful at least for that much, when one travels in the company of violent and undisciplined murderers." She'd never said a truer word. There hadn't been a single day when she'd not wondered if the two of them would live long enough to see another dawn. She glanced over to where Garred played in the corner of the room, content for the first time in days.

"I'm glad Prince Ryce was sensible enough to allow you to leave with Prince Garred," he said. "It would have grieved me if you had come to any harm in Gromwell, my dear."

"So gracious of you, when it is you who have endangered us, and still do. What you have done is treason. There will come a time when Valerian Fox loses his head to the axe."

"Madam, you have been ill-advised on the facts, I feel. I merely obey my liege lord. King Edwayn's orders were to besiege Gromwell Holdfast until such time as his grandson is returned to Throssel – as he has charged Prince Ryce to do. It was Ryce's choice to defy his liege lord. One does not do that with impunity." He nodded towards the prince, who was lining up a row of toy soldiers on top of a hassock. "Prince Garred shall be returned to his rightful home, to be acknowledged the king's heir. I assure you, Your Highness, that I have every intention of seeing the young prince on the throne one day."

"My husband is the rightful immediate heir to King Edwayn, not Prince Garred." She marvelled that her voice remained steady, but her hands were clasped behind her back to stop them shaking. "Customary law dictates that the king's eldest son is the acknowledged line of succession."

"You haven't heard the latest decree, then? No, I'm sure you have. You just refuse to accept that King Edwayn has declared Ryce unfit and therefore Prince Garred is the heir. I do believe that is the king's prerogative."

"Only because you declare it so. The king's mind, alas, is not capable of rational decisions." *Thanks to your sorcery . . .*

"Come now, my dear, surely you know your husband's failings. You will have observed Prince Ryce's lack of interest in the governing of his nation. Why, look at Gromwell Holdfast. No cannon on its walls, and yet it has been Prince Ryce's holdfast since he was eighteen, with the lands and income of the demesne surrounding its walls. He squandered the money, when he was obligated to maintain it as a bastion for the protection of the kingdom's northern borders. He is not a proper candidate for the throne."

"Indeed, I do know my husband, sir. Better than you, I think."

He shrugged. "Prince Garred can be raised differently. He has a mother to guide him in his education. You and I could raise him to be fit to take on the governing of Ardrone."

"And my husband?"

"There is no reason he cannot stay there in Gromwell, living off his own estates, if he bends his knee to his king and confirms the right of his son to succeed his grandfather."

She almost laughed in his face. Did he think she was so witless to believe that? If Ryce left the protection of the castle, he was dead. *Perhaps he already is.*

No. Don't think such . . .

"If it was the king's order to bring Prince Garred to Throssel, then why is he here, in Vavala? *You* disobey the king, Master Fox!"

"I merely do what is best for Prince Garred's safety. The kingdom is rife with disorder and treachery, whereas Vavala is mine to guard. I think we have to come to an understanding, you and I, Princess."

"By which you mean your understanding of what is best for yourself, not for me, nor Garred. What choice do I have? You have my promise of compliance to your wishes, if that is what you need. I am no more than a mother who wants what is best for her son, after all. As you say, one day he will reign."

"Accept my guidance in all things and you will be there at his side. Disobedience, on the other hand . . ." He approached her, and it was an effort of will not to flinch. He reached out suddenly and caught her chin between the thumb and fingers of his right hand. Dropping his voice to a cold whisper, he said, "There are many castles in Ardrone, where a grieving widow might live out her days behind walls. And then there are other . . . beguilements of companionship for a lady of refinement to enjoy."

She brought her forearm up and knocked his hand away, a swift angry blow. "I am aware of my position. I do not need threats to understand it. To save my son, I abandoned my husband. As I assume your ambition is to be the driving force behind the throne, I believe your legitimacy will depend on the health and longevity of Ryce's child." She nodded to where Garred sat in the corner, his eyes wide as he watched. "There is no one who will look after him as well as I do."

"And you think that is enough to keep you safe? Brave words, from a powerless woman with few friends."

He couldn't let her have any illusions, could he? Va above, he was an evil man. She felt it again then, a horrible black tarry touch that rubbed across her soul – then it was gone. Her breathing raced, driven by her terror.

"Confine your activities to caring for your son, and all will be well. Step outside those bounds, and you will be parted from him. For ever. Do you understand?"

"Your actions speak for themselves. I will do whatever is needful to keep my son alive and well."

"Then we understand one another, madam. I shall return."

Without another word, he turned and left her alone with her son.

Garred ran to clutch at her skirts. "Don't like bad man. Tell him go way."

"He's gone now."

"Me want Horntail."

"He's not here, darling—"

"Yes, is! Me see him!"

She stilled. "Where?"

"Horse." He pointed to the window. "There. Me show Mama."

She picked him up. "You saw him from there?" Earlier he had been sitting in the embrasure, looking out with his nose pressed to the glass, but the tower was in the centre of the palace. A corner of the city streets, while visible from that window, was a long way off.

He nodded. "He gone now."

She followed the line of his pointing finger, and wondered if it was possible. "I'm sure we'll see him soon, then. But he's a busy man, you know. He has to look after his horse, and sharpen his sword . . ." She prattled on to distract him.

"He's all gone," he said. "Like Papa." His sadness made her heart ache. What kind of life lay ahead for him?

"I'm here," she said. "Mama will never leave you."

She had no idea if she spoke the truth.

15

Lost in Time

Sorrel had never been to Hornbeam before. It was a port, best known for its shipbuilding and repair yards. As soon as they berthed, Lord Juster sent his officers and crew scurrying about on matters pertaining to the spice cargo, and the sale and repair of his other two ships.

As Saker and Sorrel were not involved in any of that, and Juster's only order to Ardhi was to help the other two, they left the ship together to gather information in the town. On the docks, they separated, Saker to head towards the nearest chapel to renew contacts with the clergy, and Ardhi to glean the gossip of sailors and dock lumpers in the less salubrious part of the port. Sorrel, glad the two men had accepted her ability to look after herself, searched for someone with a healing witchery. Specialist healers – such as a boneknitter or a feverbreaker – might have been hard to find, but no one was ever far from a general healer. She was soon directed to a modest shop several streets back from the wharves. The young man behind the counter was selling herbs, salves and medicines and there was no faint glow about him that would have told her he was using a witchery.

"Good morrow, sir," she said with a polite smile. The air was filled with a smell of spices, deliciously redolent of the Summer Seas, and for a moment she was transported back to the islands and the wafting scent of nutmeg flowers.

"In need of a salve, mistress? Or perhaps a philtre, a tincture, a potion, or maybe a tonic?" he asked.

She blinked, wondering how they all differed, and said, "I was told I could find a healer here."

"That'd be my father." He pulled aside the curtain that divided the shop from the back of the building. "This way, mistress. Pa, patient here to see you." He jerked his head, indicating she should enter.

The healer was a balding man with wire-rimmed spectacles perched towards the end of his nose, through which he peered at a scatter of ink drawings on the table in front of him. "Fascinating, fascinating," he said. "Look, lass, look. Your insides! The internals! Beautiful, beautiful."

She glanced at the drawings, and decided she'd rather not. Her only knowledge of anatomy involved sword slashes releasing ropes of foul-smelling guts on to the deck of a ship, and the horror on the face of a sailor who knew he was going to die in agony. She didn't need to look at pictures.

"What's the problem, lass? Indigestion? Rashes?" His gaze dropped to her waist. "Babe on the way, hm?"

"No, no, none of that."

He took a closer look at her then. "Hm. You've got a witchery glow. A fellow healer, I assume, with a question."

"No."

"Hm." Carefully he removed his spectacles, folded them up, and put them on the table. "I haven't seen anyone with a witchery, other than healers, not for half a year. Not since the shrines went."

"That's what I wanted to ask you about. When that happened, I was in Karradar, on board a ship. We've just returned to Ardrone and I'd like to know what happened while we were gone."

"Ah, hmm." He slipped the drawings of internal organs into a folder, and put them into the table drawer. "Best sit, then. Your name, hm, lass?"

She sat where he indicated. "I'd rather not say."

"Yes. Perhaps wise, given what happened to your like. Hmmm."

She muttered something unintelligible, wondering if the length of his murmurs were somehow linked to his doubts about the subject matter, or suspicion of his listener.

"Well," he said, "one day, all those with witcheries – except healers – received a message from their local shrine keeper, asking them to come to their local shrine the next day. Hmm. At first, most thought it was a note just to them, you understand. Even when they realised *all* the locals with witcheries, other than healers, were at their shrine, probably they had no idea it was happening all over the land. Hmph!"

"Everywhere?"

"Ah-hmm. All over the Va-cherished Hemisphere on the same day, so I've heard since."

"Lowmeer too?" She was utterly shocked.

"So I've heard. About the same time Vavala fell and the Pontifect was killed."

"She died?"

"That's the word on it. She died."

"But you don't think so?"

"Fritillary Reedling? Just like that? Hmm. No."

"So, they went to the shrine, then . . .?"

"Whatever they was told at the time, I'm not sure. Most came hurrying back to their homes – grabbed up belongings, food, families too some of them, but then they vanished, along with the shrines. Hmph!"

"How can a shrine disappear?" she whispered. "How was it possible?"

He shook his head. "There's just a mist there." A tear trickled down his cheek. "I still try to enter it, every now and then. Not just the main Hornbeam shrine, but some of the smaller ones as well . . ."

"And what happens when you try?"

"I see things I shouldn't. Dead people. I don't know where I am. I walk into brambles I don't see. Scratch my arms and legs until I bleed." He shook his head. "Don't ever try, lass. It's not . . . *natural* in there any more. They are haunted places now."

"And you don't know why it happened, or who did it?"

"Hm. Mayhap the Grey Lancers worked out how to destroy shrines and witchery folk all at once, in one fell swoop, or . . . Or else, someone worked out how to save the shrines and the witchery folk, all at once, by making them disappear."

"Who are the Grey Lancers? Where did they come from?"

He leaned forward and dropped his voice. "Hmm, madness, I'd call it, lass. At first, people thought they were saving us all from Primordials, from the Horned Death, from Va knows what. Folk flocked to join them or support them." He snorted. "Lost the sense they were born with, if you ask me. Now everyone is too scared to say aught, and the Grey Lancers rule."

"But the king? The king's army?"

"Don't see much o' them round here."

She was silent, not knowing what to ask next.

"Summat did happen recent-like, here in Hornbeam," he said suddenly. "The fellow who led the lancers got killed in his own lodgings, right here in town. Vicious fellow he was, sickly, with dead eyes."

"Who killed him?"

"Not sure. All kinds of tales afterwards. Some says it was a woman and her son did it, though I don't know the truth of that, or who they were. For a while afterward, local lancers were like headless hens, flapping this way and that, killing folk for no reason, arguing among themselves like they was demented. Some of the local lads among 'em crept back home, useless featherwits plucked raw from what I saw of those brought in to see me. The rest marched away, hunting another head fellow, I suppose. They haven't come back yet, but they will, I reckon. Hm."

Sorrel listened, and decided there was simply nothing she could say, so she kept silent.

He lowered his voice still further. "If I was you, I'd not admit my witchery was anything other than healing, lass. Hm. In fact, I wouldn't tell anyone you had one. Reckon any healers you meet won't blab, either."

She nodded. Her stomach roiled. They'd been sailing to other worlds, hoping to find a cure for Piper, when their own world was fracturing.

When she stood up to leave a few minutes later, she asked, "Your spectacles . . . Is there no healer here who can mend your sight?"

"Ah, 'tis only close work I need them for. I bought these from a Pashali sailor on board a trader, and they're good enough. We did have a sightmender, but she died a year ago. I was hoping an unseen guardian would find us another soon, but now . . ." His words trailed away.

Now there was no access to unseen guardians.

Sorrel shivered. Without them, there would never be another witchery.

* * *

She had arranged to meet Saker and Ardhi inside the town chapel. They were not there when she arrived, so she sat down on one of the pews at the back to wait. As she looked around, she wondered why anyone could ever have preferred such a place, built of cold stone, when they could have worshipped at an oak shrine. Her closeness to Va shrivelled in a place like this. It had a clean elegance, true, but it lacked warmth; there was no vitality, no movement, nothing alive. No beauty but its artificial symmetry.

By the time Ardhi and Saker arrived, she was almost in tears just thinking about what had happened since they had left the Va-cherished Hemisphere.

What did we do wrong, Va? Did we get too complacent, too indifferent to the suffering of others? We had a wonderful land, once . . .

When Ardhi and Saker arrived together an hour later, she insisted on leaving. "I want to get into the fresh air. Away from the port. I want to go to the main shrine now."

"So do we," Saker said. "We can swap what we've found out as we walk."

She told them all she had learned and, as she'd expected, the information they'd garnered was similar. Saker added more details about divisions within the hierarchy of Va-faith. Pontifect Fritillary, forewarned, had done her best to thwart Prime Fox, but she'd failed. "None of the clerics I spoke to believe Fox is a sorcerer, or if they do they aren't going to say it aloud. I suspect that those who did believe it went to fight for her and died in Vavala, or maybe even earlier when they first voiced their opposition to the Prime. The main problem is that the king was – and still is – on Fox's side. So moving against Fox is treated as treason."

He added, worried, "Everyone seems to think Fritillary died, which I don't believe. The idiots are *pleased* Fox has taken over as Pontifect, saying he'll do a better job of mollifying Va . . ." He kicked savagely at a stone on the path. "Fobbing lackwits. What did you hear in the docklands, Ardhi?"

"Complaints. People are really unhappy about the lack of folk with witcheries because it's affecting their livelihoods. Everyone had a tale to tell. There's a rat plague in the cargo that's stored awaiting transport, something a vermin witchery would once have dealt with in a day. The cooper used to employ someone with a witchery to bend his wood; now there's no one. Someone told me a tale of a slime mould that got into the holding sheds along the river, and there was no one with the right witchery to save the root crops stored there. A carter had his horses die of a disease that folk with witcheries used to treat. The worst of it? People aren't blaming Fox; they're blaming shrines and shrine keepers and unseen guardians."

Saker blanched. "How could things have come to this?" he asked in a murmur, not expecting an answer.

Ardhi glanced across at her, troubled. "Are you all right?" he asked.

"Miserable," she replied. "And angry too, I suppose. I thought I'd be working to protect Piper's future, and her brother's. Instead, I'm further away from her than ever, and nowhere near any solutions. Our ternion – that's all we have. And we are faced with – with—" Words failed her.

"Anarchy," Saker said. "I suppose as a one time cleric, I ought to be saying, 'Have faith. Pray. Va will provide.' And all those other platitudes."

Appalled, she asked, "You don't believe in that any more?"

"I wouldn't say that, exactly. I *do* see a land curdled by misrule and an evil man's ambition, but I also see *us*. Three people singled out – granted our witcheries and the support of the *sakti* of the Chenderawasi – for a reason. I don't know if we'll survive this, but I do know we can make a difference." He looked up into the sky where his eagle sailed effortlessly overhead. "No, more than that. We *will* make a difference."

"We don't even know how to use the plume pieces we have," she said, fingering the bambu pendant at her neck. "Unless we swallow them the way you did."

Saker shuddered. "That only worked because the sea eagle ate the other half." He paused, looking thoughtful. "Although . . . maybe that tells us something: a feather can make a connection. A ternion connection?"

"All those Chenderawasi legends speak of holding tight to a piece of feather and asking for help in dire need," Ardhi said.

"As long as you don't mind what kind of help you get," Saker added dryly.

This, she thought, *doesn't bode well.*

* * *

"That's it," Saker said, and waved a hand at what lay in front of them.

To Sorrel, it was like looking through layers of gauzy mist, all of it tinged with a golden glow resembling a vague witchery glimmer.

"I guess," Ardhi asked, in that thoughtful way of his, "that we are all seeing the same thing? No tree. No shrine. No people. It's like looking through glowing spiderwebs . . ."

They both nodded.

He said, "Strong *sakti*." He took a step forward into the beginning of the mist, but stopped abruptly. "*Adua!* That hurt! I walked into some prickles." He shook his head. "If we can't see where we're going, then it's too dangerous to try."

Saker looked up at the eagle again, and the bird spilled air from under its wings, whiffling downwards towards them. "Let's see what he does . . . I'm asking him to perch on the shrine tree."

Which wasn't there.

They watched in silence. The bird extended its feet, as if readying itself to land, entered the mist and disappeared.

"Where is it?" she asked.

"It thinks it's on the tree. But when I look through its eyes, I see only mist."

"Ask it to stay there," Ardhi said.

"I don't think we can just walk into that haze without help," Sorrel said, remembering what the healer had told her. She unstoppered her bambu pendant and took out one tiny piece of golden feather. "What we have to decide is if this is important enough to use up one of these pieces."

"We do need to discover what happened to the shrines," Saker said.

"Perhaps we can rely on connections," Ardhi said. "Links between Chenderawasi *sakti* and your witcheries."

"Physical links?" she asked.

"Yes. Maybe if Saker and I both hold the dagger, and you hold Saker's other hand with the feather between your palms. Then we'll step into the haze and see what happens. We won't ask for anything. We'll let the *sakti* decide."

That seemed as good an idea as any, so Sorrel did as he asked. Hand-in-hand they all stepped forward together. Although she could still feel their clasp, she was surrounded by a golden haze and couldn't see either of them properly.

The mist surrounded them, but it drifted by in strands, sometimes thick and opaque, sometimes parting so she glimpsed random snatches of unconnected places and people – a clump of reeds beside a stream, the glowing coals of a blacksmith's fire, a woman winnowing grain. Their progress was tentative, edging forward when they saw a safe path to take. Every time she thought they had arrived somewhere, the scene vanished and she saw another place, glimpsed different folk, heard other sounds. There was no sign of a shrine-oak anywhere.

Just when she decided that it was all completely random, she saw a child in front of her a few paces away. Shock raced her heart.

Heather.

Her distress immobilised her.

Heather, the way she had been just before she died. Beautiful, happy, with an intent expression on her face as if she were fascinated by what she was seeing.

"*Heather?*" She spoke the word, but whether aloud, or just in her head, she wasn't sure.

The child did not move. Of course she wouldn't. She wouldn't have heard.

Sorrel stumbled forward, or thought she did, wanting to gather her daughter into her arms, but when she reached out, her fingers felt nothing to clasp.

No, wait. She was still standing holding hands with Saker and Ardhi. Heather was not there.

Yes, she was. But she was still just as far away.

I didn't move. I just thought *I did . . .*

Heather was sitting as she had been, still looking at something that had her full attention. Everything about her was familiar: the tilt of her head, the way her hair wisped around her face, the curl of her lips when she smiled.

No, something's wrong. She's dead.

But I can see her.

She strained to see what had caught the child's eye. There were vague shapes in the mist. Children playing, perhaps. She thought she caught the sound of childish voices. A coloured ball, bouncing. When one of the children missed the catch and the ball tumbled towards Heather, she laughed. A boy came running to get it, a transparent figure. He did not appear to see Heather. As he gathered up the ball, he shouted at one of the other children, and Heather jumped, startled.

Sorrel closed her eyes tight, biting her lip hard.

Heather had been deaf.

An age passed, or no time at all. Saker's hand in hers, gripping her hard, and his voice, saying, "It's all right, it's all right."

When she opened her eyes, she could see him and Ardhi, but nothing more except the enveloping mist. Heather had gone.

Someone said once that in the land of the dead, the blind can see . . .

She swayed, her head spinning. Ardhi let go of her hand and slipped his arm around her shoulder instead to give her support. She leaned into him, glad of his strength. "What happened?" she asked in a whisper. "Where is this place? I saw my daughter!" *But she's dead.* "Are we dead too?" Stupid question, but nothing was making sense any more.

At least neither of them mocked her for asking it. "I don't think so," Saker said calmly, but she knew him well enough to see that he was unsettled.

"I didn't see anyone I knew," Ardhi said. "Just places and people."

"I saw Heather. She was happy, watching other children play. She didn't see me. She didn't hear me. And – and there, where she was, she wasn't deaf. But she's *dead*. I think – I think I saw her in her afterlife."

Neither of them spoke.

"Va-faith believes that you can choose the place to watch the living world from your afterlife," Saker explained for Ardhi's benefit.

"Maybe we came too far," she said.

"You mean, you think we *died*?" Ardhi asked.

"No." Saker's denial was flat and convincing. "I think I know what happened to the shrines now. Or at least what happened to this one. I think the unseen guardian's power took it and the surrounding land *out* of time. Time in our world moved on, but the shrine stayed still, stationary in its own time, which was the hour – the moment – that it disappeared."

Shaking with shock and trying desperately not to think of Heather, she considered his words. "So . . . we went to the wrong place in time. We don't belong here."

"No. And we're not in the right time for the shrine, either," Saker said. "We went too far back."

Pickle it. It was me. I took us all to the time of Heather's death.

"So how do we get to the shrine from here?" Ardhi asked.

"We try again," Saker said. "With the feathers and the dagger, as before. But this time you try to think only of me, of holding on to me, of staying with me. *I* will concentrate on the shrine and its keeper, because I've been here before. That might be enough to take us there, in the right time frame."

She shivered again, and Ardhi bent to murmur in her ear. "You can do it. Grip our hands tight and concentrate on that hold. Empty your mind of everything else."

Nodding, she took hold of their hands, closed her eyes, and thought of nothing except the clasp of the two men who had come to mean so much to her. A moment later her head was spinning, and the world around her was a blur of colour and sound and touch and aroma, all of it one amorphous mix.

16

The Shrine That Wasn't There

Saker drew in a deep breath and turned his whole being towards the destination he wanted. He knew before he began that it was problematical: he had only visited the Hornbeam shrine once, and that was more than five years previously, when he'd first started working for the Pontifect. It was hard to remember the exact details now, and the shrine could have changed. All he knew for sure was that it had vanished at a time when it should have been in leaf, so that was how he tried to imagine it. He closed his eyes and built a picture . . .

The vast oak tree, centuries old, its limbs drooping, its roots wide and thick. He recalled the man who was the shrine keeper, named for plants as most were: Wintercress. No, Wintergreen. Vervain Wintergreen. At least he wouldn't have altered much. When someone was that ancient, there wasn't much that could age. His memory of Vervain was of skin already crinkled like a withered leaf, a back bent like a wind-blown bough, hands gnarled, neck loose-skinned like old bark.

Air rushed past, clammy dampness misting his skin, and he knew he'd changed where they were. He opened his eyes.

Wherever they had landed, it was not the right place. He couldn't see it properly because of the thickness of the mist. In consternation, he whipped his head around. Nothing.

Damn you to beggary, Saker, what have you done?

All he wanted to do right then was panic, but Sorrel's hand clasped his, her trust implicit. Yet the ternion was doomed if he couldn't find a way out of this for them all.

Think, you beef-wit. Think.

They *had* moved. From the feel of the air against his face, they were still moving. Hunting for something that approximated to his recollection.

His memory of the shrine must have been faulty. Neither the witchery nor the *sakti* knew where he wanted to go. *After five years, what did you expect, you daft dewberry?*

They were moving around in an infinity of time. Va, but it was cold. Wrong season. Depth of winter. He thought of warmth, and felt the move from winter to spring against his skin, but there was still no visible oak, no shrine, no people.

Sweet Va. Help me. I am so lost . . . Don't panic, just decide: where can you get a better memory from?

The answer was obvious.

The eagle.

The bird knew exactly what the shrine looked like *now*. A bird from the Summer Seas which could drop into a tree that was somewhere in a different time. A Chenderawasi bird.

Reaching out to find the connection, he released something of his humanity in order to drift free so he could be drawn to an alien mind. It made no difference if he opened or closed his eyes; he saw nothing. He lost track of time. A few seconds? Days? He had no idea. All he could be certain of was that he was holding on to two people who meant the world to him, and he must never let go. The ternion, linked not just by magic, but forged by the courage and integrity of his companions. Sorrel, as close to him as any sister. Ardhi, the brother he'd never had in his own family. He was their only hope; they were his anchor to reality in a place which had no time.

When he groped through the gloom of his mind, he found the link, travelled down it. And was there, in an alien, Avian mind once more.

From the bird, through time, to his body, he tightened the link to bridge the interval, building it stronger, pulling himself closer. Nausea swept through him like a cresting wave. He spoke to the bird, ordering it to perch on his shoulder, and felt the lurch through his being as the eagle launched itself from the tree and dropped down, bringing the two periods of time together into one whole. His stomach heaved and then quieted. The taloned feet hit his shoulder, propelling him forward a step, then pinions brushed his head as the bird strove to balance itself and fold its wings. He opened his eyes and heard voices. Laughter. Shouting in the distance, chatter close by, men and women.

And then silence. The three of them were standing near the edge of the massive oak and the eagle was settling its weight on to his shoulder, digging its claws into his skin. People, far and near, were staring at them, rooted in place by varying degrees of shock or consternation.

Vervain Wintergreen had told him that the age of the tree was at least a thousand years. Unlike many shrines, this one did not have any walls. As its lowest branches dipped to the ground at the point furthest from the tree trunk, the sheltered area resembled an upside-down bowl with the butt of the oak at its centre. Entry was through a break between massive boughs.

"We're here," he said, letting go of the hands he held. "You can open your eyes."

When he'd visited the shrine before, it had stood at the edge of an outcrop of huge granite boulders half buried in a meadow. On the side closest to the town there had been a row of houses, but most of the tree had jutted from the boulders into a wild meadow, beyond which was a forest. He could still see the boulders and the meadow, and a little of the forest, but the houses had vanished. At the limits of the meadow everything became blurry, as if he was looking through fog. Edges of the closest trees and bushes became indistinct, those further away dissolved into the mistiness. He had the unpleasant thought that if he walked outside the visual limits, he too would lose definition and start to forget who he was, or where he was. He'd be caught in a moment that had no end.

Hurriedly, he returned his gaze to the settlement. Everything appeared makeshift, temporary. Buildings of unmortared stone, or of untreated wood and reed thatching, had been constructed against the granite boulders. A well had been dug for water.

The scene reminded him of the hovels outside a city wall. Cleaner and less noxious, certainly, but too many people living in too few buildings, all with an aura of unspoken poverty. Pigs and cows and hens and humanity, all cheek and jowl – not what anyone associated with a shrine and its emphasis on nature. There were children as well, so he guessed that some of those who had hidden themselves here had brought their families with them. Even so, he doubted the whole settlement could have numbered more than two or three hundred folk.

Someone yelled for Vervain, and a moment later the ageing shrine keeper stepped out from between the drooping branches. As Saker had expected, he had not changed much in appearance over the years.

Nor had the old man mellowed. He took one look at the three interlopers and cried, "By the oak! Who are you?" His tone was larded with suspicion and alarm as he looked from one to the other. Then, directing his attention to Saker, he added, "I remember ye. Rampion! You're the witan got hisself nulled out on Chervil Moors." He snorted. "Didn't hear your witchery was one of linking, though. To a bird, eh? That's a strange one."

Saker released his hold over the eagle, and it lifted into the air to perch in the oak instead. "Greetings, Keeper Vervain. These are my friends, Sorrel Redwing, and Ardhi from Chenderawasi."

Vervain switched his attention to Sorrel. "Ah. Heared about ye from the oakmarrow over in Melforn. That's a rare bewitching ye have."

Sorrel blinked. "You mean from the shrine keeper? Marsh Bedstraw?"

"Oakmarrow is an archaic word for unseen guardian," Saker said. His mind raced as he began to think things through.

"Archaic?" Vervain snorted. "It's the *true* word!" He stepped over to Ardhi, the gaze from his deep-seated eyes shrewd. "But you? You're a strange blood." He reached up and placed his hand flat to Ardhi's cheek. "Born by the sea and sea-borne. More the Way of the Flow than of the Oak, methinks? And your bewitching's a right odd one. What's your skill, lascar?"

"Climbing."

"The higher the height, the deeper the fall."

Ardhi smiled faintly. "Tell me something I don't know, *bapak*."

"That's a word of respect, I hope, young man."

"In my land, the elderly are always respected."

"Hmph. Beware of those high places. A slip kills."

Ardhi merely inclined his head politely; it was Sorrel who leaped to his aid. "Is that a promise or a warning, sir?"

Vervain shrugged and turned back to Saker. "We were alerted about Va-forsaken witcheries, and such is he. He's neither trusted nor welcome here." He signalled to several of the men who had been watching them from nearby. "Burr," he said, "shepherd this fellow yonder. Disarm him, and confine him well."

"He's here to help us!" Saker protested. "I suggest you listen before—"

"And perhaps *you* are gullible," Vervain snapped, contempt layered over every word. "Va-forsaken means what it deems. He's not one of us. Take him away, Burr."

"I can vouch for him," Saker said, and laid his hand on his sword.

Vervain's eyes flickered to the weapon and back to Saker's face in a glance that was dangerously unfriendly. "I am hardly likely to have confidence in an unfrocked cleric who was once nulled for blasphemy and apostasy. Especially one who's thinking to draw a blade in the sanctity of a shrine."

Va, what has happened while we were gone? Shrine keepers were never like this . . . "Do not harm him or you will face my wrath," Saker said. Pox on't, Vervain's archaic speech was contagious. "My power lies not just in my sword," he added for good measure. As the man called Burr came forward to grasp Ardhi's arm, Saker stepped between them. "Treat him as an honoured guest."

Burr glanced at Vervain for confirmation. The shrine keeper hesitated, then nodded. "We are not savages."

When Burr and another man led Ardhi away, Saker saw the kris sheath at his belt was empty. Sorrel was holding her tote close to her chest, her face blank.

"You must tell how came you here," Vervain said, addressing Saker. "I'd not thought it possible since the shrines were locked."

"I'd not thought to find them so, after returning from a journey across the face of the world," Saker said in bitter anger. "Over two years absent, and we come back to this: a land where shrine keepers no longer serve their congregation, and folk with witcheries abandon those who need them? You may find us uncomfortable visitors," he warned, his ire seeping into every word. "We want answers."

The old man spat. "You've no rights here, not to answers, not even to be fed. We don't have victuals to spare." He waved a hand at what had once been meadowland on the other side of the oak and Saker glanced to see what he was indicating. A couple of cows grazed there and an area had been walled off to keep the animals away from a vegetable plot. "No food comes in here. We feed ourselves."

"What's the *point* of all this?" Saker asked, surprising himself with the intensity of the rage he felt. As he spoke, he kept an eye on Ardhi to see where he was being taken. "The lands out there are struggling, people are frightened, with no recourse to help from shrines, while you hide in safety and grizzle about raising your own cows?"

Vervain glowered at him. "Cobble dwellers are the ones who chose to desert their shrines in the first place, favouring the stone-walled chapels in their towns and cities. So let them turn to their clerics! We owe them little."

Saker and Sorrel exchanged glances and he knew she was as appalled as he was.

"Vervain, Vervain," came a voice behind them, "calm yourself. There is no point in condemning without listening."

Saker turned to look at the speaker, a middle-aged woman dressed in cleric's garb. His glance went to the medallion around her neck; the oakleaf was edged with gold, denoting her rank. District Arbiter.

She nodded to him. "Willow Partridge, once Arbiter of Hornbeam. You want a conversation? Then let's have one." She waved a hand at the interior of the shrine. "Enter, both of you, and remember this is a sacred place. I think, Witan Saker, we have met once before, when you were hardly more than a student."

He recalled he had once made a courtesy call on her in the Hornbeam Va-faith office, but he had little memory of the event. She was a quiet, greying woman with grief-stricken eyes, and he wondered why she would have remembered him.

"I am no longer a witan," he said as they followed her into the shrine itself.

"I'm not surprised at that," she said. "You were nulled, after all."

He winced and turned his attention to the interior of the shrine. The light, filtered through the translucence of the roof of woven branches and layers of living leaves, was luminous and soft. The seating, part of the living tree, woven from roots and branches, had been smoothed and polished by the worship and pilgrimage of generations. "I have never been faithless, Arbiter Willow."

Keeper Vervain, trailing behind Sorrel, snorted. "And are we to swallow all the sweet words tripping so easily from your lips, nulled witan? Sit, fellow, and before you hear any truths from us, you tell us whence you came, and how, and what you want."

It was hard to condense their story into a tale that was succinct and still coherent, but Saker did his best. It helped that he left out everything to do with Piper, the Chenderawasi feathers, Avians and the kris, simply saying that Ardhi was a sailor with a witchery from the Va-forsaken Hemisphere who wanted to help.

"We have been there," he said. "We've seen first-hand the faith of Ardhi's people, and it's not so different from ours."

"And we are supposed to be impressed by the testimony of an apostate?" Vervain asked, furrowed eyebrows eloquently expressing his doubt.

Va-damn. That is all coming back to haunt me still?

Sorrel intervened then, saying, just as snappishly as Vervain, "May I point out just who brought the charges against Witan Saker, and who prosecuted the case for nullification?" She paused for effect. "Why, I believe it was Prime Valerian Fox!"

He blinked in surprise. Sarcasm was not something he had heard Sorrel employ, even to make an argument. She pushed on, eyes flashing, her whole body rigid with annoyance. No, with rage. "And why do you think that vile man might have done that?" she asked. "Because he knew that Witan Saker was a threat to him. Because he knew Saker Rampion was the Pontifect's agent." She shook an irate finger at Vervain. "I was *there*. I saw it."

"And who do you think warned me that our troubles might have their origins in the Va-forsaken Hemisphere?" the Arbiter asked. "Pontifect Fritillary! She had heard that there was Va-forsaken witchery loose in Ardrone, threatening her agents. Something about sorcerous feathers and daggers . . ."

Saker winced. Fritillary knew about those because he'd told her. But he hadn't known Ardhi then. Cankers 'n' galls, everything in his past was coming back to kick him in the rump.

"How did you get here?" Vervain asked. "How did you find this shrine?"

Deciding any mention of *sakti* and feathers would make Ardhi's situation worse, and that any explanation he tried to make now would only dig a deeper pit for himself, he said vaguely, "As you saw, my witchery is a connection to birds, and it was the eagle that led us here. The shrines have been taken out of our world's time, haven't they? Apparently time does not mean much to a bird." It was a weak explanation with just enough truth to make it plausible, and they appeared prepared to accept it. "What we need to know," he added before they could find holes in the explanation, "is what happened in our absence. Why are all the shrines hidden? Where is Pontifect Fritillary?"

"She is managing resistance to Fox and his sorcerers from outside," Arbiter Willow said, "in ordinary time."

"How can I contact her?" he asked.

"You folk'd be the last ones we'd tell," Vervain muttered. "We have our ways. Ancient ways, not for ordinary folk to use."

"But how long do you intend to hide the shrines?" he asked, puzzled. "For ever? Do you even understand how people will lose heart?"

"It's already happening," Sorrel said.

Arbiter Willow opened her mouth to reply, but Vervain silenced her with a gesture and said, "I don't think we hanker to discuss our plans with you. I suggest you return to the world, and keep your wagging tongue behind your teeth about all you saw here." When Willow seemed set to disagree, he added, "Can we trust them to keep silent? They came here with that Va-forsaken nut-skin!"

Sorrel sent him an indignant look. "They are your words, not Va's. There is nothing in Va-faith about people on the other side of the world not being cherished. We are *not* leaving Ardhi behind."

"Then ye'll have to stay yourselves!" Vervain said. "Locked up with him, till we get the word from the Pontifect what to do with ye. And that might be a long time in the coming."

The smug weasel, Saker thought. "You'd have to feed us then, wouldn't you? But we're not staying. If I write a letter to the Pontifect, will you send it to her?"

"No."

"Believe me, she will be anxious to hear from me."

"We're not messenger boys! We don't carry letters. It's a long walk. And a dangerous one."

Saker blinked in surprise. A long *walk*?

"We can send verbal messages, though," Arbiter Willow said, earning a furious glare from Vervain. "We have . . . ways."

Now that's interesting. "How long before Pontifect Fritillary receives such a message?"

"Might be a day or two," she said.

"Or longer. It depends," Vervain added, still ungracious.

"On what?"

"When the Pontifect visits a shrine, and which shrine it is," Willow said.

"Have you any idea where she is?"

"Last I heard," she said, "in Lowmeer. But she does move around."

Saker thought about the difficulty of a verbal message. He'd have to be cryptic and use their code words . . . He asked, "Will the message alter as it is passed from person to person?"

Vervain gave a scornful grunt. "We are not idle-headed dewberries. We can pass a coded message, if that's what you mean."

"It will be a long one."

"Just as well most shrine keepers have long memories, isn't it?"

Hog's piddle, he's a sarcastic fellow. "I'll write down the exact words. You still have not explained what has happened in Ardrone that you had to hide the shrines."

"Sorcery happened. That's what."

"Prime Fox is only one man. How did he bring about this disaster?"

"How did you know it was Fox?" Willow countered.

"Fritillary spoke of his . . . nastiness before I left for the other side of the world. And I was one of her informants anyway."

Vervain shot a warning look at Arbiter Willow. "He might be lying. He could be one of the sorcerous sons, for all we know."

His heart skipped a beat. "*What* sorcerous sons?"

"Who was your father?" Vervain asked.

The shrine keeper didn't mean anything by it. He *couldn't* mean anything by it. But suddenly Saker was remembering Robin Rampion saying, "I've always doubted you had the right to my name . . ."

Va's acorns, he couldn't be Valerian Fox's son, could he? They had all been at university together – his mother Iris Grey, Fritillary Reedling, Valerian Fox . . . and his supposed father. It was such a horrible idea that it had never crossed his mind.

"*What* sorcerous sons?" he asked again. *I don't look like Valerian . . .*

It was Willow who answered. "Some folk say Valerian Fox had at least fifty. To suck the life out of them in order to extend his own lifespan. Others act as his agents."

His heart hammered under his ribs until his chest ached. *I am not a sorcerer. The Rani would have known if I was.* His breath steadied.

"Later," she continued, "he found some of them useful as his instruments to lead armies of coerced peasants."

"The Grey Lancers."

"Yes. But it is more Fox's sons who have forced us to hide, not the lancers. The sons have the real power. The lancers are just a bunch of very nasty soldiers, twisted by sorcery into men who don't care what they do. I would hesitate even to call them human any more."

"And by *hiding* you think you are winning the battle?" Sorrel asked, arching a mocking eyebrow.

Neither of them answered that.

"What about Prince Ryce? What do you know about his situation?" Saker asked.

"He is besieged at his summer estate, Gromwell. Up near Twite," Arbiter Willow said. Her sadness never left her, and her words sounded as if she had to drag them out of some dark place to bring them to light.

"And no one helps him?"

"It is the king's decree. To go against the king is treason," the arbiter pointed out.

"Then I suspect that a little treason is in order. The king has had his brains curdled by sorcerous treachery, and it's time someone stopped him!" His indignation welled up again and he felt a strong desire to break something. Reason, though, prevailed, and he calmed enough to say, "I'd like to write that message to Fritillary Reedling, if I may."

"Come with me. I have a slate." Vervain jerked his head at Sorrel. "You stay here with Arbiter."

"*Wass lundia*," Saker muttered. "It's all right, Sorrel."

He hoped the glance he gave her was full of meaning.

17

The Foundations of Treason

Sorrel watched him go and then looked back at Arbiter Willow. "What did he say?" Willow asked sharply.

"'It's all right,'" she replied.

"Before that!"

"I think he swore under his breath," she lied. "He's rather annoyed to find that after all he has suffered for Va-faith he should be treated as if he were a threat." In fact, Saker had spoken in Pashali, telling her to keep her eyes open. He'd wanted her to take a look around. Striving to sound pleasant, she said, "We are here to help. Including Ardhi. Sorcery is a problem that will hurt both hemispheres if it is allowed to spread."

When Willow said nothing, she added, "Would you excuse me, Arbiter? It is more than two years since I had a chance to pray at a shrine. I need to seek peace with my faith, and the Way of the Oak."

The woman's face softened. "Of course, my dear. I understand. And – separating people from their shrines was not something we did callously or without thought. It was the Pontifect's order, designed to save them."

"Fritillary Reedling's order?" That was hard to believe.

"Yes. I shall leave you to your devotions." She turned and walked away, heading for the exit.

Sorrel spent a moment or two in quiet contemplation of the Way of the Oak, seeking peace from the presence of the tree and its solid strength, but mostly she was surreptitiously studying her surroundings. Saker and Vervain Wintergreen had disappeared into the area on the other side of the massive trunk, where a number of the boughs had drooped sufficiently to provide room-like structures giving privacy. Arbiter Willow, she suspected, was waiting outside the main entrance to make sure she didn't leave unseen. There were several other worshippers quietly focused on their own devotions, none paying her any attention. A cat walked by, and rubbed up against her legs before disappearing into the web of roots. There was something odd about that, but she couldn't quite put her finger on why.

For the first time in her life since she had received a witchery, it was of absolutely no use to her. Most of these folk had witcheries, which meant they could see through any glamour she chose to make. It was a long time since she'd felt so vulnerable. Chiding herself for being such a goose, she moved away from the main entrance and considered how best to leave the shrine without drawing attention. She found a place where she could scrutinise what was happening outside and for a few minutes she did nothing except observe, unseen behind the drooping branches. People were busy. Every so often there was a flare of witchery, although she couldn't see what was done with it. A dog barked in the distance, a horse neighed, chickens scratched in the dirt.

No one was nearby, so she scrambled under the skirt of branches and stood up. It didn't take her long to realise that there was no way she would ever be anonymous. There were too few people and any stranger stood out like a beacon on a barren hill. People stopped what they were doing to look at her, and others turned to see.

The back of her neck prickled in alarm. She had the oddest feeling that she was looking at a scene skewed sideways. The settlement was odd, but she couldn't quite put her finger on why, not yet. She would think about it later. Right then, several of the women were approaching her, all in possession of a witchery.

"Mistress," one of them said, "have you come from Hornbeam?" The question wasn't a hostile one; the woman appeared anxious for an answer, not confrontational. Absurdly, she was holding a cage in her hand with what appeared to be rats inside.

"Yes, I have."

"What news from the port?" one of the others asked.

Immediately there was a babble from all those gathered around her, a flurry of questions. She was appalled when she realised the implication: all of them had been cut off from their loved ones for months.

"I was only there for a day," she said, trying to halt the spate of anxious questioning. "So I don't know very much. I did hear that the Grey Lancers lost their leader, and after that they left Hornbeam. So everything is peaceful there at the moment."

"Do you know anything of Baker's Row?"

"What about the people on North Bank?"

"Are ships coming into port still?"

"Do you know Tomtit Crake?" "Jay Birch?" "Cob Reed?"

In the end, she put her hands over the ears. "Honestly, I don't know anyone in Hornbeam."

The man named Burr hurried up then, flapping his hands, saying, "You're not to talk to her! She's not to be trusted!"

"I think it's the other way around," Sorrel said. "*You* are the ones not to be trusted. We came here for information, wanting to help. We have all suffered because of sorcery. And then you take one of us away, depriving him of his freedom. Is that fair? Where is my friend? What did you do with him? Why are you so afraid of someone you've only just met?"

"Guildsman Burr was just following orders," a man muttered.

"No one will hurt him," said a voice behind her. It was Arbiter Willow again. "We just have to be careful, because he isn't one of us. We are Va-cherished and he is not."

"And so we condemn half the world because of where they live? How stupid is that? And you've never even been there! Where is Ardhi? I want to talk to him."

Willow shrugged. "You can see him if you want. Take her there, Burr."

Burr conducted her through the staring crowd to the only hut with a door barred on the outside. Sorrel lifted the bar and entered the single room, allowing the door to swing closed behind her. There was enough light filtering through ill-made walls for her to see that half of the interior was stacked with bags and barrels. Ardhi was sitting cross-legged on a burlap sack, looking at ease. She listened for the sound of the bar being replaced, but all was silent.

"This must be the food supplies they brought with them," he remarked in Chenderawasi. "When you consider how many people they have here, it's no wonder they are worried."

"They don't have that much land to use, either," she said, replying in the same tongue. "This place is like an island. Va knows what happens if anyone dares to cross over the perimeter into that mist." She swallowed, remembering her glimpse of Heather. "Anyway, let's get you out of here. At least they haven't tied you up."

"Are they going to let me just walk out?"

"Probably not. I suspect we're going to have an argument. Just remember that the shrine itself is sacred; no one can be hurt there. If they threaten us, we run for the oak."

"Is disobeying the shrine keeper and an arbiter some sort of—" He frowned, trying to think of the right word.

"Sacrilege?" she suggested in her own tongue. "After all the horrible things they said about you, I don't care. In fact, I'll climb the fobbing sacred oak if necessary."

His lips twitched. "You wouldn't."

"Oh, yes, I blithering would!"

He grinned at her. "I love you, you know," he said, reverting back to the language of Chenderawasi. "I love you as much as the waves adore the caress of the wind. I desire you as much as the ripples desire to embrace the sand."

Her breath caught. Shocked at the suddenness of his declaration, moved by the beauty of the island imagery of the words, she felt she'd never breathe again.

When she didn't reply, he gave a rueful smile. "We islanders tend to wax poetic when we love. That doesn't make it untrue, though." He stood and crossed to her side to place his hands on her shoulders, so close she could feel his breath on her cheek. Gently he moved his fingers along the curve of her shoulder until his thumbs brushed the sides of her neck under the loosed tumble of her hair. He said, "I don't want you to do anything for me that will place you in harm's way. Not now, not ever."

His gentle sincerity brought moisture to her eyes. She opened her mouth to speak, but he placed a finger on her lips, halting the words. "I couldn't bear to see you hurt, ever. But if I see you safe and happy, then the sun rises on another day – and I know I can bear the weight of the world."

"Ardhi—"

"No, no, don't say anything. I just wanted you to know how I felt. In case, in case – well, just in case it ever mattered. I know you, Sorrel. Now is not the time for you to think about this. For now, we are a ternion and we three have a job to do, and Piper to save. And her brother. That's what matters."

She paused to consider his words, and to remember the purpose of the ternion. "You're right. That's *all* that matters at the moment. But . . ." She felt her face colour up and was glad of the dimness as she strove to steady her breathing. "Thank you for saying it. To be loved – that means a lot to someone who's not had much love in her life."

Not waiting for an answer, she opened the door and walked out into the sunshine, but then was unable to resist looking back at him over her shoulder, smiling.

Reality returned with a thump, though, when she saw Willow's face darken as Ardhi emerged, blinking in the light. "You foolish girl—"

"I am *not* a girl," Sorrel said, the sound of her voice harsh. "I have been to places and seen things that you could scarcely guess at. I have been tasked with something that is beyond anything you could understand. Don't *ever* patronise me, Arbiter."

She didn't say any more because Saker was there, striding across towards them, scattering the foraging chickens. His glower indicated that whatever he'd learned had not cheered him. "Let's go. Feathers and dagger as before." He held out his hands to take theirs. "Let's commit treason, shall we? We are going to rescue a prince." His smile was grim.

"I never thought I would be so glad to leave a shrine," Sorrel said, and took his hand even as she reached out to grip Ardhi's. "This place is . . . all *wrong*."

Sorrel had worried that they'd have trouble returning to the present using the same piece of plume, but, intensely focused, and with the help of his eagle, Saker managed the return trip with ease. When she looked at the feather afterwards, it was dead in her hand. Ardhi shook his head, and she held up her palm so that the now colourless dried-up wisp was whisked away in the wind.

She could feel the undercurrent of anger and distress within Saker. He'd done what most people thought was impossible: he'd seen and spoken to an unseen guardian. His Shenat roots went deep, so to see the population cut off from the shrines of the Ways must have been especially horrible for him.

When they reached the ship, Lord Juster was not on board so the three of them descended to the empty wardroom. Saker unbuckled his sword and flung it on to the table as he seated himself on the bench.

"I've been thinking all the way back," he said. "I believe they told us more than they intended." He looked across the table at Sorrel. "Vervain and Arbiter Willow both knew I'd been nulled. Nothing odd in that. But Vervain wasn't surprised that I had a witchery. Why not? Nulled people aren't usually granted witcheries!"

"He already knew?" Sorrel asked. "Fritillary could have told Arbiter Willow, or Vervain."

"I can't imagine her doing that. I was her *spy*, for Va's sake. The less known about a spy, the better. Most of the time after I was nulled, I was wandering around in Lowmeer, under another name. And there's something else. Vervain knew about you and what your witchery was. How?"

She frowned. "I don't know. Hardly anyone knew in Ardrone. Only Mathilda, and later Prince Ryce . . . I don't think I ever used it when Valerian Fox was present. I thought he might see through a glamour, being a Prime, so I was careful. Just now I wondered if Marsh Bedstraw – the Melforn shrine keeper – might have told Vervain. She knew because she saw the witchery bestowed on me."

"Unlikely Marsh Bedstraw would have met Vervain. Shrine keepers rarely leave the vicinity of their oaks."

"Then how?" she asked.

"I think it was Vervain's unseen guardian, his oakmarrow, speaking to Melforn's oakmarrow."

"The unseen guardians *talk* to one another?" Ardhi asked.

"Well, communicate, anyway. I think that's the way they will send my message to Fritillary, one oakmarrow to another until it reaches an unseen guardian who knows where she is and can pass it on."

"Communicate how?" Sorrel asked.

"In the past, I heard folk tales about roots spreading through the earth, from one shrine-oak to the next, and over in Lowmeer there are tales about how water connects one shrine to another, through rivers and lakes and the sea. Knowledge is thus passed from one unseen guardian to another."

"That's a lovely idea," Sorrel said. "Somehow . . . comforting."

"An unseen guardian, the oakmarrow of Chervil Moors, appeared to me and spoke. It'd be nice to think that it was because I was special, but it's more likely it was because I'd been in contact with the magic of the other side of the world – that is, with Ardhi's kris. The kris was right there, with Sergeant Horntail who was escorting me. I had a sorcerer's warning mark on my palm as well. Perhaps the unseen guardian knew that Shenat power was not strong enough on its own, and recognised that in Chenderawasi *sakti* there was something that might help."

"Communication between unseen guardians would explain *how* all the shrines disappeared at the same time," Sorrel said. "But it doesn't really tell us *why* the Pontifect ordered them hidden in the first place. I mean, there's no point, unless there's a plan. They may be safe now, but who would want to stay locked away from the world? We were given witcheries in order to help others, not to keep them to ourselves."

"People still have other connections to Va-faith. They have chapels to turn to," Saker pointed out, "and the chapel clerics who run them. Many of them are not enamoured of Valerian Fox. Or they weren't when we left."

"Who are you trying to convince?" she asked. "What is our faith without Shenat shrines?"

He sighed. "I know, I know. In fact, I can tell you exactly what our faith is without them. A faith without its heart. Worse, a faith without any power that can stand up to sorcery, which is why Fox has been working towards that outcome from the beginning. When Fritillary Reedling made the decision to lock all the shrines away, she gave Fox exactly what he wanted."

"Then why did she do it?" Sorrel asked.

"She must have had a very good reason, and a plan. I just don't know what it is. Arbiter Willow told us that Fritillary is not at a shrine, which makes sense. She's out in the world somewhere. That way she can have her spies tell her what Fox and his lancers are doing. But she must have a way of keeping in touch somehow with the shrines. I suspect somewhere where there is a shrine which *hasn't* disappeared. A place where she can live, and the shrine keeper can pass on news through the unseen guardians to all the shrines, and news can come back the other way, to her. How else would they be able to send her a message?"

"Where do you think it is?"

"Ustgrind. It's a Way of the Flow shrine. How better to connect than through water? And it would be under the protection of Regala Mathilda."

Ardhi, who had been listening in silence, his chin resting on the hand propped up by his elbow on the table, suddenly sat up straight. "The message you sent – how will she reply?"

"I told her to tell the shrine keeper at the main Twite shrine to attach an answer to the leg of any eagle that landed in their sacred oak. Twite is not far from Gromwell Holdfast."

Ardhi grinned. "Good thinking."

"But that doesn't tell us what her larger plan is." Saker looked across the table at Sorrel. "You said what we saw at the Hornbeam shrine was all wrong. Why?"

"I'm not exactly sure, but I'm a farmer's daughter, and if I was trying to sustain a village of that size on land of that area, well, it wouldn't look like that."

"Go on."

"They had supplies to start with. Mostly grain and flour and fire-wood. To supplement that, they took farm animals and started a vegetable garden."

"Which all sounds very sensible to me."

"Yes. But if it was me, I'd also try to reduce things which would be a drain on resources. Dogs and cats, for example. They eat a lot. True, they protect and they hunt, but when you're confined to a tiny area like that, what would they be hunting? And there's no need for protection – yet you have to feed them. I counted at least four cats and five dogs. Why have so many? Then there were two horses. Why? Nobody's going anywhere. I suppose one might be handy to pull a plough, but when I looked at the meadow – what was left of it – it had been overgrazed. There were three cows and some goats and pigs . . . Much of what must have been lush is now eaten bare. Shenat teaching says we must protect the land, not treat it like that! It all looked so . . . wrong."

"You're right," Saker agreed, frowning. "Bad management."

"What were the people *doing*?" Ardhi asked.

"Who?"

"The people there," Ardhi said. "Some of those folk were doing what you'd expect – cooking, gardening, drawing water. But some were standing around in groups, looking at – well, that's it. I don't know. A couple of men were just staring at a barrel. Just staring at it!"

"I saw someone carrying a cage of rats," she added.

"Ah." Saker thought about that. "At a guess, they were using their witcheries."

"They had a strong witchery glow," she agreed. "I know there are vermin-catching witcheries, but carrying rats in a cage . . .?"

The door to the wardroom opened then, and Lord Juster entered with Mate Finch Aspen, calling over his shoulder for someone to bring the brandy before he expired with thirst. "A day to try the most patient of men," he complained. "I have been poking around in the most *appalling* places. I swear, I smell of gunpowder, wood shavings, linseed oil and –" he sniffed at his sleeve "– lard, I believe." He shuddered and extracted a pomander of spices from inside his embroidered doublet to wave under his nose with an expression of relief. "There are times – in fact most times – when I am unutterably relieved to have been born a nobleman. The thought of life as an artisan in some appalling backstreet quite distresses me."

"What have you been doing," Saker asked, "to have arrived at that startling conclusion?" Juster was playing the effete nobleman again. To amuse them, perhaps? No, he thought not. It was Juster's way of releasing his own unrelated tensions.

"Selling spices – which command the most extraordinary price at the moment, I might add – and then traipsing around the streets buying up every cannon, crossbow, arquebus and pistol that I can find in Hornbeam, or on board the ships in port. I do wish we could return to an era without gunpowder. I declare, it sells for about the same price per pound as grated nutmeg does at the moment. Outrageous!"

One of the sailors brought in the brandy, and Juster looked around at them all. "Well," he said, raising his glass, "are you ready to rescue that fun-loving scatterwit of a prince, Ryce of Betany, and place him on his father's throne?"

"That hardly sounds like a recommendation for the change," Saker said.

"Of course it is. Scatterwits like Ryce listen to advice. Mad kings like Edwayn do not. I foresee a golden era of government by a consensus of nobles and pen-pushing accountants! Which is surely a better way to rule." He raised his goblet. "King Ryce!"

Saker drank the toast, but he rolled his eyes, nonetheless.

18

Inside a Fallen City

The sound of the door to her prison opening unexpectedly terrified her.

The guards brought meals twice a day; Bealina was used to that. Garred, bless him, was thrilled each time. Poor wee mite, he was bored.

It wasn't those times that started her shivering with terror, almost fainting with horror. It was the other times. Like this.

Valerian Fox standing there, with that smile on his face. A predator's smirk, anticipating its prey.

Dear Va, not again, please . . . not again.

She started shaking and moved so that when Fox looked her way, Garred was out of his line of sight. The boy had fled to the corner of the room the moment the sorcerer entered, and now sat with his back to them, his head ducked. His terror of the man was so intense he refused even to look at him, and she was glad, at least, of that.

"Yes, I'm back," he said crossing the room to where she stood, unable to control her trembling. "Returned for another taste of your loveliness. Should I tell Ryce what we do, sweet, sweet Bealina? Should I tell him how you squirm in my arms?" He pretended to consider it. "No, I think not. For the moment he stays in his holdfast, which means he bothers me not at all. If I let him know you are here, and not safe in Throssel, he may do something foolish . . . But rest assured, there is one day when I will tell him, so that he dies knowing."

She wanted to scorn him, to say something clever and cutting. But always there was the memory of what he had done to her, starting a day or two after she'd arrived in Vavala. Always there was the horror to remind her.

"Tell me, has your bleed come yet?"

She wanted to lie, but there it was again. That black tarry touch of coercion, oozing into her mind, stripping it bare of any chance of rebellion.

"No," she whispered.

His smile broadened. "Let's just make certain it doesn't, shall we?"

She shrank back against the stone of the wall and closed her eyes, tried so hard to find resistance somewhere inside her, but the tar was there, making her compliant as he lifted her skirts, kneaded the flatness of her stomach and said, "Ah, yes, he calls to his father, this sorcerer. Shall we let him feel his sire, m'dear?" And then he was thrusting into her, hard and uncaring of her pain, triumphant and victorious, while the tears ran unchecked down her cheeks.

Afterwards, after he had gone, she turned to the open window. She leaned on the sill, looked down at the roof below. Was it high enough? Would she die? Anything would be better than this . . .

"Mama."

Garred was there, tugging at her skirt, his eyes wide and scared.

She wiped away the tears, smiled down at him and said, "Yes, sweetheart. He's gone. We'll play now."

Her precious son, and Fox's perfect weapon.

Gerelda shivered in spite of the warmth of the day. Vavala was a changed city and no bright sun and cloudless sky was going to bring any cheer to the streets now. Although there were no outward signs of war, there was no laughter along the thoroughfares. No smiles, no happiness, no . . . No sense of normality. That was it. No hucksters, no buskers, no costermongers promoting their wares with noisy banter. And whenever had Vavala been without its musicians on the corners? She did not need a witchery to know that there was something badly amiss in the Pontifect's marble city.

Folk put their heads down so as not to meet the gaze of those around them. Glances towards her and Perie were sidelong, a flicker of quickly averted eyes. Were people afraid, or merely cautious? Hard to tell. There was a disproportionate number of unsmiling clerics in the streets. Their clerical medallions, once just a silver representation of either an oakleaf or water, now had an addition: a gold leaping fox.

Perhaps worst of all was the absence of children. Those citizens who had returned after the battle had not brought their families with them. Which said a lot.

After passing the guards at the gate, she led Peregrine into the streets near where the oak shrine had once graced the banks of the River Ard. In its place was an expanse of dark, brooding briars and brambles, nettles and thorned creepers. Thin wraiths of mist snagged and tore on the thorns, and slithered through the leaves.

"Wait here," she said. "I'll be back in a minute."

She left him on the breakwater wall while she looked to see if there was a message from the Pontifect for her, as she did every time they passed by a hidden shrine. First, she had to locate a small plant called Shenat Blood, then find the luck-letter box. This time, when she opened the stone casket, she found a long, detailed letter in Fritillary's handwriting. She replaced it with her own coded missive summarising what she and Perie had done since her last communication.

She would need time to decipher Fritillary's code, not to mention her handwriting, for she had the habit of crossing the sheet with lines written at right angles. Shoving the letter into her tunic unopened, she replaced the casket lid and returned to Peregrine.

"Where are we going now?" he asked, slipping down from the wall.

"What can you tell me about the city so far?"

He pulled a face. "The black smutch is everywhere. It's hard to single out where it came from originally. There's a lot of Grey Lancers."

"What about sorcerers? What about Valerian Fox?"

He gestured at the building looming over the river further downstream, the Pontifect's palace. "Valerian Fox is in there. I can feel him like a big black spider sitting in the middle of his web. He's much stronger than when I came close to him before. He's . . ." He hunted for the right word. ". . . brimming with power."

"Sated on stolen lives, the canker," she muttered, her deep-seated anger spilling over into words.

"He's too powerful. If I get close to him, he'll know who I am and what I want. I won't be the one to kill him." He left unspoken the words he could have uttered: *He will kill me.*

168

She changed the subject. "And the man we were following?"

Just outside Broom on the Ardronese–Valance border, Perie had picked up the smutch trail of a sorcerer leading a small group of Grey Lancers. They'd been following that man's smutch ever since, but the group had been travelling fast and they'd never managed to catch up.

Perie shrugged. "He's here, somewhere in the city. We'll find him."

She felt a momentary satisfaction. Another one dead soon enough. But what was the use if Valerian still lived? He could keep birthing his line of tainted children. Fritillary had hoped Perie would be Valerian's nemesis, but Gerelda knew better now.

"I think we need a good meal and a good sleep before we tackle him," she replied. "Are you hungry?"

"Starving."

"We'll find a pot-house." She'd once known every good eating place in Vavala, but war had visited the city since then. "There used to be one not far from the main palace gates. It's a good place to sit and watch who comes and goes."

The pot-house had a long trestle table and benches outside the door to the street. In spite of the pleasant warmth of the sun, most of the customers preferred to sit inside. The only other person was a single man at one end of the table, leaning back against the wall, clutching a mug.

Gerelda hated to be cooped up in a room when there were lancers about, so she and Perie ordered the food inside and sat outside. Perie occupied himself with the task of demolishing everything heaped on his plate as soon as it was delivered, ignoring her interest in the visitors to the palace down the road.

After a while she began to tire of it herself. As far as she could tell, the people she saw were either servants or clerics. Of far more interest was the fact that the man at the other end of the table appeared also to be on watch. Surreptitiously she switched her attention to him. Middle-aged, bearded, greying, wearing nondescript clothes, none too clean, that spoke of a farmer or possibly an artisan. He was unshaven and his nails filthy. He looked as if he had been sleeping rough.

Of even more interest was the bundle he had with him. A tote bag of good quality leather and a coat wrapped around something which might possibly have been a sheathed sword. Alert now, her casual glance became a careful survey. There was nothing about him that suggested a fighting man or a guard or one of the Grey Lancers. Nor was there anything that suggested a soldier. He was half slumped against the table, hands curled lovingly around the mug of whatever he was drinking. All the appearance of a man down on his luck.

And yet she was sure he was watching the open gateway to the palace compound with far more interest than a casual observer.

She bent her head towards Perie's ear to ask quietly, "Is there any chance that the sorcerer we've been following is in the palace?"

He shook his head. "I don't think so. I think he's over in that direction somewhere, at least half a mile." He pointed to where he meant. "He's not moving at the moment. This whole city is reeky with smutch, though."

She opened her mouth to reply, but just then he stiffened, alert, and grabbed her hand.

"Grey Lancers," he said. "Coming from that direction." He nodded away from the palace.

"Many?"

"Twelve? Fifteen?"

"Sit tight. They shouldn't have any interest in us."

The men shambled up the road, more like a mob of unruly louts than soldiers. None of them was carrying a lance, but they all wore swords and most had daggers strapped to thighs or biceps or stuck through their belts. Not that she was foolish enough to underestimate how dangerous and unpredictable they could be. She glanced at Perie. His face was pallid, and he'd laid down his spoon.

They stopped at the pot-house, but neither she nor Perie interested them. They wanted ale. They entered the taproom and yelled for the innkeeper.

Gerelda turned her attention to finishing her meal as quickly as she could, but just as she cleaned her plate, six of the lancers emerged from inside to sit at the other end of the trestle table. A serving girl and the landlord carried out platters of bread and cheese and ale. As the men began to eat, Gerelda stood, hoping to leave as unobtrusively as possible. When Perie hurriedly scrambled to his feet to follow, one of the lancers spied the man in the corner.

"Pox on't, lookee who's here!" he called out, and his tone was gleeful. "One of them men Cap'n Fox let get away!"

The others turned to look. The man in the corner raised his eyes but didn't react, which made her wonder what was wrong with him. No sensible person thought Grey Lancers could be ignored, surely.

"The bastard must've followed us," said another, a gaunt, pale fellow with a drooping moustache, before adding with a chilling lack of emotion, "Kill him. Ought have been done on the road." All of the lancers leaped up, groping for their weapons.

It was a perfect opportunity for Gerelda and Perie to leave, unnoticed and unremarked. The man – for all that he was so casually condemned – meant nothing to her. Yet as she began to turn away, her gaze met his and something in his eyes halted her. A terrible expression of loss – not of fear, but rather the look of a man assailed by an unbearable despair. Inwardly she groaned, acknowledging that she was about to do something unutterably stupid.

She unsheathed her sword and killed the lancer standing next to her.

Before the man had even slid off her blade to the ground, an expression of astonishment and disbelief on his face, Perie had his spiker in his hand. He dropped to his knees beside her, disregarded by the lancers. Face expressionless, he casually used the dagger to hamstring one of the lancers with a slashing cut to the back of the knee. The man collapsed, his mouth gaping open in astonishment.

Without missing a beat Gerelda swung the edge of her blade into the next member of the group, cutting his sword arm to the bone. He howled, a curdling sound that mingled with a string of screamed expletives from Perie's victim. All the lancers in the taproom would be on top of them in moments.

Pickle it, you daft woman. Why are you doing this? You never interfere in things that aren't your business, you ninny . . .

Three down, but there were three to go.

Two of the three rushed at her. In the seconds she had left, she believed she was going to die because of her own stupidity.

The men ignored Perie, which was ill-advised. As she engaged the next fellow, Perie jabbed his spiker upwards into the genitals of another. The bench they'd been sitting on went flying as the man flailed in shock. Blood sprayed through the air, drenching her. She had no idea where it had come from. She was in a clinch, sword to sword, no blood drawn, and Perie's opponent was doubled over, shrieking.

The man she was fighting was huge, much stronger than she was, and he was bending her backwards over the table. She fought for balance, and lost. He had her flat to the tabletop, pressing her down with his body, their blades crossed right in front of her nose. She knew she was defeated, but refused to surrender. Given his weight, it was useless to wriggle. Instead, she used the thumb of her free hand to jab him in the eye. He yelled and drew back his arm in order to slam a fist into her face.

Before the blow connected, a sword blade was whacked into his neck and she was doused with another shower of blood. She scrambled up, blinking, and wiped a forearm across her cheek. She was face-to-face with the bearded man.

He gave a crooked grin. "Run," he suggested.

Breathless, she took in the carnage at a glance – six bodies. Dead ones, not wounded – and she had only killed one of them. Perie was already ten paces away, racing down the street, his spiker still in his hand. The remainder of the lancers were spilling out of the taproom.

She took the man's advice.

They pounded down Palace Walk, Vavala's main thoroughfare, following Perie. The few pedestrians took one look at the bloodied trio, all of them still with their blades unsheathed, blood dripping from hilt to tip, and scattered. One brief look over her shoulder told Gerelda that the closest of the lancers was maybe only fifteen paces behind them.

"Any ideas?" she yelled at the man.

"Aye – run faster!"

She did.

Perie took the first turn on the right. She knew that laneway descended to the river, but whether it was desperation or a plan that led him in that direction, she had no idea. He did not know Vavala as well as she did, and she couldn't think of any advantage in the route he chose.

Her thoughts raced. No chance to hide, not with the pursuers so close. Little chance to outrun them. Too many to fight, although Va knows, the bearded man appeared to have made short work of five lancers, only three of whom were wounded.

Perie pelted onwards. He was outstripping them, confound him.

She redoubled her efforts, cursing. The bearded man began to drop behind a little. The downward slope steepened and Perie's strides grew longer. She could see the docks in front, and what was known as Neap Pier, normally only used when the tide was so low that barges and ferries could not use the main docks.

"Can you swim?" she yelled over her shoulder. In that short glimpse behind, she didn't think the lancers were gaining on them.

"Like a whale. Why?" he asked in a bellow.

Instead of answering, she waved her sword at the scene in front of them. He muttered something about the River Ard being fobbing cold. He was right. It was fed year long by melted snow and ice.

The closer they came to the docks, the more certain she was that Perie had no real plan except to jump in the river. He was a fine swimmer, and she could swim too, thanks to Saker and their days together at the Grundorp University. Va, but they had been mad in those days. Grundorp was a cold, blustery place and the water had been about as warm as a wolf's smile . . .

Perie's feet hit the boards of the dock and he kept on going to where the pier jutted out towards the deeper flow. The Ard was half a mile across and swift at this time of year. The planks of the pier rattled under her flying feet as she followed. She saw him hurtle from the end to disappear into the waters with a splash. She didn't slow down, but followed him into the river, feet first. By the time she surfaced, he'd already been drawn away by the outgoing tide. She looked back in time to see the bearded man plunge into the water behind her.

A moment later, the pursuing lancers came to a halt at the end of the pier, gesticulating and milling around. She suspected they were trying to find someone who could supply them with a boat.

Good luck with that, you murdering weasels.

The way the river was flowing, in another minute or so the three of them would be out of sight around the bend.

* * *

Gerelda shivered as she bent to unlock the door to the lawyers' guild building, popularly known as Proctor House. The three of them were still wet from their time in the water, and the wind made everything worse. Optimistically, she'd hoped there would be some of her friends in residence, but the shutters were closed and grass grew in between the paving stones of the steps to the front door. The building was abandoned, probably since the time of the war for Vavala. Lawyers, she reflected, were too canny to return to a city under the rule of Valerian Fox.

She had abandoned her pack at the pot-house, and so had Perie, but she still had her sword, her purse, her folded up maps of Ardrone and the Principalities and, fortunately, her lock picks. Anyone searching the belongings she'd left behind would find nothing that tied them to her. She bent to insert the metal pieces into the large keyhole in the door.

"Who taught you to do that?" the bearded man asked.

"A witan."

"Is it wise to break into a building that apparently belongs to a society of writ-wrights? It feels a bit like trying to pet a bear with its foot in a trap."

"I'm a lawyer."

"Oh, good. You can argue my case when I'm arrested for breaking and entering."

"If we are found, I don't think anyone will be charging us with burglary. Murder, maybe, but burglary? I don't think they'll bother, do you?"

He tilted his head as if considering that. "Probably not. Anyway, thanks for intervening back there. I owe you."

"What's your name?"

"I've no idea, I'm sorry to say."

The lock clicked. "Ah, that's got it." The door opened and she gestured them inside, quickly shutting the door behind them. As an added precaution, she slipped the bolt across on the inside.

The entry hall, with its streaked marble pillars and marble tiled floor, she'd always thought pretentious and cold. There was evidence that the building had been abandoned in a hurry – discarded files, a dropped shoe, a half-eaten apple on the floor – and signs that it had not been occupied for a long while. The apple was withered and rock hard, the floors were dusty, the walls had mould creeping down from the ceiling and spiderwebs festooned the corners.

"There's a common room through there," she said, pointing. "If there's any wood, we can get the stove going so we feel a bit warmer."

"We don't have anything dry to wear," Perie said and rubbed his arms.

She shrugged, indifferent. "We're alive. We'll manage."

The bearded man looked around, taking in the murals on the ceiling and the gilded cornices and mouldings as they walked through to the common room, which was marginally cosier. The floor was wooden and someone had ripped up the carpet. The textured walls, once hung with portraits of past legal worthies, was now dotted with empty dark patches of unfaded fabric.

He eyed the crystal chandelier and the gold inlay of the walnut furniture and said, "I always did think writ-wrights were paid too much."

"You remember what you thought about lawyers, yet you can't remember your name?" she asked, not bothering to hide her scepticism. She lifted the lid to the brass studded box next to the equally ornate ceramic stove and peered inside. Good, there was plenty of wood. She pulled out the kindling to set the fire.

"He's been ensorcelled," Perie said. "Not recently, but I can feel the smutch on him. Maybe that's why he can't remember who he is."

Her head jerked up and she scrutinised the bearded man more closely. He had drawn his sword and was emptying out a mix of river water and blood from his scabbard on to the floor with a look of disgust on his face. "You *really* don't know who you are?"

"All I can recall is the last few days."

"What do you remember?"

"Waking up on a roadside. I was standing there, talking to a farmer bringing turnips to the market in Beck Crossways."

She picked up the flint and steel she found in the woodbox and used it to spark the tinder. "Go on."

As he told his story and did his best to clean his weapon and dry its scabbard, she tended the fire. By the time he'd finished, the logs had caught. She closed the door on the stove and brushed the wood dust from her hands. "So you saw this woman in the marketplace in Beck Crossways. You don't know who she is, or whose child she had, but the next day you followed her anyway. Did the lancers not notice you?"

He shook his head. "I'm more careful than that. I bought a horse in Beck Crossways and followed them for several days all the way here. As we came close to the city gates, I caught up a bit so I could see where they went. They entered the palace. After half an hour, the lancers rode out, but she and the boy didn't. The men we killed were in that lot. I didn't think they'd ever seen me before. I don't remember it."

"You were just sitting in the pot-house wondering what the sweet acorns you were going to do next."

He looked sheepish.

"You are making about as much sense as a hedge-born moldwarp."

"That's about right," he agreed, rubbing a rough hand over his head, ruffling his hair. "Hang me for a muckle-head, but there's naught else I can tell you."

"Show me your sword."

He showed it to her, but kept a tight hold.

"Do you know what that means?" she asked, jabbing her thumb at the insignia on the hilt.

He stared at it as if he'd never seen it before, but said slowly, "That's the Ardronese king's coat of arms. House of Betany."

"You're a king's man," she said. "And I've no time for your logger-headed monarch who has led his land to ruin."

He looked shocked at her lack of respect, but all he could say was, "I don't remember whose man I was. A soldier, though? Yes, that feels right."

"The woman – describe her. And how old is the boy she carried?"

"She's right pretty. Tiny, though. Got a waist you could circle with your hands. Dark hair. Fair skin. Hardly more than a child. Wed young, I'd say. The tyke's two, or thereabouts."

"Was she well dressed?"

"Not at all. Like a farmer's daughter. Although—"

"What?"

"Her shoes. Not the kind of thing a farmer's daughter wears. Made for walking floors, not plodding fields." He frowned, then shook his head. "I don't know." He pulled a chair up to sit close to the stove and held his hands out towards the radiating warmth. "Who are you two, anyway? Never met a picklocking writ-wright who carried a sword before, let alone one who could use it. And you speak of our king like you are Lowmian."

"I am. Or was. My name is Gerelda Brantheld. I work – I *used* to work for Pontifect Fritillary Reedling as a Va-faith proctor."

"Before the world as we knew it hopped the twig, eh?"

"Before the whole world fell off the branch," she amended bitterly.

"How can you remember some things, and not others?" Perie asked him. "That's rattle-brained."

"Been mulling over it. Reckon it's anything about me and my life that I don't remember. Learned stuff? That I recall. I could find Throssel or Betany on a map; I could tell ye how to walk from the king's palace to Faith House without missing a step – but I don't recall walking them streets myself. I'm lost, lad. Worst of all, I'm not doing what I ought because I don't remember what it is!"

"Those lancers back there at the pot-house," Gerelda said, "One of them mentioned a Captain Fox."

"Aye."

He hesitated a moment, then dug into his belt and pulled out a leather pouch. "I lost my tote back there, but the money I was carrying I still have." He opened the pouch and spilled the gold coins into his hand to show them.

Perie's eyes widened. "Fiddle-me-witless, that's a tidy nut-store."

"Mistress Brantheld, I'm trusting you. You came to my aid when I was a swordpoint away from dying, for no good reason I could see – except that you got no love of Grey Lancers. My gut tells me this money is not mine. I'm supposed to be doing something with it, but whatever it is, Va only knows. Summat important. If you can help me discover that—"

"Anything I can tell you is only a guess."

"I'll listen to any twaddle right now."

"You have a sword that bears the royal insignia. If I combine that thought with what you've told me . . . One of the nearest towns to Gromwell Holdfast, where Prince Ryce is besieged, is Beck Crossways. We were there not long ago. The siege was still in place."

"Go on."

"Could the woman and child possibly be Princess Bealina and her son Prince Garred?"

He shrugged. "I don't know."

"I'm wondering if you were sent by the king to fetch Prince Garred and return him to Throssel, with or without his mother. Prince Ryce might have agreed to it, believing Gromwell was doomed. Somehow, a Fox intervened . . ."

He looked at her, aghast. "Va help me, why can't I remember!"

It was Perie who answered that one, even though the man was not expecting a reply. "A sorcerer can make people do just about anything he wants. Kill, fight when he doesn't want to, make folk believe things which aren't true. He could make you forget. Although I would have said he was more likely to kill you."

The anguish on his face was clear and she was moved to pity. "So, Sir Nameless, where do you think your sympathies lie? With the king, or with Prince Ryce, or somewhere else?"

"I'm fobbing sure it's not with anyone called Fox," he said. "Every time I hear that name I want to spit."

She smiled slightly. "Given what happened back in the pot-house, I'm fairly certain you don't much like Grey Lancers either. I'm sure we are all agreed that giving Valerian Fox access to Garred and his education is a very bad idea."

The man nodded, frowning.

"So what do we do?" Perie asked.

"I think," she said, "we'd better find out if the princess and her son are really inside the Pontifect's palace, and if they are, then we do our level best to remove them." She looked over at the man, whose clothes were now steaming from the heat, and added, "We still have a sorcerer to kill too, the fellow we've been following, who may well be the one who ensorcelled you. Does any of that interest you?"

His frown vanished into a beatific smile. "Now that sounds like my kind of scrap and tussle! When do we start?"

Confound it, she thought. *We'll all be on the City Watch's list of criminals now.* That was going to make everything that much more difficult.

19

The Darkest Hour

Another dawn. That was something, Prince Ryce supposed.

He had learned to live with the uncertainty of whether he'd see the next sunrise. Each time he glimpsed the first light of the day creeping across the waters of the estuary, he was both pleasantly surprised and – *Admit it, Ryce* – smugly gratified. The heralding of a new day meant those treasonous whoresons had again failed to blow him to beggary overnight.

He would never have predicted Gromwell Holdfast could have lasted that long, not when the enemy had cannon. He had not realised beforehand just how incompetent the Grey Lancers were.

You can't make an army out of farmers by clicking your fingers and wishing it so, he'd thought gleefully. In his more sober moments, he determined that when he was king, he was going to make blistering sure all nobles kept a trained force of men for the Crown to call upon in times of need. If only his father had seen the danger of the Grey Lancers right at the beginning, none of this would have happened.

In fact, the miracle was how few of his men had been killed. The unknown architect who'd designed the holdfast had been skilled. The walls were stubborn and they endured still. True, they'd finally abandoned the outer bailey and the main gate, together with the landward tower, but in anticipation of that, they'd used much of the internal stonework to reinforce the inner bailey.

The well continued to supply them with sweet water, and rationing the food had extended their ability to hold on. Of course, they'd been aided by one of the cannon belonging to the besiegers exploding and killing some of them because they hadn't fully understood how to handle it.

He didn't doubt that sooner or later Gromwell would fall. Even as he stood there, watching the dawn, another cannonball came sailing towards the Seaward Tower. It missed and dropped out of the sky, ploughing into the middle of the inner bailey to create yet another hole in the ground. At least that ball had not been filled with anything explosive. Not many of them had lately, which he took as a sign that gunpowder was scarce.

Only a matter of time though . . .

He could have borne anything if he'd known for sure that Bealina and Garred were safe. Stupid, of course. Horntail must be dead, and Bealina was a prisoner. She wasn't *safe*.

"Another day."

He turned to see that Lord Seaforth had come up the steps to lean against the parapet next to him. "They seem to have trouble working out the correct elevation," Ryce remarked.

"That was another solid ball," Anthon said. "They don't do much damage if they don't hit a wall." He had a tendency to express the obvious, but Ryce knew there was no better person than Anthon Seaforth to have at his side. He was uncomplaining, equable and unafraid. His indifference to death inspired the men. Certainly his unfailing good humour was a tonic to those he commanded.

"I think the time is nearing for us to try to break out of the hold-fast," Ryce said. "I've been watching our besiegers and they are getting more and more careless. Their discipline is disintegrating. We have a chance of success. Besides, if we leave it much longer, we'll lose our fitness and strength. The next cut we make in rations will be a savage one."

"Whatever you say, Your Highness. I for one will be delighted to leave. First thing I'll do is walk into a good tavern: order some of their best ale and a plate of griddle cakes heaped with honey and cinnamon."

"The next wet night we get," Ryce promised.

"Your Highness!"

He turned to see his page boy, Caddis, gazing towards the open sea and flapping a hand in excitement. "There's a huge ship coming up from Port Spurge. Looks like it's a three-master."

An ocean-going vessel? That was odd. It could only be on its way to Twite, which was a small town, usually only a port of call for bilanders, the cargo ships plying the coastal ports. No, wait . . .

Maybe Caddis had spotted a two-masted cargo hulk, the clumsy vessels that carried timber from East Denva to Throssel and the shipyards of Hornbeam, returning up-estuary laden with textiles and fancy goods.

"Put the spyglass on to it, there's a good lad."

Caddis obliged happily, and Ryce exchanged an amused glance with Seaforth. More sombrely, he reflected that they had come to a pretty pass when the mere sight of a large ship provided high entertainment.

When he stepped up to have a look, surprise made him give a sharp intake of breath. An ocean-going vessel indeed. It was Lord Juster Dornbeck's *Golden Petrel*. He would have recognised it anywhere, even if the spyglass had not shown him the flag flying from the mainmast.

He almost wept with gratitude.

"Who is it?" Seaforth asked.

"Someone who might just be our salvation," Ryce replied.

"A sloop-of-war dead ahead," Grig Cranald said, poking his head around the door to the officers' wardroom. "Flying the king's colours."

They all turned to look at him. Saker felt excitement stir and placed his drink down on the table, thinking ruefully that when you weren't a sailor, you welcomed anything promising an end to on-board tedium. Beside him, Sorrel, who had been mending a tear in Mate Finch's coat – as a panacea for her own boredom – hurriedly shoved the needle, coat and scissors away into the tailoring box.

Juster, who had been tilted back in his chair with his feet up on the wardroom chart table and a goblet of brandy in his hand, let his feet thump back to the floor. "Who's at the helm? And how far are we from Gromwell?"

"Forrest, cap'n. He reckons we're approaching it now. Ardhi's up in the crow's nest on the lookout."

"Right. Give the order to man all guns, but keep the gunports closed. We want to look peaceful, while primed for anything."

Cranald withdrew and Juster reached for his sword belt. "Sorrel, would you mind taking charge of the sick bay in Barklee's place? Saker, the eagle, please. I want to know what there is to be seen."

Saker nodded. He'd already made the connection to the bird. It was spiralling into the sky above the ship and images of what it saw were flicking into his mind. As he ran up on to the weather deck with Juster, he said, "Good views of what I assume is the holdfast. Half-ruined, but inhabited. You ever been there?"

"Yes, once, when I was about twenty."

"It looks like they're holed up on the seaward side. Was there more than one tower? Because there's only one now, near the cliff. There's a heap of rubble that could have once been another. Men on the walls, armed. No cannon that I can see in the holdfast."

"Get us as much detail as you can on the number of besiegers and their weaponry."

Grig Cranald handed over the ship's spyglass to Juster, saying, "Ardhi says the flag the holdfast is flying is a red stag."

"Prince Ryce's emblem." Juster gave a low laugh. "Who would have thought he could hold out this long? There must be more to Ryce than we once thought."

"If that's all we have to believe the prince is still alive, I wouldn't rely on it," Saker said. "Flags can lie."

Juster focused the spyglass on the ship ahead of them. "That sloop looks to be anchored."

"Why would it be here?" Saker asked.

"To make sure nobody supplies the holdfast from the sea. I seem to remember there was a landing at the foot of that cliff there and they had some sort of winch rigged to bring goods up from boats."

Saker sent the eagle in a wider circle to spy on the besiegers. Sorrel, clutching her shawl tight as the wind whipped around the deck, asked, "How dangerous is that sloop to us?"

Juster, still gazing at it with the spyglass, said, "Sloops-of-war are small, less than twenty guns, carronades rather than cannon. Shallow draught, manoeuvrable, don't carry much in the line of supplies and don't have large crews. We could blow that one out of the water without them being close enough to send a ball that would even splash us. Her name's *Dragonfly*. Daft name. Easy to tear wings off a dragonfly."

Sorrel winced, remembering the screams of men when a galleon had burned in Kotabanta harbour. Saker said nothing. Cranald and

Mate Finch exchanged looks. Forrest, at the helm, waited for instructions as *Golden Petrel* continued on its way up the estuary.

"Va, but you bilge rats have a lot to say without even opening your mouths," Juster growled. "Do you think I like the idea of blowing another ship – and all its company – to smithereens? I served under the man who later went on to captain that vessel over there, and who probably still does. You remember Orrin Parkett, Finch? Distant relative of the Earl of Yarrow."

"Aye. A good sailor, a fair officer. A poor provider as a sire, though, as I remember."

"That's because he had to support so many small fry. Sailors used to say he had a family in every port up and down the coast."

Ardhi called down from the crow's nest just then, to say signal flags were being raised on the sloop. A moment later, a cannon on the deck of *Dragonfly* boomed, and Sorrel jumped.

"Only a signal cannon," Juster said, "to get us to look at whatever the message is. Nothing to worry about." But as the distant line of flags unfurled to flap in the breeze, his face tightened in a way which did not bode well for *Dragonfly* and its captain.

"What do they say?" Saker asked.

Juster grimly snapped out the order to heave to. "They're ordering me to pay *Dragonfly* a visit. Arrogant lubbers. And damn King Edwayn to a Va-less hell for putting us in this position."

No one said anything in answer to that.

"Launch the pinnace when we're ready, Cranald," Juster said. "Saker, if I wrote a message for Prince Ryce, could you get that bird of yours inside the holdfast with it?"

Inwardly, he shuddered. "No. If they see a bird of prey coming down to land on their walls, they'll loose an arrow at it. Especially if they're starving." He was by no means certain what would happen to him if the eagle died while the two of them were twinned.

Juster frowned and conceded the point. "All right then, keep it up high in the sky and see what else you can find out from what it sees. Finch, you're in command of the vessel. Grig, you come with me. We're going over to that sloop to see what we can do to put a hole in the hull of the captain's intentions."

As they watched Lord Juster being ferried over to *Dragonfly*, Saker said to Sorrel, "I'm going to lie down in the captain's cabin." She nodded, her face grave.

He glanced at her. "You don't much like it when I do this, do you?"

"I hate it." The venom in her tone surprised him.

"That much?"

"Saker, linking to a bird to the extent of twinning with it – I can't believe it's a good idea. You're crossing a boundary. It's an unnatural kind of magic that doesn't belong in the Va-cherished Hemisphere."

It was the first time she had voiced such a strong dislike of his connection to the eagle. "This link has saved us several times already. Would you have me reject it?"

He saw a tear at the corner of her eye as she looked away. "I'm not sure you could. In fact, I'm not sure about anything any more. How did we become so important to half a world?"

The anguish in her voice tore at him. When she turned back to look at him, he read misery in her gaze. "I just want this to be over," she said. "I want it to *end*. I want to be with Piper again. And . . . and I don't think that's ever going to happen."

"Trust in Va. All will be well—"

"Don't you dare offer me religious platitudes when you don't even believe them yourself!"

He stared at her, shocked.

"Don't look at me like that! I know you too well, Saker. Your Shenat beliefs may be strong and true, but you don't think Va answers prayers." She gave a small laugh. "That's our problem, isn't it? We know too much about each other, you and I." She sighed. "Off you go. I'll make sure you're not disturbed."

"Welcome aboard *Dragonfly*, my lord," Captain Parkett said. "I'm glad to see you again after all these years."

"Captain." Juster inclined his head in acknowledgement. "A lot of water has passed under the keel since we last met. You're looking well." It was a lie; Orrin Parkett had lost a lot of weight, to the point of gauntness. His hair had receded until he was almost bald, his beard was sparse, and his fingers were so swollen at the joints that they had twisted this way and that like broken twigs.

"This is my second mate, Grig Cranald," he added, by way of introduction.

"Perhaps you would like to stay on deck, Master Mate," Parkett said, "while I show your captain below."

Grig bowed, and Juster followed Parkett, confident that Grig would do his best to find out as much as he could above decks.

Below, the ship was cramped and dark, smelling of gunpowder, rancid oil and the mustiness of cockroaches. Remembering his own apprenticeship on a similar dank vessel, Juster had to stop himself from shuddering.

"A fine looking man, your mate," Parkett said. "Been sailing with you a while, has he?"

"Long enough. He has many skills." Knowing the remark had been barbed with innuendo, he added a barb of his own. "And may one enquire after your family? All those children of yours doing well?"

"Damning me to beggary with their needs, the little squeakers. Make yourself comfortable. Brandy?"

"That would be very welcome." He accepted the drink, served in a battered regulation naval mug, and just managed to stop himself from pulling a face as he took the first sip. "And now that we have the pleasantries out of the way, can we perhaps get down to business? What possible reason could one of His Majesty's sloops have for halting my passage to Twite?"

"Come now. I'm sure you know the situation at Gromwell Holdfast. My orders are to prevent Prince Ryce and his misguided henchmen and vassals from having contact with anyone. In particular, to prevent supplies being brought to the holdfast by sea."

"Ah, yes, I do believe I heard something about Prince Ryce refusing to give up his son to the custody of the king. I *could* say that none of that is my concern. I am merely sailing past to Twite."

"And I would guffaw. One of the prince's stalwarts, yet you intend passing by to Twite?"

"Are you accusing me of lying, captain?" He smiled in a friendly fashion.

"Va forbid! But mayhap . . . trying to flimflam me."

"Perhaps. I don't know whether you are aware, but I have been to the Spicerie in the Summer Seas and have only just returned with my *Petrel* and two Lowmian prize ships. All with their holds stuffed to the seams with nutmeg and mace, cinnamon, cloves, pepper and cardamom. A veritable treasure, in fact, considering the price of spices at the moment. Most of it is already sold, but I kept back a selection for my . . . friends."

"How exceptional for you. And your friends, of course."

"Let us return to the question of this siege. I must say, captain, I do admire your extraordinary bravery."

"You mock me, my lord? Unworthy of you. I follow the orders of my liege, and it is not meet that you should deride me for it."

"Indeed, sir, that was not my intention. It is merely that when you obey the dictates of a sick old man who may die any moment, thereby annoying intensely his appointed heir, well, I cannot help but admire your courage."

"The king's acknowledged heir is his grandson Prince Garred."

"Come now, captain! Surely you have been told how ill King Edwayn is! Why, I saw him but two sennights ago, in Throssel. He was frail in body and, alas, frail in mind. It grieved me to see him thus." He heaved a theatrical sigh. "If Edwayn passes into the keeping of Va's afterlife soon, Prince Garred will not even have reached his third birthday. I find it hard to contemplate that men of power – the nobility, the clergy, the merchants – will countenance a boy less than three years old on the throne, when he has a hale and princely father. Such a situation would be fraught with opportunity for the unscrupulous."

Orrin looked worried, but said nothing.

"For that reason," Juster continued, "when King Edwayn dies, thinking men and women will support Prince Ryce's claim because they want stable governance. Prince Ryce will be king. Where would that leave you? I do not think your position will be enviable then, Orrin. Your loyalty to Edwayn is to be commended, but I tend to think it is unwise."

Orrin Parkett sat very still, his brandy untouched. "What choice do I have? I am one of His Majesty's naval commanders, and I do his bidding. I cannot promote treason."

"I rather think that, when he comes to the throne, Prince Ryce will consider your actions here now as treasonous to him. Prince

Ryce is young and his reign will be long. Your career will soon be over and the new king could cancel your pension."

There was a long silence.

Finally, Parkett asked, "What would you do if you walked this deck?"

"There is one way I can see for you to wriggle out of this," he replied, swirling the atrocious brandy in his mug. "Resign your commission now and make your last order to your crew to sail to Twite to put you ashore. Disappear for a while until Prince Ryce gains his throne and you can claim your pension."

"And what would I live on in the meanwhile?"

He tilted his head thoughtfully. "I might have an answer to your problem." He dug the fingers of his right hand into his waistcoat fob pocket and withdrew a little packet of spices. "Smell those, Orrin." He dropped it into Parkett's palm.

Orrin raised it to his nostrils and inhaled.

When he went to hand it back, Juster waved it away. "No, no, it's yours! Keep it. I could deliver enough spices to you today that would keep your crew and yourself living in comfort for several years."

There was another long silence.

"And what would I have to do to earn such bounty?" Orrin asked finally, and Juster knew the man was hooked.

"For a start you would have to be wise. Wise enough to accept my offer and to sail up to Twite. Because otherwise *Golden Petrel* blasts you out of the water, and of course you might well drown. Or end up looking like a skinned and headless carcass in a butcher's shop."

"Right now, may I remind you, you are on my ship and in my power, Lord Juster."

"True, but my ship is out of range of your cannon, whereas your ship is well within the range of mine – and I have this." He flicked back his coat and pulled out the pistol that had been thrust into his belt. "Have you seen one of these new-fangled wheel-locks before? I bought this one in Javenka. Truly, Pashali gunsmiths are remarkable artisans. Isn't it beautiful, and so small! I loaded and primed it before I left my ship. All I have to do is to rotate the cock like this –" he demonstrated what he meant "– and that releases the safety catch. If I were to pull the trigger . . ."

He looked over the top of the pistol he was now pointing at Parkett and smiled. "Very effective."

"You are threatening me, Lord Juster? Do you think you'd get off this ship alive, if you were to harm me?"

"Probably not. But my objective right now is more to stop the siege." He shrugged. "If I die doing it, I'll look on that as a worthwhile demise. If I don't leave *Dragonfly* safely in the pinnace in the next few minutes, my crew have their orders to blow you out of the water. We could have done that anyway, but, well, given that I once served under you . . ."

Parkett said nothing.

"I think I will leave the ship now and I suspect you will let me. You could blast my pinnace to pieces as I sailed back to my ship, or you can send your own boat across after me to pick up the spices I promised, and then you could sail away. We will be watching. When Prince Ryce is king, I will personally see to it that your pension is paid as well. Now doesn't that sound like a pleasant retirement?"

20

The Biting Gadfly

"I know something that might help," said the nameless bearded man. He was sitting next to Perie, at the table in the kitchen of Proctor House, but it was Gerelda he addressed.

She cocked her head, ready to listen. They had been discussing plans and suggesting ways to disguise themselves for over an hour, as often as not discarding an idea as impractical or too dangerous. She was inclined to trust the fellow, although apparently even he could not be certain of his own loyalties.

Fiddle-me-witless, I'm not usually this accepting after a mere day's acquaintance. It was muckle-headed, but she *liked* the man.

"Sailors firing off the cannons say the noise on a gundeck blisters their eardrums," he said, "so they make themselves a pair o' plugs. Softened candle wax, bunged in the earhole. If a man can't hear, then he can't be coerced. Right?"

She brightened. "Wax, that's an idea. Sometimes you remember the darnedest things, Sir Nameless. I doubt wax would stop Valerian, but his sons? Worth a try."

"Be plenty of candles here, Mister," Perie said. He pulled a face. "I can't call you Mister all the time! Not if we're comrades."

"He's right. We have to think of a name for you," she said.

Perie grinned. "We get to choose?" From the mischievous look on his face, he was about to suggest something inappropriate, and a pang of guilt racked her. He was still so young, and he so seldom had fun, or even smiled. *Sweet Va, what have we done to this lad?*

"*You* don't get to choose," she said, tapping him on the wrist. "Sir Nameless chooses."

The man thought for a moment and then said, "Gadfly."

"Why that?" Perie asked.

"Because gadflies are obnoxious biting bastards that annoy every man and his horse into apoplexy. And I feel like being a gadfly to them Grey Lancers. Fact is, I'm fobbing angry with something. Or someone. Or maybe the whole world, if only I knew why."

"I hope you're not going to bite us," Perie said.

"I'll settle for tormenting sorcerers instead. This fellow you've been after, he can be the first."

"You carry the black smudge on you," Perie warned. "The one that tells sorcerers to know you for an enemy."

Blistering grubbery, she thought. *How are we ever going to get out of this city alive, let alone rescue a woman and child who might possibly be the future of this land?* Her next stray thought was that Ardrone might be better off without a king.

Oh, fiddle. I'm becoming a revolutionary like the Primordials. She tried to imagine lawyers doing a better job of governing, and failed. She laughed inwardly, sure that writ-wrights would be a barrow-load more unpopular than even nobles, and went to find a quiet spot to decipher the Pontifect's letter. She had already perused it, but reading a page of crossed lines was never easy, and this one was written in code as well, so she needed to ensure she'd understood it properly. In the end, Peregrine came looking for her, and found her sitting on the servants' stairs in the dark.

"I'm pondering," she explained. "The letter was from the Pontifect."

"Reckon you don't like what was in it, then."

"She asks us to kill any Vavala sorcerer sons here, and then stay on. She needs us to find out as much as we can about Princess Bealina and her son."

"So that really be the princess who Gadfly saw?"

"Probably. Fritillary was here a day or two back. We just missed her. She wants us to wait for her return." She crumpled up the letter and began to walk downstairs to the common room so she could throw it in the fire. She wasn't about to leave it lying around, code or no code.

"Delivery from the Pontifect," Perie said to the maid who answered the door to the servants' quarters. He offered her the small sack he held, raising it in front of his face so she couldn't see him properly.

The sack contained nothing more than unshelled and mouldy walnuts bought cheaply in the local street market, but she wasn't to know that.

"For a, um, Master Endor Fox," he added. They'd asked around until they discovered the name of the man they had been following.

As a delivery boy, he'd used the area steps down to the servants' quarters of the sorcerer's house, and he was hopeful that no one in the street above would notice him – or see Gadfly and Gerelda where they waited pressed to the house wall out of the maid's line of sight. They had their hair tucked up under knitted caps and their faces muffled in unseasonably warm scarves. Both of them had wax stuffed into their ears.

He took a pace forward towards the maid, stepping up on to the doorstep. Surprised, she backed away, and when he thrust the sack towards her, she took it in self-defence, clutching it to her chest. All he noticed about her was that she was scrawny, no older than he was, with rough, red hands and grease-spattered clothing.

He leaned against the inward-opening door so she could not close it.

She glared at him around the side of the sack. "Very well. I shall see he gets it." Pointedly she grabbed the door edge with one hand and jerked it to dislodge him.

He didn't move, but Gadfly and Gerelda did. They barged into the house, brushing past him and the maid, to plunge down the passage towards the kitchen. The maid squealed and tried to stop them, but what with juggling the sack and trying to close the door on Perie, she failed even to slow them down.

They left her yelling after them. "Wait! You can't go in there! Git outta it. Master Corncrake! Help!"

Perie closed the door, and tapped her on the arm. "Do be quiet. Naught will hurt you, if you do what we tell you."

Her mouth dropped open.

Loathing himself for being the cause of the fear in her eyes, he tried to smile at her, but that only made things worse. She scudded away from him, running after Gadfly and Gerelda, squealing. He pulled his own muffler up over his face.

By that time, Gerelda and Gadfly had barged through into the main kitchen. Perie burst into the room hard on the heels of the maid, who was crying out as she ran, "Master Corncrake! Master Corncrake!"

At the kitchen range, on the far side of the room, the cook, a tall, thin man with the curliest sideburns Perie had ever seen, turned to look. His soup ladle dripped sauce on to the brick hearth, unheeded.

To his right, the kitchen skivvy dropped a pile of clean dishes on to the flagstones in fright. She flailed her hands like a frightened chicken trying to fly, torn between the horror of broken crockery and the entry of muffled strangers.

The only other person in the room was a man, smartly garbed in a footman's uniform. He had more gumption than the others and spun around wildly looking for a weapon, finally grabbing an iron roasting spit.

"Ah now, my man," Gadfly said, "don't be like that, else I'll be forced to run you through the belly." He waved his sword point to reinforce the threat.

The man blanched, but didn't drop his weapon. He poked it at Gadfly, then realising how futile that move would be, raised it over his head as if to use it as a bludgeon. Gadfly laughed and pinked the man's hand before tweaking the spit from his hold.

Perie ran across the room, flinging open all the doors – except the baize one, which Gerelda had warned him would lead into the main living area of the house. He was looking for the room she'd said every kitchen had, a walk-in pantry.

"Here!" he yelled when he found it, then remembered that neither Gadfly nor Gerelda could hear him. He pointed instead.

Gadfly gestured with his sword. "All of you, in there," he said, his voice a menacing growl. "Right now. Do as you're told and nothing bad will happen to you."

The servants exchanged frightened glances. The maid stopped squealing, but when Gadfly's blade swung in her direction, panic started her breath rattling in her throat.

"Go on!" Gadfly growled.

She picked up her skirts and fled into the pantry.

The cook took no notice. He looked at Gadfly, incredulous, and asked, "Have your brains run out through your ears? Don't you know whose house this is?"

As neither Gerelda nor Gadfly could hear, it was up to Perie to reply. "Yes, we know. Where is he?" he asked.

"As far as I know he's upstairs," the cook replied. His tone was contemptuous, but Perie noted his hands trembled. "I'm blistering sure you coves are about to breathe your last, all of you, unless you git out of here."

"Into the larder. Now." He tried to sound authoritative, but wasn't sure he succeeded. "Otherwise one of these people is going to damage you with their swords. We have no argument with you – if you do as we say."

The cook shrugged and jerked his head at the young footman and the skivvy. When the skivvy didn't move, he grabbed her by her upper arm and yanked her into the pantry with him. Gadfly closed the door after them. There was no bar, so they pushed the heavy kitchen table against it.

"Let's get going," Gerelda said and made for the padded baize door, Gadfly close behind. Perie followed. They found themselves inside the main hall, where stairs led up to the bedrooms. On the lower floor, closed doors led to other rooms.

Gerelda looked at him. "Which way?"

Concentrating, he took a deep breath. He could feel the horror of the man trickling down from the floor above. He pointed.

Bounding up the steps two at a time, he led the way. At the top, he halted briefly to reassess. Powerful waves of wrongness almost made him gag, but he continued on, turning to his right. He ignored the first three doors opening off the corridor and stopped in front of the fourth, jerking his head to indicate that it was the room.

They had rehearsed several different scenarios, so there was no reason to wait. Gerelda and Gadfly stood on either side of the door. Once they were in place, Perie flung it open with his left hand. In his right hand, he held his spiker out of sight behind his back. He cleared his mind of everything except a driving need to kill something that had no right to live, and stepped into the room. Behind him, Gerelda and Gadfly entered side by side, Gadfly breaking to the left, Gerelda to the right.

Perie gaped, taken aback by the size of the chamber they'd entered. The cottage he'd lived in as a child would have fitted in this bedroom. The bed it contained was large enough to have slept a family of six. He jerked himself back to his danger.

In front of the large marble fireplace, a manservant was holding a coat, about to help his master – the sorcerer – into it. Both men whirled to see who had entered without knocking.

"Sorry to disturb you, sir," Gadfly said politely. "We have an important message from the Pontifect. If you would be so good as to listen—"

"Stop right where you are," the sorcerer, Endor Fox, said calmly.

In that brief moment when both men had their attention focused on Gadfly, Gerelda slammed into the servant, sending him flying into Endor Fox, who sprawled, off-balance, against the bed.

With a single sweeping move, she pulled the cover from the bed and flung it over the shocked servant.

Endor yelled, ordering them all to be still. Perie felt the coercion like a splash of icy water, shocking, but without power. His heart sank nonetheless. With yelling like that, wax in the ears was not going to be enough to stop them hearing the duress.

Gerelda halted in mid-step. Gadfly, who had leaped up on to the bed to approach the man from the other side, was suddenly unbalanced and uncertain.

Stumbling as if by accident, Perie took another step forward, his hand still behind his back.

"Stop right where you are!" Fox cried. There was more annoyance in his voice than fear. "Who are you? Answer me!"

As neither Gerelda nor Gadfly heard him, neither replied. Perie used the time to take a step closer.

Endor smiled. "Wax in the ears, I suppose." He gave a derisive snort and yelled once more. "Take the wax out of your ears! Now!"

Gerelda and Gadfly, still halted by his earlier shout, heard and obliged, and Perie hurriedly pretended to do likewise.

"Who are you?" Endor asked, the oily coercion of his tone painful, even to Perie.

They all started speaking at once, telling him their names.

Although he felt no compulsion, Perie said, "Peregrine Clary, sir."

He felt serene, as he often did at moments like this. The killer of sorcerers, coming into his own. He smiled, remembering the words of the unseen guardian. *No pain in your heart, only hard oak.*

Seeing an unarmed lad, the sorcerer turned his attention to Gadfly and Gerelda. "Drop your weapons!"

The two blades fell from their hands, followed by daggers drawn from their belts. And Perie acted.

He took that last step forward, and swept the spiker from behind his back in one swift upward movement. It plunged into Endor Fox's stomach, the soft organs parting easily before the sharpness of its tip. Not his normal killing stroke, but it didn't matter.

Fox gasped and both his hands went to push him away.

Perie stepped back, leaving the blade buried to its cross-guard.

The man, trying to remain upright, clutched the hilt, attempting to pull it out. His face was a picture of disbelief. "How—?" he asked.

"An unseen guardian sent me. I am your fate," he answered as Endor fell, first to his knees and then on to his side. Scooping up Gerelda's sword from where it lay, Perie stabbed the man in the chest, hard. "If not me, then your sorcery, or your father, would have sucked you dry. Perhaps this is more merciful."

"I don't think he heard that last bit," Gerelda remarked, stepping forward to retrieve her blade. "Thanks, Perie. I owe you. If there is one thing I hate above all else, it's being coerced." She poked at the sorcerer to make sure he was dead, then glanced to where the servant had managed to wriggle out from under the bedcovers. He sat on the floor, shaking.

"Stay here until we leave," she told him. "After that, I'd leave Vavala today if I were you."

Gadfly, rather sheepishly, jumped off the bed. "Pickles 'n' pox, that was horrible. How can someone take away your will so easily?"

"Makes you have some pity for the Grey Lancers, doesn't it?" she replied, cleaning her sword on the bedcover.

He shook his head. "Ah, I wouldn't go as far as to say that. They had a choice and they chose to reject Shenat teachings long before they met a sorcerer. Ignorance, greed and gullibility. Fobbing horrible combination."

She looked across at Perie. "You all right, lad?"

"I'm fine. Killing sorcerers always makes me feel good." He straightened up with the spiker in his hand, having wiped it clean on the bedspread.

"Then let's get out of here," she said. "We've done what we came to do. And as an added bonus, we now know your name, Master Gadfly. Or should I say, Sergeant Buttercup Horntail? Nothing like a spot of coercion to bring memory to the fore, is there?" She smiled sweetly.

"Tell me I didn't say that," he growled, an appalled expression on his face. "That can't be right, surely!"

"Buttercup?" Peregrine asked. "*Buttercup?* You can't be serious. Did he really say that?"

Gerelda adjusted her scarf over her face once more. "Loud and clear. I heard him. And we all know you can't lie under coercion." She opened the door and peered out into the passage. "All clear, Buttercup."

"Shut up, you leprous lawyer!"

As they ran downstairs again, Perie had a hard time muffling his laughter.

21

Reunion

The defenders of Gromwell Holdfast watched in joyous disbelief as *Dragonfly* sailed away in the direction of Twite, leaving the waters at the foot of the cliffs unguarded for the first time in almost a year, all without a shot being fired. *Golden Petrel* was now anchored where *Dragonfly* had been.

Prince Ryce celebrated on the eastern wall by broaching the very last bottle of the castle's brandy with Beargold and Anthon Seaforth. "Here's to freedom," he said. "The siege will be broken within a sennight, mark my words!"

"How is one ship going to break the siege?" Beargold asked. "They could supply us, I suppose – or help us escape by boat. No more than that."

"Juster will find a way," Ryce said. "You'll see."

Beargold gave a derisive snort. "That inane fop? What does he know about sieges?"

"We'll find out soon." He should have known Beargold's innate pessimism was not so easily dissipated.

"They've just launched a boat," Seaforth said, looking through the spyglass. "They're sending somebody across to us."

"I imagine that'll be Lord Juster," Ryce said, and curbed a sudden sadness. If only Bealina and Garred were there to see this.

"It's close to three years since you saw him," Beargold said. "He could be dead, and the ship in the hands of someone else. Besides, he's renowned for his inconsistency. They call him 'Jiber' about town, did you know that? From some sailing term, meaning to change direction."

Ryce hid a smile. "I don't think that word has been applied to him because he changes *loyalties*, Beargold. More to do with whether

197

his bedmates have tits or pizzles. Here, Anthon, give me that spyglass."

"Va's galls, they had better be bringing some food with them," Seaforth said. "I am so sick of weevils in my biscuits, and I swear I've forgotten what fresh fruit looks like."

"Pickle me sour," Ryce said. "Can't you two stop complaining? Help has arrived!"

He rested the spyglass on the top of the wall to steady it against the wind and peered through. It took him a while to pinpoint the longboat in the expanse of blue water, but when he did, the first person he saw sitting astern was the flamboyantly dressed Juster Dornbeck, his topcoat embroidered around the sleeves, his hat resplendent with peacock feathers and gold pins. One hand clutched the hat to his head; the other was clasped around the top of a cane – gold-knobbed, Ryce wouldn't have minded betting.

He shifted the spyglass to take a look at the second passenger in the longboat, seated in the prow. "Blister me speechless," he muttered. *That can't be Saker Rampion, surely?*

But it was. Not in a witan's garb, but smartly dressed in clothes of a foreign cut. The witan was still all sinew, whipcord and muscles, by the look of him, sword at his side, long dark hair tied at his nape. *It really is him.*

He started to laugh. The last time he'd seen Saker, the man had been naked up on Chervil Moors . . .

"That's madness. Cock-eyed madness."

Saker leaned against the wall of the *Golden Petrel*'s wardroom, listening as Prince Ryce – of all people – protested Lord Juster's plan to end the siege. The prince had obviously sobered in the years since they'd seen each other; he'd once been game for anything, especially if it involved recklessly risking his own neck. Now, after being brought down from the holdfast to a meeting on board ship, he was demonstrating caution and restraint.

The air in the cabin was heavy with the reek of the three unwashed men: Lord Seaforth, his cousin Sir Beargold and the prince himself. Compared to the others in the cabin – Sorrel, Lord Juster, Mate Grig Cranald and Mate Aspen Finch – the three from the besieged castle were hollow-eyed, gaunt and filthy, their clothes not far from rags. There was an intensity about them too: the tight comradeship of men who had lived with the fear of death and prolonged deprivation.

Outside the sun was slowly sinking behind the cliffs, leaving the estuary a bruised plum hue under a blood-dark sky. Luckily the wind was slight and the tide was at the neap, because out on the water the *Golden Petrel*'s boats were still ferrying the holdfast's occupants across to the ship. Ryce had agreed that, now they had a safe escape route for all the besieged, there was no point in holding Gromwell any longer.

Lord Juster's plans, however, did not mesh with the prince's. Juster wanted to take every able-bodied man and attack the Grey Lancers from behind, whereas Ryce wanted to raise an army of his own to seize Throssel and ensure the safety of his wife and son – before engaging the Grey Lancers.

"What if there's still a sorcerer among that lot?" the prince asked.

"You just admitted you haven't seen a sorcerer since Bealina was taken," Juster pointed out. "You've also said that the lancers don't bother to keep watch on the cliffs because they think *Dragonfly* had this escape route sealed off. We have a way of spying on them, thanks to Saker's witchery and his eagle. We also have someone here with a Shenat glamour witchery. I'm told you already know that."

Ryce glanced at Sorrel, inclining his head. "We've met," he said dryly. "The last time under somewhat trying circumstances, for which I apologise."

She smiled at him, eyes twinkling. "I'm sure our future relationship will continue to be beneficial to us both, Your Highness."

Seaforth's eyes widened at her obvious lack of deference, but Ryce returned her smile before replying to Juster. "We have very little ammunition remaining. We have scraped the bottom of our last barrel of gunpowder and we have one working longbow and ten arrows. We do have a number of crossbows and we've been making our own crossbow bolts. We burned the beams we salvaged from the wrecked part of the holdfast to keep the forge alight."

There was an intake of breath followed by an appalled silence in the wardroom.

"Sweet Va," Juster said finally. "You were that close to—?"

Glenda Larke

"We even reconfigured a number of crossbows to shoot stones," Ryce said.

"*Stones?* You've been throwing stones at men in armour?"

"What armour?" Ryce countered. "Juster, these lancers are rabble. Dangerous rabble, but still rabble. Undisciplined, half mad, wretched farmboys and illiterate street sweepers. Ensorcelled and pitiable, but also totally pitiless. There is no honour in them, but no initiative either. The sorcerer told them what to do, and as far as I can see they will keep doing it until they die. They were never given armour and they don't know how to make it. This is a mad war, my friend."

"I think you're both forgetting something," Saker said into the ensuing silence. "Your Highness, you think that if you return to Throssel, you will find your family safe under your father's protection. But Lord Juster has not long seen and spoken to the king. Believe me, he's incapable of offering protection to anyone."

"I'm afraid that's true," Juster agreed. "He's very ill, and not in full command of his faculties."

"Valerian Fox would not have any interest in placing Prince Garred with him," Saker continued. "If he's seeking some kind of legitimacy for his temporal rule, then he will want control of the prince himself. I imagine we will find that he has been declared the young prince's guardian. It's very possible that Your Highness's son is under his wing in Vavala."

The prince scowled. "No. I refuse to believe that."

"What makes you think Fox cares about legitimacy?" Juster asked in support of Ryce. "He's an amoral sorcerer!"

"Why bother to have an election to become Pontifect, unless it was to seek legitimacy?" Saker asked. "Your Highness is correct when you said this is a mad war. We have to rid our minds of past history and think how this battle will be *won*. Not how it can be fought, but how it can be won. By *us*. I never liked Valerian Fox, but I did once underestimate him. Never again. When a man holds a hot branding iron under your nose and the expression on his face tells you what he'd like to do with it—"

He had their full attention now.

"We are all scared of sorcery, but he is only one man and he is reluctant to be profligate with his power. Each time he uses it, it is diminished. He can replace it by killing one of his sons, or by sucking the life out of a newborn. That has to complicate his life. These sorcerous sons you've told us about? They are his power – but they're also his weakness. Kill them, and you leave Valerian Fox without weapons and the Grey Lancers without leaders. We can defeat a leaderless rabble."

They were still silent, absorbed by what he was saying, so he continued.

"A large army is not going to win this war, because there never will be a single army to fight, or a single battle. There will only ever be small forces put in place and eventually left to their own resources – like this group of besiegers. I think we should fight them, vanquish them and move on, to do it again and again every time we encounter Grey Lancers."

"Harsh words from a witan," Lord Seaforth said, frowning. "I was always taught to show mercy in victory."

"From what I've learned since I returned, they will never be normal men, or happy men, or kind men. Perhaps it is a mercy to bring their lives to a close. If they want mercy, all they'd have to do is surrender."

"I agree with Saker," Ryce said. "Small companies of soldiers scattered all over the country, ready to respond. Mounted, trained, armed, led by men like Lord Seaforth and Sir Beargold."

Saker nodded. "An important, deadly task, but even so, a task that is only secondary to a different kind of battle – which is to kill all sorcerers."

"How?" Ryce asked. "We've stayed alive and Gromwell did not fall because we were able to keep the sorcerer at a distance. He never had a chance to ensorcel us." He eyed Saker with a puzzled frown. "And how is it that you think you know so much about these sorcerers when you apparently haven't been in the country for the past two years?"

"There was another land which had an infestation of sorcerers in the Summer Seas. The present rulers were kind enough to tell us how they defeated their enemies."

"How?"

But Saker wasn't about to spill Chenderawasi Avian secrets, and speak of magical plumes, or a kris containing *sakti* distilled from a Raja's bones and blood, its blade laced with barbules from his feathers. "Those who had power united," he said vaguely. "They used a combination of witchery artefacts and ordinary warriors. Ardhi has access to some of their magic which we believe may aid us."

"You trust them? People from the Va-forsaken Hemisphere?" Ryce was incredulous.

"Oh, yes. They have already helped us with their witcheries. 'Va-forsaken' is a stupid term coined by people who have never been to that part of the world."

Ryce folded his arms. "All right. Go on. What next?"

"We have to find out who killed a sorcerer in Hornbeam, and how they did it. We have to use the same method."

"And how do we find that out?" the prince asked. He was looking more and more worried.

"We've heard that Fritillary Reedling is alive—"

"Are you sure of that?"

"As sure as we can be without actually setting eyes on her. We've been inside the hidden Hornbeam shrine. We've seen what they are doing there and they as good as told us that Fritillary was behind it. She has organised resistance from without, using shrines as centres to train people to use their witcheries to fight."

The look on Ryce's face was a mixture of relief and astonishment. "I'll be beggared," he said. "Witcheries as *weapons*?"

"I suspect she might know how that sorcerer died and how to kill more of them. We need to contact her as soon as we can, and I believe we can do that through the Twite shrine."

"If we are to attack these Grey Lancers here and now – where do we get weapons and ammunition?" the prince asked.

"In the hold," Juster said. "I spent part of our spice money buying everything I could find in Hornbeam. We have enough to arm every able man that you've brought on board. I'm with Saker on this. We deal with the besiegers first, then see what we can find out from Pontifect Reedling, then we set about finding Prince Garred and his mother."

Saker looked back at the prince. He read more resolution in his expression than had ever been there when Ryce was at his father's court. He was a different man. Harder, sadder.

But then, they had all changed.

In his heart, he wasn't sure if that was a good thing, but he did know there was no going back.

22

Prince, Pirate and Ternion

The following day was spent in preparation. Two hours after sunset, *Golden Petrel* weighed anchor and headed up the estuary, all lights dimmed. On the weather deck, Juster and Ryce watched the crew go about their work as, four hours before dawn, the ship edged closer to the coast. Clouds filtered moonlight into an unpredictable glow, allowing only occasional glimpses of the white froth at the base of the cliffs.

Ardhi was up in the crow's nest because he was deemed to have the best night vision. On the portside, working without a lamp, a seaman was counting off the knots on the leadline to measure the depth they still had under the keel. Everything around them was in darkness. Along the eastern horizon, the first pre-dawn light must have been creeping into the sky, but it was obscured by heavy cloud cover.

Below decks in the crew's mess, the sailors and the prince's men were checking weapons, sharpening swords and daggers, distributing the shot for the arquebuses and pistols and apportioning the crossbow bolts.

Sorrel was in her cabin. She had dressed in her men's clothing and boots for ease of movement, idly wondering whether she would ever be comfortable in cumbersome skirts and thin-soled slippers again, when someone knocked at the door. It was Saker.

He took one look at her, and said, "What do you think you're doing? You aren't going ashore!"

She waved him inside with a sigh. "We have had this argument before. I'm tired of it."

"A battlefield is no place for someone untrained in combat. It will be chaotic out there."

"Don't patronise me. Do you think I don't know that?"

"Your glamour won't help you! You may not be seen, but a ball from a pistol, or the slash of a sword, could kill you nonetheless. And if Ardhi and I are worried about you, then it will have an impact on our effectiveness."

She wanted to be angry, but saw his anguish. "Women agonise when their menfolk are in danger, but you men don't stay at home because of it. I'm not brave. I don't want to go. But I'm not the wife or sister or mother who waits at home, either. I'm part of our ternion."

He winced.

"I'm right, aren't I?" she persisted.

"Are you sure your presence in a battle is the best use of your talent?"

She considered his words with all the dispassion she could muster. "I'm not going out there to spike a cannon or run a sword through a lancer's belly. I'm looking to see if there's a sorcerer among the Grey Lancers. If there is, this battle will be lost unless he is identified and killed quickly."

"Are you sure you could recognise one?"

"I think all three of us could, because of our witcheries."

He shook his head. "That can't be right. You had a witchery back when you first came across Prime Fox in the palace in Throssel. You never knew what he was! You've raised Piper and you've sensed nothing in her, either."

Doubts shafted through her like needles of ice. "That's – that's true. But perhaps Fox is powerful enough to hide what he is. Besides, back then I was careful to keep out of his way. I don't think these sons of his are like him. From what Prince Ryce told us yesterday, they are pale approximations who fade a little every time they use their witchery."

"We're not sure all folk with witcheries recognise them for what they are."

"We're different. We're a ternion that has both witchery and *sakti*."

He thought about that. "The Rani did say that a man who imbibed too much *sakti* became their first Chenderawasi sorcerer. Sorcery here could just be too much stolen witchery perverting and twisting those who were never granted it by an unseen guardian."

"I'm going out there, Saker. All three of us are going. We will only succeed as a ternion. Piper depends on us, and Va knows how much else. I won't take it for granted that I'll recognise a sorcerer." Mischievously she added, "Although it may be easier than we know. Prince Ryce says the ones who command the lancers wear black, not grey!"

He gave a reluctant laugh. "Don't rely on that either!"

From somewhere above came the sound of footsteps thudding on the deck, then the scraping rattle of the anchor running out. She stepped into his arms, and he enfolded her in a hug. "Take care. We both need you," he said.

She leaned back slightly to look at his face, her worry breaking through. "You're going to twin with the bird, aren't you? I don't know how you do it. Living in two heads . . ."

"Sometimes I don't know either."

He gave a lopsided smile, but she wasn't deceived. He was struggling and there was no way she – or anyone else – could help him.

Sorrel and Ardhi disembarked three hours before dawnbreak with the first group of fifty men leaving the ship, led by several men who'd grown up in the area and been employed at the holdfast. As they assembled at the edge of the cove, it was like watching a pack of dogs aching to start a hunt. Listening to their soft chatter, Sorrel knew they relished the chance to wreak revenge for the prolonged siege. Their destination was the far side of the holdfast. They would have to loop around out of sight, travelling in the dark, aiming to be in position at about the same time as the second, larger and better armoured contingent under Prince Ryce arrived close to the main gate.

Ardhi was not only barefoot, but bare to the waist. He'd oiled his body with something he had brought from the Summer Seas. An advantage, he told her, in one-on-one combat, not only because it made his skin slippery, but because it helped prevent infection of wounds.

A surge of fear washed through her. For him – for all of them. She had to resist an urge to touch him, to tell him how much she cared. Instead she said, "I've decided to wait for the next group."

He tilted his head, considering, assessing.

"Really?" he asked, and even in the dark, she could see he'd arched a disbelieving eyebrow. "They have Saker to tell them if there are any sorcerers."

She did not reply.

"You want to look on your own."

"Yes."

"Ah." He undid the sheathed kris and handed it to her.

She could have said he needed it more, but he carried a staff, an ordinary dagger and a sailor's cutlass, so he was well-armed even without it. Besides, she had an idea that either she accepted it, or he insisted on staying with her.

She took the kris.

"*Seri* guard you," he said. *Seri*, the living soul of the land and sea, the foundation of all that was Chenderawasi life. The closest concept they had to Va.

She smiled her thanks.

"Are you intending to start a – a—" He searched for the word he needed, but couldn't find it so he substituted a word in Chenderawasi.

She made a guess at its meaning. "Diversion?"

"That's it."

"It did cross my mind that one might help. Prince Ryce estimated they have five times the number of men we have. We need every tiny advantage we can get."

"Tents usually burn well," he remarked. Behind him the other men were already filing off the beach in silence.

She gaped at him. How the rattling pox did the irritating man know that she was carrying a lighted coal?

A question for another time.

"*Before* the signal from Saker's eagle would be best," he continued. "It's going to drop a stick on us when it is time to attack." He turned and vanished into the darkness, hurrying to catch up with the others.

I swear, he reads my mind . . .

She fished into the purse at her waist to check on the lit coal placed in a mullein stem, the cook's customary way of keeping an ember going for a fire. Peeping inside the hemp wrapping, she made sure it was still alight. The cook had been helpful, but he must have

207

told Ardhi what she had asked for. Rot them, there was not a man on the ship who didn't try to mollycoddle her!

Shaking her head in a mixture of exasperation and affection, she started down the path leading from the cove to the main gate of Gromwell Holdfast. Used for years as the cart track between the sea and the castle, even in the dark it was well-defined, twin lines of pale sandstone through the coastal tussocks. She walked it at a steady pace, not needing a guide, knowing she'd be at the Grey Lancers' encampment before Prince Ryce's contingent. With her glamour, she could walk openly.

Just after the sun had risen, she reached a rise overlooking the outskirts of the camp and stopped dead, shocked to have arrived without encountering any guards. Arrogant overconfidence on their part, surely, to think guards were unnecessary.

Bisected by the cart track, a line of scattered tents straggled along the banks of a tiny stream, extending to her left and right as far as she could see. The tents closest to the track were the largest, some with outside shelters and rough-built trestles and benches.

The track she'd been following crossed the stream over a stone bridge. No one was using it now, although there was a four-wheeled dray pulled off to the side, still loaded with half a dozen casks. They had been covered by canvas, now partially loose in the wind, exposing enough for her to recognise them as the size of gunpowder kegs. Stacked under a makeshift shed on the other side of the track were larger casks and barrels. Pickles and wine, she guessed. There was no sign of any horses, mules or oxen.

Directly below her, the camp was waking in a leisurely fashion. Campfires burned and the first meal of the day was being prepared. Some men were at their morning ablutions along the stream. No one talked to anyone else, or even interacted much. When she looked to the top of the opposite slope, she could see the cannon mounted on their gun carriages on either side of the track, and a few scattered sentries on watch, their gaze focused on the distant battered walls of the holdfast and the remaining pock-marked tower. The walls were bare of sentries, but the reason for the lack did not appear to have occurred to any of the lancers on watch.

She moved away from the track, searching for any hint of smutch.

A stench of rot assaulted her nostrils, enough to make her gag, but she didn't think it was anything to do with sorcery. The slope down to the tents had once been covered in vegetation, but the trees had been cut for fuel, and the meadow grasses and bushes were dead. As she walked on, it was clear the slope was now a midden heap. Human and animal excrement was mixed in with rotted food and carcasses. Some of what she cracked underfoot included human bones. Sweet Va, they did not bother to bury the dead.

The horror crept up on her, one little piece at a time. The insidious stink that soaked into her clothing. Images for personal nightmares: the broken grin of a skull; a disembodied arm with the flesh falling into green shivering slime wriggling with maggots. The grating buzz of flies and bluebottles disturbed from their feasting, blundering into her face and crawling into her ears and eyes. The boldness of the rats, their sharp whiskered faces glaring at her. The nauseous way the ground oozed underfoot where the rot was alive with slithering things.

This was the worst thing she had ever had to do with her glamour: match herself to that revolting background.

She cast aside her squeamishness and replaced it with burning rage.

Prince Ryce, Lord Juster at his shoulder, headed the main group. Leaving the cove at dawn, they followed the coast towards the castle, and then cut back inland, walking just below the crest of a rise through a low line of scrub, out of sight of the besiegers. Saker travelled with them. The sea eagle hated flying before the cool of the night had dissipated and it could catch the rise of warmed air, so it was an hour after dawnbreak before he could persuade it to leave its perch on the crosstrees of *Golden Petrel* for a preliminary look at the configuration of sentries – only to find that there were none, at least not at the besiegers' rear.

"Told you," said Ryce. "Undisciplined rabble. How far are we from the camp?"

He sent the bird cruising higher above the rolling hills and closed his eyes the better to concentrate, receiving disjointed glimpses of what it saw as he gave it directions it didn't fully comprehend, let alone want to obey. Asked to look at humans, it was indifferent and didn't understand what they were doing, or how many there were. Hungry, it was more interested in the glint of water than in the doings of men.

"Ten minutes," he told the prince and opened his eyes. "I'm not going to get much detail, but I've seen enough to wonder what kind of soldiers they are. No rearguard, no sentries, and their camp looks like a midden!"

"What would they fear? The local folk are terrified of them. Besides, they supposedly represent the king, and to fight them is treason." He smiled bitterly at Saker. "You are a wanted man now."

"I already was. And now I've tied my future to yours, Your Highness, whether you like it or not."

"A-ha, I always said you'd be my Prime one day!"

He smiled. "I don't think I'd be a good exemplar for the faithful."

"Good," said Ryce. "I like sanctimonious clerics about as much as I like sorcerers. Let's push on."

One of Prince Ryce's scouts warned them that they were approaching the besiegers' line of tents. They crawled up the rise that overlooked the camp and lay flat on their stomachs at the top.

"Va-damn their fobbing cheek," Ryce muttered, looking through his spyglass. "Some of those tents are from the Royal Games we held in Twite a couple of years back. I recognise the colours. How far are we from the track to Gromwell?"

"About a mile," the scout said.

"I've never seen anything that looked less like a disciplined company of men in my life," Juster said. "This should be an easy battle."

"A dangerous assumption," Ryce snapped. "They're not cowards. They fight like madmen bent on killing as many people as they can before they die. I've lost count of the number of times they tried to scale our walls. The worst fight – the one that lost us the main gate and the outer bailey – lasted a night and two days, and they fought with a savagery not easily forgotten."

Beargold, lying on the other side of Lord Juster, grunted his agreement. "They don't respond like normal men," he said. "Think of . . . cornered animals, but unlike animals their aim is to slaughter with as much pain as possible. Give no quarter, because you'll get none. They don't know fear. Worse, they prefer *not* to kill cleanly."

They all heard the touch of remembered horror in his voice.

"No sorcerers that I can feel," Saker said. "Sorrel is down there somewhere, though."

"I thought she was going with Ardhi," Juster said.

"So did I. I'm not sure exactly where she is, but she's somewhere on this side of the holdfast. The glow of her witchery – it's over there." He gestured in the direction he meant and sighed. "She does tend to do what she wants, not what we want, and usually does it fobbing brilliantly too."

Prince Ryce grunted. "I remember. But what does she think she's doing down there now? If we attack, she might be killed."

Saker, who'd been attempting not to dwell on that same nauseating thought, rolled over on to his back. "Your Highness, I'm going to twin with the eagle rather than just link with it. That means my body will appear as if I am in a deep sleep. If you can, wait for me to wake up before you order an attack."

He did not tell the prince just how vulnerable flying with the bird left him, but Juster said with the faintest of smiles, "I'll ask one of my men to keep the ants off you while you nap."

Closing his eyes, he sought the mind of the raptor circling above, almost beyond the range of a human eye. His heart soared at the thought of flying, and he wondered if there would come a day when he wouldn't want to return.

23

Gunpowder and Blood

After descending to the edge of the encampment, Sorrel found a cleaner spot to hunker down while she watched and waited for the right moment to make her move. There was nothing to indicate a sorcerer anywhere nearby. No smutch that she could detect, nor any faint glow of a perverted witchery.

She kept an eye on the largest and most impressive of the tents, which had a grubby flag featuring a red fox flapping tiredly on a pole at one end. Her patience was rewarded when a man emerged and walked to the nearest of the cooking fires, where he seated himself on a bench, demanding food and drink. When it didn't come fast enough for him, he swore. She was accustomed to the swearing of sailors, but the language he used was so vile her eyes widened.

As the soldiers scuttled around to bring him what he wanted, she opened up the bark around the mullein tinder, exposing the hot coal to the air. Once the outside skin of the ember brightened and the mullein started to scorch, she approached the tent. She heard nothing from inside, so she sidled around to the opening at the front, moving slowly to maintain her glamour easily.

The wailing cry of an eagle made her look up. The dark shape of the raptor was high enough to avoid any shot from an arrow, too high for her to see any details, but when it waggled its wings in a gesture that was more Saker than bird, she knew he was there. She raised a hand in acknowledgement and pulled a face at him that an eagle's eyesight would see. With a deep flap of its wings, the bird turned in a tight circle. She pointed up the slope to where she had entered the valley, and then raised two fingers.

Two minutes.

She hoped he would know what she meant, and indeed there was another waggle, before it sailed across the holdfast, heading to where Ardhi's company was waiting for the signal to attack the encampment on the other side.

Turning back to the task in hand, she twitched the tent flap far enough to peer in. The space inside was empty.

A quick glance over her shoulder at the Grey Lancers told her she was still unobserved, so she slipped inside. The tension she'd felt since leaving the cove was taking its toll. For a moment, safe within the canvas walls, she let her glamour drop.

She expected to see some comforts inside; after all, for months this had probably been the home of someone senior – an officer – but there were no cots, no table, no chairs, just a single wooden chest and an untidy heap of bedding strewn on dirty straw.

Wasting no time, she placed the now smoking tinder in the middle of the bedding, and turned to go.

The same man who had left a few minutes earlier was in the tent opening, frozen by shock in a half-stooped position.

She was still unglamoured.

They stared at each other. It must only have been a moment, but it felt like an age.

He moved first. He stepped inside and let the flap drop behind him.

Her thoughts raced. He wasn't a sorcerer, just a dangerous man – that went without saying. Middle-aged. Unafraid. Dirty. Not wearing a sword, but with a dagger thrust through his belt.

His eyes narrowed and his lips twisted upwards at the corners. A predator's smile.

He failed to notice or smell the tinder smoking in the bedding.

It would be useless to try to disappear behind her glamour; that wouldn't deceive him now that he'd seen her just a pace away.

As one, they both drew their daggers, but she glamoured the kris into a shorter, blunter instrument and hoped he wouldn't notice its real shape. It felt comfortable in her hand. She returned his smile.

"Well, well, well. Someone's gifted me a fobbing mawk! Whose whore are you?" he asked.

"The prince of Gromwell's. Are you going to be man enough for me, or will you look for the pox on the gift?"

He blinked, wondering just what she meant. Which must have been difficult, given that she was spewing the first words that came into her head. He reached out to grab her arm with his free hand. The kris reacted even more quickly than she did, slashing past his outstretched fingers in warning.

"You have to catch me first," she said and danced sideways. She broadened her smile, wanting to appear harmless yet enticing, even as she held the dagger between them.

"Playing hard to get? Come here, my sweet, and explain just how you got in here, or I'll carve off your pretty tits!"

Va-damn him. How was she going to extricate herself without alerting the whole camp?

Even as she hesitated, the tinder on the bedding flared. The wool of the blanket scorched, fibres curling black, smoke rising. The lancer turned his head to look. The kris jerked forward. He saw the movement out of the corner of his eye and moved to deflect the blade with his own. She held tight as he resisted the forward movement of the kris. Her wrist bent under his strength and his dagger moved closer. The kris twisted at the last moment, slashing his hand and angling upwards. He gave a curdling cry. She tried to flinch away from his blade, but unbalanced and off-kilter, she fell into him. The point of his weapon passed between her left side and her arm, slicing through clothing, then deeper. Pain erupted across her ribs.

They fell together, entangled. Her grip was still tight on the hilt of the kris.

Pushing herself away from him, she felt the blade slide into his flesh. She had stabbed him under the chin, the blade passing through into his mouth. He was still alive, thrashing underneath her. The hilt of the kris was jammed tight.

Next to them, the bedding was alight and the tent was filling with smoke.

Still gripping the kris hilt, she pulled hard and leaped to her feet. Blood followed the path of the blade, gushing from his mouth and neck. She struggled to form her glamour. Smoke swirled, flames licking at the tent canvas. She coughed and pain made her howl. Her assailant thrashed at her feet, spasming, spattering blood. She found the tent flap and staggered into the open air, gasping. Everything had happened so *fast*.

Outside, she tried again to form her glamour. Her side *hurt*. She needed to see what was wrong. When she touched her clothing, her hand came away sticky and red. She slipped the kris still covered in blood back into its sheath.

Ardhi wouldn't like that. Sri Kris wouldn't like it either . . .

If only she didn't hurt so much.

Glamour.

Blend into the ground. Into the colour of the stones . . . soil . . . dead grasses. Run towards the cart track. Easier. Uphill, but not nearly so steep.

Anything rather than go back over that awful midden.

She stumbled to the road, aware her glamour was patchy. She couldn't concentrate.

Someone yelled behind her.

She risked a glance. Men were running this way and that. Shouting too, but not at her. At least she didn't think so. They were looking at the tent. Smoke was pouring out of it. The wall on one side was charring; she could see the flames licking through the holes.

Of the man she'd stabbed, there was no sign.

When she reached the track, she ducked down behind the dray to catch her breath. Slipping to her knees on the dried ridges of the sun-baked wheel ruts, she leaned her forehead on a wooden spoke, pressing a hand to the wound in her side. Blood escaped through her fingers. No pulsing, just oozing. That was good, wasn't it?

Her side was a throbbing mess of pain. Peering around the tailboard, she saw lancers converging on the tent, beating at the flames. Two men were carting water from the stream in buckets. Someone had pulled the officer out of the remains of the tent, but he was clearly dead. Her mouth went dry. She'd killed again.

Don't be stupid about it. If he wasn't dead, you would be.

Flames licked through the dried grass, and there were frantic shouts as men realised the fire could spread to the rest of the encampment. One of the men gestured towards the wagon, saying something urgently to another, and they both turned to look.

And saw her.

215

She could no longer hold her glamour. She felt as weak as a butterfly in a storm, close to passing out. Thinking was increasingly difficult. Fuzzy around the edges.

The two men stared, shocked. No, *fearful*.

Why?

The answer came on the heels of the question. They weren't scared of her. It was the gunpowder.

The kris was in her hand again, although she couldn't remember drawing it out of its sheath. She smiled, knowing just how to use it this time. She reached up to one of the casks, broke the wax seal around the edges of the wooden bung and levered it out. She pulled the keg, one-handed, over the edge of the dray. It hit the ground and began to roll down the slope, bouncing and tumbling, leaving a trail of gunpowder behind. One of the men turned tail and fled. The second, braver, tried to stop it before it reached the spreading grass fire around the burning tent.

As he ran to intercept it, she edged the bung out of a second keg and pushed it to the ground, where it tumbled down the slope after the first. The third was harder. Her strength was dying, as if it was draining out of her with her blood. And why were her ears pounding so? The third keg she toppled to the ground without bothering to remove the bung.

She didn't see where it rolled. Her knees gave way and she fell.

Her last coherent thought was that she had to flee. Something about gunpowder and a fire. She was no longer clear about the details, but it seemed important. She started to crawl along the rutted track, intent on putting as much distance as she could between herself and the dray.

Nothing else seemed to matter.

As usual, Saker had to battle the eagle for control, and also as usual, he won and then felt guilty.

It took him a moment to adjust to the view of the world from above. His customary joy in flight lifted his spirits until he was flooded with wonder that he alone knew what it was like to fly. The bird – it, he, Saker – spiralled upwards, deep, strong wingbeats that he felt to the very core, rejoicing in the first touch of uplift, of air that swept his form higher without effort. Oh, the lightness of it, the glorious freedom! He tilted his wings with the merest adjustment of feather fingers, rising on the warm air until he felt he was out of the range of even the luckiest arrow shot. He eyed the land below, revelling in the perfection of an eagle's vision, in its ability to see the tiniest of field mice in a meadow. It was hungry, and Saker felt its hunger gnawing at his insides, scorning anything except fish or sea snakes.

Careful. You are Saker Rampion, not a bird. Remember your humanity. But, oh, sometimes that was difficult.

He followed the thread of the stream, banks littered with tents, to where he had seen the glow of Sorrel's witchery. There he found the cart track trailing across the low hills like a ribbon heading straight to the castle door. He spotted her glow again, near a dray drawn up just past the bridge, and found her outside a tent.

Fear cut across the duality of his mind, and the bird pressed to be allowed to go, to find the sea . . . He imposed his will and it turned its frustration into a screaming cry. Below, Sorrel lifted her face to look at him. At the bird. At them.

He waggled his wings. Eagle wings.

She raised her hand to point away from the camp, away from the holdfast, then gestured with a raised two fingers. It was a signal Juster's crew used on board ship for a lapse of time when the noise of cannon fire drowned out voices.

Two minutes. She would be out of there in two minutes. She was smiling. He tried not to think about what she was going to do, or of all the things that could go wrong.

He waggled his wings again and shot across the sky looking for the second party from *Golden Petrel*. As he flew above Gromwell, he marvelled at the damage done and the way Prince Ryce and his men had bolstered the walls from inside with dirt. Deep holes dug in the baileys told the story.

From this height, everything was laid out like a map, and his keen eyesight soon picked up Ardhi and the other men from the ship. Well away from them, he pulled in his wings and swooped fast, aiming for the copse of trees behind the lines of besiegers. Once there, he levelled off and overflew the copse, implanting the idea of what he wanted in the bird's mind. He'd watched sea eagles building nests in Karradar, and he knew what he asked was possible.

The bird flew low over the leafy canopy, searching, then circled back. This time it dipped to grasp a suitable dead twig in a taloned foot as it passed. Dry and rotten, it snapped off. Gripping it, the sea eagle flapped to gain height. It struggled to rise with the unwieldy stick in its claws, but gradually, with strong beats, it found the rising air. With another screeching call to gain the attention of the men on the ground, the stick was dropped, the message relayed telling them Ryce was in place, ready to attack.

He set the eagle to return the way they had come, promising it the chance to go fishing soon. Within a minute or two he was back over the Grey Lancers' encampment, searching to make sure Sorrel was gone.

The large tent where he'd seen her only a few minutes before was on fire, and the fire had spread. Flames and sparks shot high into the air, followed by billowing smoke and a booming sound. Two more explosions followed, blossoming outwards in violent paroxysms of fiery air. When the smoke cleared, there was only a cloud of shredded matter left, floating gently down like petals in a world that had caught its breath.

On the ground a massive hole was surrounded by a circular band of devastation, littered with dead bodies and pieces of bodies, and burning or flattened tents. Even the road was scattered with debris. There had been a dray, there, he remembered. With kegs. Gunpowder kegs, obviously.

It had only been minutes since he'd left. Ten at the most.

Perhaps Sorrel hasn't escaped.

He sent the eagle a little lower, searching the scene with a raptor's sharp vision. There were spot fires burning, and a scattering of unopened kegs. The dray had been overturned by the blast, not destroyed. If – when? – the fire spread, there would be more blasts . . .

He could hear screaming now. Shouting. Crackling of fire. He was directly over the encampment, still searching, when he caught a flare of witchery. No, wait. That wasn't witchery; it was *sakti*.

But Ardhi wasn't there, and the small pieces of feather Sorrel wore in her bambu locket had never glowed like this.

It had to be the kris, Ardhi's kris, glowing because its power was in play, as bright as a beacon in the vision of a raptor. He curved the eagle around in a tight turn to take another look, homing in on the glow at the edge of the road about thirty paces away from the bridge.

This time he saw her body. She was either dead, or unconscious, lying face-down, her arms bent forward on either side of her head. Her right hand clasped the kris. She was not far enough away from the fires, or from the unexploded powder kegs, to be safe. *If* she still lived.

The eagle screeched, and he saw her through its eyes. Her left side was drenched in blood, the florid ruby of Betany roses.

His heart turned over.

He wanted to ask the bird to land. His need to go to her was overwhelming, but he stopped that insanity before it took hold. Inside an eagle, what could he do to help her?

He turned and flew as fast as he could back to his body.

24

Revelations

A footman, after tapping on the door of the Regala's retiring room and being bade enter, handed Regala Mathilda a note. "For Your Grace," he murmured, and effaced himself from the room in a sidle that Lowmian servants had perfected over generations of servitude. Mathilda found it both ridiculous and oddly pleasing.

Sometimes the Lowmian court drove her to distraction with its exaggerations. It was surprisingly difficult to change anything, even when the presumption was that she had the power of life and death over the palace staff. Odd, that. She'd thought being the Regent would mean she could do exactly what she wanted.

She waited until the footman had gone before heaving a sigh, feeling certain that the note was from Chancellor Yan Grussblat requesting a meeting about her recent order to proceed with the execution of Merchant Uthen Kesleer. That upstart fellow deserved to hang for what he'd done to Regal Vilmar, but Grussblat had urged clemency, saying Kesleer's wealth would fall into the wrong hands if he was dead.

Another decision to make, just when she'd been enjoying a moment of peace, so rare in her life now. There was never enough time to spend with her son, let alone just be quiet by herself. Always some affair of state begged for her attention, or an argument had to be won with her Council, or a decision made about fiscal matters, or a draft of a law to peruse. Always *something*.

Now, when she opened the note, she found her assumption had been wrong. It wasn't from Yan. It was Sister Genet Bitterling's writing. Her handmaiden had been gone for almost two sennights, and this was the only time she'd heard from her since she'd left. Not that such an absence was unusual; the woman was constantly disappearing, saying she was on Pontifect Fritillary's business. To her court ladies, Mathilda explained Genet's absences as convent retreats.

Your Grace, she read, *I request an audience urgently on the Pontifect's business. Your obedient servant, Sister Genet Bitterling.*

She snorted. Genet was neither her servant, nor particularly obedient. Mathilda had few illusions about the nun's loyalties; they lay with the previous Pontificate, not with the Lowmeer Regality. There was something unusual about the wording. A subtle lack of deference, perhaps? Yes, that was it. Although, she had to admit, a reverence for those above her was always noticeably absent from Genet's character.

She pulled the bell rope. The door opened almost immediately and the same footman returned. "Who gave this to you?" she asked.

"Sister Genet, Your Grace."

"Where is she now?"

"In the chapel, I believe, Your Grace."

"Fetch her."

While she waited, she stood looking out of the window over the garden – the same window through which she had pushed Aureen to her death.

She came here from time to time. Her penance for Aureen's death, perhaps. She cared not one whit about Regal Vilmar Vollendorn, murderer of babies – but Aureen? Aureen had been an innocent whose death was necessary. The woman had known too much about the birth of the twins, and if she had been questioned she might possibly – probably? – have spilled those secrets.

Mathilda's guilt stemmed from the reality that she would never know for sure if the maid's death had been necessary, and thus she *needed* to remember her, to stand there at the window and feel regret, as if the act of mourning her victim meant she wasn't entirely a monster.

Still, being in that room alone made her uncomfortable. The view out of the window nagged at her like a sore tooth. It was a punishment. She pondered on the oddity that the death of a mere servant should be the one thing in life she regretted. All the rest she could justify, be proud of – but Aureen's death? That besmirched her. Her conscience would have rested easy if she could have been sure that Aureen had threatened her son's safety.

"Your Grace?"

She turned to see Genet in the doorway, inclining her head in greeting.

"Come in, Sister. Close the door. It's been a long time without word from you. Have you seen Fritillary Reedling? What news do you bring?"

The wretched woman didn't reply immediately. Instead, she asked, "Are we likely to be disturbed?"

For a moment Mathilda was tempted to scold her for presumption, but something in the woman's tone made her change her mind, and she rang for the footman yet again, to tell him they did not want to be disturbed under any circumstances.

"Now what is it?" she asked when he had gone. "You have news from Pontifect Fritillary?"

"Not exactly. I *am* Pontifect Fritillary Reedling."

The words dropped into the stillness of the room like a stone into the mirror surface of a pond, sending out ripples to shatter the reflection. The words changed everything; the ripples they created broke Mathilda's peace into a thousand clanging pieces.

She stared at the nun.

Her tone was not Genet's. Her shoulders no longer slumped. Her skin might have been crinkled with age, but the years seemed to have fallen away from both her stance and her voice. From under the shelter of her wimple, her eyes met Mathilda's gaze with unflinching, critical perusal.

A cascade of emotions raged through her. The impudent harpy had been living in the castle on and off for months, *deceiving* her? Fury predominant, she raised her hand to slap that smug face.

A slight smile twitched at the corner of Fritillary's lips, daring her, and Mathilda was reminded that this woman had once wielded a power greater than any mere monarch. She dropped her hand, feeling a smidgen of admiration.

There was no question of the truth of what the woman said; she saw it all now. Where else was there a safer place to hide than under everyone's nose? Preceded by two other handmaidens, who would question a third? No one looked at a nun. In particular, no one questioned a sister of the Order of the Veil. By the time "Genet" had arrived, most people thought Fritillary Reedling was dead. Few people in Lowmeer had ever seen her in person anyway, except for Prime Mulhafen, and he must have been in on the deception from the beginning.

Oh yes, the impudent hag had chosen a hiding place well.

"Consign you to a choiceless hell," she said. "How *dare* you deceive me! Regal Vilmar would have beheaded you for less. And so could I, if I wanted."

Fritillary smiled. "You could, I'm sure. If you were very silly. But I think perhaps you have never been that."

"Why did you not *tell* me? Why did you not trust me? I am the Regala and the Regent!"

Fritillary raised an eyebrow, and said, "Exactly."

Had the woman just said that she wasn't trustworthy *because* she was royal? The insult left her speechless.

"We have too much to discuss to waste time in argument, my dear. I have news to impart."

"What news? From whom?" Va, how she wanted to wring the woman's scrawny neck!

"From the hidden shrines, sent via the oak roots and the streams."

She pressed her lips together, not trusting herself to speak, and nodded.

Without asking if she could sit, Fritillary took a chair next to her and continued. "But first, let me say this. I have decided that it is time to uncover the rest of the shrines here in Lowmeer. Lord Herelt Deremer has confirmed that the land is clear of sorcerers."

"I hate being beholden to that man for anything."

"I sympathise. I should warn you though, some of the shrine keepers and many of those with witcheries have agreed to be part of my fighting force elsewhere."

"But shrine keepers never leave their shrines for more than an hour or two, surely?" she asked when she had gathered her wits long enough to reply. "What if they die?"

"Then the unseen guardians will choose another, as they have to do anyway, from time to time. Shrine keepers may be long-lived, but they are far from immortal! Shrines will not be safe here while there is sorcery elsewhere. They understand the necessity. You should too."

Galls, but the woman was insolent. "Go on."

"The rest of my news is just as . . . unsettling. It appears that Lord Juster Dornbeck has returned from the Summer Seas. He is about to lift the siege of Gromwell Holdfast. Perhaps he already has. He has Saker Rampion and Sorrel Redwing with him. So your daughter is safely back in Ardrone. All that is the good news."

She dragged in a breath, incapable of speech.

"Unfortunately," Fritillary continued, "there is also bad news. I have had unsettling word from Proctor Gerelda and Peregrine Clary. It seems that the Princess Bealina and your nephew Prince Garred are in Valerian Fox's hands in Vavala."

Poor, silly Ryce! He couldn't even take care of his own heir. She sat motionless, trying to assess the implications of that.

Fritillary gave her no time. "Your Grace will, of course, be anxious to know more about your daughter. Her name is Piper. She is well. However, she is also a sorcerer."

She stared at Fritillary, her fears crowding in and her stomach churning. She whispered, "How can anyone possibly know that? That boy Peregrine couldn't say that much about Prince-regal Karel! That's all supposition. It *must* be."

She read something in Fritillary Reedling's eye that spoke of pity and a touch of contempt. The ugly old termagant!

"My dear," the Pontifect said in an infuriatingly patronising voice, "I think you had better admit the truth so that we can move on from there and deal with the consequences."

"I don't know what you mean."

"Your Grace, there can be no shame. Prime Valerian Fox seduced you into his bed, that much is now clear. It is the only thing that can explain why both your children bear the mark of sorcery. Certainly neither Regal Vilmar nor Saker would have fathered a sorcerer."

She knew her cheeks had flooded with colour. *Fig on them all!* "No one has said Prince-regal Karel is a sorcerer. Someone gave him the black smutch, that's all. And that's probably exactly what happened to my daughter too. In fact, it must have been my maid, Aureen. She's the only person besides Sorrel and myself who touched both babies. She committed suicide later. Threw herself out of this very window in the middle of the night. None of us could work out why. If she'd been coerced by a sorcerer into doing something terrible, like infecting my babies, that would explain it! She couldn't live with her crime."

Heat spread from her neck into her face. The lie was audacious, but Fritillary had never met Aureen and didn't know what an innocent simpleton the maid had been.

Please Va, grant that she believes the flush to be a sign of righteous anger, not an admission of guilt.

She sat straight in her chair and met the Pontifect's gaze, unflinching.

"No." Fritillary's negation of the idea was as flatly emphatic as her look. "Your Grace, we *know* that Fox bedded you. You as good as told Sorrel Redwing that. Fox is the father of the twins. Acknowledge that, and we can move on. No one is *blaming* you. You were helpless under his coercion. You were raped, in effect."

That flap-mouthed Shenat witch! After all I did for her! Damn her to beggary – I saved her life!

She tried desperately to keep her expression impassive. If Fritillary was willing to accept that interpretation – coercion, not part of a plan to wriggle out of her unwanted marriage – then at least she could hold her head high. But that fawning bitch, Sorrel. She must have told Saker . . .

Pox on't. Denial was not going to be believable.

Capitulating, she allowed a tear to slip down her cheek. "I was so alone. I didn't know what to do. He was the Prime! I was powerless in his hands. I prayed so hard that I would not have his child; why did Va not answer my prayers?"

There was the faintest flicker in Fritillary's eyes which could have meant anything at all. She placed a hand over Mathilda's. "Who knows the mind of the Creator? It is not ours to question. But rest assured, no one is going to blame you. In fact, no one else is going to realise. Content yourself with the knowledge that this man will fail, and that those who bring about his humiliation will be those he hurt most – you, me, Saker, Prince Ryce."

Mathilda couldn't move, couldn't for a moment even speak. Her thoughts tangled, jumping from one possible consequence to another.

"What we have to decide now is where we go from here," Fritillary was saying. "We cannot have Lowmeer ruled by a sorcerer."

"He's a baby. A child! You've seen him, you've played with him, you know! How you can think that he – that he—?" Her terror was so intense her hands began to shake. He was a prince. He deserved to rule. Besides, without him – without the regency – she would have nothing. Worse than nothing. If the Lowmians found out she had tricked Vilmar into acknowledging another man's son as her own . . . *Dear oak.* She was dead.

"We know that the only way to become a sorcerer is to be born to one," Fritillary said, as if she was explaining something to a child. "The twins are Fox's children, Mathilda. And we have to deal with that calmly."

"How can I be calm about the murder of a child? Because that's what you're saying, isn't it? You want to kill my son!"

"I don't. Remember to whom you're talking, Your Grace. How can I – as the true Pontifect of Va-faith – justify the murder of a child, *any* child? This country has already gone down that road once and it will *not* happen again. Fortunately, Saker has intimated that he and Sorrel may have something which can buy us some time."

"Go on." In her panic, she could barely articulate the words. *Saker knows of this too?*

"I don't know the details. I haven't yet talked to Saker. He sent a coded message and much of what it said was obscured by his need to keep matters private. I think he's saying that they have brought back some kind of witchery from the Va-forsaken Hemisphere, which has proven to be effective against sorcery over there. So do not give up hope; Prince-regal Karel might indeed be a sorcerer, but that doesn't mean there isn't a way to change that."

Dare she hope?

I will not let anyone harm him. Ever.

Fritillary did not wait for her to answer. "True, he is not Regal Vilmar's heir. He has no *legal* right to inherit the Basalt Throne."

"*I* am royal," she snapped. "Karel comes of a royal line. The House of Betany is as ancient as the Vollendorns!"

The woman raised both eyebrows, then leaned back in her chair. "Listen to me carefully, Your Grace. I don't really care if Prince-regal Karel comes from a royal line. I don't particularly care if he comes from the Vollendorn family, or from a long line of Sprot butchers or Rog sprat-catchers. The Vollendorns are one of the most horrible murderous regimes the hemisphere has ever seen. We are all well rid of them."

"What – what are you trying to say?"

"The only thing that really counts is the suppression of any sorcerous elements in Prince-regal Karel. Saker appears to think this is possible with Va-forsaken witchery. So, we watch him like a hawk as he grows up. We educate him to be a fine upright young man who will inherit the Basalt Throne when reaching his majority. If we can do that, you can continue to be his Regent in the meantime. I would prefer that solution. The alternative could be unrest and a civil war erupting between rival families, a mass of warring estates fighting like dogs over a bone, because there wouldn't be a clear line of inheritance. And you would be the first casualty."

Fritillary stared at her, a hard implacable gaze.

Fob it, she's a woman who's been just as powerful as any monarch. Don't underestimate her. She chose her words carefully. "Very well. But all three of you – you, Saker and Sorrel – will hold a secret that could cause great upheaval if it was ever known. It is also a secret that begs for blackmail. So I will say this, just the once, to you. I will *not* be blackmailed. There is nothing more important to me than to see my son on the Basalt Throne. If needs be, I will destroy you all to achieve that end. Do not thwart me, Fritillary Reedling. Because there would be a price, not one you would want to pay."

The confounded woman's expression did not change. "I'll remember that. But you should also remember that Saker, Sorrel and I hold the only hope that Prince-regal Karel possesses to be a man not tainted and twisted by sorcery. Destroy us, you also destroy him and possibly Lowmeer as well, because he will be another Valerian Fox."

Mathilda stood up abruptly. "This conversation is at an end. You may go."

However, when Fritillary was already at the door, Mathilda halted her. "Sir Herelt Deremer – that day you were both here, did he know who you were?"

"We've known each other for thirty years," Fritillary said.

"I loathe being made a fool of," she said. "You'll pay for that. Both of you."

* * *

227

Fritillary Reedling emerged on to the street in front of Ustgrind Castle and halted a moment to relax the tension in her muscles. Va-damn, but that uppercrust hellion was going to give them all problems in the future!

She sighed as she crossed the market square. Her assertions to Mathilda had been emphatic, but she was not certain of their truth. She had exaggerated Saker's confidence that he and Sorrel possessed the means to halt the development of sorcery within the twins. Only time would tell. The thought of being dependent on Va-forsaken magic made her shudder anyway. Was it to be trusted? She had no idea. Would it last? She had no idea of that either. Too many questions, too few answers.

Barden was waiting for her on the corner of the marketplace when she emerged from the castle. "You look as if you have been hit by a charging bull."

"A good analogy," she said, "although the bull is actually a rampaging cow with very sharp horns and a mother's rage to protect her calf. However, I've done my best and now we have work to do. We're returning to Vavala, Barden. This is where we begin our real war."

25

Aftermath

Saker leaped to his feet.

The transition from eagle's brain into his own body and mind was shockingly abrupt, roiling his stomach and jerking his heart into an erratic pounding.

He snatched up the crossbow and quarrels he'd brought from the ship, yelling at Juster and Prince Ryce, "Attack now!"

"What was the explosion?" Ryce asked. They were all on their feet and fully armed, ready to advance.

"Gunpowder kegs, near the bridge. Sorrel's there, hurt."

He didn't wait for a response, but as he turned and ran he heard Juster shouting, "Don't blow up any more gunpowder! We need it!" And then, "You, sailors, get after him. Go on, run!"

The bird's-eye view of the shortest route to where he'd seen Sorrel was impressed into his memory. A mile, he estimated. He hurled himself at the terrain, taking a straight line by leaping rocks and tearing through bushes. It had been only seconds to fly back; now he was returning on foot. His last glimpse of Sorrel, still unmoving, told him to expect the worst. When he spared a glance behind him, it was to see the two tars given the task of following him falling farther and farther behind. He was vaguely aware of gunfire echoing and the battle cries of attackers hell-bent on slaughtering the Grey Lancers.

When he hurtled across the rise overlooking the bridge and the burning encampment, Sorrel was still where he'd last seen her, unmoving. A Grey Lancer, skin and clothes black with ash, was bending over her, trying to prise the dagger from her hand.

As his gaze swept the scene, Saker readied the crossbow by touch. He had practised with the weapon for months on board ship, and

Juster's ire if a bolt hit the ship's woodwork encouraged good marksmanship.

No one was looking his way. He shot the bolt and the man slumped sideways, dying silently without fuss. Saker crouched for a moment, looking for any immediate danger. Nothing.

Most of the men who'd survived the initial explosion had fled or were still fleeing. When he realised why, his puzzlement changed to horror. The overturned wagon was burning fiercely. Further away there was a crater where the earlier detonation had taken place, but there were several more kegs, still unopened, some of them surrounded by flames, staves already charring. If one keg exploded, the flash and concussion would set fire to the others.

He was far enough away to have a possibility of surviving. Sorrel, if she was still alive, was certainly doomed. He sped across the intervening scrub as he'd never run before. As he raced, he dropped the crossbow and fumbled at the bambu segment he wore on a leather thong around his neck. By the time he reached Sorrel, he'd unstoppered it and grasped the remaining feather segment inside.

With a clarity born of terror, he knew he had no chance of carrying her away in time. Instead, he flung himself over her body, curling his fingers around the feather fragment with one hand and grasping the dagger blade in the other. He thought of being cold and wet and safe. He whispered in her ear, "Live, Sorrel, live."

Out of the corner of his eye, he saw the beginnings of the explosion burgeon in a cloud of yellow and red and gold and orange and a roar of sound. Instinctively, his hand tightened round the kris. He didn't feel the pain because right then sound and light blurred and melted into one, and it felt as if the air itself was bruising and crushing him.

So this is what it is like to die.

It didn't happen. He was still there. *Cold*, not burned. Freezing. Shivering. Still lying on top of Sorrel. He could feel the rise and fall of her breathing, but otherwise she wasn't stirring. His hand, slick with blood – his blood – was still wrapped around the kris blade. His palm was cut. When he opened his other hand, all that remained of the feather was a heap of gold-coloured dust that sifted through his fingers.

He tried to rise, but couldn't lift himself more than a couple of inches. He turned his head to look sideways. What he saw mystified him. He was looking at . . . glass? Flawed glass three or four inches thick! No, wait, that made no sense. He touched it with a finger. Va be poxed, it was *ice*, not glass.

Turning his head still further, and wriggling sideways slightly so he could look over his shoulder, he saw it above him . . . more ice. He was *cocooned* in the stuff. He thought back to the moment before the explosion: he had asked to be cold and wet and safe.

One thing about witcheries and *sakti*, he decided: they could be far too literal.

A minute later, one of the sailors from *Golden Petrel* was battering at the ice with a rock to break their prison open.

She was wrapped in fog.

"I've done all I can." Grig Cranald's voice. Muffled, as if it came from a long way away. "We need Surgeon Barklee, or better still a witchery healer."

"It will be hours before we get to Twite, even if this wind holds." That was Lord Juster Dornbeck. No mistaking his beautifully articulated drawl.

"She is strong." That was Ardhi. Good, he was still alive. And so was she. Sorrel felt a surge of gratitude.

She opened her eyes, and saw him standing there, the brown of his skin muddy and blotched as if he was ill. He was holding her hand. She couldn't make sense of anything because there was a hole in her memory. The last thing she recalled was gripping the kris and running. No, trying to run, and being unable to do more than crawl. The essence of a nightmare. Before that? A man, a dagger. He'd cut into her side; she remembered blood and pain. Yes, there it was again. Stabbing along her ribs.

Yet surely she was on board ship now, and wasn't this the captain's cabin? Someone was dribbling sugar water into her mouth. She swallowed to avoid choking.

"Don't move." Mate Grig Cranald's voice. "You have a wound deep in your left side and you've lost a lot of blood. That's why you feel so weak. I've stitched it up, but it's important that it doesn't start bleeding again, so you mustn't move."

She wanted to agree with that, but the words would not come. She closed her eyes and drifted away.

When she awoke again, it was dark outside. The familiar sounds of a ship on the move were comforting. The ropes sang, the masts creaked, the hull whispered – a hundred different sounds she'd come to recognise over the months. And in her nostrils, the saltiness of seawater, the tang of wet rope – and the smell of the fragrant oil that Ardhi used on his hands to stop them being chafed by salt-soaked wet ropes.

She smiled. The aroma reminded her of so much that was good in the world. "Ardhi," she said without opening her eyes.

"I'm here. Don't move too much."

More water dribbled, and she drank greedily this time. She cracked her lids apart. "I feel so tired."

"I want you to drink more." He pushed a straw between her lips and she sucked up something sweet. She drank as much as she could, then pushed it away. "How did I get back here?"

He smiled at someone standing to her side. "Saker."

She turned her head slightly to see him. "Dear friend." She smiled weakly. "Should have listened to your nagging."

"Probably. But your messing with gunpowder did the trick in the end. The explosion and the resultant fire killed almost everyone in that particular encampment, and it distracted the other lancers elsewhere. They thought they were being attacked by a *huge* force of men bombarding them with cannon. Many dropped their weapons and ran away. We dealt with the rest and our casualties were low. The besiegers have vanished and I gather that the local farmers are exacting revenge for the months of pillage of their farms by dispatching the deserters. *You* are the hero of the battle."

She laughed, winced and decided not to do that again. Va, but she was weak.

"There's one . . . not so good thing," he added. "I used another piece of feather. We had six between us, and now we've used three. Yet we haven't come close to Fox – and we have Piper and her twin to think of too. Perhaps we need a feather piece for each of them."

To kill or to cure. If they could.

He rubbed a hand over his head. "I don't know why the Rani couldn't have told us more about how they could be used."

"I don't think she knew herself how they would work in the Va-cherished Hemisphere," said Ardhi. "How could she? She wasn't familiar even with your witcheries, let alone the origins of your sorcerers."

"Then maybe she should have given us something more powerful."

Ardhi quirked an eyebrow. "Like a whole regalia plume—?"

Saker sighed. "Yes, I know. That would have been madness. She did her best, and she risked much to trust us."

"You haven't said *how* you used the feather to save me, Saker," Sorrel said. "My last memory was terror that the gunpowder was going to explode and I was going to die."

He handed her the water with a warning look. Hastily she started to drink.

"When I reached you, the kegs were already on the verge of exploding. I had no time to carry you out of the way. All I could think to do was to hold the feather tight, grip the dagger, and think of anything that could save us both."

"Like what?"

"I thought of being safe and cold and wet and protected. There was no time to be more specific."

"Sweet cankers, Saker! Just tell me what happened!"

"I'm not sure you are going to believe it."

"I've been to a land where birds rule and can talk inside your head, I've seen age-old shrines disappear – and you think I will have trouble believing what you're about to tell me?"

"There was a stream a few paces away, remember? The water came out of it, surrounded us, and turned into ice." When she stared at him, startled, he said, "I *told* you it was hard to believe."

"*Ice?*"

"A wall of ice, a hand-span thick. Part of it was smashed by flying debris, and the heat of the explosion melted some, but enough was left to keep us safe."

Ardhi added, "A connection between the *sakti* of my islands and the Way of the Flow in yours. A combination that saved you."

"Thank you," she said to Saker. "You risked your life for me."

He smiled at her. "Just returning a favour."

"Where are we going now?"

"We need to find a healer for you, so we're sailing to Twite. We don't want that wound of yours turning septic. We'll be there tomorrow morning. After that, we are going to the main Twite shrine. If I am right, we will have a message there from Fritillary Reedling."

The Twite healer forbade Sorrel from leaving her bed for at least a day, so when Lord Juster, Prince Ryce, Saker and Ardhi set off from *Golden Petrel*'s berth to walk to Twite's main shrine-oak, they left her behind.

Prince Ryce grumbled all the way, much to Saker's irritation, saying he didn't understand how anyone could communicate with an invisible keeper at an invisible shrine. "This is a waste of time," he muttered as they strode through the streets of the port. "I want to ensure the safety of my wife and son. I ought to be confronting my father!"

"Deposing a king is not a step to be taken lightly," Juster said.

Ryce looked at him in surprise. "Do you really think there's a question about who is more important to me? King Edwayn betrayed not only his own family, but also his country. As far as I am concerned my father is but the shell of a king. He needs to be deprived of his throne." He caught the look Saker gave Ardhi, and added, "Master Witan, not a word, please."

"No, Your Highness," he said dutifully.

As he'd expected, the place where the oak had been was now a mess of prickles wreathed in mist. Lord Juster looked over at Saker. "I suppose this is where you do your stuff with the eagle."

At least the bird was not hungry this time, so it didn't fight him as he cajoled it down to the ground. When he tied his letter to its leg, it did however stab at him with its beak, drawing blood. He calmed it with a soothing sound in the back of his throat, and sent it on its way.

"What did you write?" Ardhi asked as the bird took off.

"Just that we are here, and asking if they have a message for us from Pontifect Fritillary. Oh, and I said the siege of Gromwell had been lifted and that His Highness is with us."

"And how long will we have to wait for a reply?" Ryce asked.
Saker shrugged.

"That look," Ryce said, "bordered on disrespect, witan!"

"It was supposed to," he replied cheerfully. "I figure that we all can treat you as a bosom comrade for at *least* three years on the basis of lifting the siege."

"Absolutely," Juster agreed. "Possibly even four. In fact, I expect to have my next foray into privateering funded out of the royal treasury."

"You fobbing bastards. As penance for your disrespectful perfidy, I can make you all walk barefoot dressed in sackcloth from here to land's end at Gilly Point!"

"That wouldn't worry me too much," Ardhi replied, looking down at his unshod feet. "I've already walked barefoot from Lowmeer to Ardrone once."

"He's not joking," Saker said. "He did."

"Then maybe your penance would be to wear shoes?" Ryce suggested.

Juster laughed. "He's got you there, Ardhi."

Ryce looked at Ardhi, interested. "You're a sailor and yet you walked? Why?"

"A long story," Ardhi said.

"Some day I hope to hear it." He sobered, and added, "I may never be able to repay you all for what you've done. I won't forget the risks you have taken, nor your loyalty. I have no idea what I will be able to offer you, any of you, but I will tell you this: if you help unite me with Princess Bealina and my son, you can name your price."

"Oh, in that case, I am sure we will oblige," Lord Juster said, "although did I not once warn you about making too many promises to your ne'er-do-well friends?"

"Who said any of you were my friends?" he countered, arching an eyebrow. "A nulled witan, a reckless privateer, a trickster hand-maiden – who mysteriously now has a name other than Celandine Marten, which no one has explained – and a shoeless Va-forsaken islander? You jest, Juster. Whatever could a disinherited and discredited penniless prince, with only a cannon-battered ruin to his name, possibly have in common with such a passel of reprobates?"

Juster studied his nails thoughtfully. "A love of perilous adventure? An absurd hankering to cross swords with a sorcerer? Believe me, even the handmaiden doesn't seem averse to tackling doomed ventures—"

They never heard the remainder of what he was going to say, because just then the world around them began to change.

The untidy tangle of vegetation shivered, as if in a breeze, then dissipated, like a painted scene melting in the rain. The eagle rose up into the sky, calling in alarm, circling higher and higher until it was just a dot in the sky.

And there, where the furze and holly and brambles had been, the oak tree shrine began to appear, first just as an indeterminate vagueness, and then in living detail. A solid oak, hundreds of years old, clad in the young leaves of late spring when they should surely have begun to turn, surrounded by outbuildings, vegetable gardens, people and livestock – a whole complex that had more in common with a monastery than a shrine. People with witcheries had been living here in hiding, just as they had in Hornbeam.

Waiting at the entrance to the shrine was Fritillary Reedling.

She looks so much older, Saker thought in shock. Her hair was completely white.

"Well," said Juster, sounding pleased, "it seems your note must have said exactly the right things, Saker."

26

An Assembly of Heroes

Afterwards, when he had to describe the scene to Sorrel, Saker remembered the confusion of that moment. They all had questions to ask, and answers to give, and explanations to make. There were also secrets to keep.

Saker's greatest confusion, though, came from the Pontifect's appearance. She had aged badly. Apart from the change in her hair, her face was lined and her once beautiful hands were covered in liver spots and wrinkles.

Gall 'n' acorns, it's what – only three years since I saw her last, and she looks at least fifteen years older!

For her benefit, he sketched a bare outline of what had happened since he'd last seen her, but serious conversation was postponed until the shrine keeper, an elderly, dark-skinned man proud of the Pashali blood mixed in with his Shenat ancestry, led them into his private section of the shrine. Living roots had been twisted in their growth to form seats, but there were only four, which meant that someone had to sit on the beaten soil. Ryce, Fritillary and Juster all took a seat as their right. Saker and Ardhi grinned at one another and said nothing. Saker, knowing that Chenderawasi folk regarded chairs as something designed for discomfort and used for formal occasions when brevity was to be encouraged, let Ardhi sit on the ground.

The shrine keeper served elderberry wine in wooden cups. As he was withdrawing to leave them alone for their discussion, he caught Saker's eye, deeply distressed.

Change, Saker thought. Everything was changing, and even those keepers who had dealt with several hundred years of history found the present challenges unprecedented. Oak shrines, supposed to be places of peace and comfort, had been caught up in violence and war. Some had even been destroyed.

After the shrine keeper had left, Lord Juster took a sip of the wine and spluttered. For a moment Saker thought he was going to spit it out, but his good manners prevailed and he swallowed it with a pained expression, muttering something that sounded like "Hog's piddle."

Ryce looked at him quizzically."Really?"

"Some other time, gentlemen!" Fritillary snapped. "We have much to do. Keep your stories relevant and as succinct as possible. Details can wait."

When no one volunteered to go first, she began, detailing what Gerelda Brantheld had been doing with Peregrine Clary – whom Saker had never heard of – to kill some of the sorcerer sons of Valerian Fox. Saker didn't know whether to be appalled or impressed. The idea that Gerelda had been embroiled in so many murders, however justified, grieved him for her sake. Sweet Va, how life had changed in the Va-cherished Hemisphere! Va-cherished? That had become a laughable epithet for their land.

Fritillary then moved on to tell the full story of Sir Herelt Deremer and the Dire Sweepers, and how Deremer had discovered the truth about the Horned Death – thanks to Saker's preliminary discoveries. "The Sweepers, aided by Lowmian guards, have eliminated Fox sorcerers from Lowmeer. Deremer believes the only ones left are those in Ardrone, East Denva, Valance and Vavala, which is excellent news."

Saker kept silent on the question which bothered him most about Deremer: why had the man tried so hard to kill him at that small village in the south of Lowmeer?

Of everything that was said that morning, it was the story she had to tell about how the shrines had been hidden, and why, that interested him most.

"We had no way of fighting Valerian Fox in the beginning," she explained. "His sorcerer sons were everywhere."

"Fobbing grubbery, he must have been jumping in the bed of every Fox female on every Fox estate for years, from the Principalities down to our southern shores, to have had so many sons," Juster muttered with a tinge of reluctant admiration. "Surely half of his offspring were girls?"

"I wonder if he used sorcery to ensure otherwise. Not important now. Coercion made it easy for him to raise an army; Fox money armed them. His problem was more how to take men who'd never held a sword or a bow in their lives and turn them into soldiers."

"Which is why he's relied mostly on lances, pikes, crossbows, staves," Prince Ryce said. "Easier to train them to use those things than to make a longbow archer or a swordsman."

"Surely Fox could buy pistols and cannon and arquebuses from Pashalin?" Saker asked. "He's rich enough. Not much training needed. Pashalin is where black powder is made, too."

"Oh, he did," she said. "But their rulers started to worry whether the arms could be one day turned against them, so they stopped their open export. But we shouldn't be complacent. Fox is destroying Va-faith from within."

"So you decided to hide the shrines and hide the shine keepers, and save the folk with witcheries," Juster said. "But what's the point in that if ordinary people don't have access to shrines?"

"It was a terrible thing to do," she said. "I know that. But we needed time to prepare in safety." She glanced at Saker. "I supposed you guessed what we were doing."

"You've been training people how to use their witcheries to defend themselves and others, or as an act of war."

Prince Ryce protested. "Can you do that? Use a witchery to harm or kill, and you lose it, that's what we were taught!"

"True," Fritillary agreed. "However, I was indirectly given a lesson from the unseen guardian of the Great Oak. She – or he – gave a witchery of sorts to my secretary, Barden, who has no Shenat roots, and that witchery is aggressive in its defence of him and me." She heaved a heartfelt sigh. "There's a time when you have to fight to preserve what is good and true. Oak shrines were attacked and burned. Water shrines had their springs poisoned. Keepers were murdered. We had to stop that."

"I'm glad to hear it," Prince Ryce said.

"I still don't see how witcheries can be used to fight and kill," Juster said.

"Of course they can," Saker said. "Take, um, a man with a wood-working witchery. He can bend staves for a cask, curve planks for a hull—"

"We know what a woodworker does," Prince Ryce interrupted. "So what?"

"Think of all the things made of wood. Bridges, crossbows, wagon wheels, gun carriages, trees, boats, buildings. A woodworker could break any of . . ."

"Woodworkers never break the wood they work with!"

"Only because no one employs them to do so because it's cheaper to use an axe or a saw! But that doesn't mean they *couldn't* do it."

Fritillary nodded. "They have in fact been perfecting their abilities to do so."

"There's one problem," Saker said. "There must be many more Grey Lancers than folk with witcheries."

"Yes. But a coerced army tends to lose their focus with time. Whenever a Fox son goes off to coerce more farmers' sons, the lancers he leaves behind start to fall apart."

Ryce nodded. "We noticed that. They became increasingly slovenly. So what now? Are we ready to do battle?"

"We can't keep the shrines and witchery folk in hiding any longer," she said.

"I don't understand how you did it in the first place," Ryce said.

She stirred uneasily. "Let's just say that the unseen guardians are entities with very strange abilities. They can travel time, carrying a place with them."

"What the blazes does that mean?" Prince Ryce asked.

"They can take their shrine and keep it stationary in that moment, while everywhere else time advances as usual. They become islands stuck in our past."

"That doesn't make sense," Juster said.

"It doesn't have to make sense to us. The point is that unseen guardians can do it."

Saker had an uncomfortable thought. "How did you get here?"

"There have always been paths and streams that link one shrine-oak with another – the spiritual, natural connections between the phys-ical parts of Shenat faith. Unseen to us and unused except by the unseen guardians. If the shrine-oaks stay in another time, so do their links. Unseen guardians have made them visible to a select few of us, so that they can be walked. Or sailed if they are water shrines. I've done enough walking over the past year or two to a last a lifetime! Be grateful to Va that it is possible."

"I agree," Ardhi said suddenly. "You don't want or need to know any more than that. And you don't want to know what price was paid, either."

Saker looked at Fritillary's wrinkled hands and felt queasy.

There was an uncomfortable silence, which Prince Ryce broke, saying, "All I care about is rescuing Bealina and Garred. I must return to Throssel as soon as possible."

"Bealina is not there," Fritillary said. "They were taken to Fox in Vavala."

Aghast, the colour draining from his face, Ryce said, "They are in *Fox's* hands? Saker was right?"

"I had word," she said.

"What about Horntail? He was with them—"

"Ah, that bearded fellow was yours? He lives, but was ensorcelled and remembers nothing. Gerelda Brantheld told me he is with her and Peregrine, hiding in Vavala. They've been trying to find a way to free your family."

Ryce groaned and jumped to his feet. He slammed his palm flat to the bough of the oak, over and over, with the full force of his arm behind the blows.

Fritillary stood and went to lay a hand over his to force an end to his pounding. "Princess Bealina is probably safer there than she would be with your father," she said, "King Edwayn is unpredictable and violent. At least Fox is rational in his behaviour, and at the moment it is in his interest to protect your son."

"We'll go to Vavala, then," Ryce said, addressing Juster.

"For *Golden Petrel* to get there from here would take a month or even more, depending on winds."

"We'll go overland."

"Not advisable," Fritillary said. "A whole company of armed men couldn't approach Vavala unheralded. Besides, it's more important that—" She stopped, face flushed.

Glenda Larke

What, Saker wondered, was so embarrassing that she hesitated to say it? *Ah of course.* "You want King Edwayn to abdicate first."

"It is better to do this with a semblance of legality, as well as unity. I've already primed the northern princes to follow your lead when you are king, Your Highness. Mathilda will support you, too, of course."

"But my son and my wife!" Ryce cried. "They are in the hands of that monster!"

Lord Juster stood up to take Ryce's arm and ease him back on to his seat. "So what do you advocate, Your Reverence?"

"You sail back to Throssel." Fritillary was addressing Prince Ryce, but they knew she was speaking to them all. "You take the city and the castle. You *could* force the king to abdicate on the grounds of insanity."

Juster and Ryce glanced at one another, faces without expression. Saker sucked in a sharp breath. Blister it, with that slight emphasis on "could", had she just given Ryce free rein to do what he liked with his father?

"With the city and Throssel Palace secured," she continued, her tone as calm and measured as always, "you get the Arbiter of Throssel to crown you king. Then you travel overland to the port of Betany. That way you save several weeks at sea. Once there, you seize the navy in the king's name and sail to Vavala."

"The navy is in Betany?" Juster asked.

"Edwayn has been trying to blockade Lowmian ships, part of his daft plan to control the spice trade," she said. She gave Lord Juster a sidelong look before adding, "He had reports from Karradar. Something about the Lowmians attacking *Golden Petrel* on your outward voyage. He was not only furious, he was bent on revenge. Fortunately the news of that didn't arrive until after Regal Vilmar had died, or the troubles with Lowmeer could have been worse. At my request, Regala Mathilda showed restraint."

Juster burst out laughing. "Now that's one outcome of our skirmish in Karradar I would never have predicted!"

Fritillary ploughed on. "When you arrive in Vavala, you will be joined by the Dire Sweepers and Lowmian troops, as well as forces from the Principalities. Before then, Gerelda and Peregrine will have rescued Bealina and Prince Garred so that neither your wife nor your son will be hostages to your behaviour."

242

For another hour, the conversation continued, thrashing out details of what could or could not be done. Most of the discussion was between Lord Juster, Prince Ryce and Pontifect Fritillary Reedling.

Commerce, royalty and religion.

Saker was bemused by his own attitude, halfway between uneasiness at the thought of deposing a king and facing a sorcerer, and rejoicing at the idea of battle. Ah, how much he wanted his revenge on Fox.

But how strong were the Prime's powers now? If he could suck the life out of others to extend his own, did that mean he could – barring accidents or murder – live indefinitely? If he was injured, even mortally, perhaps he could cure himself by dragging the life out of those around him. He looked down at his palm. The black smudge was there again, now that he was under a shrine tree. Time, or perhaps the counter effect of his contact with *sakti*, had faded it a little.

Lord Juster broke up the discussion, announcing he had to arrange for supplies for *Golden Petrel*, after which they would sail back to Throssel. He and Ardhi and Prince Ryce then headed off on foot to Twite, leaving Saker and Fritillary Reedling standing side by side in the shrine.

"Sorrel will be glad to reach Throssel," Saker remarked. "She's been fretting because it's been so long since she saw Piper."

"I will be interested to meet her. She sounds like a remarkable woman."

He chuckled. "She is."

"She's the only person in the Va-cherished Hemisphere at the present time who has a glamour. She must have been special from the beginning. An unseen guardian saw something in her that few people have. Are you in love with her?"

"What business is that of yours?"

"Well, you still work for me."

"I haven't been paid for the past three years!"

"Even so, I don't recall ever receiving your resignation."

"My heart is still not your concern."

She levelled a stare at him, without speaking.

Rot it, she had a way of chiselling information out of you, just by looking . . . Worse, he could not lie, or even prevaricate, because her witchery meant she could read him like a book.

He sighed heavily. "Sorrel Redwing lost a daughter under horrible circumstances. She has little place in her heart at the moment for anyone except Piper."

"You care for her, nonetheless."

"Of course I do! You have no idea how much we have been through together, side by side. I love her as much as it is possible to love a friend without going that one step further."

"She doesn't care for you?"

"Not in that way, no. I've been aware of that for a long, long while. Perhaps even longer than she has!" He smiled. "The attraction was there initially perhaps, but there was also always something missing. Now it's not something missing, but rather something . . . inserted. Somewhere along the line we've become more akin to siblings. I feel like an older brother always trying to protect her because I got her into this mess, at least partially. And she's the younger sister telling me she's not a child any more and can look after herself."

Fritillary shook her head and waggled a finger at him. "That's not a good basis for a marriage."

He laughed. "No, it's not. So it is just as well we aren't contemplating one, isn't it?"

"Tell me about Piper."

"She's a delight. Intelligent, charming, pretty. Everything that a parent would want in a daughter. But – but there is no doubt that she is Valerian Fox's child and that she is also a sorcerer."

"Who else knows that she is the Regala's child?"

"Ardhi. Juster guessed. He knew about devil-kin and guessed we took Piper from Ustgrind to save her life."

"Who knows she is Fox's child?"

"Possibly the midwife who delivered the twins. Apparently Mathilda said something during her travail—"

"That woman's dead."

"Then, if she didn't tell anyone, just Sorrel, myself, Ardhi and Lord Juster."

"You told Lord Juster?"

"We needed his help. So that he would give it, we had to tell him why it was necessary. Ryce, on the other hand, knows nothing. He has assumed she is Sorrel's, born of some Lowmian liaison. He's too polite to ask for details."

"I think it best that neither Ryce nor anyone else ever find out Fox sired the twins. What else should I know?"

It was an order, he knew that, but he had also to give thought to the responsibility he and Sorrel had to Ardhi's homeland. "The future of the Va-forsaken land depends on our secrecy."

"I can't make promises when I don't know what I'm promising!" she said. "The only thing I can say is that I won't do anything with the information you give me that runs counter to your wishes without discussing it with you first. I will also take all you say seriously, because I trust your judgement in this."

With that, he had to be content. He leaned forward and dropped his voice as he began to tell the story of the Chenderawasi.

By the time Saker had finished the tale and answered all the questions, it was dark outside. The shrine keeper brought some food, but both of them only picked at it. Fritillary was silent for a long time as she considered all she had learned.

"I am relieved," she said at last, "that you feel the two hemispheres are linked through our beliefs and that their *sakti* is not so very different from our witcheries. When I first heard about the dagger, I was afraid of the opposite. That it was linked to the sorcery and the curse of the Horned Death."

"I'm even wondering if the Chenderawasi Avians are so very different from our unseen guardians. They *are* more visible, but like unseen guardians, they dispense magic."

She looked intrigued. "An interesting thought!"

"Ardhi mentioned a price for hiding the shrines. Was it the unseen guardians who paid it?" *Or was it you, because you have been walking those unseen paths?*

"Some of the older oaks are dying," she admitted. "There will be new trees, new guardians."

His insides lurched uncomfortably. "But a young guardian of a young oak . . ."

". . . can't grant witcheries for many years," she finished for him. "We will all pay in the end. Fewer witcheries granted for several generations."

And you chose *to do that.*

She smiled faintly. "I believe we would have lost more if the trees had not been hidden. Shrine keepers and witchery folk were being targeted."

Dear Va, what a decision she had made, knowing how much she was damaging the future of the whole hemisphere. Heroic? Presumptuous? He gazed at her, half of him admiring the resolution and courage of her decision, the other half appalled at her gall.

And she knew it, damn her.

27

The Splitting of the Ternion

By the time the others returned to the ship that night, Sorrel was almost spitting with impatience. She hated being confined to bed, even if it was in Lord Juster's luxuriously appointed cabin. There was only just so much admiring she could do of the Pashali embroidered bedding, the gilded porcelain chamber pot with the dragon handle, or the intricate carved panelling that had been installed in Javenka to replace the damage done to his cabin by the Lowmians.

"I'm sure I'm well enough to get up," she told Grig when he looked in on her as she was having her lunch, brought to her personally by the cook a few minutes before. "Can you bring me my clothes?"

He looked uncomfortable. "I could," he replied, but his tone told her he was reluctant to do so. "Saker would be upset with me if you don't stay in bed, though."

"Saker does not dictate what I do," she said crossly.

He grinned. "He does try, nonetheless, doesn't he?"

"And are you abetting him?"

"Well, in this case, it's more what the healer said, which was that you should stay abed today."

"I could go up on deck in my nightgown . . ."

"The dock lumpers would love that."

"I could glamour myself some clothes."

"Believe me, you'd be chilly up on deck without a cloak." When she glared at him, he relented. "If you are that determined, I'll fetch your clothes – but I'd hate to see my embroidery of your wound ruined by you climbing the steps to the upper deck. Really, Sorrel, it's better you don't."

She heaved a sighed. "All right! All right! I'll stay in bed."

"I thought you'd be sensible about it." With that infuriating remark, he left, leaving her to twiddle her thumbs and curse her well-meaning male friends.

When Saker did return it was already dark. He knocked and poked his head around the door when she answered. "Are you respectable? I've brought your clothes from your cabin. Grig tells me you think you are well enough to get up."

She glared at him. "I've been well enough all day long. What happened? Have you any idea how hard it is to lie here and not know—?"

"Everything's fine." Briefly he sketched what had happened and the decisions that had been made. "Pontifect Fritillary wants to meet you, so when you're dressed, come to the wardroom."

"She's *here*?"

"Yes. Stop complaining and get some clothes on. Do you want any help?"

"No!"

"I didn't mean—"

"Out!"

He grinned and left the cabin.

Pulling on her clothes hurt, but once it was done she found she could walk normally, although she was careful not to move her arm too much. She stepped out into the companionway to hear a woman saying, "And you want to protect these islands from *us*?" The door to the officers' wardroom was ajar.

Saker replied, "From rapacious traders and fortune hunters, yes. We have a window of opportunity now, before people like Uthen Kesleer and his trading company—"

She reached out to knock on the door, but pain gripped her side as the movement stretched her newly healed skin. She was forced to lean back against the wall to catch her breath.

"Kesleer is languishing in jail at the moment," the woman said. Pontifect Fritillary, she assumed. "He may already have been executed."

Saker grunted. "Really? Can't say I'm distressed by that news."

"I will speak to the Regala about drawing up trade treaties. You talk to Prince Ryce when you have the opportunity. If I am successful regaining my place as Pontifect, I can do more, by appealing to religious scruples. However, let's win our war first."

"Thank you, Your Reverence."

She raised her hand again to knock, but halted when she heard his next words.

There is something else worrying Sorrel and me—"

"The twins."

"Yes. I'm not sure we know how to stop them growing up into sorcerers."

Sorrel could see Saker's profile through the crack of the open door. He dug into his belt purse and fished out the second of the circlets the Rani had given them. "Prince-regal Karel must wear this. Always. The Rani hoped it will stop the development of his sorcery. Piper already wears hers."

She took the gold circlet and ran a finger over the softness of the feathers that had been use to weave it. "Regal enough for a prince, isn't it? I will give it to Regala Mathilda as soon as I can. I do have to go back to Ustgrind. Tedious place. Mathilda fights the starched-collars of the court as best she can, but they are such *dour* men. Copper-counting, figure-toting merchants, all! She is having more luck with some of the women, fortunately. Offer them freedom they've never had before, and there will always be a few who'll snatch it with joy."

He smiled and Sorrel wondered if he was thinking of her, climbing the rigging, hiding behind her glamour, dressed as she was now in a sailor's garb and revelling in the freedom it gave her.

"I need to speak to Sorrel," Fritillary said.

And that, she thought, *is as good an entrance line as any.* She stepped into the wardroom. "Your Reverence," she said. "I am here."

The woman was impressive: taller than Saker, filling the space around her with the power of her presence. Even her stance as she rose to greet Sorrel commanded attention, though her dress was unadorned and her wiry white hair escaped untidily from under a net snood. Saker had once told her she was about fifty. Well, she looked older. The startling whiteness of her hair was unexpected.

"Mistress Sorrel, a pleasure indeed to meet you. Saker has outlined your adventures since the two of you met. I fear your life has been overturned by this witan of mine, for which I apologise."

"Oh, I think my life had been turned upside down before we met."

"Either way, I fear there will be more adventures. I have need of your witchery. Saker is going to Throssel with the prince and Lord Juster. Prince Ryce's wife and son have been imprisoned in Vavala by Valerian Fox and they must be extricated so he cannot use them to influence Ryce's behaviour. Someone with a glamour, to help rescue Princess Bealina and her son, would be appreciated."

She was speechless; Saker was not. "Wait a moment," he protested. "We do know – or we think we know – that Fox can't coerce someone with a witchery, but he could probably see through a glamour. Of what possible use would Sorrel be? She'd be captured the moment he laid eyes on her!"

"He's also seen me before," Sorrel said. "Although he might not recall my face."

"There's another thing too," Saker added. "We were told by the Rani of Chenderawasi that we are a ternion and it is in that unity of three that our strength lies."

Fritillary's gaze didn't waver from Sorrel's face. "This is your choice. But hear me out before you decide. Of course, I can't force you. If you go to Throssel, there is nothing much you can do that others cannot. Ryce will rely on his friends to get inside the castle, after which there will be fighting."

She was beginning not to like Fritillary. After all she had been through, this woman thought she was useless? She wanted to say that Juster had found her very useful last time he'd needed to see the king, but instead she listened, feeling the muscles of her face hardening into a glower that she didn't bother to disguise. Saker shot her a glance in warning, but then quickly looked away.

"In Vavala," the Pontifect continued, "I need somebody who can get inside the palace unseen, warn the princess what is going to happen, tell her what to expect. If she doesn't know, the plan might fail."

Her gut wrenched in protest. "I need to go to Throssel. Piper is there. She is my responsibility." Her voice wobbled, but even as she spoke, she wondered if Fritillary understood. *Do you know what it's like to leave a child? Do you understand that I think of her every day, all day, and dream of her by night?* She bit the words back.

"Once Throssel has fallen to Prince Ryce, Piper can be brought to Vavala under Saker's care," the Pontifect said.

She battled her disappointment. No, her *grief*. "And how do you intend that I get to Vavala?" She wasn't sure why she even asked. She would *not* go.

"With me, via the timeless route from shrine to shrine. We must free Prince Garred and his mother before Fox gets any inkling of what is happening in Throssel."

Her throat tightened. She could hardly breathe; to have the prospect of returning to Throssel snatched away from her was more than she could bear. She shook her head with more violence than was needed. "No. Oh, no. I won't go."

Fritillary stared and she stared back. "I'm sorry to have to remind you of unpleasant facts, Mistress Sorrel, but Piper is not your daughter and you have no rights in her life. In fact, I believe Regala Mathilda told you to bring her to me. I am aware that you have risked your life more than once to keep her safe. From what Saker has told me, you've cared for her with love, but that still does not mean you have any authority over her disposition. Mathilda intended that I be her guardian."

Her throat swelled with pain, preventing her from venting her protests.

"We know she is not really a princess of Lowmeer any more than Karel has a right to be the Regal," Fritillary continued. "It is probably best that Piper's connection to him is kept secret."

She swallowed back the lump in her throat. "I – I am aware that ultimately Regala Mathilda will dictate what happens to Piper. But what are you trying to say? Because I'm not sure that I am prepared to keep my mouth shut if it means a sorcerer will sit on the throne of Lowmeer."

"That is indeed unthinkable. You would do well to remember that. I will leave you two to discuss this." With that remark she turned on her heel and left them alone in the wardroom.

Trembling, Sorrel sat down. "Sweet Va, what did she mean?"

"That both of them might have to be killed," he said. The grief she read in his look was not reflected in the flat tone of his words.

"Was she – was she threatening Piper to make me compliant?"

"Va, no!" He was appalled. "She's not like that! No, it was just a warning so—" He couldn't go on.

"So that I am prepared to lose her. One way or another. What are we going to do?" She dropped her face into her hands, not weeping, but so tired she felt she couldn't keep herself upright.

He didn't reply.

Surprised by his continued silence, she lowered her hands to look at him. "Pox on't," she said, "you think I shouldn't go back to Piper."

He turned away, refusing to meet her eye. "She's right. Your glamour won't be needed in Throssel. Prince Ryce will seize power there by force with his battle-hardened men. In Vavala, though . . ."

"But . . . Piper."

"I know."

He took her hand and held it. "I will bring her safely to you. I promise."

She managed to nod, but she wasn't sure he could do all he pledged.

Lord Juster insisted she remain in his cabin that night because the bed was more comfortable than her own, but she couldn't sleep. Sometime after midnight, she rose and dressed to go up on deck. As she stepped out into the open air, she glamoured herself and walked straight past the sailors on watch. To keep out of their way she climbed up the shrouds to the crow's nest, only to find it occupied.

Ardhi, leaning on the railing, looked down at her, head cocked to one side. "We have a saying, 'When in child-bed, obey the midwife.' I think it can be extended to mean, 'When sick, obey the healer.' I find it hard to think he suggested you climb the rigging."

"No, but he did say Cranald had done an excellent job with the stitching, and his witchery was just to speed the healing along. Is there room enough for me in there?"

"Of course." He helped her in, and she leaned against the railing opposite him, the space so narrow that they were almost touching. "I'll leave if you want to be alone."

"Please don't," she said. She hadn't been looking for company, but when she'd seen him there, she'd felt a wave of gratitude. "Isn't it lovely tonight!"

The cold air was clear. The port and bordering town were in shuttered darkness, so the sky's meadow of stars blazed bright. As they watched, folds of green and gold played across the northern horizon.

"We don't have that moving light in the skies of the Summer Seas," he said, "although I have seen it before, in Pashalin."

"We call that the Night Queen's Drapes. Legend says she draws them across the sky when she wants to sleep, but the Sky Queen of daylight hours keeps trying to open them. Eventually, in the morning, she succeeds."

He gave a low laugh. "They wouldn't help me sleep! I'd stay up all night, just to watch."

"I'm going to Vavala with the Pontifect."

"Yes. Saker told me."

"I don't want to."

"I know. I will come with you."

Surprised, she asked, "Are you sure?"

"I don't think I'd be of much help in Throssel. Saker's eagle eye is needed there, but my climbing skill? Not this time. On the other hand, I hear the Pontifect's palace has high walls and high windows that are not barred . . ." She saw the flash of his smile. "Sounds like a place for someone whose witchery is the skills of a chichak."

"What's that?"

"A house gecko. They climb even better than me."

"We'll be splitting the ternion. Didn't the Rani say those who fly alone, die alone?"

"Saker won't be alone." But he was worried, she could tell.

"The Pontifect might not agree to take you with us through the shrine paths."

"I won't ask," he said matter-of-factly. "I'll tell her I'm coming." He turned her around to lean back against his chest, facing the sky. "Look up, and watch," he murmured, lips close to her ear. "We believe that when danger threatens we appreciate everything more. Do you remember the way the ripples glowed blue at night in the Summer Seas?"

She nodded.

"In Chenderawasi, we have a saying:
When the sea is darkest
And the storm cloud frowns,

When the moray hungers
And the reef shark prowls,
Then ripples shine their brightest . . ."

He stopped.

She waited for him to finish, feeling that there had to be another line. She turned in his arms to face him. "Go on."

"Maybe now is not the time."

"Yes. Now. There may never be a tomorrow."

"Then ripples shine their brightest,
And our hearts meld beneath the stars."

He ran a finger down the side of her face from her temple to the corner of her lip. "I love you."

His whisper was so light that the wind whisked it away almost before it was heard – but it had been said and etched into her memory nonetheless, every nuance. He'd said it before, when there had been no time to think about it. Now there was. Now she could revel in the joy, in the way time stopped as if the world had held its breath, as if breathing was unnecessary. She could have sworn that the air between them thickened, saturated with their longing.

Yet it was she who shattered the moment. "If you love me, then you know what I will say."

He gave a sad smile. "Yes. And I honour you for it. I could not love you half so well if you did not put Piper first."

"And I, you, if . . ." She waved a hand instead of enumerating all his obligations.

They laughed together, softly, ruefully. He said, "We both have our – what's the Ardronese word? Pri – prio-something."

"Priorities. I will tell the Pontifect that I will only go to Vavala if you are with me." She turned to climb down the rope ladder to the shrouds, but at the last moment she glanced back over her shoulder. "I do love you, you know."

She saw the flash of his gun by starlight and heard his intended, "I know," whisper on the breeze.

28

Connections

The following day, Ardhi, Sorrel and Fritillary Reedling began their journey at the Twite oak shrine. Before they started, Fritillary lectured them on what it would be like, her stare as hard as her voice.

"This will be dangerous," she said. "Do not leave the path. It's the root of a shrine-oak, or perhaps the spiritual essence of it, reaching through time. Its connection from this tree to the root of the next will keep us safe. Leave this living path, and you will never find your way back. Tonight we'll sleep in the Shenat Hills, in another hidden shrine. The next night we'll be at the shrine on the border, then somewhere in Valance, and by the end of the fourth day we'll be in Vavala. I suggest you look neither right nor left. If you need to relieve yourself, drop back, but *do not leave the path*." She looked from one to the other and they both nodded, infected by her solemnity. "Do not interact with anything. Whatever is here inhabits a different timeline."

Sorrel remembered how close they had come to losing themselves searching for the shrine at Hornbeam. She remembered her glimpse of Heather. Or maybe not Heather, but an image taken from her own hopes and fears.

She shivered. Ardhi reached out and touched her hand. "I'm all right," she said and tried to smile. They were still standing under the outer canopy of the Twite oak, on the far side from the entrance, looking out through a break in the foliage. If she let her gaze wander, she saw those who had been living in hiding around the oak. If she looked straight ahead and focused on the path, the beginning of which was a knotted root underfoot, she saw a straight pale line stretching into a colourless nothingness.

They moved off in single file, carrying only water. Fritillary was in front of her and Ardhi behind.

She tried not to look to either side. They were walking through a blank whiteness. Not a mist, she decided, because it lacked clamminess and had no hint of water. *A fog of forgetting, perhaps.* That thought skittered a shiver up her spine again. Occasionally, she saw figures off to the side, or heard people calling, or laughing, or weeping, but if she did glance sideways, she could never bring anything into focus. Fritillary walked with a steadfast pace, her gaze fixed straight ahead.

If she can do that, Sorrel thought, *so can I.* She squared her shoulders and disciplined herself not to look, even when she thought she heard Heather's voice calling to her.

Nothing changed, not the light, not the mist, not the path. The passage of time remained strangely unfelt. It wasn't until they reached the next shrine that she realised they had neither spoken to one another nor stopped to rest throughout the whole journey. She had no idea of how long it had taken them. Fritillary collapsed on to a bench in the shrine, her face drawn and tired.

The shrine keeper was blind, a man old beyond normal reckoning if his archaic speech was any indication. He felt his way around as he fetched them water and food and bedding. He evidently recognised Fritillary by her voice, because he greeted her, saying, "Your Reverence? Ye've done come agin so soon? Daft as a rabbit, are ye? Ye walk these paths and the years run away from ye like tears down your cheeks! How much longer will ye last, be ye skipping through time?"

She did not reply.

"An' tell me, lady, how much longer are we to be hid here, liken us were rabbits in the warren too scared to wave a whisker in the air, else the fox snap at it? What's old Mother Alder going to do iffen her heifer gets sick again, when Hyacinth Knapweed is the animalmender around about and she be sittin' yonder, twiddling her thumbs, instead of caring for the village kine? When can we open up the shrine again?"

"Before winter arrives," she said and patted his crinkled hand with its bulbous knuckles and crooked thumb. "I promise."

His blind eyes held on to their opaque blankness, but his face lit up. "Earth and oak," he said, "thanks be! To serve folk, one must be *among* folk, no?"

"Contain your joy, old man," she said gently. "War is coming. All those with a witchery, the ones who can walk, must travel to Vavala by the timeless paths before then – or else fight here in Ardrone. Walking the paths once or twice is not going to hurt anyone."

"And how many miles have you walked through the timeless lands?" he asked.

She shrugged. "Who knows?"

After they'd eaten, picking at the food for none of them was hungry, Sorrel wanted to sleep. Fritillary had other ideas. She wished to know all about Ardhi and about the Summer Seas and the Chenderawasi Islands, their politics, people, trade, climate, belief systems and everything that had happened to them there. Sorrel, her eyelids drooping, struggled to stay awake, and left most of the answering to Ardhi. When the questions were too awkward, he pretended he hadn't understood and went off at a tangent, enumerating the advantages of a regulated trade between equal partners. Sorrel doubted Fritillary Reedling was deceived by Ardhi's veneer of an innocent and gullible islander with nothing to hide.

The next day, and the next, were much like the first. On the final day, when they sighted the Great Oak through the mist and knew they were arriving in Vavala, Sorrel found herself weeping with gratitude. That misted world with its long periods of silence punctuated by occasional ghostly cries or whispers of truncated conversation, the long tedious hours of walking, followed by penetrating questioning from Fritillary – she felt worn thin, like the sole on an old shoe.

Ardhi slipped his arm around her shoulders as they stood on the path and stared ahead at the leaves of the greatest oak of all. His breath shifted the strands of her hair as she leaned into him.

"The kris is aware of the ancient *sakti* of that tree," he said. "The wood is alive and strong and true."

"But we are only flesh and blood." She feared, but didn't want to give words to her dread. What if the ternion died? What then, for Piper?

His arm tightened about her, the hardness of his muscles both a comfort and a tantalising seduction. "Together we are strong," he said as he wiped away a tear on her cheek with his thumb. "I will never leave you."

Fritillary, standing in front of them, turned. "Come," she said, "let's find out what's been happening in Vavala."

Sorrel grasped Ardhi's hand as they stepped under the canopy of the Great Oak.

In Proctor House, Horntail and Gerelda were training, yet again. Day after day, always training, honing their fighting skills. Horntail had taken it upon himself to teach her what he called a battle mind.

Perie watched as they fought each other with practice swords they'd found in the basement. *Lunge, parry, thrust, interrupt the beat . . . Try this, try that, go for the unexpected, expect the bizarre . . .*

In war, Horntail said, there were no rules. Everything was not only possible, but desirable. If you could cheat, deceive, kick, bite, scratch or throw boiling water at your opponent, then you did it. What mattered was winning, not rectitude. What mattered was surviving to fight another day, not dying heroically.

Come to think of it, that was a philosophy Perie had once agreed with wholeheartedly, but no more. Now . . . he wasn't so sure. There'd been too much killing. Too many deaths. Now he just wanted it all to be over. More than anything, what he desired now was peace and rest in a place where there were no more sorcerers. In his bleakest moments, he dreamed of a quick death. When he confronted those thoughts, though, he found the idea of an overgrown grave beneath an oak tree more comforting than gloomy.

"No, no, no!" Horntail said. "Don't wait for your opponent to recover. Catch him off-balance!"

Poor man, he still didn't know who he was and he swore black and blue that he couldn't possibly have a name like Buttercup. When he wasn't practising with her, he prowled the rooms like a frustrated cat looking for a way out.

"How much longer?" Horntail asked, as he brought the practice bout to an end. He rubbed his already dirty sleeve over his sweaty brow. "Proctor, I'm be lard-bloated if I have to stay inside a moment longer. When is this confounded Pontifect of yours coming back? Yesterday, you said today. The day before that, you said yesterday . . ."

"You know as much as I do," she lied, examining the damage he had inflicted on her knuckles. "She got my message and said she'd contact me in about ten days. Which was up yesterday."

"She knows where we are, though."

"Yes, Buttercup. I sent a message. And I'm just as impatient as you are. I think we've found out all we can about the palace without actually going inside. I don't think you'd be so impatient to leave the building if you knew what the streets are like out there." Fear saturated the city. No one smiled in Vavala any more.

That night, as the three of them sat around the fire in the common room in gloomy silence, someone rapped at the brass knocker on the main door.

Horntail gave a grunt that could have meant anything. "So," he asked as he strapped on his sword belt, "how do we tell if that's friend or foe?"

"Open it?" Gerelda suggested.

Perie snatched up his staff and made sure his spiker was accessible. "It's not a sorcerer."

They all trooped out into the main hall. Gerelda and Horntail stepped to either side of the door.

"You're the sacrificial chicken," Horntail said to Perie, grinning. "Open it and then get out of the way."

The precautions were not needed. Fritillary Reedling stood in the doorway, with two people behind her.

"Good evening, Perie Proctor," the Pontifect said. "May we come in?"

Even as she asked, she was already stepping into the hallway, the two others close behind her.

Peregrine's first thought was *Pox, she's got so old!*

He didn't know the other two people. One of them was a woman and the other was brown-skinned and barefoot.

"We've been walking all day," Fritillary said. "So, as you can imagine, we're tired. We just stopped long enough for me to find your message at the shrine. This is Mistress Sorrel Redwing of Ardrone, and Ardhi, from the Summer Seas. Friends of Saker Rampion."

The woman's face broke into a smile as they followed Gerelda to the common room. "Sergeant Horntail! Prince Ryce has been worried about you. He will be so glad to know you are still alive."

Horntail looked at her blankly. Gerelda explained and there was an awkward silence before he mumbled, "I have no idea who you are."

"Oh, nobody important," she said. "You probably never knew who I was anyway, but I remember you. You headed Prince Ryce's personal guard."

Horntail continued to look blank.

"Maybe you can settle an argument for us," Gerelda said as she gestured for them all to precede her into the room. "Is his first name really Buttercup?"

"What? Whose? *Buttercup?* Sergeant Horntail, is that *true*?"

He sighed.

The mattress on Sorrel's bed had a musty smell of damp. She picked up the pillow for a closer look, which revealed it was covered in mildew. She pulled a face, threw it across the room and decided it was better not to examine the rest of the bedding.

Hoping Ardhi would seek her out if he saw a light under her door, she left her candle burning, climbed into bed – and woke hours later when the morning sun streamed in through the long windows.

She groaned at her tactless inability to stay awake and hoped desperately that he had not come after all. How could she have been so – so *feeble* as to fall asleep the moment they had a chance to be alone? Someone had been in the room already that morning; there was a ewer of hot water steaming on the washstand. When she poured it into the washbowl, white scented flowers floated to the surface. She touched the petals with a finger, blushed, then laughed.

After flinging on her clothes, she hurried downstairs to find Gerelda in the kitchen chatting to Ardhi. Outside the door, Horntail was talking to Fritillary in the kitchen yard, his heavy frown an indication that the conversation was giving him trouble.

Gerelda had an odd expression on her face, as though she was not sure if Ardhi was making fun of her. Sorrel shot a look at him. His innocent smile told her that Gerelda was right to be suspicious.

"I think your friend here," Gerelda growled, "should've been a lawyer. He is an expert at saying a lot without actually telling you anything."

"Oh, he probably did study law! He seems to have done everything else: oceanography, hydrography, cartography, navigation, astronomy—" She glanced at him. "What have I forgotten?"

"Pilotage."

"Right. So you were having fun at my expense." Gerelda glared at Ardhi. "He told me he was a swabbie."

"That too, for a time. Also third mate on Lord Juster's privateer. Do you have anything to eat? I'm ravenous."

Gerelda cut her some bread and cheese. "Fritillary told me you've been with Saker. I haven't seen him in so long, not since before he was nulled. We went to university together, you know." The smile that lit her face spoke of pleasant memories.

She hadn't known, and felt a moment's pique, as if no one had the right to have known Saker longer than she had. *Ninnyhead.* "You were good friends?"

"The very best at one time. We squabbled a lot too, as I remember. Fun student days, you know. And I met him once since too. Let me think . . . three years or so back? No, more. Just before he went to Throssel Palace as spiritual adviser to the young royals."

"He's coming here with the prince and Lord Juster Dornbeck – and an army. Soon, we hope. In the meantime, we have to rescue Princess Bealina and Prince Garred," she said.

"Just like that?" Her sarcasm was undisguised. "How? I mean, we haven't had any luck at finding out where they're being kept, let alone worked out a way to rescue them."

"Oh," said Ardhi wearing his innocent expression again, "that's Sorrel's job. She'll just walk in the front gate. It's what she usually does."

Gerelda's eyes narrowed. "Why, oh why do I have the idea that I really ought to believe that?" She sighed. "Who the pox are the two of you?"

"The answer to your prayers," said Fritillary, appearing in the doorway.

29

The Rescue Begins

Fritillary Reedling's knowledge of the layout of the palace was key to their preparation. Gerelda unearthed rolls of used parchment from a chest in Proctor House and the Pontifect drew up detailed plans of every storey on the back of the sheets. She took them through the diagrams, room by room, detailing what they might reasonably expect to see in each.

The building, erected in stages over three hundred years, had started as a castle and evolved into a much more elegant edifice, with glass windows instead of arrow slits, and charming archways and statuary instead of a portcullis and drawbridge. The original curtain walls remained only along the river edge. The wall that divided the palace grounds from the city was more decorative than protective, topped as it was with a stonemason's delicate lacework.

The palace interior, a maze of floors at different levels, had its integrity interrupted by the later addition of five elegant towers of varying heights, the tallest of which, built originally as a prison, was in the centre of the building. Fritillary thought that was where Princess Bealina was most likely to be incarcerated.

Peregrine, armed with a scoop and a broom from the Proctor House stables, posed as a street sweeper and kept watch on the main gate of the palace. He reckoned the busiest time was first thing in the morning.

"Of course it is," Fritillary said. "That's when the functionaries arrive to start work in the city's administration offices on the ground floor and when the palace servants return from the market. Then there's an influx of palace clerics from early morning services at the city chapel. Perusal of those entering will be perfunctory. Don't be too confident, though, Sorrel. They'll know almost everybody who comes and goes on a regular basis. If they see you, there will be questions asked."

"They won't see me." *Although Valerian Fox might.*

Ardhi, studying the walls, concluded that the most vulnerable area was the most visually formidable: the ramparts of the curtain wall along the river. "There are no guards there," he said. "The rest of the walls are patrolled, day and night, by men with firearms."

"They assume attackers won't come from the river," Gerelda said, "because boats would soon be noticed."

"Tides to worry about, too," Ardhi said. "Certainly, they don't think in terms of a single swimmer being a danger."

"What are you considering?" Fritillary asked.

"Climbing up from the water during the darkest part of the night. From the top of the wall, I can get on to the roof."

"Only if you can climb sheer stone," Horntail said, not bothering to hide his scorn.

He shrugged. "I can."

"He's already done it," Sorrel said. She'd found that out when she'd gone to his room on their second night in Vavala, only to find him gone. He'd returned at dawn, his hair still wet from his swim.

Fritillary looked thunderous. "What? You jeopardised this whole endeavour by—?" Words failed her.

Ardhi shrugged, not at all contrite. "If they caught me, what would have happened?"

"You'd be dead, that's what!" Horntail folded his arms and glowered at him. "No guard is going to believe that a lascar has any business scampering about the Pontifect's palace! You'd be killed on the spot."

"No one will see me up on the roof, even during the day. Most of it is not visible from the ground. I just wanted to see if it was possible, and it is."

"And what good can you do up there?" Horntail asked, still dismissive.

"Look, the problem is not how Sorrel will enter, or leave. The problem is how do we get a woman and a child out of there."

At last Horntail began to look interested. "And your giddy-brained idea is—?"

"Lower them by rope into the water. Have a boat waiting. At night."

"Hmm." Horntail considered that. "Go on."

That night, Ardhi took Sorrel up on the roof of Proctor House through a dormer window. Once they were sitting on top of the ridge in the moonlight, she asked, "What's all this about?"

"I miss having the rigging to climb. There's nothing like being up high. Look at the view!" He'd lapsed back into his own language, as he so often did with her. He waved a hand at the dark shapes of the rooftops, at the palace towers which were now just shadows blocking the stars, and at the river, slick and black. "When I was a boy, I was always up in the trees. Anyone who wanted young coconuts sent me up the trunk to twist the fruit down."

They sat in companionable silence for a while, her head on his shoulder.

"You know what I envy Saker most for?" he asked some time later. "Being able to see the world from up there, in the sky! What I wouldn't give to have his witchery . . ."

"He hates it."

"No, he doesn't. He hates taking command of a wild creature and making it a slave to his wishes. That's different to hating flight." He sighed. "Sometimes I wonder if witcheries are not granted as a test, as much as a gift. Saker recognises the potential of the power he commands over birds. In a war with this sorcerer and the Grey Lancers, he could have an army of birds darkening the sky . . . His dilemma is that as a witan and a believer in the Shenat Way of the Oak, he is supposed to care for your animals and trees, for the – what's the expression?"

"'Oak and acorn, field and forest, farm and flow.'"

"Yes. And yet, if he commands such an army and wins a battle, how many birds would die? If he doesn't, how many of *us* will die? That's his dilemma. His test."

She thought about that, and felt a little sick. "And your test?"

"How much should I help you all, knowing I risk Chenderawasi's future. If your nations grow strong and are not threatened from within by internal conflict, will you turn on us to seize our spices and our magic?"

"We will all do our best to stop that. Prince Ryce and Regala Mathilda will have reasons to help us, as well."

He smiled at that. "Ah. Yes. You and Saker can be very . . . persuasive."

"And my test? What is mine?"

"I think you already know."

A whisper, because it was too difficult to say the words out loud. "Piper. And Prince-regal Karel. Two sorcerers who cannot be permitted to live . . ."

He reached out and wiped a tear from her cheek with his thumb. "We will find a way. We must." He leaned forward and kissed her lightly on the lips. It was she who deepened it, took it to another place where there was nothing but themselves and the stars. Enclosed tight in his embrace, she felt them both start to slide down the slate tiles and abandoned the kiss for laughter, never doubting that he would keep her safe. Their feet hit the pitched roof over the dormer window, and they came to a halt.

"I think we had better go inside," she said, rolling on to her back. "I have to sleep tonight. And you— Oh, look! A shooting star! And there's another one!"

He looked up. "In Pulauan Chenderawasi we say the giant who sleeps on the moon, guarding his wealth, has rolled over and kicked some of his jewels into the sky. Those that fall to earth burn as they travel and become the sky-iron we find in our mountains. Some of that is in Sri Kris." He touched the tip of her nose with his forefinger. "Be careful tomorrow, Sorrel. I'll be watching."

"I'll be all right. I've memorised the layout of the whole palace, I swear."

"Take care."

"*You* take care, not just because we need the ternion . . ."

He smiled and whispered, ". . . but because we've barely begun our journey together." He kissed her again, leaving no doubt in her mind of what he meant.

When she stood outside the gates the next morning, her heart beating wildly, she found her trepidation oddly pleasurable. It made her feel *alive*, bringing back memories of her time at court when spying for the Lady Mathilda had been her one escape from the tedium of court life.

She shot one last glance over her shoulder to make sure that Peregrine was there, leaning on his broom, watching her. After sidling along the outside wall until she was close to the gate, she waited until the guards were distracted by a couple of cloth merchants wanting to gain entry, then slipped through.

The forecourt of the palace would have been bewildering if not for Fritillary's coaching. The broad marble stairs on the left led up to the open terrace in front of the Pontifect's quarters. The archway directly ahead led into a long barrel-vaulted passage through to the stables, the kitchens and the servants' quarters. To the right of the archway, there were three smaller entrances, one to the administration areas, one to the Grand Hall and public audience rooms, and the third to another stairway that led to four of the five towers and all the private rooms.

All these entrances to the building were guarded.

She stayed close to the outer wall, watching for the right moment to move across the forecourt. Glancing upwards to the roof, she couldn't see Ardhi anywhere, but from the configurations of the towers, ramparts, walkways, windows and balconies, it was obvious that there were plenty of corners and nooks out of sight from the ground.

Dropping her gaze once more, she saw a groom leading a horse through the archway into the forecourt. Behind him walked someone in better quality clothes, a couple of large fellhounds at his heels. Once out from under the archway, the man mounted his horse, whistled his dogs and headed towards the gateway. His servant followed on foot, a look of tired resignation on his face.

She wasn't worried, even though they were going to pass a few paces in front of her. Her concentration was total and she was sure her glamour was flawless. Anyone looking her way would see the uninterrupted stone wall of the forecourt.

Then one of the hounds scented her. In Throssel Palace all the dogs had known her and ignored her, but here? *Va-damn, why didn't I think of that?*

The dog halted, raising its snout, nostrils twitching. Neck thrust forward, it turned to look straight at her. Its nose told it she was there. The other dog, incurious, still trotted obediently after its master.

Sorrel stayed still, barely breathing.

The nearer dog growled a warning, a deep rumbling. The rider didn't notice anything, but the servant called out, "Heel, Brute! Heel!"

Brute. Right. And it's not taking any notice.

It lunged at her, front paws thudding into her just below her shoulders, its weight slamming her back against the stonework. Lips drawn back in a snarl, it sniffed at her face. She was terrified. Whatever happened, she knew she must not drop her glamour. If she did, she was dead. The fellhound's lips curled back, displaying its fangs and gums so close to her chin that she could feel the animal's bad breath on her face. Her throat was less than a finger's width away from being ripped out by the yellowed teeth. Saliva dribbled down her tunic top. And if ever a dog had looked crazed, this one did.

No doubt about it, her attempt to locate Princess Bealina looked like ending in disaster almost as soon as it had begun.

Keep your glamour going. Don't let it slip. Whatever you do, don't let it slip, not for a second.

Unless her glamour was absolutely perfect when she moved, people staring so intently might notice *something* was wrong; a distortion perhaps, or a gauziness in the air.

Every head was turned her way. Faces registered incomprehension at the dog's behaviour, apparently clawing and snapping at the wall. A group of kitchen servants stared from the gateway, where they had just arrived with baskets of vegetables and a handcart laden with pig carcasses. Hands on swordhilts, the gate guards watched, alert but reluctant to leave their posts when they could identify no real cause for alarm.

The dog continued to whine and snarl. The groom grabbed its collar and tried to pull it away. Even though he was close, he was so preoccupied with the dog's odd behaviour that he still didn't see her. The horseman dismounted and stalked across, shouting angrily at the hound and cursing the servant for not controlling it.

For a moment she thought it might all subside without anyone noticing her.

It was the second dog that spoiled everything.

As the servant pulled the first one away and its master walloped it with his riding crop, the second bounded forward to see what was so exciting. It sniffed and clawed at her shoes. People watching began laughing at its antics. When the dog's nose encountered the leg of her trousers, it snapped at it and sank its teeth into the cloth. It began to pull.

Out of the corner of her eye, she saw several of the guards on the archways abandon their posts to head in her direction. Her mouth went dry.

She built herself a different glamour, making herself appear to be a larger, more ferocious hound than the one tugging at her trousers. The real hound was not fooled; it knew exactly what it had in its teeth. Her aim was to confuse the folk watching. Where there had been only one dog, they now saw two, the smaller of which was tugging at the leg of the other.

Wide-eyed and panicked, the huntsman and his servant lashed out at both animals indiscriminately, apparently unwilling to admit that a moment before there had only been one. Sorrel winced when the blows hit her arms. The real hound turned tail and fled, so she vanished her canine glamour by changing it into the wall behind her. Once she was invisible, she stepped sideways, which left her assailants even more confused. Several who had been approaching within a pace or two of her hastily backed off.

She blessed the rarity of her witchery; a cleric or shrine keeper might have thought of a glamour to explain what was happening, but not these folk. Edging slowly away along the wall, she watched the chaos of the forecourt until she thought it was safe to walk briskly towards the smaller arches. She thought she'd got away with it. No one was now guarding the door ahead. No one was following her, or even looking her way. Behind her, a hysterical servant screamed about dogs that vanished. The horse, unhappy at all the noise and babble, panicked and started to dance out of the gateway, scattering guards and visitors, barely under the control of a servant who had grabbed its reins. But a moment later, when she glanced back over her shoulder again, she saw the first dog racing across the forecourt towards her.

Smelling her fear, its muscled body was a projectile that would have had her on the ground before another breath was drawn. She threw herself down on the cobbles and rolled just as it leaped. The breath whooshed from her lungs and she lost her glamour.

Run, Perie, she thought. *Go tell them I failed . . .*

The dog missed and whipped around to leap again. And then, whirling from above, singing its flight song, a dart of greyish silver plunged into its shoulder.

The impact she'd expected never came. The animal twisted in midair and fell to the cobbles, where it mouthed at its shoulder in distress. The dagger that had brought it down dislodged and fell close to her: the kris, an arm's length away.

She built her glamour again and reached out to hide it under her hand. Glancing up, she glimpsed Ardhi peering over the roof edge, just before he ducked away. Slowly, she stood up and looked around the forecourt. It was as if time had stopped. Everyone was stilled, like run-down clockwork figures. Every head was turned her way, every gaze blank with shock, every voice silenced by bafflement. A moment before they had seen her; now there was nothing.

Right, all of you, stay like that . . .

She walked slowly away towards the door that would lead her upstairs into the castle. The centre of her back crawled with fear, as if there was a target drawn there. She waited for a ball to be fired, an arrow to be shot, a lance to be thrown.

Nothing happened.

Behind her noise burgeoned once more: screaming, barking, footsteps running, orders shouted, the clunk of the gates being shut.

Pox on't, if a knowledgeable cleric hears about this, everyone in the entire palace is going to be looking for a glamoured woman.

Out of sight of the forecourt, she pounded up the stairs as fast as she could flee.

30

Never a Queen

Peregrine knocked at the front door of Proctor House, using the rhythm that was a signal between themselves. When Horntail answered, he stumbled inside, gasping, dragging in breath as best he could.

Horntail closed the door and shot the bolts. "What happened?"

"I think . . . she's in a real bad pickle." He bent over double, gasping.

By the time he'd forced those words out, the Pontifect had arrived, grim-faced, followed by Gerelda, strapping on her sword.

"Everything went widdershins after she entered the gate," he said. "At first I couldn't see her because she was out of my line of sight, but I did hear barking and people squawking."

"Dogs," Horntail muttered. "Fob it."

"People running and flapping this way 'n' that. More barking and bawling and such. Bit later I actually saw her, still glamoured, hurrying across the forecourt, but she didn't match herself to the background very well. There was a sort of wavering in the air folk might have seen. Reckon she was going too fast. Anyway, this great big dog was after her. She fell and lost all her glamour. Folk saw."

He gulped, dragging in another breath.

"Saw Ardhi, too, I did. Don't think anyone else did though. I was looking for him, like. He was up on the roof and threw something. Reckon it was that wavy dagger of his. It hit the dog. That's when she glamoured again. I don't know what happened after that, because they closed the gate, but I think she got away."

He looked around at them all. "There'd be more dogs, I reckon," he said.

Fritillary Reedling nodded calmly. "Indeed. Time for the boat . . ."

* * *

270

She had made *such* a botch of this. No point at all in moping about it, either. *So snap out of it, you dewberry* . . .

At the top of the stairs, Sorrel emerged into a long corridor with rows of doors on either side. If all had gone as planned, she'd have had as much time as she wanted to wander about and observe. Fritillary's suggestion – that she loiter until she saw where meals for Bealina and Garred were taken after leaving the kitchen – had been a good one, but now she had to hurry.

Guards would already be scouring the palace for her. She'd been seen, and sooner or later Fox would understand they had an intruder with a glamour witchery. A moment more thought would tell them that the uninjured dog could find her again in minutes. As soon as they got themselves organised, she was in trouble.

There was no one in the passageway and all the doors were closed, making it ill-lit. She glamoured herself again, but this time she wore the robes and the face of a male cleric, an elderly man with a bit of a humpback and a cast in one eye, which was about as different from herself as she could conjure up.

She hurried on, hoping she was heading in the direction of the central tower. When she rounded a corner and saw a housemaid dawdling down the passage carrying linen, she put on her most imperious voice, deepened her tone, and said, "Lass, I'm looking for the quarters of Princess Bealina. I have been sent to give spiritual guidance, but there is such a *disgraceful* to-do downstairs and my guide was called to help deal with it. They are all concerned with some intruder, or something equally worrisome. Which way should I be heading?"

The maid's eyes widened. It was obvious she hadn't heard of the trouble downstairs. "Oh, reverend sir, I don't rightly know! But the laundry maid says she takes her clean linens to the central tower." She pointed. "That's down that way. Walk to the end, then upstairs."

She thanked the woman, dismissed her with a wave of the hand and walked on, hurrying as soon as she was out of sight. A narrow staircase led to a room where two bored guards were playing draughts using peach and apricot seeds on a board drawn in chalk on a desk. They both looked up the moment she entered.

"I've been sent to offer the princess the solace of Va and lead her in prayer. Have I come to the correct place?"

They exchanged glances and then the older man said, "We haven't heard anything about that!"

"I don't care whether you've heard about it or not! Those are my instructions. She is to be weaned away from her attachment to Shenat and I've been told to come here and talk to her about the state of her spiritual life. And I certainly don't intend to discuss the matter with mere guardsmen. Well, what are you waiting for? Give me entry to the princess!"

She flicked an arrogant hand to hurry them, and then added, "Oh, and I think one of you should go below and help the search."

"*What* search?"

"There's an intruder in the palace, some woman with a hunting dog, I believe. She overturned a cart. Or something like that," she added vaguely. "Anyway, they were asking for all guards to scour the building. One of you should let me in to see the princess before I get tired of waiting. And I think – if I were you – I'd be very careful about disobeying His Reverence's orders. He does not take kindly to that."

The older man scowled. "Go and see what all that's about, Jecho. I'll deal with this."

The younger guard unhooked his sword belt from where it hung on a wall hook and left the room as he buckled it on. The other took a key hanging on the wall and walked over to the door at the side of the room. "I will lock the door after you. When you are finished, bang on it and I will let you out."

He flung it open and indicated she was to enter. As she went to walk past him, she staggered.

"Argh! This fobbing knee of mine!" She clutched at him, wincing with make-believe pain. "Ah, help me to a chair, my man."

Taken unawares, he did what she wanted, assisting her into the room as she leaned on his arm. Without warning, she dropped her glamour and wrenched him forward so that he lost balance. Before he could react, she pivoted, bending and lunging so that she hit him with her full body weight in the midriff. As he fell forward over her back, she yanked his arm, flipping him. Behind her, someone screamed – Princess Bealina, she assumed.

The guard crashed down, falling awkwardly head first, ending up flat on his back.

Thanks, Ardhi. All that practice on board ship really worked.

She whirled to wrench the key from the lock and pull the door shut, which shoved the guard's body fully into the room. After locking the door from the inside, she turned her attention back to the man. When she knelt beside him, the kris in her hand in case she needed it, he groaned and looked at her without comprehension. His head was bleeding on to the floorboards and his eyes were glazed.

The young woman who'd been sitting at a table when she entered was now standing, white-faced, with a small boy clutched tight in her arms. "Who are you?" she asked in a high-pitched squeak.

"My name wouldn't mean anything to you, but if you're Princess Bealina, I've come to get you out of here." She took a closer look at the guard but he appeared to have passed out. She relaxed a little and sat back on her heels, to look around properly for the first time. "I rather think he's going to be out for a while, but we need something to tie him up, just in case."

"Who *are* you?"

"Pontifect Fritillary Reedling sent me."

"She's dead! Fox told me he'd killed her."

"He lied. She's here, in Vavala. I saw her this morning."

The room was more spacious than she had expected. There were windows on three sides, and a privy on the fourth. The furnishings included a canopied bed, a chest, a small table and chair. She stood up and strode over to the bed.

"Good news, Your Highness," she said, using the kris to cut the frill from the canopy curtain. "The siege of Gromwell Holdfast has been lifted. And I've come to get you out of here."

"You're curdled crazy! I'm not going anywhere with someone I don't know. There was a cleric, and then— What *happened*?"

Dear oak, she is so young! Barely out of the schoolroom. "We've got to be quick." They had so little time before their situation moved from critical to dire . . . All her fault.

Explaining the situation as she went, she crossed back to the guard and began to bind his legs, then his wrists. He didn't move. "Listen carefully. What you saw was a glamour witchery. I glamoured myself as a priest; that was how I got in here. The problem is how to get you both out of here before somebody realises."

"I'm not going anywhere until I know who you are! It – it looked like sorcery to me. No one's been granted a glamour for – for centuries!"

"Look, I can be myself, like this, or I can look like anyone. Even Prince Ryce."

She glamoured up his likeness. It was a mistake, because Prince Garred cried out, "Papa!" only to burst into tears when she banished the image.

"How *dare* you!" Bealina cried.

Oh tush. Not another princess with an overblown idea of their own importance.

"Sorry. But we have so little time." Opening one of the windows, she looked out over the roof. No sign of Ardhi. She thrust the kris outside, hoping he would sense it. He'd followed the dagger across the hemisphere once . . . "You have to escape," she said. "Otherwise Prince Ryce can't move against Valerian Fox. We were going to do it under cover of darkness tonight. This was supposed to just be a preliminary reconnoitre to find out where you were being held, and to warn you in secret, to be ready for later." She sighed. "I made a mess of it. Everyone knows I'm here, so you're going to have to leave now."

The princess's expression was one of agonised indecision. "That's clay-brained! How can I trust you?"

"Would you rather trust the man who put you in here?" This was one scenario that hadn't occurred to them: that the princess would be in such a state of fear that she would refuse to trust her rescuers. "Did Ryce ever tell you about the Lady Mathilda's handmaiden, a woman called Celandine?"

"No."

Pox on't, he wouldn't, would he, confound his princely pride. She sighed. "Then I think you are going to have to take me on trust. A friend is coming to help us in a minute. He has a witchery too – a climbing witchery."

"That's ridiculous. Who's ever heard of a climbing witchery?"

She gritted her teeth. "We have to escape out of a window, on a rope. You, me and Prince Garred. Who is an absolute darling, by the way, and he has his father's eyelashes. If you won't come with me, the consequences will be dire for Prince Ryce."

"I can't risk Garred's life to strangers with a rope!"

She had a point.

In the distance, a hound bayed. *Oh, rot it.* "Pontifect Fritillary was sure you'd trust someone with a witchery. I guess none of us thought you'd think a glamour was something a sorcerer might do."

"You don't understand! He can coerce me into doing *anything*. How can I be sure he's not coerced me into thinking up all this?" She waved a hand at her and the guard. She was one step away from hysteria.

"I don't think he could do that. He's made you think he's more powerful than he really is."

Bealina stared at her, bewildered. "I don't know what to believe . . . I've been so . . . so *alone*."

Empathy overwhelmed Sorrel. The poor woman. What Va-less hell had she and Garred had to endure? She softened her tone. "I know, I know. Maybe I can think of something that Prince Ryce knows and Fox doesn't. Um, did the prince ever tell you King Edwayn ordered him to kill the nulled witan, Saker Rampion, and Prince Ryce rode up to Chervil Moors to do it, but then deliberately let him go?"

"I don't know what you are talking about!"

"I'm here, Sorrel." It was Ardhi's voice at the window. They both turned to look as he hauled himself up on to the sill, a coil of rope over his shoulder.

"What's happening?" she asked.

"Guards are rushing around in a panic on the ground floor," he said, "and they've closed the gates. All's well, though; I saw Peregrine hightailing it up the street as soon as things went wrong."

That meant their back-up plan was about to be implemented. Relief quelled her panic, at least in part. "Have you seen Fox?"

"He's down there. They're bringing up the dogs from the kennels. I think you'd better get out on to the roof as quick as you can." He swung himself over the ledge into the room. "You go first." He was already tying one end of the rope to the solid wood frame of the double bed. "Your Highness, Horntail made a harness, and I'm going to lower you both down, one at a time. When it's your turn, you can hold on to Prince Garred yourself to keep him calm."

"*Horntail?* Horntail's with you?"

Bless you, Ardhi. Why didn't I think of Horntail?

"He's waiting for us outside the palace," Ardhi said. He sounded cheerfully confident. "With the Pontifect. The real one. Sorrel, I want your shoes and your kerchief, as well as the kris."

She didn't waste time asking why. The kerchief was the one Saker had given her so long ago, but she handed it over without a word. He held out the harness to her. She slipped it over her head and tied it firmly. They had practised this, just in case.

"It's not far," he said, "but you might spin a bit. Just concentrate on fending yourself off the wall. Use your feet. When I send Bealina down, there'll be a tail of rope below her. Grab that as soon as you can. You keep it taut, away from the wall, and that will stop her from grazing the stonework as I lower her. When you and Bealina and Garred are all at the bottom of the tower, don't wait for me. Go to the – what are those things called again?"

She guessed he meant the roofed turrets projecting out over the river from the curtain wall. "Bartizans."

"The southernmost one, as planned. I've opened the watch port and anchored the other rope. It's too short, though."

She nodded. "Right. Has anyone seen you from below yet?"

"Not that I know of."

Bealina watched him suspiciously. "You're a Pashali," she said at last, and made it sound like an accusation.

"No, I'm not," he said. "I'm what you would call a lascar."

"Would it make you happier to know that he belongs to a ruling family and has a university education that far surpasses anything you or I possess?" Sorrel asked, hauling herself up on to the window ledge.

Ardhi raised an eyebrow at her, but she didn't apologise. She was so weary of people making stupid assumptions about him. Mathilda and Ryce had both irritated her with their innate belief that their birth made them automatically better people, and it looked like Bealina might be the same.

Royalty. Pah! "I'm ready," she said. "Your Highness, I beg you, for the sake of your son and your husband, trust us."

Bealina gave her a weak smile and nodded.

Ardhi had been right. She did spin and she bumped her knee once, hard enough to give herself a bruise, but she was down on the roof in seconds. He hauled the rope up, and it wasn't long before she was steadying Bealina's descent as Ardhi paid out the rope from above. The silly woman had her eyes closed, and if Sorrel had not warned her, she would have landed with a thump.

"I thought I was going to die," Bealina said.

"Garred seems to think it was fun." Indeed, the boy was chortling. "Again!" he shouted, and they both hastened to shush him.

Ardhi loosed the rope and it dropped down from above. Bealina jumped. "How will that fellow get down?" she asked.

"His witchery," she said. "No, don't take the harness off. You are going to need it again. Come, we'll wait for Ardhi in that bartizan over there. We'll be out of sight."

"And then what?" the princess asked.

"A boat. That's why we need the rope."

"But—"

"Quick." She grabbed Bealina by the arm and hustled her across the roof. It sloped slightly downwards to the parapet walk of the curtain wall bordering the river. The door to the bartizan stood open and once inside they had a view through the wooden watch port, now propped open, while remaining concealed themselves. Back through the doorway, Sorrel saw Ardhi climbing down the outside of the central tower, using no more than his fingers and toes.

At her side, Bealina shivered. "He looks like a spider. Why doesn't he wear shoes?"

"People don't where he comes from. There is little need to, for the weather is always warm."

"How do you know that?"

"I've been there."

Bealina's eyes widened. "How brave!"

She didn't reply. Instead of joining them, Ardhi had disappeared behind the tower.

"You don't like me very much, do you?" Bealina's whisper was barely audible over the sound of wind and waves and the distant barking of dogs finding a scent.

Fiddle me witless, what's bothering her? "I don't know you, Your Highness. Forgive me if I was rude. I am scared too, because we are running out of time. Right now, I'm worried about my friend as well." She managed a smile. "Don't worry. We'll have you both safe soon."

She looked around the interior of the bartizan. Ardhi had already anchored a rope on the solid bracket of the door bar; she needed to to make it long enough to reach the water. Fortunately, sailors' knots came easy to her after her time on board ship and she began to knot her rope to his.

"This will all be over soon," she said, working at the task. "Prince Ryce is coming to Vavala with an army." She sketched in all that had happened to Gromwell and why the prince had gone to Throssel first. "So, you see, it was our job to rescue you. I'm sorry I made a mess of it and the guards and Prime Fox have been alerted."

"He will never let me go," Bealina whispered. Her face was as white as bleached linen.

"Fox? He won't have a choice in the matter. As soon as the boat appears, we go down the rope to the water. And then we take you to the Great Oak shrine. In the many months the shrines have been hidden, not one has been found by Fox's men. You can wait there in safety for the prince's army."

"The guards will find us any minute."

"That's what the rope is for. To lower you into a boat. We planned for every contingency. The boat will already be on its way, manned by loyal Shenat boatmen all arranged by Pontifect Fritillary." All the boatmen had needed was a word from Peregrine – and Ardhi had seen him leave.

"Me look!" Garred said, pointing to the lookout window.

Hounds in the distance bayed and Sorrel suppressed a shudder as she bent to pick him up, glad of the distraction.

"And you've spoken to His Highness?" Bealina persisted, frowning.

"Prince Ryce? Yes. He's been fretting about you and Garred. He adores you, doesn't he?"

Her words didn't appear to cheer Bealina. She looked sick.

Garred wriggled in Sorrel's arms as he leaned out of the window. "Water," he said.

She tightened her grip on him. "Yes. That's a river." She looked across his head to Bealina. "You'll be safe soon, and together with your husband. You'll be queen before you know it."

"I can't see a boat." Bealina's shoulders slumped. "Fox controls everyone. You can't fight him. You just can't, no matter how hard you try . . ."

"We have witcheries on our side."

"There was a time," Bealina said, so softly that Sorrel had to strain to hear, "when all I wanted to be was Ryce's queen. But sometimes dreams die, and evil men win."

"Fox hasn't won yet," Sorrel said.

Princess Bealina gave a bitter smile. "Fox saw to it that I will never be a queen."

Oh, blister it. What does she mean? She made a guess. "He's . . . hurt you? That won't make any difference to Prince Ryce. Have faith in him, in his affection for you. He spoke of his admiration for your courage during the siege, and how his men adored you. There is nothing that would ever change that, truly."

"You don't understand anything."

"Try me."

Bealina was silent.

"Ah, look – I think that's them now." A small sailboat was battling a moderate headwind towards the palace seawall. "I do believe that could be Horntail in the prow!"

The princess fixed her eyes on the boat. She began to shake. "It's a long way down," she whispered.

"It looks further than it is," Ardhi said, entering the door behind her. "I think I've confused matters a bit for those searching the palace. I barred the door to that guard room, so they won't know what happened inside and will have to spend time breaking it down. The guard is still out cold."

"My shoes?" Sorrel asked.

"I dropped them, and the kerchief, from the roof on to three different levels below to confuse the dogs. They found the first shoe almost immediately, and that diverted the search to the other side of the palace." He turned to Bealina. "This time, Princess, you go first. Sorrel is stronger and Garred is obviously fine with her holding him, so she will take him down after you. Let's get you ready for when they arrive underneath us."

Sorrel watched as he tied the rope to the harness Bealina still wore.

She would have understood fear, or panic, but the closer rescue came, the more the princess appeared subdued and miserable, rather than scared. "Don't worry. I'll take such care with Prince Garred," she said. "He's the most precious of cargoes. Ryce will be so proud of the way you have kept him safe."

The look the princess gave her was unreadable, and it worried her. Something was not right.

They both helped Bealina over the sill of the watch port the moment the boat arrived underneath. Ardhi began to pay out the rope as quickly as was safe. At least this time there was no danger of her hitting the wall; the bartizan projected far enough over the water to make that unlikely. As soon as the men in the boat caught the tail rope and began to haul her in, Sorrel stopped watching to turn her attention back to the roof, in time to see guards stepping out from a dormer window on the far side. Quickly, she closed the door.

"Guards coming," she said, putting Garred down on the floor. "At least three."

"Did they see you?"

"No."

"The moment you arrive in the boat, I'm going to throw the rope down and jump," Ardhi said, watching as the princess was helped out of the harness and seated next to the mast.

Sorrel nodded, aware they might not escape in time.

He hauled the rope up the moment the harness was free, and she put it on while he wound the other end around the bracket for the door bar to keep it taut while she climbed out through the window opening. He handed Garred to her and started to unwind the rope.

"Ardhi," she called out as she began to descend. "There are another two men running along the parapet walk!"

The rope dropped shockingly fast, and her stomach lurched in protest. Garred squealed as they spun. Eager hands grabbed them as they reached the boat.

As soon as she was safely seated, Horntail snatched the boy into his arms, laughing with joy. "I remember you, lad!" he cried.

Garred grabbed the sergeant's beard and began to prattle about whizzing round and round.

Sorrel only had eyes for Ardhi. He splashed into the water beside the boat almost immediately. "Get out of here!" he cried as one of the sailors hauled him in. "They've seen us!"

The helmsman in the stern was already pushing the tiller over for the sail to catch the wind, the boat heeled and Ardhi tumbled in over the gunwale.

"Get down!" Horntail yelled, and bent protectively over Garred. Sorrel thought he was warning them about the boom swinging over, and ducked, but at the same time there was the bang of an arquebus being fired up on the wall, followed quickly by a second.

Bealina gasped and flung herself down between the seats, Sorrel spreadeagled on top of her. There was a silence, and then more shots. The boat scudded on.

When Horntail raised his head a little later, he said, "It's all right. We're out of range now."

Sorrel pulled herself on to the seat, and bent to help Bealina up. The princess's face was ashen and she was clutching her chest.

"Did you hurt yourself?" Sorrel asked.

Bealina looked down and pulled her hand away.

Her dress was torn. Blood stained the edges of the tear.

For a moment Sorrel was uncomprehending, until she realised the first ball fired must have hit the princess. She hadn't flung herself down for safety; she had been toppled by the shot.

She looked up at Sorrel, and then leaned against her, gasping. "I feel strange." She sounded surprised.

"Let me look." Sorrel slipped an arm around her back to hold her upright, and the princess slumped against her, coughing.

"Va save!" one of the sailors said, appalled. "That's blood!"

A froth of red bubbles spattered down Bealina's dress.

Aghast, Horntail handed Garred to the sailor and scrambled over. He ripped up his own shirt to make a pad of cloth to press against the small wound in her chest, but it was obvious to them all that the real problem was internal. "We need a healer!"

"Garred needs you. Stay with us," Sorrel said into her ear.

"Va knows . . . better . . ." Bealina's words were faint. Blood dribbled from her nose. She began to cough again and this time there was much more blood. In between the spasms, she tried desperately to draw in air.

Sorrel clutched at the bambu around her neck, fumbling for another wisp of feather. Ardhi dived at her, rocking the boat, to stop her from opening it. "No," he said. "No, Sorrel. That is not what it is for."

"Saker did it for me!"

He didn't reply, but his hand tightened over hers, clamping the stopper in tighter.

"Tell . . . Ryce . . ." Bealina whispered. She closed her eyes as if she was too weak to keep them open. She dragged in more air in rasping gulps between each word as she murmured, "Love . . . always . . . but . . . better . . . this . . . way. Tell him I won. For Garred . . ."

Garred pulled away from the sailor to clutch at his mother's knee. The final movement she made was to touch a finger to his cheek – and smile.

Sorrel held her close, resting her own cheek against the princess's. Each breath wheezed into Bealina's lungs, a ghastly sound, and was expelled in a haze of blood. Each breath was further and further apart.

Somewhere before they reached the shore, life was gone.

Sorrel exchanged a look of despair and guilt with Horntail over the top of Bealina's head. His face was ashen. "I remember everything," he whispered. "Everything."

31

Rage

Bealina looked tiny in death. More girl than woman and mother. A Staravale princess who had fallen in love with the man she'd married, dreamed of becoming a queen – and died far too young. The shrine keeper, Akorna, laid her on one of the shrine-oak's great boughs, close to the trunk. In the subdued light filtering through the oak leaves, her body lacked substance, as if in death it had begun to fade away into its surroundings.

Sorrel stood by the body grieving and wretched, shaken, wishing she had done things differently, knowing that if she had fled out of the gate after the dog attacked instead of going to look for the princess, Bealina might still be alive.

My mistake killed her . . .

Ardhi came up and slipped his hand into hers. He pulled her away to where they could speak privately. "It wasn't your fault."

She buried her face in his shoulder. "If only I had–"

"Valerian Fox was to blame, the guards were his instrument – and it was just appalling bad luck that a stray ball hit her the way it did and did the damage it did. It could have been you. Or me, or Horntail, or one of the sailors."

"I thought I could use the feather to—"

"We can't save everyone, Sorrel."

"Saker saved me with one of his!"

"And the power disappeared from it for ever. You are part of the ternion; Bealina was not. Your life is key to success. But using it to save you has left us with only three pieces – and there are three sorcerers in this world who have dangerous access to power because of who they are: Valerian and Mathilda's twins. The feather pieces were granted to us to rid this world of sorcery. We have to use them where they are most effective."

She wiped away her tears with the back of her hand. He was *right*, confound it. "I don't like the idea that my life is worth more than another's . . ."

"I know." He didn't speak again until her tension dissipated and she took a deep breath and stepped away from his hold.

"What was it the princess said to you?" he asked.

She revisited the horror of the moment in the boat. "She knew she was dying. Ardhi, she was *glad*! She said it was *better*. She meant it was better to die than to live. She told me to tell Prince Ryce. It was horrible."

"What would make her say that?"

"I don't know. Maybe she was ashamed. I think Fox raped her."

He frowned. "But if so, that wasn't her fault!"

"No, but women of her class are taught to hold to their virtue as though it's their exclusive responsibility."

"Maybe she thought Prince Ryce wouldn't want her back. That he'd blame her," he suggested.

"I don't think he's like that. And I don't think she thought he was."

"No, there's more to it than that."

The remark came not from Ardhi, but from Peregrine, who had come up behind them with Gerelda and Pontifect Fritillary. "There was more than just the smutch of Fox's touch on the princess," he explained. "When I first saw her body, I knew there had been something sorcerous alive inside her."

He was blushing and it took her a moment to understand what he was too embarrassed to say. "Oh, sweet Va. Another Fox," she whispered. "She was pregnant."

None of them said anything.

"Hang me for a muckle-top. She *knew*." Sorrel hid her face in her hands. "That's what she was trying to tell me. She was terrified of giving birth to another sorcerer."

"More than that, perhaps," Fritillary said. "If she had another boy, Fox could have passed him off as Ryce's, killed Bealina and Garred and put his own son on the throne as the supposedly legitimate king."

Sorrel shuddered. "Oh, Va, that man is so vile."

"Why don't we shoot him?" Gerelda asked.

"It has been tried," Fritillary replied. "And it doesn't work."

"Why not?" Peregrine asked.

"The would-be assassins killed themselves instead of him."

"He coerced them from a distance?" Gerelda asked.

"None came back to tell us how he did it, but it is certain that he has built his power to a level that we really know nothing about. Fortunately, he doesn't use it much because of the cost to him."

"But if he's in extreme danger from us," Gerelda said, her tone dry, "he wouldn't count the cost then."

Sorrel walked away. On the other side of the oak, she stood and laid her forehead against the bark of the trunk, but there was no respite there. Her thoughts circled the same path: *What if I had . . .? Or maybe if I'd . . .?*

It was Fritillary who found her and laid a hand on her shoulder, saying, "We pay a terrible price for the gift of life: pain, grief, death and mortality."

"Then is there any point to all this?"

"Of course there is. Life itself! Have faith in Va, my dear. We make a mistake when we expect Va to intervene in our lives. Belief gives us hope and strength. Witcheries give us help. The Way of the Oak and the Way of the Flow bring us peace and tranquillity and a glimpse of our eternity as part of creation. Expecting anything else is arrogance. In our arrogance, we pray for help, when what we should be doing is working on our moral strength to live good lives. Believe that, and you'll be happier and your life will have more meaning. Perhaps Bealina knew that. She died a warrior and a hero, knowing she was offering Fox a defeat of considerable measure. If she had ever given birth to a son of his, she would not only have brought another sorcerer into the world, she would have condemned Garred to death, and she knew it."

"She was so young."

"Perhaps she was also wise beyond her years."

"What will happen to Garred now?"

"I will take him to his father through the timeless paths. I will tell Prince Ryce her last words."

"I could take Garred and tell him myself." *And I would see Piper . . .*

"You are needed here still, whereas my presence is required in Throssel now. The Ardronese need to know I am alive."

The words shredded Sorrel's surge of hope.

"Garred clings to Horntail," Fritillary added, "so I think it best that the sergeant comes with me. He has regained his memory, you know. In the meantime, I'll send a nun who knows the timeless paths to take a letter to Ryce. He said he'd pick up messages at the Seaforths' home in Throssel."

Fifteen days after leaving Twite, *Golden Petrel* anchored in Throssel Water, a short row from the coast, just after dusk. Over the next hour, the ship's boats ferried men quietly to land, where they began the ten-mile walk to Throssel city. Among those who left the ship were Prince Ryce and all his men, Lord Juster and half his crew, and Saker.

By dawn, separated into different bands, they had all reached the city's walls, where they mixed in with the crowds entering through the five gates. Ryce's men, dressed as sailors and with strict orders not to catch the eye of any of the town guard who might recognise them, joined the jostle of fringe dwellers, day labourers and hustlers surging into the city alongside the farm carts bringing produce to market. Throssel was a busy port, and sailors were no uncommon sight.

Saker and Grig Cranald travelled together, and once inside the city the two of them headed for the Barklee house. As they approached the docklands, an uncomfortable tightness developed in Saker's chest. The closer he was to finding out how Piper had fared, the worse it grew.

He need not have worried. As soon as she heard his voice greeting Surgeon Barklee at the door, she hurtled out of the kitchen and raced into his arms. She snuggled there as if he had never been away, so loving and so totally forgiving of his desertion it was hard to believe she had a drop of sorcerer's blood. The tenaciousness of her clutch, though, did indicate she would be reluctant to have him disappear again.

He looked over her head to where Barklee and his wife watched. "Thank you for taking such good care of her, both of you."

"She was no trouble," Mistress Barklee said with a tender smile. "A little charmer, she is. Just smiles and my boys do anything for her.

She'd be welcome to stay for ever. I'll miss her when she goes, for sure."

"I'm afraid we will be leaving Throssel soon," Grig said. "I'm sorry we have to take your husband away again. And Banstel too." He grinned at the ship's boy, who had followed Piper from the kitchen. "That is if the lad still hankers after the sea."

"Aye, sir!" Banstel said.

Mistress Barklee tousled his hair. "He's mad keen on being a privateer, this lad. Barklee is another, chafing for a deck beneath his feet! That's sailors for you."

Saker looked down at Piper and touched the Chenderawasi circlet she wore. "Did you remember not to take it off, sweetheart?"

She nodded, her curls bobbing in her enthusiasm. "Papa not go away again? Never, ever, ever?"

"Not Papa, dearest," Mistress Barklee said, and blushed. "I'm sorry. She's been hearing the children talk to Barklee, and so she started calling him Papa too. Then of course, the bairns told her he wasn't her papa, so she decided *you* were."

"You my papa!" Piper cried.

He smiled at her. "Oh, not exactly. In fact, you're a lucky girl. You have lots of papas. Lord Juster and Ardhi and Mate Finch and Mate Cranald and—"

"And you?"

"And me too."

"I want Mama. Where's Mama Sorrel?"

"You'll be with her soon, sweetheart. And she won't go away again, I promise." *Va forbid.*

"Time to go," Grig Cranald said. "We've business in the city. Barklee, Banstel, you're wanted too."

Five minutes later they were on their way to the Seaforths' townhouse on the other side of Throssel, where everyone was to reassemble.

Originally, Saker had wanted to leave Piper with Mistress Barklee, thinking she would be safer there, but Ryce had insisted that she be brought to Seaforth's residence. "Saker, if we fail," he'd explained, "Barklee's house won't be a safe place for her."

That was a disputable excuse if ever he'd heard one, but Ryce had made it an order.

Saker chatted with Piper as they walked through the city, but he was preoccupied, his thoughts churning. Pox on't, what was that canker of a prince up to? He'd always thought Ryce needed to assert himself more and take charge – but now that the man was showing leadership, well, his intentions were worrying.

When they arrived, Ryce requested his immediate presence, so he left Piper with Barklee and was conducted by a servant to the library, an impressive room lined from floor to ceiling with shelves of leather-bound books. When he entered, he found the prince leaning against the mantel of the fireplace, talking to Juster. Both of them had evidently been fitted out with clothes from the Seaforth family's wardrobe, because they looked immaculate in outfits that had seen neither a siege nor a sea voyage. In fact, Saker thought they'd both not only had the benefit of a bath, but had received the attentions of a barber as well, rot the two of them.

"You wished to see me, Your Highness?" he asked.

"Yes, indeed. Brandy? Seaforth's cousin keeps a splendid cellar."

"No, thank you." Unless he had sadly misjudged, this was a meeting better attended cold sober.

"I've decided on the best way to get into the palace with my men," Ryce said, "without killing too many people. I want to dress Piper up as Prince Garred, and tell the guards on the gate that I am surrendering my son into the king's care, thereby relinquishing my own claim to the throne, as he has requested."

He gaped at the prince, his rage rising.

Juster had the grace to look abashed but Ryce was unfazed. "Juster has not long informed me that she is my niece, rescued by you and Sorrel from all that Lowmian codswallop about twins and devil-kin. For which I am very grateful. I was seeking a way to enter the palace without a fight, and this appears to be our only chance to have the guards open the gates for me and a group of armed men. Edwayn declared Garred his heir, and the heir to the throne is granted a company of forty guards."

You bastard, Juster. "You would risk her *life*?"

"If there is a fight, I risk my own, and those of my men. However, everybody knows that the king has ordered me to deliver Prince Garred to him. If I arrive at the gate with a child in my arms, I think there is a good chance he will grant me entry. In fact, there's a chance I could persuade the guards on the gate to open it without even consulting the king."

He stared at Ryce, aghast. "May I point out that Piper is a year older than Prince Garred. She's also a girl, and surely the palace guards are familiar with Prince Garred's visage!"

"Piper is small for her age, and Garred is large," Ryce said calmly. "Their colouring is not dissimilar. They are cousins, after all. Moreover, it is over a year since anyone here saw Garred, and growing children of his age alter rapidly. And who's going to look in the pantaloons to see if the child is a boy when I tell them it's my son?"

He tried to subdue his fury. "What if the king has already heard that Prince Garred was taken to Vavala?"

"Oh, he has heard. Fortunately Seaforth's brother is still welcome at court in spite of his connection to me, and he knows what happened. Edwayn sent an outraged letter to Fox, who denied the rumour and said Bealina and Garred are still in Gromwell with me. The king believed that denial. He has not yet heard that the siege has been lifted — we are about to inform him."

The idea of Piper being used with such casual disregard for her safety was an abomination. He swallowed back his bile. "Your Highness, what will happen to Piper if your plan fails?"

"What do you think will happen to any of us, Saker? We die."

"Piper is a child, and she doesn't have a choice. And as you've said, she is a legitimate royal princess of the Vollendorn line." It wasn't often he uttered such outright lies to a friend, but he didn't care. Piper *mattered*.

"We are all in Va's hands, isn't that what you clerics tell us? May I remind you, Saker, that you do not have any say whatsoever in Piper's well-being. She is evidently my niece. In the absence of her mother, and given King Edwayn's madness, I am her nearest relative. I am also your liege lord, I believe, seeing that you have arraigned yourself at my side rather than my father's. She goes with us tomorrow to the palace."

In desperation, Saker shot a glance at Juster, but he appeared to be studying his newly manicured nails and would not meet his eye.

Nor had the prince finished. "You will stay here tonight. Neither you nor Lord Juster will accompany us to the palace tomorrow. You are both too well known as traitors."

He had to put his hands behind his back, else he might have been tempted to swipe a fist at the prince's jaw. "Who will take care of Piper?"

Juster spoke then. "Surgeon Barklee. He's not known at the palace, and Piper adores him."

Ryce gave a curt nod of acquiescence. "I am sure Piper will be quite safe, Saker. None of us will put her in any unnecessary danger. As soon as we are inside the walls, Barklee can take her somewhere safe. For all the king's madness, his guards are sane enough, and not in the habit of harming tots any more than I am of not caring for the welfare of my blood relatives."

Not trusting himself to speak, Saker inclined his head.

"As early as possible," the prince continued, "you and your eagle will tell me all you can about the positioning and number of guards within and outside the palace walls. The more we know beforehand, the safer everyone will be."

"Yes, Your Highness."

"Perhaps I could send Grig Cranald with Barklee," Juster suggested. "To keep an eye on Piper's safety. He's not known to any of the palace guard any more than Barklee is, and he's a good man in a tight spot."

"Very well, if it makes you happier." With that, Ryce drained the last of his brandy, and left the room.

Juster eyed Saker warily.

He said, keeping a fragile hold on his rage, "Leak on you, Juster, what did you have to tell him for? It was Regala Mathilda's secret, for her to divulge if she wanted, not our prerogative to do so."

"I thought it would *stop* him from wanting to use Piper! He was going to do it anyway. I felt sure if I told him she was his niece, he'd think twice about it." He held his arms up, palms outwards, in a gesture of surrender. "I was wrong. I am sorry." He looked towards the door, and the expression on his face was one of reluctant admiration. "Va knows whatever happened to the Ryce we used to know, because fiddle-me-witless, the man has become a king while we've been away!"

"If that's how kings behave, then damn them all to beggary!"

290

"Whoa, my friend! Be careful who you say that to, or your head will be on the chopping block." He clasped Saker's shoulder with a firm hand. "You aren't a lackwit. You know that in order to rule, a monarch has to have a heart as cold as steel. Ryce would have been a terrible king when he was eighteen. Now maybe he's a monarch strong enough to make good decisions, even when it means someone gets hurt."

"The theory sounds fine. But when it involves his own niece, who's not quite three—!"

Juster released his hold and turned to the side table in order to splash a measure of brandy into a glass. "Here, drink this and pray that Ryce succeeds tomorrow, because if he doesn't, we'll all be running for the border."

32

Long Live the King

A flick of flight feathers, a tilt of the tail to change direction to pass over the Throssel Palace walls, a counting of guards, an assessment of how relaxed they were . . . The sensual feel of wind through feathers, the joy of flight, the shimmering vibrance of colours and their subtle gradation, the wide panorama of his field of vision.

That glorious world of flight, where he was always in danger of losing himself and his humanity.

Saker concentrated on the scene below. That rabble supposedly guarding the southern wall were playing dice behind the grapevines and there was even one fellow pursuing a housemaid across the pump yard, the lout. Horntail would have made short work of those layabouts.

Juster was right. If a king was weak and ill and almost blind, then good government crumbled. Ryce would have a tough task bringing Ardrone back to its former glory.

Idly Saker wondered whom the prince would rely on. He'd need a chancellor who could knock the civil servants into shape, a treasurer with a sharp eye for theft and waste and corruption, a Prime who could take on the mess Fox had left behind, a guard captain to bring the armed men up to a decent standard with a military command thinking in terms of guns and cannon rather than swords and crossbows. It was ridiculous that ships used gunpowder and yet most armsmen on land did not.

He was grateful that Ryce's talk of Saker being his Prime was only a joke. The idea of having to deal with the horror of Fox's chapel clerics and their hatred of Shenat . . . If he hadn't been flying with the bird, he would have shuddered at the thought.

One last look to make sure he had all the information Ryce wanted and he closed his twinning connection to the sea eagle. When he opened his eyes, he was back in his body, lying on the divan in the library, where Barklee was keeping an eye on both him and Piper.

When the three of them rejoined Ryce, it was to find a crowded room. All the men who were to lead the foray into the palace were there: Juster and Grig, Sir Beargold and Lord Seaforth and members of their extended families, most of whom Saker knew at least by sight. He also spotted the king's chief physician, Emerling. For a moment he puzzled over that, until he realised that if Ryce could persuade Emerling to say Edwayn was incompetent to rule, he would have a way of legitimately deposing his father.

Edwayn's hatred of witchery healers, stemming from the death of his queen, meant that he never allowed them into the palace. Emerling was just a physician. Sadly, there had been no witchery healer to give a warning of, let alone treat, the king's madness. Saker suspected that the hope of any cure was long gone.

"Ah," the prince said on catching sight of Saker, "you have information for us?"

"Indeed, sire," he said and told them all he'd seen through the eagle's eyes.

With a grim smile, Ryce turned to the listeners, saying, "Are you ready?"

A rousing acclamation of assent rose from those in the room, with a number of the younger nobles drawing their swords and waving them in the air.

"Then let us go and reclaim a throne!"

Under cover of the enthusiasm, Saker murmured in Barklee's ear that he hoped Prince Ryce was not overconfident.

"Whatever happens, I'll make sure Piper's safe," Barklee promised.

"Let's go," the prince said, but as he turned towards the door of the room, one of the liveried servants entered, carrying a sealed letter and a letter opener on a salver.

"Is that for me?" Lord Seaforth asked.

"For the prince, my lord," the servant replied, and approached Ryce.

Frowning, Ryce took the letter and slit it open. It was a single sheet, and whatever news it contained, it was sufficient to turn his face a sickly colour. He read the contents twice. The room fell silent, everyone staring, rooted to the spot. For Saker, it was an age before Ryce crumpled the paper in his hand and looked up – at him.

"Your wretched friends! They've killed my Bealina with their fucking boneheaded incompetence!"

The letter dropped from his shaking hand. He looked around the room. "My queen is dead, killed in a dastardly attack by Valerian Fox's men. Prince Garred is unharmed and on his way back to Throssel." His voice had wavered, but he threw back his shoulders as he added, "Today we fight for this land so that never again will it fall into the hands of sorcerers! Today we start the battle by wresting rule from the hands of a mad king who does a sorcerer's bidding. My father has long been as good as dead, and today we avenge him and release him from the Va-less hell of sorcery. Are you with me?"

This time, the foot-stamping ovation clinked the porcelain on the glass shelves of the display cabinets.

As Prince Ryce's party left the house a little later, Piper, dressed as a boy, cheerfully told everybody she was a prince and she was going to sit on a throne and have lots of pet dogs. She hugged Saker and waved to him as Barklee carried her away. In his own farewell, Juster threw an arm around Grig Cranald's shoulders and said something in his ear, which prompted Grig to smile at him with an eloquent look of tenderness.

When they'd all left, the crumpled letter still lay on the floor where Ryce had dropped it. Saker picked it up, recognised Fritillary's hand and shamelessly skimmed the contents. The account of Bealina's death was stark. Heartbreaking. But all he felt was relief that Fritillary made it clear that it was Ardhi and Sorrel who had brought Prince Garred to safety.

They were still alive.

"Pickle all princes," he said to Juster. "If anything happens to Piper—"

"Grig's there to take care of her. But who will take care of him when I'm not there?" Juster sighed and poured them both a generous glass of the Seaforth brandy. "Drink up," he said. "We both need something to allay our fears."

"I thought you preferred to remain heart-whole," he remarked and sipped the brandy.

Juster sighed. "That was my intention. Never thought someone would come along to upend my profligate life. Dammit, Saker, loving someone is worse than sailing a ship with a hull covered in barnacles. You can't scrape love off and sail away. It's a joy, yet it ties you in knots of fear. Poor Ryce." He drank more of the brandy, then swirled the glass, watching the liquid spin. "And you know what? There is nothing I hate more than sitting around, worrying about other people. The . . . *waiting*."

"I know. It gets you every time."

"You've lost Sorrel, haven't you?"

"She was never mine to lose."

"More fool you."

He shrugged. "There was a moment when we could have gone down a different pathway, but it never happened. Not sure why. Maybe because she once watched me make a fool of myself over the Lady Mathilda?"

"That was exceedingly stupid. Was *that* what was behind your nullification?"

"It was the excuse. Anyway, Sorrel has become the sister I never had, and I can't imagine it any other way now."

Juster drained his glass and reached for the brandy. "Come, have a drink with me."

I'll always have the ternion. Always. What he wasn't sure about was whether he'd always have Piper. "No, thank you. I'll twin with the eagle to see what's going on in a minute, and I need to be sober for that."

"A drunken eagle would certainly be something to behold . . ."

"And I'd rather you kept sober enough to watch over my body, if you don't mind."

Juster sighed again and put down his glass.

Ryce approached the main gate at the head of his men. He attempted to look like a broken man, but he wasn't sure he succeeded. Inside he was churning with a passion he could hardly contain.

This is for you, Bealina. You and Garred.

Bealina. Before she left Gromwell, she'd become so thin, so pale, and yet she'd always been cheerful, so certain they would win. It had broken his heart to see her struggling with the lack of amenities, never complaining, always greeting him with a smile, always loving and passionate, even when she was hungry and tired and frightened, and anxious about Garred.

You did that to her, Father. You did that to your grandson. You could have had the siege lifted any time. Oh, Fritillary could blame Fox, if she liked, but it was Edwyn's distrust of Shenat that made the kingdom vulnerable in the first place. The king had deliberately sought out a Prime who wanted to rid the nation of Shenat clerics. He'd chosen Fox before he'd even met him.

Ryce glanced behind to see Barklee, dressed in borrowed clothes so as to resemble a nobleman rather than a ship's surgeon, carrying Piper. She was wearing a velvet suit with lace trimming which delighted her, and she waved at him happily.

There were two men on duty outside the closed gates of the palace, both armed with pikes. They stepped forward and called the group to a halt.

Keeping his shoulders slumped, his gaze indirect and his expression abashed even as he seethed inside, he approached the foremost guard.

"Your Highness," the man said, at a loss.

"Open the gate, guardsman. I bring my son, Prince Garred, to the king, as requested. Gromwell has fallen."

The two men exchanged glances. "I'll speak to the captain of the guard," one of them said.

"By all means," Ryce said. "I'll come with you."

The guard hesitated.

"Come now, man. You can hardly expect me to wait out in the street like a tradesman!"

The guard banged at the wicket set into the main gate, and it opened from the inside.

"Wait here," Ryce said to Seaforth, the words only for show, as Seaforth had been instructed to do no such thing. Ryce waved the guard inside and the man, flustered, preceded him. As they had planned, Sir Beargold entered on his heels then halted in the doorway, so that the wicket could not be closed behind him.

The guard dithered, not knowing what to do.

"Well, go on, man," Ryce said, "get the captain, quickly now. Is that still Captain Rollin?"

The man gave a nod, remembered whom he was addressing, and stuttered, "Yes, Your Highness." He scurried away across the forecourt between the gateway and the palace buildings, heading towards the main guardhouse. The four guards on duty inside the gatehouse looked from Ryce to one another in consternation as one by one his men began to file in through the wicket.

"Your Highness," said the one in charge, "we have no instructions from the king—"

"Of course you have! The king has ordered my return and I am here. These men are Prince Garred's bodyguard. As you know, the heir apparent is entitled to a company of forty men . . ."

While he was speaking, the men who had entered behind him flung open the main gate, to allow a flood of soldiers inside. Some of them greeted the guards by name and clapped them on the back as old friends. As more and more men entered, they milled around, blocking the view of the guards. Ten of his men stole away, one at a time, their destination the postern gate. If all went well, they would soon be opening that gate to the bulk of his men already gathering in the street outside.

Captain Rollin came running up, still shrugging himself into his coat. Ryce greeted him effusively, spilling the same nonsense about why he was there. He rested a friendly hand on the man's shoulder. "Don't worry, Rollin, the matter between my father and me will be settled today, without further argument. And right now I will take my son up to see his grandfather. Come, Beargold, let us leave the good captain and Lord Seaforth to sort things out here."

With that he simply turned his back on the guards and started walking towards the main building with Beargold, chatting as if they were perfectly at ease. Barklee walked a pace or two behind, beside Grig Cranald. Piper was sulking because Barklee wouldn't let her walk by herself. Inside, Ryce was a mixture of nervous tension and sheer, blinding rage. How dare his father put him in this position in the first place! With a little luck, Rollin was already confronted by an irreversible situation: forty men inside the palace grounds, without anyone offering any physical resistance to their presence.

As they walked, every nerve was screaming at him either to hurry or to look around to see what was happening behind. He did neither. Just before he stepped into the palace building he looked up. There was an eagle circling above.

Saker, watching over Piper.

The king's solar was always guarded, but after explaining to the two men on duty that they were there to deliver Prince Garred, they were ushered into the reception room.

While one of the sentries fetched the king's chamberlain, Conrid Masterton, Ryce murmured in explanation to Grig, "That's Prelate Masterton. Can't make up his mind whether he's a cleric or a king's man. I wouldn't mind at all if he wasn't alive at the end of this day." He turned to the remaining guard, asking, "Where's the king?"

"I don't know, Your Highness."

Ryce looked at Grig and Barklee. "Let's find out, shall we?"

He opened the door to the audience room and marched inside. The others followed, with the guard attempting – respectfully – to insist they wait for the chamberlain, but quite unable to decide just how to achieve that when they all ignored him. Ryce almost laughed at the man's predicament.

The room was empty so he just continued on into the king's private apartments through the door on the other side. In the king's sitting room, a footman was winding up the ornate clock on the glassware cabinet. His eyes widened when he recognised the prince.

"Where's the king?" Ryce rapped out the question in a tone that brooked no evasions.

"Y-your Highness. Ah – dining room?"

Ryce strode on and flung open the dining room door. King Edwayn was seated at the table with a spread of dishes in front of him. He did not appear to have eaten much. He was huddled into his chair, more frail and ill than when Ryce had seen him last. He could almost feel a twinge of pity. Almost.

The guard who had gone looking for Masterton was just inside the door. Masterton was standing at the king's side, speaking urgently into his ear. He straightened and fixed a smile on his face when he saw Ryce and his party.

Ryce ignored him and turned to the guard. "Out," he snapped.

The guard did not need telling a second time.

"That includes you, Masterton."

"Your Highness, the king is not well. He needs—"

"Whatever he needs, it is not you. Now get out, or my man here –" he indicated Grig "– will skewer you for me."

Masterton looked at the king.

Edwayn glared at his son. "I've no secrets from Conrid," he said in a thin waver. His one good eye dripped liquid down his cheek.

"Then you most certainly should have!"

Masterton intervened, saying smoothly, "And you should have more manners. Anyway, who are these two . . . persons . . . with you, that you should want them to be privy to a conversation with your monarch?" He frowned at Barklee, with Piper in his arms, and Grig, who had been following hard on his heels.

"They are my son's physician and his bodyguard. However, now that you have seen that I have brought Prince Garred to you, perhaps we can dispense with their presence." He waved a hand to indicate that Barklee and Grig should leave the room. Both moved to comply. "I suppose if you *really* wish to stay, Masterton, I am not averse. You won't like what you hear, though." He laid a hand on his swordhilt in a more bellicose invitation to leave.

Grig indicated the open door they had used to enter the room and raised an eyebrow at Masterton, who took the hint and hurried after Barklee. Piper chose that moment to struggle in the surgeon's arms, dislodging her hat.

"Down! Me want down!"

Masterton grabbed hold of Barklee, wrenching him to a halt. "This isn't Prince Garred!" He stared at the child. "What piece of chicanery is this? Who's this brat that you want to fob on to the kingdom?"

Ryce nodded to Grig, the merest of movements. Grig didn't need a second invitation. His sword whispered out of its sheath. There was no room to manoeuvre in the doorway, so he sliced the edge of the blade across the side of Masterton's neck. It wasn't the best of strokes, but there was enough power behind it to send the man sprawling to the floor, blood spurting in a shower. Traumatised, Piper started screaming. Another thrust from Grig and Prelate Conrid Masterton was dead.

Piper shrilled even louder. Ryce grabbed Barklee and pointed at a door across the dining room. "Servants' passage," he said, and Barklee fled towards it with the child, clutching her tight and burying her face into his chest so she couldn't see the horror behind them. The king, trying to lever himself up from the dining chair, shouted at him as he ran past, but he took no notice.

Grig moved the other way, back into the sitting room.

The two guards leaped at him, drawing their swords as they came. Grig pushed a chair in the way and when the first man stumbled over it, Ryce deftly flipped that man's sword out of his grip. Confident that Grig would manage the other guard, he was about to turn back to deal with his father when another seven or eight guards burst into the sitting room.

Ryce opened his mouth to call Grig back into the dining room when there was a flash, a retort and a puff of smoke. One of the newcomers had fired a pistol. For a moment Ryce thought the ball had missed, then he saw: a ragged hole in Grig's shirt, blood blossoming over his chest.

Grig looked down at himself, in disbelief. He fell slowly, his sword dropping first, his body languidly slumping as his knees folded and he bent over at the waist. Ryce knew a dead man when he saw one. He leaped back into the dining room and slammed the door shut behind him. About to grab a chair to shove under the handle, he noticed bolts had been put on the door. He shot them across, top and bottom, guessing they were a result of Juster's incursion into the palace with Sorrel.

He turned to face his father.

The king cowered back in his seat at the table. His face was ashen.

They stared at each other in silence. His first thought was that there wasn't much left of the man. His back was humped and his flesh loosely draped over a bony frame; his eyes were faded things without a spark of vitality.

"If that wasn't your son, why are you here?" Edwayn asked at last.

Sheathing his sword, he crossed to face his father from the other side of the table, knuckling the polished board as he thrust himself forward in confrontation. "Prince Garred was taken by Valerian Fox with his mother. That sorcerous Prime of yours never had any intention of returning my son to you or anyone else. He has foully murdered Bealina! Murdered the mother of my son! What you have done is unforgivable."

The king's expression didn't change, although he seemed to shrink still more. He was just a sick old man, with nothing to offer anyone. "I'm your liege lord," he said, the words a quavering mockery of what he had once been.

Ryce felt nothing. The father of his childhood was a tarnished memory, and this once-king had brought the land to its knees. Perhaps he'd never had a choice after he'd brought Valerian Fox into his household. Perhaps Fox had coerced him right from the beginning, or perhaps he hadn't needed to, but none of that mattered now, and Ryce could not bring himself to care.

He pulled the wheel-lock pistol from his belt, where it had been hidden by the fullness of the skirt of his frock coat. It was primed and loaded. All he had to do was cock it and fire.

Edwayn mumbled, "I never thought you had it in you."

"You were wrong."

He shot his father through the heart.

An hour after Edwayn's death, Saker's mind tumbled back into his body. He was sweating and his hands were clenched. Far above, he could still feel the eagle, crying its triumph at having rid itself of its human burden.

Not so easy to escape, is it? You poor thing.

He moved his head to the side carefully, as his dizziness and disorientation dissipated.

Juster was sitting beside him. "You're back?"

He began to nod, changed his mind and sat up. Wordless.

"What happened?" Juster asked.

"It's over. They won. The king is dead."

"How do you know?"

"I flew down to the palace grounds after it was all over. Barklee spoke to me. Well, to the bird. Ryce shot Edwayn and killed Masterton.

All the courtiers are now polishing Ryce's boots. Most of the guards are delighted, and those who weren't are either dead or keeping their noses clean."

"Yet you're upset. What went wrong? Is it Piper?" He gripped Saker's arms as if to shake him.

"She was in the middle of it, but she's not hurt."

"Then it's Grig."

"Yes."

It took him several attempts to say it. In the end, he blurted, "Oh, blister it, I'm sorry, Juster. They shot him at close range. Ryce said he was dead before he hit the floor."

Juster sat motionless, staring at him. Then he shook his head, trying to deny the truth.

Saker opened his mouth to express sorrow, condolence, but Juster held up his hand to halt any further words. "There will never be anything you could say that would help. Don't try."

Grig Cranald wasn't the only death. Several of Prince Ryce's men who had gone to open the postern gate died in a skirmish there. Taken overall, though, it was a surprisingly bloodless victory. Fox had never ensorcelled the guards; there had been no reason to do so, and Saker assumed it would have sapped too much of his strength. As they were loyal to the king, all Fox had to do was to keep Edwayn under his thumb, and everyone else followed.

Most of the king's men knew and liked Prince Ryce. They'd once shared barracks with his men, so they were loath to fight them and proved reluctant to die in the service of a king known to have been losing his mind, especially when there was a young and handsome prince appealing to them to follow him instead. Still, Saker thought, it didn't feel like a victory when one of the men who'd died had been a friend. He and Grig had shared so much since they'd first met in Karradar on *Golden Petrel*, including bunking down in the same officers' cabin when Grig wasn't sharing Juster's bed.

As he watched Prince Ryce organise the palace in the days that followed, he found it hard to reconcile this prince – no, this *king* – with the man he had known before. Ryce had hardened. He cared little about his murder of his father and wasted no time in introspection. Instead, he threw himself into the administration of his kingdom, or rather, he organised others to do it for him.

The mark of a good administrator, I suppose. Who would have thought?

Somewhere along the line, presumably in the microcosm of Gromwell Keep and its manor lands, Ryce had learned.

Lord Seaforth, heading the Privy Council, was organising the Ardronese nobility's support for the new king. "It's not so hard to be the *head* of the Council," he confided to Saker. "All I have to do is ask the king what he wants, then choose the right people to do it, and then get them to do the work."

"And how do you know you have the right people?" he asked, curious.

"Oh, they are the ones who are happy to give advice, but who don't question the king's decisions."

Right. He had a point.

Beargold was appointed Lord Lieutenant and given the task of organising all matters to do with the military, the King's Company and the King's Guard. Some orders he issued were brutal. Grey Lancers were to be exterminated on sight. The Fox estates were to be confiscated, all of Valerian's children executed and all their assets seized.

Lord Juster was appointed the Minister for Trade and Navy, a task he reluctantly accepted for a limited time. As Prince Ryce's previous adviser on naval matters, he was already cognisant of much that needed to be done. "At least I can put the proper procedures and plans into place," he told Saker. "But I'm a sailor and I will *not* spend the rest of my life on land."

The new king's instructions to Saker, given on the day of Edwayn's death, were to proceed immediately to Faith House with a company of Ryce's men, to make sure no one removed any documents, or anything else. He was to take over Fox's living quarters there, as well as his office.

"Your first job," Ryce continued, "is to root out all the clerics who supported Fox because they did not like Shenat ways. Any such clerics are to be defrocked and their personal assets investigated to see if they were illegally obtained. You always wanted an emphasis on our Shenat roots; you've got it now."

"I'll do what I can until we leave for Vavala. But I'm not your Prime, you know."

"We'll see about that later. Just get to Faith House before Fox's priests destroy evidence, or steal the silver."

"Gladly," he said. "I'll take Barklee and his family with me. They can look after Piper until she's reunited with Sorrel."

Ryce stared at him in genuine surprise. "What do you mean? She's a princess and it is not appropriate for her to be in the care of a surgeon and an unmarried cleric. She'll stay here in the palace where she belongs."

"Your Majesty – Ryce – she's been under Sorrel's care since the day she was born. She has *thrived* in our care."

"Pickle it, Saker, she's my niece! Of course she will stay here in the palace with me. I will employ suitable staff for her. A gentlewoman of noble family—"

No. Think. You've got to find a way to keep Piper with us.

"Your Highness, ah – sorry, Your Majesty, you cannot acknowledge your relationship to Piper until you consult Regala Mathilda. If Piper lives at court, folk might notice the resemblance between her and Prince Garred. Or between her and the Lady Mathilda when she was a little girl. That may result in embarrassment to the Regala. She is in a difficult position as it is: an Ardronese princess acting as Regent to her Lowmian son. I'm not sure she would ever be in a position to admit that she concealed the birth of twins. It could even call into question the legitimacy of Prince-regal Karel's birth."

Ryce thought about that, and finally nodded. "I suppose you're right. But make no mistake: Piper is royal and should be brought up as such. Select a nun of a high-born family to give respectability to her nursery in Faith House. When things are more settled I'll send a letter to Mathilda about it. In the meantime, take her to Faith House, but bear in mind that it is not in your interest to become too fond of her."

His heart sank. *It's far too late for that. Cankers and galls, what will Sorrel say if I don't bring Piper back to her?*

"When are we leaving for Vavala?" he asked, changing the subject.

Ryce sighed. "I thought we could leave immediately Edwayn was dead, but it's not so easy. People are begging for our guards to deal with the remnants of Grey Lancers here, in Ardrone. I thought—" He was interrupted by a knock at the door. "I asked not to be disturbed. See who that is and tell them to go away."

Saker opened the door, where a flustered guard was flanked by Fritillary, who looked exhausted, and Sergeant Horntail carrying a small boy.

Oh, oak and acorn, he thought. *That's got to be Prince Garred.* The boy struggled free of Horntail's arms and ran across to his father, calling, "Papa, Papa!"

"Your Majesty . . ." Fritillary's tone said it all.

Saker could only watch while Ryce fell apart in a heartrending mixture of joy and raw, rekindled grief, while Sergeant Horntail prostrated himself before his new king in abject despair.

33

Lives Upended

That night, Saker, Fritillary, Piper, Banstel and the whole Barklee family slept in Faith House. There were no clerics in residence, but the ordinary lay servants had remained. Fritillary insisted on questioning them closely, using her witchery.

"No problem with any of them," she told Saker as they sat alone in the dining room of Fox's private quarters, chatting over the remains of their meal after the others had gone to bed. "They're all glad to be rid of Valerian Fox."

He gave her an exasperated look. "They are not my servants. I'm not going to be living here. This is just temporary."

She snorted. "We'll see."

"Now that we're alone, tell me the details of what happened to Princess Bealina."

"Not a happy tale," she admitted. "Sorrel blames herself for Bealina's death. Pointless guilt, really. In fact, had she lived, I think Bealina might have killed herself anyway."

He listened, appalled, as she detailed the circumstances. "That's horrible," he said. *I hate that man more than I have ever hated . . .*

"Her death is a great loss to Ardrone and to Ryce. But the baby? Its unborn state can only be a good thing."

"I hope you don't think we should kill Piper and Prince-regal Karel, simply because they are Fox's children?"

To his horror, she paused before answering. "I don't know, Saker. When they are adults, will they agree to wear those circlets? Can we be sure that those things will even work?"

He wanted to protest, but the words stuck in his throat. No one could be sure.

She said gently, "I do know there have been far too many deaths of children in this whole sorry business."

"I try not to remember. It bites too deep."

"This has been hard on all of us."

"You're looking more than just tired. Are you all right?" he asked.

"Oh, that's probably all the walking through timeless places," she said. "It certainly turned my hair white."

"Are the paths still necessary?"

"In Lowmeer, no. Their shrines are back in real time. But elsewhere, witchery folk trained at hidden shrines are walking those paths to Vavala and Staravale where our armies are gathering. The Great Oak in Vavala is still hidden, but it connects to what used to be the Water Purifiers Guild building."

He knew the place; it wasn't far from Proctor House.

"We'll go to open warfare against Valerian and his remaining sons soon," she said. "Our folk are already using their witcheries to weaken Fox's army in numerous ways."

"For example?"

"Horse charmers have been appropriating his army transport. Grey Lancers don't treat their mounts or their packhorses well. Easy for a charmer to winkle horses away at night, or better still, liberate a whole pack-train, including the supplies."

"And where is Sir Herelt Deremer now?"

"Near the Valance border in Staravale, leading his Dire Sweepers, other Lowmians, plus soldiers from Staravale and West Denva. He'll cross the River Ard soon to join up with my forces. He's sent word that he believes there are no sorcerers remaining west of the river. He had the advantage of starting earlier, before Fox's sons had experience. And being ruthless helped too. He thinks nothing of burning whole buildings to kill one sorcerer."

"Not a man of kindly disposition."

"He's brutal, Saker, make no mistake about that. But then, we're fighting a brutal foe."

"Where is Valerian now?"

"In Vavala still. A number of his sons are gathering there too."

"I'm not sure Ryce will help us, Your Reverence."

She paled. "He's not given any indication when he'll bring his men north?"

He shook his head. "He's plunged straight into Ardrone's problems. I think he's appalled at what he has found, so his focus is on repairing the kingdom and building his own reign."

"I was counting on him. And on the Ardronese navy for carrying supplies . . ."

"I doubt it will happen."

She rose and started to pace as she talked. "Sometimes I wonder at myself. I'm a woman of faith, a proponent of harmony, and all I can think about is war. How will we win without Ardrone? Herelt's men are tough, but they are more used to operating furtively in clandestine ways. Apart from them, we have a few reluctant soldiers from the Principalities, all with little training and no experience. There's only one Peregrine. You and Ardhi and Sorrel – one ternion. A few Chenderawasi magical objects of unknown value. A reluctant sea eagle."

He tried to joke. "Don't underestimate my eagle."

She stopped dead. "Will you come north with me?"

"Of course! The ternion has to be together. And we are your best chance to bring down Valerian."

"I have proof that he's increasing his power on a daily basis by draining others of life – mostly very young children. There's been a spate of kidnapped babies. Several of my people have tried to assassinate him. They never got the chance." She started to pace again. "You thought he was bad enough when you knew him. That's nothing to what he is now. Nothing."

Her fear shocked him. Fritillary, frightened? He repressed a shiver. "Do any of his sons know how to prolong their lives the way he does?"

"We've seen no evidence of that. But would we know?"

"That secret might die with him. Our ternion will kill him."

"Every sorcerer has to die for us to be sure we are safe." She turned to face him. "Every single one."

"I will never countenance killing an innocent child, just to be 'sure'. That's what Deremer and his Sweepers used to do. We will keep an eye on the twins."

"Will that be enough?" Her gaze locked on his. "You will die of old age before the twins do. You've got to do more than 'keep an eye on them'. You have to find a way to *cure* them."

She left the alternative unspoken and he wasn't foolish enough to ask what it was.

"When are you returning to Vavala?" he asked.

"Not tomorrow. I need to rest one whole day."

"I'll go with you, but I have a horrid idea Ryce won't be happy. He wants to appoint me as his Prime."

She raised her eyebrows. "That's quite a promotion."

"It's ridiculous. There's never been a Prime so young."

"There's always a first time. You've grown up, Saker. You've seen the world, thought about life. If you're concerned about protecting the lands of the Summer Seas from rapine, what better position to be in than spiritual adviser to a monarch in this hemisphere?"

With that remark, she left the room and went to bed.

The following morning, Ryce spent three hours closeted alone with Fritillary. Saker was busy in Faith House, but around midday a servant came to tell him he was to partake of luncheon with the king and the Pontifect. A number of other notables, including Juster, Beargold and Seaforth, were also there, and Saker was unsurprised when Ryce announced that he felt there was far too much to be done in Ardrone for him to send any forces to the north.

"We have a remarkable opportunity to defeat the Grey Lancers left behind in Ardrone," he said, "because Fox has called all his sorcerous sons to help him against Deremer's army in the Principalities. Without sorcerers, Ardronese Grey Lancers are leaderless. I want every single one of them dead."

He has a point, Saker thought, wondering nonetheless if it was wise to stay at home and watch Fox make firewood and mincemeat of Deremer's army, or, worse still, of Fritillary's secret one. However, his opinion was not asked. When he met Juster's gaze across the dining table, it was clear the buccaneer didn't think much of the decision either, but Juster was Ryce's man. He would not be taking the fleet north.

After the meal was finished, the king kept Saker and Fritillary back. "I want to tell you," he said, addressing Fritillary, "that I intend to make Saker my Prime."

"I've no problem with that," she said calmly.

"*I* do!" Saker protested. "I don't have the experience for such a post. Moreover, I'm going north with Pontifect Fritillary. I have to fight this war, even if Your Highness's – Your Majesty's forces may be better employed elsewhere."

Ryce frowned. "In Fox, we had an experienced arbiter, an older, much respected cleric – and look where it got us. You can't be worse than he was, Saker. It's not possible."

Fritillary rose from her chair. "I think it best if Your Majesty would give me leave to retire. This is a matter for you to settle between yourselves."

Ryce nodded his agreement, and the two of them were left eyeing each other across the table with the remains of the meal still in front of them.

"Your Majesty, I do not want to be your Prime. Someone of my age and experience would not garner the respect of the clergy, the very people a Prime is supposed to lead."

"Saker, the very first king of the Betany line, the man who persuaded ten warring dukes to give up their ducal power and unite into one kingdom, was twenty-two years old when he was crowned king."

Saker clenched his fists at his sides, not in anger, but in resolution. He would *not* take on the position of Prime of Ardrone. "Va-faith in Ardrone is in turmoil," he said. "There have been too many arguments, too much division and too much distrust. There is still a problem with Primordials in the Shenat Hills—"

"Everyone knows now that Fox is a sorcerer and an evil man," Ryce interrupted. "Those who followed his spiritual leadership are scurrying away from his legacy like rats trying to hide in dark holes. They aren't going to present any problem to you. They want everyone to forget what they did and what they believed."

"Perhaps, but there are still town clerics who believe Shenat is superstitious nonsense and that we should be ridding ourselves of shrines and strengthening Va worship. Va-faith in Ardrone needs to be led by a man or woman of stature, someone capable of uniting clerics, witans and shrine keepers. I am not that person. It wasn't so long ago that I was accused of apostasy and blasphemy, and may I remind you that my nullification was the decision of a king's court."

"That's exactly why I think you will be accepted as my Prime. You suffered personally from Valerian Fox's evil. Your conviction will be overturned by a royal decree and news of your innocence will be spread by public notice in every town and village. Your part in the battle against sorcery will be acknowledged and you will be rewarded. A title will be in order, of course."

"Oh, for Va's sake, Ryce!" he cried, dispensing with formality. "You aren't listening to me! *I do not want to be the Prime.* I'm not the kind of man who likes to sit behind a desk dealing with paperwork, back-biting clerics and details of religious doctrine and liturgy. You *know* that. And I don't give a hog's piddle about titles!"

"Yes, so I've noticed, from the infrequency with which you use mine. But I need you, Saker. I need a man I can trust. I need a friend keeping an eye on our faith. I have to surround myself with people who have power, and yet don't have to be watched every minute of the day to make sure they're not stabbing me in the back. Do you understand? By now, everyone knows I killed the king! Regicide *and* patricide – have you any idea how many of the nobility are ready to turn on me because of that? I have a second cousin who will stir up trouble, for a start, and I can't touch him. Your very reluctance to take on this post tells me that you won't fail me."

It was a plea from the heart which Saker felt as a physical pain in his chest. Ryce needed him. But the thought of a lifetime of admin-istration and dealing with either quarrelling nit-picking clerics or stubborn shrine keepers? *No, please no.*

"The Pontifect supports your appointment."

"Then she too is going to be disappointed. I'm sorry, Ryce, I can't do this. May I have your leave to withdraw?"

Ryce waved a hand in acquiescence, so he stood up and bowed. However, before he turned away, Ryce asked, "What *do* you want to do?"

"Right now? Go to Vavala, kill Valerian Fox and help win the battle against his Grey Lancers and his remaining sons. After that, Sorrel and I want to pick up Piper and take her to Lowmeer. Regala

Mathilda has to decide what's to be done about her future. What happens after that, I'm not sure."

"I wouldn't bring Sorrel into Ardrone again if I were you."

"Pardon?"

"After I talked to her on the Chervil Moors that time, when you were nulled, I made some enquiries about her. The name Celandine Marten never led anywhere. Mathilda and I were in Melforn when she took on Celandine as her handmaiden at the Melforn Shrine. Oddly enough, there was a woman who murdered her husband in the area the night before. I found out her name. Sorrel Redwing. There was a witness. She pushed her husband down the stairs. And lo and behold, when I met you in Twite, there's Celandine suddenly being called Sorrel."

Oh, blister it.

"No one is taking Piper anywhere," Ryce continued, "least of all a woman wanted for murder. The child is my niece."

Saker stood stock still. "I know about Sorrel's husband's death. He killed their daughter and was about to murder her. He fell down the stairs when they struggled. She has risked her life to save Piper. I've travelled with her for more than two years, most of that time on board ship. You get to know someone really well in those circumstances. I owe my life to her. You owe her as much as you owe me. She was one of those instrumental in lifting the siege of Gromwell."

"She was responsible for my wife's death!"

"She *rescued* her! Princess Bealina died because one of Fox's men shot her. You heard what Her Reverence said. You heard what Horntail said. He was *there*."

"I also heard what Sorrel promised me about my wife and son." Ryce ran a hand through his hair in a gesture of anguish. "I can't bear the idea of that woman caring for my niece."

"She's the only mother your niece has ever really known!" Saker was at a loss. Would it help Ryce if he knew that Bealina had thought it better to die, and why – or would it make it all worse? He swallowed the temptation. He couldn't do that to the man.

"I *have* been thinking about what you said earlier concerning Piper's existence being an embarrassment to Mathilda," Ryce said. "I will write to her and ask what she wants to be done. I suspect that

Mathilda might be happy to have her daughter under my care in Ardrone. Don't you?"

Perhaps. But that would mean telling him Piper was Fox's daughter. Whoever raised her *had* to to be told that, because she possessed the potential to be a sorcerer. If Ryce did know, what would he do? Order Piper's killing?

He might.

Rather than find out, Saker said instead, "Right now, Piper needs the woman she thinks of as her mother. The only person who has the right to deny her that is the Regala Mathilda. The Regala placed Piper in Sorrel's care with the understanding that she was to be taken to the Pontifect, and that Fritillary Reedling be the one to decide her fate because she was a twin and possible devil-kin. No one expected Sorrel would have to flee for her life because she was unjustly blamed for a theft. Perhaps we ought to consult Fritillary on this matter. She does know the entire story."

"We could do that," the king said quietly. "Or we could come to some arrangement."

Saker felt himself go cold. *Beggar me speechless, Ryce, you can't mean what I think you mean . . .*

Ryce looked down at his hands and fiddled with the large ring he wore. Not long ago, it had adorned his father's hand. "If there is a Prime Saker Rampion, then I will expedite Piper's removal to Lowmeer, in Sorrel's care, for Mathilda to decide her fate. Be my Prime, Saker, commencing right now. You owe my family. You bedded my sister, took her virginity, risked her life and her marriage – any marriage – for the sake of your pizzle. You owe the Ardronese Royal House of Betany and I'm claiming our debt."

He was frozen, held tight in a web of his own making, knowing there was no escape. When he found his tongue, it was to say, "I have to go to Vavala with Fritillary Reedling. I believe that my presence there forms part of your only chance to see Valerian Fox dead."

"And if I say you can go, will you promise to return with all possible expediency?"

Piper. Sorrel. Mathilda's rights as a mother. The moment of silence lengthened even after he knew there was no way out.

"Five years," he said finally, his voice husky. "I'll be your Prime for five years."

"Ten."

He was locked in the prince's gaze. The breathless silence felt as sharp as the honed edge of an axe about to fall. He wanted to bargain still further, but Ryce's watchful narrowed eyes stopped the words.

He bowed his head. "Very well. Ten."

Ryce breathed out, and the tension eased. "You are lucky I call you a friend, witan. You may think this blackmail if you like; I call it justice. Don't hate me for it. I *do* need you, and you will be well-recompensed. Ten years." He smiled, all charm. "Agreed."

He bowed his capitulation. "Thank you, sire." *Fig on you!*

"Thank *you*, Saker. I appreciate your sacrifice." He paused. "Tell me one more thing. Is Piper yours?"

A loaded question if ever there was one, with its obvious corollary. *Is the next Regal your son?*

"I don't believe so."

"Pity." His lips curled up. "I would have found that . . . amusing."

"Pox on you, Ryce."

The king grinned.

He was beaten and he knew it, and all he could do was grin back at him, shaking his head.

Curdle me sour, the royal whelp is going to be a fobbing remarkable monarch. Who would have thought it?

34

The Eve of Battle

Saker returned along the timeless paths to Vavala with Fritillary, followed by a long line of clerics, healers and artisans with witcheries. When they emerged into the Water Purifiers Guild building, the first person he saw was Gerelda Brantheld. He paused, watching her talking to a lad, surprising himself with the depth of the joy he felt at seeing her again. She was leaner than he remembered and her bare arms were all muscle. Spittle damn, but she was beautiful.

When he crossed over to her, she greeted him with a huge smile. "Saker Rampion! Fritillary told me she'd been in contact with you. By the oak, it's good to see you!" Grabbing his hands, she looked him up and down, then gave him a bear hug, which he reciprocated.

"It's been too long," he said, and meant it.

"You haven't met Peregrine, have you?" She released him and indicated the lad hovering at her side, a lanky, dark-haired Shenat youth. "Perie, this is Witan Saker Rampion. He's a hedge-born Shenat hayseed, but not a bad fellow for all that."

"Take him over to Proctor House, Gerelda," Fritillary said. "We've got a couple of hundred witchery folk following us in. This place is going to be crowded. Fill him in on the latest news on the way, if there is any."

"Yes, Your Reverence." She grabbed him by the arm and headed for the exit. "Proctor House is where your friends are. Sorrel and Ardhi. Perie and I were on our way out, anyway. We have to buy some supplies."

As they stepped out of the building, he wondered at the casualness of their exit into the streets of Valerian Fox's city. "Isn't this a little dangerous?" he asked. "Strolling around, wearing a sword openly?"

She grinned at him again, and he remembered her love of tight spots. "We've had some narrow escapes, but Perie has a wonderful witchery. He can sense the black smutch of Grey Lancers and sorcerers a mile off, and identify one from the other. Anyway, most of them left the city this morning for the north. You could almost hear the collective sigh of relief . . ."

"Where were they going?"

"To battle Deremer's army, who are, by all reports, about to cross the River Ard from Staravale. Perie and I are supposed to be joining them soon."

"And Valerian?"

"Still holed up in the palace. We think he's going to join the army to lead the battle, but soldiers move slowly, and he'd rather stay a few extra days in palace luxury and follow them later."

"And what about Sorrel and Ardhi?"

"Ardhi's fine. That man has to be the most phlegmatic fellow I've ever met. If you dumped me down in Chenderawasi and said, 'Survive as best you can, Gerelda,' I'd be insane in a month. He just grins and sees through us as though we were made of glass. Sorrel? I like her a lot. But go gently with her. She took the princess's death very badly. Ah, I think I had better warn you: she thinks you're bringing that girl with you. Piper. Who is she? Is she yours?" She appeared more intrigued than worried by the thought.

"No. We're responsible for her, though. And . . . we grew very fond of her. King Ryce wouldn't allow us to take her out of Ardrone. Long story."

"*King* Ryce?"

"That's right."

"Interesting times. You'll have to tell me all, later."

They reached the open street and conversation halted as she walked purposefully at a brisk pace and Perie indicated he wanted to concentrate on hunting down any trace of smutch. Five minutes later, she knocked on the door of an ornate building on a quiet backwater of a street.

"No smutch anywhere?" he asked Peregrine.

"Well, there's Valerian and his remaining guard of Grey Lancers. And there's another sorcerer son with him."

"Nasty fellow called Ruthgar, by all reports," Gerelda added.

Saker glanced up at the facade. "I remember this building. I was here once on the Pontifect's business."

"Remember the rhythm of the knock," she said. "And keep your lock picks handy in case no one is home. Perie and I will be off now." As the door was opened by Ardhi, she and Perie hurried away.

Sorrel came running up when she saw who was on the doorstep. She looked over Saker's shoulder in expectation, her face lighting up. "Piper?"

He shook his head. "I'm sorry. I had to leave her with the Barklees."

The bitter grief on her face as she turned to Ardhi cut him to the core.

The rest of the morning was spent in exchanging information, pretending the three of them could be content without Piper as long as she was safe. Their conversation became strained after Saker said he might accept the post of Ardronese Prime. He didn't say why, and the possibility unsettled them. "It's what I want," he lied. "It's my best chance of influencing Ardronese policy towards Chenderawasi."

"But what about the ternion?" Sorrel asked. She sounded hurt.

"Being Prime won't make any difference," he assured her, even though he wasn't certain that was true.

At lunchtime, Fritillary sent around a messenger with a note asking Saker to check on an East Denvian army that was supposed to be approaching the city.

He sent the bird up, nudging it gently to follow the main road from Vavala to the east, and indeed there was an army a day's march away, pitifully few ill-equipped men carrying the colours of both Valance and East Denva.

Ryce, your Ardronese army will be missed.

He sent a note to Fritillary, telling her what the eagle had seen.

"One man," he muttered to Ardhi and Sorrel, "and he has done so much damage. How was it possible?"

"Not one man; one *sorcerer*," Ardhi said.

"He was clever," Saker said. "For years he used the Dire Sweepers to clean up his own sorcerous wreckage. He exploited our weaknesses. He divided Va-faith. He turned a king against his heir. He made people fear one another. He set things in motion and then watched people dance to his music of misery."

"The ternion will defeat him," Sorrel said, "because we listen to a different tune."

"That's true," Ardhi agreed. "*Sakti*, the Ways of the Oak and Flow give us the agency to bring things back into balance."

"Us," said Sorrel. "*Us.*"

They exchanged glances and he knew they were all thinking the same thing. *Why us? We're so ordinary. It's the things we have that count: the kris, pieces of a plume, a connection to birds, a glamour, an ability to climb.*

Was that enough?

It felt . . . puny.

"Fritillary has made it quite clear that we have to find a cure for the twins," he warned. "Just killing Valerian and his sons is not enough."

Ardhi smiled at Sorrel as she picked up the lamp to light their way upstairs. "It's a beautiful night," he said when they reached the first floor. "I'm sleeping up on the roof, under the stars."

She felt a sharp stab of fear. "Don't roll off!" *Stupid, he never falls . . .*

"There's a sort of wooden parapet with a balustrade on the far side, overlooking the river."

"Sounds like a widow's walk."

"What's that?"

"A sailor's wife would have it built so she could watch for her husband's ship to come into port. Sometimes she'd not know she was already widowed."

"Ah. Well, I can think of a happier use to put it to. I've placed a couple of quilts up there."

Desire gripped her so strongly she couldn't move.

"Careful." Gently, he took the lamp from her hand and put it down on a side table.

"No," she said, suddenly vehement. "I don't *want* to be careful. Tomorrow I could die. Or you could. I'm done with being careful, or proper, or any of those things. Tonight I want to lie naked in your arms under the stars and be totally wanton . . ."

He blinked, startled, and then started to laugh. He grabbed her hand and together they ran to the spiral staircase that led up to the roof.

Later that night Saker was still awake in the darkness of his bedroom when someone knocked at the door.

"Come in!" he called.

He sat up in bed and turned to look. There was little light but he recognised the silhouette in the doorway. "How did you get in downstairs? Oh, right. I once taught you to pick locks."

"You also gave me a set of lock picks," Gerelda said, closing the door behind her. "You don't mind me dropping in, do you?"

"Curdled hells no!"

He stood up to light a candle beside his bed. "I've been lying here awake. Thinking about you, actually."

"Really? It's been a while and I wasn't sure—"

"It was another world then," he replied quietly. "I wouldn't even know where to begin to tell you what I've seen, and heard, and felt." He looked up when the wick caught and flared. Their shadows danced and merged on the walls, even though they themselves had not touched. "Rot it, Gerelda, what about you? You've spent a couple of years killing sorcerers for a living?" His voice shook as he thought of it. "I wish that weren't true. That it hadn't needed to happen."

"So? I gather you've been flying around inside a bird's head! Pox on't, how do you deal with that?"

"Not very well sometimes. Probably about as badly as you deal with helping a lad as young as Perie kill sorcerers."

Her hands shook. "It hasn't been easy. Seeing you again is good, though. A reminder of better times."

"I was thinking of them. Those university days. We had something good then."

"We didn't appreciate it! One never does at that age." She sighed and crossed the room towards him. "The intervening years have not always been kind to either of us, I think."

"Not to us, not to our world, either. Although there was one very memorable night in the Shenat Hills before I was nulled!"

"Ah, yes. That reminded me how much I'd missed talking to you."

Glenda Larke

"Do you want to start over?"

She walked into his arms as if she had never been away. "Very much. Hold me, Saker. Just hold me. I need to weep on the shoulder of a friend."

Saker woke in the morning with Gerelda's naked body snuggled into his side, her hand resting on his chest. He stroked her back, enjoyed for a moment longer the sensuous curve of her muscled body, and revelled in the wonder that for a time it had been his. She had indeed cried. He'd held her and listened. He'd heard her grief and shared his own, stripping his soul bare in a way he could not have done to even Ardhi or Sorrel.

"We had such hopes for happiness. What happened?" she'd asked, but he knew she neither wanted nor expected an answer. Certainly, he had none to give. Life had left a darker mark on their souls since their student days, and the depths were deeper and less certain.

He said, "Look forward. Not back. Ahead lies victory."

"How do you know?"

"Because it's the only destination that will allow me to live." Win or die. There was nothing else.

As they'd talked, they both knew how the night would end.

Now, while she still slept, he dressed and went to stand at the window, casting about for the touch of the eagle. It was perched nearby waiting for the warmth of the sun, restless as it began to feel the first pangs of hunger. Gerelda rolled over sleepily. He looked at her and smiled, affection flooding through him.

"You are beautiful," he said.

She opened one eye. "You must like muscular women."

"This one, certainly."

"I have a few more scars."

"Not scars. Badges of courage."

"No matter what happens today," she murmured, "last night was spectacular. Were we so good when we were younger?"

"We *thought* we were. We thought we knew all sorts of things that no one else did."

"Ah, yes, I remember. The arrogance of youth."

He laughed. "We are fully, what, ten years older and wiser now?"

320

"I really don't know why we don't do this more often."

He smiled at her. "Maybe because we don't meet up enough? Perhaps we ought to work on that. Although I'm not sure being a companion to a witan is much fun."

"That sounds halfway to a marriage proposal!" she said, laughing.

He sobered suddenly and said, "I can't imagine ever wanting to marry anyone else."

Her eyebrows shot up. "Beggar me speechless, Saker, we haven't seen each other for what, over two years? No, wait. Well over three! And you come up with a declaration like that?"

"Hm-mm," he agreed. "They've been hectic years, cluttered with enough disasters to curdle anyone's insides."

"I'm not sure if that's sufficient basis for marriage."

"Maybe not. But how would you like the idea of being a Prime's wife anyway?"

"How would you like the idea of being a lawyer's husband?"

They both laughed and he knew that one day, if they lived, they would return to that conversation. Before then, though, she and Peregrine intended to join up with Deremer's forces, and the ternion had to tackle Valerian.

As he watched her don her clothes, his appreciation overt, he said, "No matter what happens, I shall remember last night. There is something . . . clarifying about knowing how close one is to death. It brings what's important into focus. When I think of the future, the idea that appeals most to me is that you are there somewhere, in my life."

She didn't reply, but she did give him a smile, and when they made their way downstairs, there was a buoyancy to her step that had not been there the night before.

Two hours later he persuaded the eagle into the air. There was no time to wait for it to catch its own breakfast, so he bought a fresh bream from fishermen on the docks and threw the half-stunned fish into the water while the bird watched from a rooftop. Feet extended and with leisurely grace, it dipped down to where the bream flapped feebly on the surface. Its fierce triumph as it returned to its perch and its greedy anticipation as it tore into the flesh roiled his stomach.

Curbing his own impatience, he walked back to the Water Purifiers Guild building where the others waited.

From the moment he saw Ardhi and Sorrel, he knew that they had spent the night together. It was there in the little things: the touches, the smiles, the softening in the gaze when they exchanged a look. He saw it, too, in the fear they tried to hide from each other. Two people in love, on the cusp of building a life together, yet having to postpone it, to pretend it didn't matter because it lay in the darkness of a great shadow.

Please don't let anything happen to them, he thought. It would tear him to pieces. A ternion wasn't a group of three; it was a union of three. If one died, they would all shatter. They were family.

As he greeted them, Fritillary came over with Barden, who was almost hidden behind the expanse of an unfolded map in his hands. "Is that bird of yours ready yet?" she asked in a tone that suggested she was chiding him for tardiness.

"Half an hour," he said equably. "It's feeding."

"Come," she said, heading for the large table in the guild's dining room and waving Gerelda and Peregrine over to join them. "Postpone your journey north, Proctor," she ordered. "We may need you."

Saker rescued the map from Barden, who needed at least one hand to lean on his staff.

An ostentatious fountain sat in the centre of the table, reaching high into the domed ceiling. It held no water now, but was still impressive as an exuberant ceramic confection.

"Giddy-brained Lowmians," Fritillary muttered under her breath so only he could hear. "Take them out of Lowmeer and they forget all about the austerity of their culture and order falderals like this. On guild money, too." He thought her exasperation was more that of a fond mother than the censure of authority.

She gathered them around one end of the table, well away from the fountain, and asked Saker to spread the map in front of him. It showed the northern routes from Vavala to Enstrom in Valance, and to Peith in Muntdorn. As he did so, a subtle change occurred in the sunlight entering the room, as if the shadow of a cloud had passed across the building. He wouldn't have thought anything of it except that the floor shivered subtly at the same time. He looked around at the others, to find them all wearing startled expressions.

Except for Fritillary.

"The shrine of the Great Oak is shifting through time towards the present," she said. "We are close enough here to feel it. As soon as Valerian dies, or when he leaves the city, we will bring the shrine out of hiding altogether." She gave Saker a shrewd look. "Where will you tackle him? You'll only get one chance."

"In the palace," he said. "If we can. Too many unpredictable possibilities if he leaves. He'd be surrounded by Grey Lancers all the time then, and he could steal or use the power of any number of his sons. Whereas Perie says there is only one son in Vavala at the moment."

"Our problem is how to kill him, not where," Ardhi agreed. "Do you know just how he sucks the life out of others for himself?"

"We know a little," Fritillary said. "He can't hurt those with witcheries. His victims all seem to be either children or his own sons. That's either because they offer him the most power, or because they are easier to kill. We know he can coerce anyone he can see, but to gain their longevity, we believe the victim has to be close by, possibly even within his physical grip. What do you know about how *we* can kill *him*?"

"Chenderawasi legends and history tell us that it was . . ." he groped for the right words ". . . a blending together that brought victory. Witcheries, *sakti*, artefacts, people, all interwoven and focused."

"So?" she asked.

It was Sorrel who answered. "We have Ardhi's kris and his climbing witchery. A small piece of a tail plume, nothing like as powerful as breast feathers. There's Saker's command over birds. My glamour witchery. Pitifully little, in fact."

"It's not what we have," Ardhi said, reaching out to cover her hand with his. "It's how we combine them that counts."

"There are many local people with witcheries who can't be coerced," Gerelda said. "Can you use them too?"

"Not directly against Valerian," Ardhi said in flat denial. "They aren't powerful enough. Believe me."

"Then it's just us. The ternion," Saker said.

"And that's all?" Gerelda asked. She sounded dismayed.

"There's me," said Barden.

They looked at him, blank-faced, then at one another in fidgeting embarrassment.

It was Fritillary who broke the silence. "He could just be right," she said slowly. "Barden has no Shenat blood, yet the Great Shrine-oak of Vavala gave him his staff, made from its own wood, contrary to all custom. The staff can make decisions and attack by itself, just as you've said your Va-forsaken dagger can."

"The kris is not Va-forsaken," Sorrel said quietly.

Fritillary nodded. "Right. You're right. I'm sorry. That is an expression born of unthinking arrogance and I must remember not to use it. Anyway, the staff is another weapon we can use."

Ardhi's face had lit up as she was speaking. "Made from an oak tree of great venerability," he said, "containing *sakti*, wielded by a man of great wisdom – yes! A weapon worthy of this battle. That gives me another idea. What about smearing the sap of an oak shrine on our blades? Would Fox find that . . . unpleasant?"

"Worth a try," Barden said. "A tiny wedge in a pie of weaponry. Who knows which slice he'll find lethal?"

"Who's going to use your staff?" Gerelda asked.

Barden's rheumy eyes glared at her. "I go where my staff goes," he said. "Naturally."

"And I'm going with you," Fritillary said. When Saker opened his mouth to protest, she held up her hand. "Not just because I'm the true Pontifect, either. Listen. Just before Valerian launched his attack on Vavala, forcing us to flee, there was a black smutch in the sky, evidently some kind of sign to his scattered forces. An extravagant gesture that must have expended much of his power, when he could surely have used an easier, more ordinary way."

"Vaunting his power," Saker said. "Just like him." He touched his cheek in memory, fingers catching on the roughness of the skin that he could feel but no one could see.

"My point is what happened next," she said. "While we were watching the smutch, I touched Deremer, he winced and I felt as if my fingers had been stung. I looked at them and they were glowing, even though I wasn't consciously using my witchery. At the time, I thought it was something about Deremer. Now, I think I had it wrong.

Sir Herelt winced because my witchery flared as it reacted to that smutch."

Saker was interested now; they all were.

"I think there's an added layer to my witchery. Once, when Fox tried to coerce me in the Pontifect's palace, something unsettled him. I felt then as if I was sucking his horrible smutch into my body. And on that day of the sky smutch, just possibly my witchery reacted to the overwhelming amount of sorcery by trying to change it to a harmless witchery glow. There was too much of course, *but something did alter*. We have to think of a way to exploit that."

"You're our Pontifect. You may die if you face Valerian as if you were a – a combatant," Gerelda said.

She snorted. "So? I'm not indispensable."

"My people believe the Chenderawasi sorcery was just too much witchery in the wrong hands," Ardhi said.

"Sorcery and *sakti* are not so different then?" Fritillary asked. "Now that is worth thinking about."

"What about our first problem?" Sorrel asked. "How do we get anywhere near Fox without him knowing?"

"Especially," Fritillary said, husky-voiced, "as we have indications that he has boosted his power through the murders of children."

Saker, trying to thrust that image out of his mind, stared at the fountain. He imagined water trickling down from the top, splashing into the numerous flamboyantly decorated bowls on every level before spilling over into the next through flutes and channels. When it was in operation, the sound of the water would have drowned conversation, and the cascades would have obscured anyone sitting opposite. *Such a stupid ornament . . .*

"How do we get into the palace this time?" Sorrel asked. "They've increased the number of guards tenfold."

Fritillary looked around the table. "Any ideas?"

"Divert attention away from what you want to hide, to something else," Gerelda said.

"That's where other witchery folk may be just the thing," Barden said. "Diversions."

"Water witcheries," Saker said suddenly, ideas cascading. "Your Reverence, do we have Lowmian Way of the Flow folk?"

"Of course. What do you have in mind? No, wait. Can we get your eagle into the air again first? I want to make sure that everything is proceeding as I had hoped in the north."

Saker sat still, with his hand on the map and his eyes closed as the eagle launched itself from its perch. He was linking to it, rather than twinning. The bird found a funnel of hot air rising over the ovens in Baker Lane, and spiralled effortlessly upwards, happy to follow Saker's gentle nudging since it involved little energy. When it was high enough, he encouraged it into lazy circles over the northern end of the city while he watched through its eyes.

"The barracks are a mess," he said, surprised. "The roof has fallen in by the look of it, and most of the walls have toppled. Can't have happened very long ago because folk are still pulling people out of the rubble. Most look to be dead."

Fritillary nodded complacently. "Our woodworkers concentrated their witcheries on bringing down the main beam that supported the lancers' sleeping quarters. Our healers gave the barrack servants soporifics to put in the evening hotpot so the lancers would sleep well."

The eagle began to edge out over the expanse of Ardwater, but Saker prompted it to circle back because he'd caught sight of something else interesting. "There's a disturbance at the lancers' stables. People arguing outside."

"That will be about what happened to the horse tackle last night. A plague of rats and mice. I imagine they chewed through every piece of leather in the place." There was more than a hint of amusement in Fritillary's answer.

As the eagle flew on, he could only marvel at the ingenuity of those who had been in the hidden shrines for so many months, inventing and perfecting methods to use their witcheries in unaccustomed ways. The previous afternoon he'd heard about Fox family ships springing leaks and sinking at their moorings, while Lowmian clerics had used the Way of the Flow to divert a small stream to flood Fox's gunpowder warehouse. Vavala's Faith House, used as the living quarters for Fox's clerics, was plagued by mould that rotted everything from shoes to the food. He assumed that was the work of a plant healer whose usual task was to control mildew and fungus in stored grain.

The eagle left Vavala behind and followed the river northwards, and Saker opened his eyes to show the others at the table where it was on the map.

The Ard was navigable only as far as Vavala. After that it began to narrow, and bridges linked the Principalities of Valance and Staravale.

"First bridge now," he told his listeners. "The eagle is not keen to go farther."

"What can you see?" Fritillary asked.

"Grey Lancers on this side of the bridge."

"How many?"

"Birds can't count. It's more worried about leaving the open water behind."

He was battling the bird's instincts and the detail on the ground was obscured because it wouldn't concentrate. "I'm guessing there's well over a thousand Grey Lancers on our side of the Ard. On the other side . . . I don't think there's more than a couple of hundred men – Deremer's, I assume. They've built some earthworks as protection. They aren't trying to cross."

"Move to the next bridge."

The view there told the same story. Many Grey Lancers on the east bank, a few soldiers on the west. Where was the bulk of Deremer's army?

"Fly on," Fritillary ordered.

The eagle resisted and he had no way of insisting. Instead he hinted it go higher, and it obliged.

"I can see the beginnings of the border country," he said. From there on, the valley was steep and the river swift. No one could have brought an army across the water, not easily. And then he saw what he'd almost missed.

He laughed and let the eagle fly free to return to Ardwater.

"Ice," he said and jabbed at the map. "Here. Deremer has got his water witchery folk to build a bridge of ice. At this time of the year! That's crazy. How did they do that? They are already on our side of the river, readying themselves to attack the Grey Lancers from behind."

"Deremer always was a very smart man," Fritillary remarked. "Way of the Flow witchery folk can do many things with water. And what, after all, is ice but frozen water?"

Ardhi smiled across the table at Sorrel. His kris had thought of ice too.

35

Stalking the Fox in his Den

Guided by Ardhi, they spent the best part of the next day weaving ideas into a focused strategy. Ardhi relentlessly hammered the central concept: action based on a combination of *sakti* and witchery and artefact, with cooperation the key. Finally, they had a plan.

Early the following morning Sorrel donned clothes that gave her the most freedom of movement – sailor's breeks, tunic and shoes, a cloth belt with a dagger thrust through the waist. She completed her outfit by weaving her hair back at the nape and tying the end.

Ardhi was taking a different route to the palace, so she said goodbye, knowing that before the day was through one of them – or both – might be dead.

And then what will happen to Piper?

Saker had tried to cheer her, saying Prince Ryce already thought of Piper as his niece, and no matter what happened to the ternion, the child would be cared for, but Sorrel found that knowledge more unsettling than consoling. It was just another warning that Piper was not hers to rear. A hint that she was going to lose her second daughter.

The thought cut deep, bleeding grief into her bones.

She's not Heather. She's alive and well. She has a future. Be grateful.

She left Proctor House with the others, to find the streets already thronged with city folk going about their daily routines. An early morning service at the stone chapel was the first stop for some; others called at the open market to buy foodstuff brought into the city at first light from nearby farms, while a few headed to the docks to haggle over seafood sold by the night fishermen.

Gerelda had grumbled, saying that she hated elaborate plans. "So many more things can go wrong. And if you ask me, there are far too many people involved in this. Which means infinitely more mistakes are possible."

"Too late to change anything now," Saker replied, smiling in a way that told Sorrel much about his affection for the proctor.

Gerelda sighed. "I know. Trouble is I've got used to it being just me and Perie. But today we've witchery folk involved that neither you nor I have ever met. Rainmakers, woodworkers, animal charmers . . . There are just too many unknowns."

"Spoken like a true writ-wright fact-chaser," he said cheerfully.

"Oh, muzzle it. It's fine for you lot. I'm the only non-witchery-endowed person involved here today. I feel like a moulting goose in a herd of thoroughbred warhorses."

When they reached the meeting place, a shadowed laneway pinched between two overhung buildings, Sorrel looked around the rest of the armed group gathering there, and realised Gerelda was right. Even Barden had a witchery of sorts, with his oaken staff. The others had all been chosen by Fritillary on the basis of their witchery talents. Most of them she did not know.

Someone was distributing pieces of sacking and gave her one. "What's that for?" she asked.

"To keep the worst of the rain off," the man replied.

It wasn't raining then, but a storm was part of the plan.

No one spoke much. Now and then Gerelda would look at Peregrine with a raised eyebrow. Every time he shook his head, meaning he sensed no lancers, and no sorcerers other than the two men in the palace. "A large black spider sitting in the middle of his web," he said, "with his son scuttling about on the edge."

"So confoundedly arrogant," Fritillary muttered. "So sure his hold on the eastern lands is secure that he thinks to destroy the Dire Sweepers and Lowmian strength in one great battle. He believes it possible to destroy all opposition from the Va-cherished Hemisphere with the fell broom of war." She and Barden were disguised as beggars, and her ragged clothing, stinking like a knacker's yard, did not match the eloquence of her pronouncement.

Perie, screwing up his nose, asked, "Did you roll in the fish midden down on the docks? 'Cause that's what you reek like."

"No better way to stop people looking too close," she replied.

"Barden and I have faces half of the city would recognise, if they cared to glance our way, so this seemed to be the best chance of making sure they *didn't* look."

Just then one of her clerics came hurrying up the street. "They're on their way. The driver and two men, as usual."

Fritillary gave a nod, and most of the group melted away into the surrounding alleys. Although all were bound for the main gates of the palace, they split up to take different streets and back lanes to get there. Fritillary, Barden, Perie, Gerelda, Sorrel and Saker remained, as did four others, all well-armed witchery folk.

Saker glanced across at Sorrel. "Sure you can manage a horse and cart?"

"I was a farmer's daughter, remember?"

She peeked around the corner of the building in the direction of the market. A couple of housewives with laden baskets stood chatting on a corner, some apprentice artisans hurried along to their work-shops and two schoolboys dawdled on their way to dame school, pushing and shoving each other as they went.

When the cart approached with two cook's assistants walking behind, Fritillary and Barden stepped out into the middle of the roadway, arguing. Sorrel hugged the wall and studied the driver. A man of fifty, greying stubbly beard, rotund pot belly, thin face with sunken cheeks, black coat stuck with bits of spilled food, filthy trousers tied over the bulge of his stomach with a piece of frayed cord . . . Easy to glamour all that as long as she didn't have to make herself smell as malodorous as it looked.

The driver yelled at the arguing couple. "Shift your arses, ye lay-abouts! I'm on palace business!"

Neither of them moved and he was forced to halt the cart.

Perie ran to hold the horse's head. Saker and Sorrel separated and approached the driver from different sides. Gerelda and the other men moved towards the assistants walking behind.

Saker pulled his dagger and leaned towards the driver. "We're stealing the cart. Get off and we won't hurt you."

The man gaped at him, then down at the dagger pinking his ribs, his face a picture of disbelief. "We're from the Pontifect's palace! Are you beef-witted? He'll see you dead in the wink of a gnat's eye!"

Saker reached out and pulled him from his seat to the ground. Even as the man tumbled, arms flailing, Sorrel was climbing up on the other side into his vacated seat. By the time she'd gathered up the reins, she *was* that unattractive, pot-bellied fellow.

The man yelled for help at the top of his lungs. Saker drove a fist into his stomach, which promptly silenced him.

"We are going to tie you up," Saker said in his ear as he doubled up on the ground. "I suggest that afterwards you disappear quietly. Don't go back to the palace this morning."

The assistant cooks took one look at the grim-faced armed men and allowed themselves to be frogmarched away into the alleyway by Gerelda and the witchery folk, where they were tied up.

Barden and Perie immediately set to pushing vegetables and goose carcasses from the back of the cart on to the ground. They left the heavier side of beef where it was. When there was enough space cleared, the two of Fritillary's men who were woodworkers lay down on the boards, while Perie and Barden pulled sacking up over their supine bodies.

"Rot it, couldn't you have got rid of the beef first?" one of them muttered.

By then, Saker had pulled the cart driver to his feet and was hustling him across the street to be tied up with the others. The man was pale, gasping as if he was about to faint, and he dragged Saker to a halt as he fell to his knees. "Can't walk," he whimpered.

Saker looked away from him, to Gerelda. "Give me a hand, will you?" he asked. As she came towards them, he bent to haul the carter to his feet with one hand. He still held his dagger unsheathed in the other.

The cart driver's weakness was faked. He threw himself at Saker, reaching with both hands for his neck. Instinctively, Saker swung his dagger up. The driver's impetus drove the blade into the base of his own midriff.

Saker swore, but it was too late to do anything about it. He pulled the knife out and blood and innards gushed.

Sorrel kept a tight hold on the reins, but the horse was apparently inured to the smell of blood. The street was now devoid of pedestrians. Far from coming to the aid of the carter, everyone had melted away.

It paid not to see anything in Fox's Vavala.

"Blister it, Saker, did you have to make such a mess?" Gerelda said, hauling the dying man off into the alley while Fritillary muttered a hurried prayer for him.

When Sorrel flicked the reins to start the horse on its way once more, a forlorn pile of discarded fruit and vegetables and a pool of blood remained to tell the tale. Barden, Fritillary and Peregrine dropped behind to follow at a distance, the old man lurching, his crooked back and arthritic knees giving him a gait like a crab missing half its legs.

Saker, now walking beside Sorrel, rubbed at the red spatter on his clothing. Both he and Gerelda were wearing an approximation of servants' livery in the hope that from a distance they would be able to fool the guards on the palace gate.

"That was messy," Sorrel said.

"Unfortunate and unnecessary," he said with a sigh.

"Put it out of your mind," Gerelda said. "What's the eagle seeing?"

"All quiet. No signs of alarm."

"Your seagulls?"

"All in place. No one appears to have noticed there are hundreds lined up on the roofs. But then, most people never do notice birds."

The horse plodded stoically on its way, needing neither guidance nor encouragement, unworried that its usual master had been replaced by a glamoured version. Sorrel looked up at the sky, overcast from horizon to horizon, which was fortunate because it meant the dark glower of the rain cloud now emptying its load of water immediately over the palace did not stand out as something inherently unnatural.

They felt the first few spatters just as they turned the corner into the stretch leading directly to the main entrance of the palace. The towers were almost hidden behind a falling wall of water. Rain lashed the gate and the two guards on duty outside huddled on either side, drenched and miserable.

She draped her piece of sacking over her head and shoulders like a cape.

"Is it one person doing that?" she asked Saker, nodding to the squalling rain. Control of water was specific to the Way of the Flow, and it was normally small-scale: a shower where a crop especially needed it, or the opposite – pushing away rain from where it wasn't wanted. But this? This was not a summer shower; it was a torrential storm.

"Four," he said. "Lowmian witans, one on each side of the palace. They are taking water from the river to make the cloud."

There was a simple brilliance to it: even if Fox did look out of his window, he would never see any of the glow of their witcheries through the rain.

The full blast of the water hit them when they were thirty paces short of the gate. The guards, obligingly, started to open it so they could drive straight through. Saker bent down to speak to the two woodworkers. "We'll be in position in about a minute. How's it going?"

"Fine. Just give the word, and don't go over any bumps until you're ready . . ."

"Did you hear that?" Saker asked her.

"No bumps."

She waved a hand in thanks to the Grey Lancer sentries as the cart trundled through the gateway. Saker ducked his head to hide his face.

There were another six guards in the sentry hut immediately inside the gate. When she was level with the gate hinges, she pulled the horse to a halt and held tight to her seat.

Saker cried, "Now!"

From underneath the cart came the sharp crack of shattering wood. Sorrel's seat slumped to one side. As it sagged, the weight shifted and there was another even louder crack. This time there was no doubt of what had happened. The axle had broken. Just as they'd planned, they were positioned so the gate could not be closed. Sorrel jumped down and glamoured herself to disappear. The two woodworkers leaped out at the same time.

The cart was tilted at a sick angle. The horse neighed and panicked as the shafts tugged uncomfortably at its shoulders. It bolted, dragging the remains of the load behind it, shedding pieces as the axle scraped the cobbles and the wheels broke away. The side of beef slithered to the ground.

Both Gerelda and Saker had killed a man before any guard had time to draw a weapon. Peregrine was the first of their company to race in through the gateway from the outside, followed by Fritillary and then a slew of the other witchery folk. Within seconds, noise erupted through the driving rain: the clash of swords, the screams of men, the shouts of alarm.

Barden's staff whirled into the attack, cracking a guard over the head. Fritillary, gripping Perie by the arm, started running for the stairs leading up to the terrace. Drenched by the rain, Sorrel and Saker followed, taking the steps two at a time. Sorrel abandoned her attempt at a glamour. At the top, she glanced back at the forecourt.

Pandemonium. Men fought. Seagulls swooped and screamed and clawed. Dogs, street curs urged inside by dog charmers, were yapping and leaping up at the guards spilling out from the building. A horde of rats scampered underfoot, running up the legs of guards to bite their hands and disappear inside their clothing. The rain continued its deluge, obscuring details, but she thought she glimpsed the main gate splintering, sending shards of wood through the air like arrows. A woodworker, standing with his hand on a gatepost, was grinning.

She couldn't see Ardhi anywhere.

Ardhi had quarrelled with Sorrel the evening before, which upset him, but he'd refused to change his mind. He'd decided not to go with them through the main gate and nothing was going to budge him from that decision.

"When you steal a cobra's eggs," he told them as they sat around the fire in Proctor House, "it pays to have someone keep an eye on the mother snake. Much better I enter the palace my way, over the wall. Then if anything goes wrong I can divert Fox's attention from the rest of you."

"And what if we don't meet up? If we come face to face with Fox without you?"

Sorrel's words were calm and rational, but he heard her dread, and his heart ached. *She's been through so much, and still we ask for more.* "I'll be there," he said. "I won't let you down." When she looked dubious, he added, "Remember that from the time the kris was made, it has worked towards keeping Chenderawasi safe. It is *still* intervening in our lives, still helping us rid the world of a sorcerer. Find Fox tomorrow, and you'll find me. With Sri Kris's help, I'll be there before you are."

Sorrel said nothing to that, so Fritillary expressed her exasperation instead. "You *can't* know that. You're asking us to believe in a power that no one can see or feel, manifesting itself in something as outlandish as a curvy dagger and *feathers*?"

"Va-faith does that all the time. With oaks and unseen guardians and things as outlandish as a witchery to influence rats."

Sorrel muffled a laugh and Saker sucked in his cheeks.

Fritillary breathed out heavily. "Ah. I suppose an oak tree with an unseen guardian must appear somewhat . . . peculiar to you."

"You must trust the *sakti* here today."

"Does that mean you think such a trust guarantees success?" she asked, her sarcasm still to the fore.

"No. If anything was—" He couldn't find the word he wanted, so he used a Pashali word and asked Saker to translate it.

"Predestined," Saker replied.

"If everything was predestined, then we'd lose an element of choice. I run a risk; we all do. I do believe if I die getting to Fox, the dagger and the *sakti* will still try to help you."

"You won't know where Fox is," Gerelda said. "You don't even know what he looks like! Peregrine's the one who can sense the smutch."

He said dryly, "I think Sri Kris can find a sorcerer."

"But how will you get into the palace?" Sorrel asked. "They watch all the walls now, all the time."

"Trust me," he said. "I can do it."

The rest of the night, with Sorrel in his arms, and with both of them pretending nothing could ever harm them, had been a joy.

As they left Proctor House in the morning, Saker lingered to say, "Kill as many of those guards as you can on the way in. It will make things simpler."

"That is my plan," he said.

"I thought it likely. Take care, swabbie."

"Look after yourself, squab!" He left then, laughing, before Saker remembered that a squab was an unfledged pigeon.

He set off for the river. He was gambling that the guards on watch would spend most of their time on the lookout for boats approaching the wall, not swimmers. No one, he thought, would be looking straight down, especially in the rain.

Clad only in his brecks and a headband to keep his hair tidy, with his kris thrust through the waistband on one side and an ordinary dagger on the other, he waited dockside until the rain had started, then lowered himself into the water to drift downriver. By the time he reached the foot of the palace wall, the rain had changed from a heavy shower to an onslaught that reminded him of Chenderawasi afternoon downpours. He smiled and started to climb.

As ever, his fingers found the crevices and the roughness of stone, the tiny imperfections that gave him a hold. Long before he reached the top, he was climbing with his eyes closed. If he opened them he was blinded by water anyway. Only when his fingers felt the ledge at the top did he take a look. He levered himself up until he could see both ways along the parapet walkway, but there was no one in sight, and the doors on the bartizans in either direction were shut.

He hoisted himself over the wall on to the walkway. He ran then, through the rain, to the bartizan door on his left, kris in his hand. There were two Grey Lancers inside. One had gone to sleep seated on the floor, propped up in the corner. The other was looking out over the sea through the viewing port, a bored expression on his face. The rain was rattling down on the roof so loud he did not hear the door open. Ardhi came up behind him, kris in his hand.

Cutting throats was messy, but it did mean that the victim didn't have much chance to call out. Ardhi lowered the dead man to the floor and turned to the other, who died without ever waking.

There were four bartizans, each overlooking the river. He visited every one of them. Every Grey Lancer who died would be one less at Fox's beck and call.

When he stepped out into the open after the last killing, the rain washed away the sticky mess of blood spatter on his arms and chest.

He moved across the roof to the edge which overlooked the forecourt. Thanks to the weather, no one was looking upwards, but none-theless, he hid behind a decorative gargoyle that was funnelling water from the roof at the corner. Everything was quiet, and there was no sign yet of Saker or Sorrel or any of the others. He was about to edge away and search for Fox when the gate cracked open. As the gap widened, he saw the kitchen cart approaching. He lingered a little longer, until he was sure that it was a glamoured Sorrel driving it.

Good, everything was on schedule.

He moved across the roof to the servants' quarters at the back of the palace, aiming for a dormer window he'd seen there on his last visit. Ramming his foot against the wooden window frame, he burst open the latch and climbed through on to a bed. The room was neat and frugal, with three cots, a wooden linen chest and nothing else. Dripping water everywhere, he whipped a cover off the bed and dried himself before peeking out into a long empty corridor. With the aid of the kris balanced on his palm, he oriented himself before padding barefoot along the passage. As he'd expected, all the servants were busy elsewhere.

The kris pointed him down the servants' stairs to the next storey and into a narrow ill-lit service passage which accessed all the public and private rooms. He counted off the doors on both sides, matching them up in his head with Fritillary's sketch plan. Filing room, treasury, clerk's office, the archcleric's chambers . . . Finally, the rooms that had been Fritillary's.

Ahead of him, a servant entered the passage from one of the rooms and started walking his way. He opened the door on his left and stepped inside. A gamble, but the kris was quiescent. He found himself in an empty chamber, dimly lit because of the heavy rain outside, silent except for the ticking of a clock. Elaborate candle sconces studded the patterned silk wall coverings. The polished inlay of the floor was mostly smothered by the pile of a thick carpet. A predominant theme of a leaping red fox was repeated everywhere, from the velvet covering the chairs to images painted on vases. A moment's nostalgia made him long for the simplicity of his home on Chenderawasi, where opened shutters turned bare walls into vistas of the natural world outside.

The quivering of the kris dragged him back to the present. The room had three doors, the unobtrusive one he'd used, an ornate one leading to the main corridor, and another, which stood slightly open, linking the room to an adjoining chamber where a conversation was taking place. The kris pointed in that direction, red streaks blazing angrily in the metal of the blade. Silently, he crossed to position himself behind this third door so he could peer through the crack near the hinges. A cleric, clad in a black robe adorned with gold jewellery which he'd been told was the garb Fox favoured, was leaning over a map spread on a table. The kris struggled frantically in his hand, leaving Ardhi with no doubt that this was indeed Valerian Fox. He was addressing another man, middle-aged and richly clad.

Sri Kris, this is where we've been heading since we left Chenderawasi. This is the moment . . .

The conversation meant little to him because Fox was explaining the disposition of the Grey Lancers along the banks of the Ard and the place names were unfamiliar.

Impatiently, Fox picked up the map and walked out of Ardhi's view. "Why is it so slumbering dark in here?" he growled. "Pull the bell, man, and get a servant to light the candles! This fobbing rain—"

Ardhi opened the door a fraction more to enlarge the crack. Fox had moved over to the window and was now staring out through the rain-streaked glass. "What the blistering pox—?" His face changed, twisting in rage. "That's a witchery rain! What is that Va pickled hag up to now? Alert the guard!"

Ardhi hurtled into the room. As he tore across the carpet, he flung the kris at Fox, but lunged for the other man to stop him raising the alarm. The fellow was reaching out to the handle of the double doors on the main corridor when Ardhi crashed into the back of his knees. Taken completely unaware, he didn't even have time to break his fall. His head cracked against the unopened door. Ardhi reached for his second dagger and stabbed him without checking to see if it was necessary.

Rolling to his feet in a half crouch, dagger dripping blood in his hand, he turned to face Fox. The sorcerer was still standing at the window, looking down at the kris sticking out of his chest. The table was between them.

He should be dead.

The kris had surely entered his heart up to the crosspiece of the haft. The sorcerer was as pale as buttermilk, yet he still stood. He raised his head to look at Ardhi, his expression one of black rage, tinged with disbelief. He tried to grip the hilt of the kris, but it burned him when he touched it and he snatched his hand back. Then, with a chilling lack of fear, he pulled off the chain around his neck with its Va-faith symbol of oakleaf and water, topped by his own addition, a leaping fox.

Ardhi attempted to step towards him, but couldn't. He felt as if he was buffeted by a gale so strong that forward movement was impossible. It wasn't wind, though; it was waves of sorcerous power, rushing at him, snatching his breath. It was all he could do to clutch the hilt of his other dagger, to refuse to let it be swept away by the wash of vile potency.

Coercion?

He didn't think so. This was just raw power. Power sucked from the innocence of children, power purloined from sorcerous sons – the man was keeping his own injured heart alive using the lives he had stolen.

Winding the chain around the hilt of the kris, Fox yanked it out of his chest without touching it with his fingers, and it flew back to Ardhi's free hand. The sorcerer smiled. "I don't know who you are, or what that dagger is, but it will take more than that to kill me."

Ardhi wiped Fox's blood away on the flank of his trousers and looked down at the kris. The feather flecks in the blade had blackened.

Seri protect us . . .

36

In the Fox's Den

Saker raced across the terrace to the Pontifect's entrance to the palace building, Gerelda at his shoulder, Sorrel and Perie just behind. A Grey Lancer guard stood on either side of the open doorway, each armed with a pike. Faced with people waving swords running towards them, they both stepped away from the door into the open, gripping their weapons in an attacking stance.

A sword was not much use against a pike, so Saker skidded to a halt, Gerelda at his side. They both had their wheel-lock pistols primed, and at this range it would have been easy enough to kill both men – but reloading would have to wait until they were inside out of the rain, and would take about a minute. A minute they might not have once they entered the building.

"Leave this to me," said a voice at Saker's shoulder. He turned to see Barden, his wrinkled face crinkling into a smile that displayed several missing teeth. He stepped forward jauntily, still leaning on his staff.

Saker went to grab his arm, but Fritillary shook her head at him.

The guards exchanged a puzzled glance. "Well, well, what have we here?" the younger man asked. "An old codger who wants to play?" He lowered his pike, intending to poke him in the stomach with the spearhead. "Are you sure you got legitimate business with the Pontifect, Grandpa?"

"More certain than I am that you ever went to school," Barden replied, and swung his staff. It whirled out of his hand and smashed into the shaft of the pike so hard that the weapon clattered to the marble tiles. The guard scrabbled to pick it up, but bent over he presented a perfect target. The staff cracked the defenceless man over the head. Sorrel winced. Barden chuckled.

Gerelda looked impressed. "Now why can't I have a walking stick like that?"

"Maybe when you're long enough in the tooth?" Saker suggested.

The other guard stared, disbelieving, but not for long. He levelled his weapon, roared his anger and charged at Barden. Once again the staff was there first, slamming down on the pole behind the metal reinforcing of the spearhead. The shaft broke in two. The guard, enraged, tucked what was left under his arm and ran at the old man as if the shattered end was a battering ram. But the staff hadn't finished yet. It tripped the guard up. Barden hobbled forward, grabbed it and brought the end down hard on the back of the man's skull.

Fritillary nodded her appreciation. "Nicely done, Barden. You always were the perfect secretary."

"One is never too old to learn a new skill." He pulled a face at the bloody mess on the head of the staff and tried to wipe it clean on the guard's coat.

Saker peered through the door. "Get a feather piece ready, Sorrel."

She removed the stopper from her bambu pendant and took one out.

"Perie, let's go," he said. "Gerelda, you guard the door. Do your best to keep everyone out."

Sorrel waited for Saker to enter the building first, followed by Perie who calmly stepped over the two bodies to join him. Barden, leaning on his staff again, was next. She hung back momentarily, staring at the lancers. They looked to be dead. "I'll never get used to this."

"You're not supposed to," Fritillary replied. "Acknowledging the tragedy of death is what makes us human." She hoisted her ragged skirts up to keep them out of the blood and strode forward, unarmed and straight-backed. "Come on, my dear. You've seen worse than this before."

The passage opened up before them, doors on either side. Perie ignored the first few, then stopped short and pointed. "That one," he whispered. "He's in there."

Saker nodded. "The son?" he asked in a whisper.

"Not here. Downstairs."

"Go kill him." He pointed back to where Gerelda waited.

Perie nodded and returned the way they'd come.

Sorrel came forward. She was to be first in the door, a glamoured version of Harrier Fox, Valerian's father. As Barden was the only one who remembered the man well, he'd helped Sorrel perfect the likeness, right down to his favoured facial expression. They hoped the shock of his sudden appearance might buy them a few precious moments before Valerian saw through the glamour to the woman beneath.

There was still no sign of Ardhi. "Shouldn't we wait?" she asked, hiding her despair.

Saker checked his pistol. "No. Have faith. He won't let us down."

Sorrel put her hand to the doorknob, turned and pushed. The door caught and did not fully open. When she peeked inside, she could see it was blocked by a dead body sprawled on the floor. Not Fox, she knew that immediately.

Saker came to her aid, putting his shoulder to the door. The body slid across the carpet, smearing a pool of blood and allowing them both to step into the room, Fritillary and Barden on their heels.

Fox and Ardhi faced one another, Ardhi strangely stilled, his kris in his hand, wet with blood.

She stared straight at the sorcerer, maintaining her glamour. For that precious moment he was transfixed. Saker was given the time he needed to level his pistol and pull the trigger. The flash, the smoke, the deafening noise that left her ears ringing . . .

He should never have missed. They were so close. Saker was a good shot. And yet, Fox still stood, unmoving, untouched. Saker dropped the useless pistol and drew his sword.

It was then she felt it, the black tarryness that made breathing difficult. With disbelieving eyes, she saw the ball from the pistol hovering in the air just a handspan from Fox's chest before it fell to the floor in front of him.

She struggled to make sense of it. Saker hadn't missed.

Not coercion.

A sorcerous barrier. No wonder assassins had failed.

"Kill each other!" Fox yelled at them.

She knew the order for what it was, and dismissed it.

"Don't be so witless, Valerian," Fritillary remarked. "Your sorcery does nothing to us. Today is the day of your death."

She's buying time for us, Sorrel thought, amazed at how calm the woman sounded, even as her face was draining of colour, and her breathing became increasingly laboured.

"Fritillary Reedling?" Fox asked, incredulous. He looked her up and down. "I thought you were long dead. In fact, you *smell* dead. Is that a burial shroud you're wearing?"

"I have the strength of the Way of the Oak and the Way of the Flow behind me, remember? And I've come to claim back the Pontificate."

"And you brought along that old fool secretary? What, will he write out my resignation?" He appeared genuinely amused, rather than worried. "Barden, use that staff of yours to kill her."

Barden shook his head. "You can't coerce me, you botch of nature."

For the first time, Fox appeared disconcerted. He knew Barden had no Shenat blood, nor Way of Flow roots, and should then never have possessed a witchery. Yet the old man rejected his coercion with a smile. Saker and Sorrel used the moment to step forward to Ardhi's side.

Saker's identity registered with Fox then, his eyes widening as he took an involuntary step backwards. "*Rampion?*"

"That's right."

"No, it can't be. Your face was scarred."

"Shenat looks after its own."

Nonsense words: anything to make Fox doubt his ascendancy.

As the others caught Fox's attention one by one, Sorrel manoeuvred herself into position close to Fritillary and between Saker and Ardhi. She let her glamour fade and grabbed Saker's free hand, enclosing the piece of the feather between his palm and her own. With her other hand, she gripped Ardhi's bare upper arm. He showed her the kris, and she saw, to her horror, blackened streaks in the blade where once there had been fiery gold.

She struggled to breathe. The air felt thick and foul, and she choked on it. More than that, it was saturated with sounds, the cries of people struggling to live, the terrified protests of sorcerers knowing they were betrayed by the man who had sired them. At the fringes of her vision she saw a curling darkness, like the scorching edge of parchment before it flamed in a fire. This was what Perie called a tarry smutch, and it was full of the memory of dead voices, sucked up by Fox along with their lives. She tried to speak, but no words came. Ardhi turned to look at her, and she read both love and despair in his gaze. He'd refused to die under that onslaught of power, yet neither could he break free.

Fritillary reached out and placed a hand on the back of Sorrel's neck, fingers tingling, her skin-to-skin touch soothing. Somewhere, far away, the woman's voice taunted Fox. Sorrel poured all her strength into turning her head to look at Fritillary, less then an arm's length away. Her witchery was glowing. It outshone Saker's, although every now and then there were flashes of a nasty mustard colour staining it, like dirty smoke obscuring sunlight.

"Sorrel." Saker, trying to say something. His hand tightened on hers, pressing the feather into her flesh. "Remember."

Remember the plan. Remember the unity.

Feather, kris, Avian, oak, glamour, witchery, transformation.

"I don't know what any of you think you are doing." Fox, mocking them. "Your puny power cannot conquer mine. You're an old woman, Fritillary, raddled before your time, while I have so many fresh young lives in me. And you, Rampion? Can you fight me? I stopped a pistol ball. Do you think your sword can reach me?"

Sorrel tried not to hear, not to think about his power. She reached out to Saker and to Ardhi, and began to build another glamour. But what was the point if the power of the kris was gone?

No, mustn't think that.

"I don't need a sword," Saker said. She thought he was speaking between gritted teeth. "I have the power of the Way of the Oak flowing in my blood."

Remember. The soft mistiness of the mountain top of a distant island, the cascading beauty of a Chenderawasi call, the perfume of the nutmeg flowers . . . Remember the glorious beauty of the Chenderawasi birds. The young Raja, the plumes, the talons, the spurs, the magnificence.

Piece by piece, she built her glamour. The most special, difficult one she'd ever attempted because it had to be perfect. It had to *live*. Beside her, Saker was gasping for breath as Fox made him the target of his flow of dark sorcery. The sorcerer didn't notice what she was doing, not immediately. He had already dismissed her as someone with a harmless witchery. Come to think of it, he'd never even noticed her when she was Mathilda's handmaiden. Had he even paid her attention except in the courtroom?

"Who are you?" Fox asked, switching his attention to Ardhi. "What's an ignorant nut-skin like you doing here in the civilised world?"

"Killing you," Ardhi said, speaking for the first time. "We put something on that blade."

Sorrel felt a flutter then, an interruption in the outflow of sorcery smutch. She seized the chance to draw a breath of clean air into her lungs.

"Rubbish!" Fox snapped. "I would know. I would feel it . . ."

"You will. You do. Your sorcery wouldn't recognise something from the Va-forsaken half of the world as a danger, would it?" Ardhi, bless him, aiming to confuse the vile man.

Another fluttering interruption in the smutch. Sorrel seized the moment to adjust the glamour she was building. The image of a Chenderawasi Avian.

The next words Ardhi uttered were spoken to Saker in Pashali and then repeated in his native tongue for her. "It's working. I can feel it."

Fritillary was transforming sorcery to Shenat-based power and feeding it to her, and from her to Ardhi and Saker. Sorrel felt Fritillary's witchery glow spreading through the air; she felt the gentle but resolute power of it in her bones. It was what they'd hoped for on the basis of so little evidence: the day that Fritillary had transformed some of Fox's sky smutch and made it her own.

Her joy was short-lived.

"It is killing her," Saker whispered in her ear. "Be quick."

Even as he said the words, Fritillary began to sink to her knees, her fingers skidding down Sorrel's back.

"Ready," said Sorrel, and for the first time ever she prepared to step away from her own glamour. "*Now!*"

Saker took hold of his witchery, and moved into the world of birds. This time he called not on any living species, but on the Avian essence, on their nature, their substance and the kernel of their existence. He reached through Sorrel to Ardhi and back again, channelling via the *sakti* they held in the feather, using Fritillary's Shenat power, and Sorrel's, and his own. He groped for the *sakti* in the blade of the kris, but failed to find it.

"The hilt," Ardhi whispered in Pashali.

He remembered then: the handle of the kris was carved from the Raja's bone. He had not thought to look at the hilt, and neither apparently had Fox when he'd quenched the blade. The power he wanted was still there, in the Raja's bone, more *sakti* even than there would have been in the feathers forged into the blade.

The moment Sorrel said "*Now!*", he reached out to the glamoured image, showing it the essence of a Chenderawasi Avian enshrined within the hilt of the kris and the piece of feather. When all the elements fused, the glamoured image of an Avian was imbued with temporary, magical life.

The air shimmered. Glitters of misty gold and flickers of colour coalesced into a vibrant, living, solid presence. There, in the room with them, was a Chenderawasi Avian male in breeding plumage, as tall as a man, spreading its glorious tail and wings of iridescent colour, flexing its dewclaws and the cruel curve of its talons, unsheathing the spurs on its legs with the sharp sibilance of a weapon leaving its scabbard. It was real, the *sakti* of its essence fighting the sorcery in the air. Valerian Fox fell back against the wall in stark horror.

Saker, weakened, collapsed, dragging Sorrel with him. He glimpsed her face, white and shocked. Beyond her, he saw they had all been felled. Fritillary was lying on her side, only half-conscious. Barden was on his hands and knees, still clinging to his staff. Ardhi was kneeling, trying and failing to stand.

We won! We did it! Saker wanted to say the words aloud, but no sound came out of his mouth. He scrabbled for his sword. If he could put a blade through the man's heart while he was vulnerable . . .

The Avian was standing on it, one great taloned and spurred foot clamping it to the floor.

Va, why was he so feeble? He had his hand on the hilt, but couldn't budge it.

He could feel Valerian fighting back. The tar-brush touch of sorcery was still driving outwards from him, now focused on the Avian.

They had not won, not yet, and he didn't know what more he had to offer to the battle.

The Avian struck Fox with his beak, opened up a gash on his cheek, ripped the skin along the bone of his jaw, but still the man did not fall. It clawed at his leg and dug its talons deep into Fox's thigh until he screamed. Even then, the sorcery still poured out of him, attacking the *sakti*.

Va help us, he is so strong . . .

Already their construct was beginning to disintegrate. The colours of the feathers began to fade. Oak and Avian, *sakti* and Shenat . . .

Think, Saker.

The old Chenderawasi tales Ardhi had related: the Chenderawasi Avian who stabbed the Chenderawasi sorcerer with a Chenderawasi kris . . .

We have a kris but it is damaged. And our sorcerer is not a Chenderawasi islander.

Then he had it. It had to be a weapon of Shenat oak for the enemy of Shenat.

The oak. They'd used the oak sap on the kris blade, but had not yet utilised the wood.

His frantic gaze located Barden's staff. It showed no signs of life. Even if it had, none of them had the strength to wield it. No, wait. That didn't matter. It had to be a combination of *sakti* and witchery.

He couldn't move. Sorcerous power pinned him to the spot.

"Barden. The staff . . ." It took the last of his strength to whisper the words. "To the Avian!"

And Barden, the old man who had dreamed of having a Shenat witchery all his life, disregarded by Fox, heard and responded. He crept forward on his hands and knees, pushing the oaken staff along with his gnarled hand.

The Avian fought on, clawing and stabbing with its beak while Fox sent waves of corrosive darkness to eat away its insubstantial flesh. He could see it, blackness eating into the plumes, the skin of its legs . . . Feathers flew, blood streamed, the bird screeched its hate and Fox raged.

Saker saw Ardhi through a blur. The lascar was dragging himself upright, panting, groaning, inch by painful inch until he climbed to his feet, swaying.

Barden edged on. When he reached out with his staff, trying to touch Fox, he fell flat. Even then, he didn't give up. He pushed it until it nudged at the bird's foot. Golden light, the colour of a low afternoon sun, rippled across the Avian's feet. It looked down, saw the staff and gave a ringing cry of challenge, that flawless liquid song they had all heard carolled across the Chenderawasi forest. The Avian bent and clasped the staff in the dewclaws of its right wing.

Fox stared, unable to believe what he was seeing as the bird tossed the staff at his chest. At the same time, in perfect unison, Ardhi flung his kris.

Staff and kris thudded home side by side, impaling Fox against the wall next to the window. For a moment he hung there, staring at them, his incredulity at what had happened registering on his face. For one stark moment they could feel him trying to snatch the breath and the heartbeats from them all – and failing.

The murkiness in the air vanished as the sorcerer turned all his power inwards in a last desperate attempt to save his own life. Saker staggered to his feet, propping himself up on the table. His legs felt boneless.

Fox was still alive. He looked from one to the other of them, incomprehension in his gaze. "Who *are* you?" he asked, puzzled.

Saker smiled. "Your death, and the end of sorcery."

"No, not quite," Fox whispered, and smiled. "There's still Ruthgar. He knows." He coughed then, and blood poured out of his throat into an ever-widening pool as his eyes closed.

The staff in his chest flared with burning light, so bright that they turned away. When they looked back, Barden's oaken stave had turned into a heap of ash and Valerian Fox was a half-burned corpse with the kris still lodged in his breastbone. Ardhi leaned over and pulled it out.

"Ruthgar?" Saker asked. He was still gasping for air, as if he'd been running. "What's so important about this Ruthgar?"

As Ardhi wiped the kris blade clean on one of the drapes, the gold streaks in it began to flicker back into life. "Just before you came in," he said, "Fox told me Ruthgar was his chosen heir, and he'd given him the secret of how to extend his life and power."

"Do you think he told the truth?"

Ardhi turned to look at him. "No reason to lie to me. He thought I was about to die."

"Then we have another sorcerer with the same potential as Valerian."

"I'm afraid so."

37

The Price of Victory

Shaken, Saker looked around the room. Both Barden and Fritillary were lying flat to the floor. Sorrel scrambled to kneel at Barden's side and take his liver-spotted hand in hers. Saker moved over to Fritillary.

"Are you all right?" he asked, lifting her up into a sitting position.

"He almost sucked the life out of me." She gave a weak smile, and leaned against his chest like a child.

"I'll see what's happening outside," Ardhi said and headed out the door, his kris in his hand. "Perie might need help."

"You did it, Secretary Barden," Sorrel said as the lascar left. "He's dead, and it was your doing."

The old man smiled and his fingers pressed hers, the tiniest of movements. "A fine witchery," he whispered. "Worth this old life."

"Barden!" Fritillary snapped. "Don't you *dare* die on me. You have far too much to do!"

His lips twitched in the beginnings of a smile, but he closed his eyes. "Whisht, now, woman," he said. "All things, the fine and the rough, come to a rightful end." They watched while his chest rose and fell, and finally stopped.

"Whatever will I do without him?" Fritillary asked, ragged-voiced. A tear rolled down her cheek.

She sounded so lost and frail that Saker's concern became an ache under his breastbone. *Don't you dare die on me too, you infuriating woman.* "Your Reverence—"

"Saker, I can't feel anything below my waist. His power burned me out inside. Or maybe I just used too much of my own."

He struggled to find something to say, and finally blurted, "Well, you did say you'd done enough walking to last a lifetime."

"You tactless muckle-top," she said, but his words had brought the ghost of a smile to her lips. "Indeed, I will miss Barden more than my legs . . . Take me into the next room. I saw a sofa there."

He picked her up in his arms, surprised at how light she was, and carried her there. "Now go see how Gerelda and the rest are doing," she ordered as he settled her. "Look for this Ruthgar. If Perie can deal with him before he grows in power, that would be . . . a comfort. But I'm not hopeful. Sorrel will stay with me. If it's all under control out there, you can send some of the clerics in. We need to claim back the Pontifect's palace and the administration of Va-faith . . ."

"I'll get a healer."

"It won't make any difference. It's not that kind of wound, Saker. It doesn't even hurt, you know. There's nothing there to give pain. You need to check what's happening downstairs. Now off you go!"

Sorrel, who had been listening, nodded to him, and he left them both.

After returning to the other room to pick up his sword and reload his pistol, he stepped out into the passage. There was no one around, but he heard shouting in the distance. Once on the terrace he had a view of the forecourt, and felt more at ease. No one was fighting. The only Grey Lancers he could see were dead ones. Seagulls, bloodied and belligerent, were feasting at the wounds in the dead flesh. Fighting his revulsion, he banished them to the river and swallowed back his bile.

By the time he found Gerelda, he knew the opposition inside the palace had been broken. Her eyes lit up when she saw him. "You really are alive! Ardhi said you were, but I so needed to see you with my own eyes. He said Valerian-fobbing-Fox met a nasty end."

He nodded. "Barden's dead, though. And I'm not sure Fritillary will walk again."

"Oh. Oh, pox. That's bad. Are you sure Valerian—?"

"Very, very dead."

"Barden. I liked that old man."

"So did I. At the moment, Fritillary doesn't seem to care much that she can't walk. You? Perie?"

"Everything under control. That sorcerer son what's-his-name escaped though."

"Ruthgar." *Fuck.*

"Didn't even *try* to fight! He just fled out the postern gate, apparently. He was gone by the time Perie and I came down the steps." She looked puzzled. "Not interested in what happened to his dad, that's for sure."

"We think Valerian passed on to him the secret of how to prolong his life."

"Oh, fobbing grubbery! No wonder he didn't stay. No reason to remain loyal to a father who has a record of killing his sons!"

He looked around the forecourt. A crowd of servants lay facedown on the paving, encircled by a line of rats. He raised a querying eyebrow.

"We didn't quite know what to do with them," she explained. "The servants, I mean. So we asked the vermin handler to guard them. This was her solution. Those rats are really vicious when she tells them to be. Fritillary can decide what to do with them later. And those witchery folk who came with us? They completely demoralised the guard! Do you know how many strong men go berserk when rats crawl up their trousers? Then there was one big bully of a man fainted when cockroaches got into his hair and down his collar."

"Any reinforcements of theirs arrive?"

"Nary a one, thanks to what Fritillary and her woodworkers did to the barracks."

"I want a healer to look at Fritillary. She doesn't seem to think it's urgent, but still . . . And where's Ardhi?"

"Up on the roof. I sent him there to guard Perie while the lad checks to see if we got all the Grey Lancers. The healers are scattered, working on the wounded. I'll send one to look at the Pontifect. Where is she?"

"Third door on the left upstairs. Did we lose anyone?"

She nodded. "Some. We haven't done a count of the dead yet. Too busy with the wounded. Most of them will recover, I think."

"Fox left us with far too many to mourn." And tomorrow they would have to set off to find Ruthgar. Not to mention helping that leery Sir Herelt Deremer and his army defeat other sorcerer sons and Grey Lancers.

More deaths to come.

She echoed his thoughts, asking, "When does all this end? I've had enough."

He put his arms around her, cradling her head on his shoulder. "Not much longer."

She relaxed into him, as if she belonged there. "You know what? I'll be glad to settle down to some nicely dull legal work. I'm tired, Saker. I've seen enough killing. I've had enough of watching a lad slide his spiker between a man's ribs, as if it's the most normal way to spend a day. I want to be *bored* for a change."

"Are you in pain?" Sorrel asked.

Fritillary lay back against the cushions with a sigh. "I wish it *did* hurt. I can't feel a thing."

"That sounds serious."

"Well, permanent anyway."

"But still, a healer—"

"Oh, don't look so upset, woman. We triumphed! I *expected* to die – and I didn't. I even wrote a farewell letter and left it with Keeper Akorna. Tell me, that . . . that bird. Was it *real*?"

"Does it matter? What matters is that it was a combination of *sakti* and witchery. What matters is that we did it together – Ardhi, you, Saker, Barden, me. Using the magic of both hemispheres. What matters is that we were able to kill a powerful sorcerer because the Chenderawasi helped us. Without that, we'd all be dead right now."

Fritillary regarded her with a thoughtful look. "You want to go to Piper, don't you?"

"Saker says we can't. Not until the last sorcerer is dead. I suppose he's right. Ruthgar comes first, then the other sorcerers." Emotion wrenched her at the thought of Piper and she had to clear her throat. "Your Reverence, we – we don't have any spare feathers for this Ruthgar. We are saving the last two for the twins. We can't kill Ruthgar the same way wc killed Valerian."

"Valerian took over forty years to get as powerful as he was. Ruthgar may be easier to vanquish."

"I hope so. We miscalculated. We thought Valerian would never risk telling a son the secret of prolonging life . . ."

"It wasn't a mistake. It's just . . . unfortunate. The secret is to pick yourself up off the floor and continue. You *must* solve the problem of the twins."

"Yes. And *you* must make sure that people like the Lowmian merchant, Uthen Kesleer, don't treat those of the Summer Seas as slaves or enemies, because if they do, the next time we need help it won't be there for us."

"People are greedy for spices. They'll do anything to get them."

"You have to control that. We need a strong Chenderawasi. In fact all the islands of the Summer Seas need protecting from our merchant fleets."

"And what do you think *I* can do about it?"

"You're the Pontifect. If you can't do anything, who can?"

Fritillary gave the ghost of a smile. "Well, kings, princes and Regals, for a start. However, I understand what you are saying."

"I can tell one thing you can do right now: ban the expression 'Va-forsaken'. They aren't forsaken. Their underlying faith is like ours in many ways."

"What an experience that must have been! To see the other side of the world, and such wonders." There was a wistful note in her voice. "Ah, here are some of my clerics. Thank you, Sorrel. For everything. Now go and find that young man of yours." She patted her hand. "He is very good-looking. But then, I always did enjoy looking at men stripped to the waist."

With that, Fritillary Reedling sat up straighter, raised her chin and squared her shoulders. She was the Pontifect again, a woman of substance, who tolerated no nonsense from anyone, and Sorrel decided she rather liked her after all.

38

Uneasy Allies

"So we meet again, witan."

Saker stared at the speaker standing under the canvas cover strung between two trees. There were other armed men there, talking to one another, and a field table strewn with maps of the area, but Saker had eyes only for the man who'd spoken to him.

This was the primary field post of the Dire Sweepers now that they had crossed the River Ard, and the man facing him was Sir Herelt Deremer, their general. He'd probably been good-looking once, but now his face was lined and drooping with fatigue. This was the man he'd known as Dyer, who had ordered his death, for no apparent reason, in a tiny Lowmian fishing village. His first taste of the Dire Sweepers. A hellish week of being confronted with the Horned Death and not being able to help its victims, then being attacked by Deremer's men: it wasn't a pleasant memory.

"Sir Herelt," he said, with only the slightest inclination of his head. "It was dark last time we met. I would not have recognised you."

"I have changed."

"So I would hope, considering what happened last time. I can't say I'm all that pleased to meet you again, even though we are now on the same side." *This*, he thought, *is a daft conversation . . .*

"There is a discussion we must have, but it can wait. Right now, I'm glad to see you alive and well. Fritillary sent word of Valerian's death. You did what I never could!"

"There were five of us in that room, confronting him. We were all needed."

"She told me Barden died."

"Did she also tell you she can't walk now?"

He looked stricken. "No. She didn't!"

"I doubt she'll ever walk again."

"She's not *dying*, is she?"

"No. But she paid a high price for our victory."

Deremer took a deep breath, then exhaled. "She says your people can help us locate the remaining sorcerers. And that there's a particularly dangerous one abroad, a fellow called Ruthgar Fox. But I am remiss. Do you have tents and supplies with you? How many are you?"

"Two hundred and twenty-eight. We're the last batch of the Pontifect's witchery folk. Some of your men are already helping us to set up our own camp about a mile to the south. We have everything we need."

"Good. Let me guess your witchery – something to do with birds, I imagine?"

"Indeed."

"One of my men lost his life that night in Dortgren," Deremer said. "Had his throat ripped out by an owl. Another was blinded by a bird's claws. They were formidable weapons."

"You may recall that I almost lost my life too."

"Let's hope our cooperation is more beneficial than our enmity."

He shrugged. "It was your actions which were those of an enemy, not mine."

"Enough of the past! Tell me the details of what you've got, so I know how best to deploy you all." Deremer signalled to several of his officers to come and listen.

For the next hour, the conversation was impersonal as Saker outlined their plans to use witcheries and learned more about the fighting that had already taken place. When he'd finished, Sir Herelt conducted him personally to a vantage point to view the disposition of the Grey Lancers' army.

From the spur of a ridge overlooking the floodplain, they could see the swift, cold snow-melt of the Ard churning its way to the sea. Between the ridge and the river, the Grey Lancers' army sprawled for a mile or two in each direction, the full extent of it indicated only by the smoke of campfires curling up through the scrubby line of trees.

"Even without Valerian," Sir Herelt said, "victory should be easy for them. They have the larger army by far, and most of their soldiers are ruthless, hardened killers used to travelling in small companies led by the most brutal among them. With sorcerers who can coerce the enemy to turn their swords on themselves, or persuade an enemy officer to give the wrong orders, how can they lose?"

"I suspect you think they can be beaten nonetheless."

"Of course. As you can see, we have them pinned down along the riverbank. We hold the ridge above them. To break out, they have to run uphill under a shower of arrows and gunfire, or retreat across the river – which would be costly to them in men, weaponry and supplies." He smiled. "We spent days manoeuvring them into this position."

"You tricked them by crossing the Ard in a place where it should have been impossible."

"How did you know that?"

"An eagle told me. You said they've charged you, up this slope, twice?"

"And we had sufficient guns to repulse them. We're now low on ammunition, though. One of those Fox sons infiltrated our lines after dark. He coerced our own sentries into killing our men. It was a mess until we managed to kill him. A lucky shot in the dark, quite literally."

"We can put Peregrine Clary on watch at night."

"That's a good idea," Deremer said, turning to look at him. "But he's only one lad. We all have wax to block our ears, but the men are reluctant to use it. They hate being deaf."

"It's a stalemate, isn't it?" Saker said. "You can't attack because you fear their sorcerers and they can't attack because you're up here on the ridge."

"We've been whittling away at the sorcerers. A lucky shot every now and then. We estimate fewer than ten remaining."

"Perie thinks five. Scattered along the valley from one end to the other. One of them is Ruthgar Fox. We followed him from Vavala, immediately after Valerian's death. He left the usual trail of smutch that Perie senses. In fact, I think you were very lucky we were hard on his tail, or he might have cut a swathe through your lines last night. It could have been your undoing, but Perie was able to warn your men, and our dog-charmer sent a pack of hounds after the fellow. He escaped down the slope about midnight."

"Oh. So that's what that skirmish was all about." He heaved a sigh. "Sorry to hear he got away. Ruthgar is a sneaky varlet if ever there was one. Clever, manipulative, always one step ahead of us."

"He's Valerian's chosen heir. He knows how to extend his life and gain power. He killed three children between Vavala and here."

"Sweet Va." Deremer turned to stare out over the valley once more.

"Perie knows exactly where Ruthgar is at the moment. Two miles to the south of where we are now."

"If the lancers know Valerian is not coming to lead them into battle, it will damage their morale. Does Ruthgar know Valerian is dead?" Deremer asked, his frown deepening.

"I should think so. The lancers are in for a bad night, anyway. A plague of rats will be on their way at nightfall, to eat into their supplies. Cockroaches, midges, fleas, snakes, spiders and ticks are already making their lives a misery. And wasps. Mustn't forget the wasps. Tonight, Fritillary's witchery clerics are arranging a diversion to distract their sentries while woodworkers sneak into their camp."

"To do what?"

"To weaken or break all the wood they find. Lances, pikes – they usually stack them up outside the tents at night, right? Kegs, barrels. Carts. Tent poles. Boats. Anything they leave unguarded."

"I like your way of thinking! What happened to the idea that you lost a witchery if you misused it?"

"Who says this is misusing?"

Deremer tilted his head thoughtfully. "What about using birds, the way you did back in Dortgren?"

"I won't do that except as a last resort." Deremer raised a questioning eyebrow, but Saker didn't want to explain his reluctance.

The eagle called then, high above their heads. Saker thought it a haunting sound of loneliness, for there never was a reply; there never could be, not here.

"Is that yours?" Deremer asked.

"In a manner of speaking."

"Can you send it to see if it can pinpoint precisely where the sorcerers are?"

"I can try. How best can I tell them apart from their soldiers? Are the lancers still wearing only grey coats?"

"No, these days they wear whatever they can get their hands on. They don't wear jewellery, though, because they don't like anything ornamental, whereas I've yet to see a member of the Fox family who wasn't adorned with enough gold to please the greediest of bawds."

"Perie and I will see what we can do." He inclined his head and, without waiting for an answer, walked off.

By the end of the day, with the help of the sea eagle, he thought Perie was right. There were five sorcerers down in the river valley, and no more. That night, two of them attempted to climb up out of the valley on to the ridge. Perie knew they were on their way long before they were close enough to coerce the sentries into betrayal. He directed Deremer's archers, and in the morning the bodies lay on the hillside, and the crows gathered to pick out their eyes.

The next few days crawled by after that, with very little happening.

Gerelda muttered that she had no idea war could be so boring. She was also worried about Perie. They all were. He spoke less and less to any of them, and spent much of his time under a young oak tree growing about a mile away. It wasn't a shrine-oak, and when Gerelda asked why he spent so much time there, he replied, "Because it was born on the same day as me," and lapsed into silence once more.

"He could be right," Saker said later, after he'd seen the tree. "It would be about the same age as he is."

"I'm losing him," Gerelda said. "I can feel him slipping away, day by day."

"You think he's dying?" he asked, alarmed.

"More . . . fading into a place I cannot reach. Oh, Saker, there has just been too much sorrow and death in his short life."

He felt the cold pang of bitter failure. He was a witan, yet he didn't know how to help Peregrine Clary. They all tried: Sorrel, Ardhi, the other clerics, but Perie remained distant and unconnected to life.

"Perhaps when this is finished . . ." Sorrel suggested. "This battle, I mean. Then things might be more normal. What's Deremer *waiting* for? It's driving us crazy!"

"He doesn't want to relinquish the advantage we have, so we wait for them to come to us," Saker replied. "And believe me, they will eventually. They are sleepless thanks to all the bites and itches. They are scared because they must now know Valerian is dead. They are hungry because no one is supplying them. The supplies they do have soon rot or are eaten by rats and other vermin. All they have is the fish they can catch."

"So how do you think it will end?" Gerelda asked.

"I think the sorcerers will coerce their own men to embark on a frontal assault. All or nothing. And we are going to make it nothing."

Even as he said the words, though, he felt ill. Deremer had made it clear that Saker was to stay out of the fight. His duty was to twin with the eagle and keep everyone informed of what was happening over the entire length of the river-flats. If Deremer had that information, he could command the placement of the archers and the men with arquebuses for the most effective result. Intellectually Saker knew that was good strategy; emotionally he felt like a coward. Gerelda, who could be coerced, would be fighting, and so would Ardhi. Sorrel could be out there on the battlefield too, but even with her glamour, there were still so many ways she could die.

All the while, he would be relatively safe.

"You don't like Deremer, do you?" Sorrel asked Gerelda the next morning as the two of them broke their fast.

"Never had much time for noblemen," Gerelda replied. "Too much good manners and not enough heart, or so I find. Deremer is worse than most because he was raised to *have* no heart. Then he found out it was all for the wrong reasons. He's a mess."

Sorrel took a sip of the hot drink the cooks had been ladling out and grimaced. She had no idea what had been used to flavour it, but it tasted like spinach. "You know what I find ironic? The Foxes were wealthy and powerful and respected, but what they wanted most of all was to live for ever. Yet most died young, killed by their own children, or by their fathers. Even the really long-lived ones didn't die in bed of old age. They were murdered." She shrugged. "Got to be a lesson in there somewhere, but they never seemed to learn it."

"Oh, pox on't." Gerelda peered into her mug, her face screwed up. "This drink is horrible. Why didn't you warn me?"

"It's hot. I guess that has to be enough on a cold morning like this one."

"I just saw Ardhi carting water, barefoot *and* bare-chested! Doesn't he feel the cold?"

"Not often." She smiled. *All I have to do is think of him, and I feel happier . . .*

Gerelda looked at her oddly.

She shrugged. "Can't help it."

"You've been travelling with those two for how long? Well over two years? Can I ask you an impertinent question – why Ardhi, and not Saker? I mean, you and Saker have so much more in common and I know you are fond of each other. You're from the same faith, you're both Shenat, both from farming families . . ."

"Well, I could say: for the same reasons that a Lowmian lawyer falls hard for an Ardronese witan."

"Now who told you that?"

Sorrel grinned at her. "No one. But I think it's true, nonetheless. It doesn't have to make sense. You look at someone and something just . . . *fits*." She was silent for a moment, before adding, "Saker never *needed* me, not to share his life, his dreams and troubles. Ardhi *does* need me that way. And I need him." She thought about that, and then added, "Come to think of it, that applies to you and Saker. He needs *you*. Or someone like you. Someone . . . practical, political, knowledgeable. You share things that you both understand." When Gerelda didn't answer, she added, "Let me give you an example. When Ardhi and I look at Piper, we just see a child we love. That's *all*. Nothing else matters. Saker loves her too, but he also sees a Regala's daughter, a future Regal's sister, a king's niece, a potential sorcerer – and all the ramifications of that."

Gerelda nodded. "Maybe you're right. He's certainly the only man who's made me think settling down might be something to consider." She shrugged. "But first, there's a battle to win. Will you be fighting?"

"I don't fight. I use my witchery, but I don't think that's going to be much help in this. A sorcerer isn't usually deceived by a glamour. Grey Lancers tend to kill everyone who isn't another Grey Lancer. If I were to try to scare them with a monster, they'd kill what they saw without a second thought. If I disguise myself as a Grey Lancer, then I'll get killed by one of you. I thought I might be more use helping the healers—"

A blast from a horn echoed from the edge of the ridge and was almost immediately taken up in the distance to both the right and the left.

"An attack," Gerelda said, dropping the mug without a second thought. "At last."

Saker saw it all.

He also did something he'd never done before: he switched every few minutes between being in his body and twinning with the bird's, stretching his strength and his hold on reality to its limit until his mind was spinning, his thoughts confused and his stomach rebelling. Back in his body, he spoke to Deremer, who would then give orders to his runners, or to his trumpeters, so that the message would go to his fighters.

". . . There's a group of Grey Lancers trying to circle through the marsh and attack from behind."

". . . More men needed to reinforce the slope near the birch copse to the north."

". . . The three remaining sorcerers are still separated. The one to the north doesn't have many guards. Might be the best target . . ."

"Ruthgar is not moving . . ."

Grey Lancers died under a wave of arrows and gunfire. He watched as weakened lances shattered and pike staves splintered. A few made it through that barrage of arrows to the top of the slope, only to fight hand to hand with a coercion-inspired madness that brought down far too many good men. Gerelda was in the midst of it, and fear for her gripped his stomach. Ardhi, bare-chested and barefoot, fought alongside her, his kris sometimes whirling from his hand and returning, dripping blood.

He saw one of Fritillary's witans sneak down the slope during the fighting, until he reached the central camp of the lancers. Once there, he loosed their horses from the picket line. Saker watched from the eagle as a sorcerer was trampled to death, unable to coerce a man with a horse witchery.

Another Fox son dead.

Two more remaining . . .

And one was Ruthgar. He knew what the fellow looked like now; unprepossessing. Thin, medium in height, narrow across the shoulders, dressed without much of the usual Fox flamboyance and display of wealth. The only gold he wore was the Fox family emblem in the form of a brooch at his throat. A man, therefore, who put more store by his safety than by any need to declare his position, or boast of his wealth. To Saker, it was a mark of the man's intelligence, an indication of how dangerous he was.

Hour after hour as the morning wore on the eagle circled overhead and Saker spied.He surveyed the battlefield with an aching heart, as the fight flowed down the slope when the Dire Sweepers succeeded, then ebbed upwards as the Grey Lancers recovered. He watched while people died, or slipped into some place between life and death. He saw the blood, the splintered bones, the guts, the decapitated bodies, the missing limbs. The stench of war and death, the screams of the wounded, the details of the dying – they reached his Avian senses too easily, far too vividly, etched into his memory by an eagle's enhanced sense of sight and smell.

"We may not be losing this," he told Deremer on one of his return trips around midday, "but we aren't winning either." Dizziness gripped him, and his words were slurred, as though he had lost the art of speaking. He wondered if he was using his tongue correctly. "Ruthgar is keeping well away from any fighting and he's well-guarded. No one can get anywhere near him from any side."

"Drop a rock on his head then," Deremer said.

It was a ridiculous idea, of course. Any rock an eagle dropped was unlikely to hit its target, or be heavy enough to do much damage if it did, and it would certainly attract the kind of attention Saker didn't want.

"Nothing short of a grenade ball would do the job," he muttered. *Grenade ball.* The words were familiar from somewhere in his past, but his memories were strange, interspersed with recollections of long hours of gazing at blue ocean far below, wrinkled with waves . . .

Deremer frowned. "I've heard of those. Gunpowder-filled balls they use in sea battles, right? I'll talk to my gunner . . ."

"A grenade would be far too heavy for the eagle!"

"I'll see what he says."

The next time he returned to report, Deremer introduced him to his gunner, saying, "Makie here thinks he can solve the problem. He's taken a ceramic vinegar jar from our supplies, stuffed it full of black powder and horse nails, popped a slow match of woven flax through the cork and tied a loop of string around the neck." He held up the jar to show him, dangling it from one finger through the loop. "He reckons your bird could hold the string, no problem." He weighted it in his hand. "Bit heavier than the fish that bird of yours catches, I suppose, but not much."

"It's a horrible idea." The dizziness had gone, but as he stretched his fingers, he wondered why they felt odd and too short.

No feathers.

"I didn't say it was nice. Will you do it?"

"We can try." Agreement didn't make him feel any better. How long before the flame reaches the charge?"

"Five minutes after it's lit," the man said cheerfully. "That's long enough, isn't it?"

39

Rebirth

Sorrel had been working in the area of the camp where makeshift platforms were built under a shade cover for the treatment of the wounded. There were fifteen healers, but she found plenty to do fetching and carrying, or washing wounds and cleaning up after a healer had finished working on a patient. If there was a lull, she sat with those who had already been attended to, offering water or comfort.

Midway through the afternoon, a soldier with a sword cut on his biceps said he thought the tide had turned. "If we can gut the two remaining bastard Foxes, we'll have this fobbing battle won. Sir Herelt and some of his Sweepers are preparing to ride after one of the sods. His best mounted men, wax in their ears, riding down the slope at neckbreak speed. Vermin handlers are going to distract the sorcerer with an attack of wasps." He shook his head in wonderment. "Dizzy-eyed scramble that'll be, down that bitch of a slope. Ouch! Have a care, you mucking skin-stitcher! That's my slubbering arm you're squeezing!"

"And the last sorcerer? Who will get that one?" the healer asked, winding a bandage over the man's wound.

The soldier nodded to Sorrel. "Your witan's yellow-eyed witch-bird. It's going to drop a fobbing grenade ball on his fobbing head."

"Where is he?" she asked, all her fears emerging once more to battle her calm.

"Oh, they were heading up to the north, about a mile, on the ridge. Overlooking that stinking marsh."

She left the tent and headed north at a jog.

It was easy enough to find them; all she had to do was follow the supply trail that snaked along the back of the ridge, just below the crest, until she saw them. The gunsmith was there, about to light a slow match, the eagle was perched on an old tree stump and Saker had thrown down a thin pallet to lie on while his mind was with the bird. She wasn't surprised by that; the more comfortable his body, the better his twinning to the sea eagle.

"What are you doing here?" he asked.

"You need someone to guard your body while you're doing something as dangerous as this!"

"Who told you?"

"I think the whole camp knows by now."

"It's no different this time to all the other times I've flown."

"Oh, yes, it is. You're asking the bird to carry a grenade ball." She squinted at what the gunsmith was doing. "Although it looks more like a vinegar jar to me."

"It is. And thank you for coming. I'll come straight back after I've checked if the grenade killed the bastard. We only get one chance, and it won't be a huge explosion. He's out in the open now, dealing with a wounded lot of Grey Lancers. I think he's coercing them into not feeling the pain of their wounds before sending them back into the fray."

"Do you really think shards of *pottery* will kill him?" she asked.

"It's got horseshoe nails in it, mixed in with the black powder."

"Oh. Suitably nasty, then."

The slow match spluttered into life. Saker lay down on the pallet while the gunsmith, a little nervously, held out the looped cord to the eagle.

"Take care," she whispered as the bird seized the loop and launched itself from the stump, its huge wings beating the air to gain height as it sailed out over the valley. It strained under the weight of its burden and had to labour to gain height. Sorrel's mouth was dry until she saw it hit the first updraught of air and cease its flapping.

"One minute," the gunsmith said. He was staring at his pocket watch.

She glanced at Saker's body. He lay on his back with his eyes closed, unmoving, apparently composed. Only the rise and fall of his chest told her he was still alive.

"Two minutes."

The bird was soon circling so high she could no longer see the grenade, let alone the glow of the slow match. She shuddered, remembering another time when someone had miscalculated and a ship had been blown to pieces . . .

"Three minutes."

She watched the speck in the sky until it made a circuit at a lower level, and the next after that, lower and tighter. It had spotted its prey. Behind her, Saker did not move.

"Four minutes."

After he left Sorrel, his rational thinking mind began to disintegrate, one tiny muddling piece at a time.

He was in the air again, looking down on the battlefield. There were fewer Grey Lancers still fighting on. He saw Sir Herelt and his horsemen, six of them all together, galloping down the steep slope, the mounts sliding on the loose soil, almost sitting on their rumps in that mad rush. One fell, toppling his rider. Grey Lancers pounced on the poor fellow and he went under, flailing, his sword wrenched from him, blood spurting, red and bold and salty.

Rot it, that was an eagle's thought.

He could smell the burning wick he held in his claws. The bird's claws. Fobbing grubbery, he was so confused. And he'd lost track of his count. Was it nearly five minutes since the eagle was swearing at him as it was lit, back in the camp? Well, swearing as only an eagle could, with a cold yellow look of pure hatred, as if he was the next meal.

Eagles knew nothing about time.

The bird was clutching the string and hating the smell of the slow match, and the hot red end burning towards the jar top. He – it – bent to look to see how far the match had burned. At a guess, three minutes.

Wings beating, steady, powerful.

Your last task, my beauty. After this, you fly free, I promise. Can you return to the warmth of the Summer Seas on your own? Do you know the way? Do you remember the splendour of the islands? Find a mate there, as magnificent as you are. Think of talons locked in courtship as you topple together through the air in your bonding . . .

There he was, the Fox sorcerer, a glint of gold at his throat, the red fox emblem he wore. Standing, surrounded by half a dozen of his guards, watching the wounded men he'd just sent back into the fray. Frowning, as the men he'd sent to die did just that.

It's over, Master Fox. Your father is dead. He might have told you how to live past your prime. But in so doing, he doomed you to an early death. You are too dangerous to be allowed to live . . .

He took another look at the burning slow match. This would be difficult. How close to the sorcerer did it have to be? Would it roll? How long would it take to drop through the air? There was a wind blowing and it could affect the trajectory.

He urged the eagle lower.

Much lower.

Ruthgar looked up. Sensed the *sakti* he carried in the bambu pendant perhaps? Or alerted by the faded black smutch on his palm?

The sorcerer shouted something, but the words were snatched away on the wind, and Saker-eagle did not hear them.

Eagle eyes saw the archer who came out from under a canvas shelter in the camp with his crossbow in his hand. Human understanding acknowledged the danger.

Now, Saker told the eagle.

Curved talons dropped the string.

They banked, man and raptor, wings beating deep, tail ruddering them away. Neither man nor eagle saw the jar explode, but the eagle's vision saw both the tumbling jar and an archer releasing his arrow.

Excruciating pain shafted into Saker. He looked down and saw the arrow's fletching protruding from his breast. And that was when he fell out of the sky.

Sorrel did not notice the grenade jar drop. All she saw was an explosion on the ground and the eagle toppling through the air, over and over, like a dead thing.

She didn't see the bird hit the ground either. All her attention was on Saker. Screaming his name into his ear, seized his body in her arms, shaking him hard. He shuddered, his whole body spasming, limbs jerking, as if the moment of the bird's impact with the ground registered on his prone body.

His eyes flew open, and he uttered a cry of anguish. And then death. A blanking out of life as though his inner self had drawn a curtain across his gaze.

"NO!"

The word was wrenched from her on a wave of negation and violent rage. "Oh, no, Saker you won't do that to me! Not to *us*."

She seized him by the shoulders and shook him, shouting at him to come back. She slapped his face, hard, but his body was unresponsive and limp. When she put a hand under the lacings of his tunic to rest on his breast, she could not feel a heartbeat.

Around her neck there was one more wisp of feather, and around Saker's yet another. One for Piper, one for Prince-regal Karel. If she used either to save him, then how would her choice reverberate through the ages? And if she didn't – then the ternion died. Saker died.

Oh, Va.

She couldn't make the choice. She *couldn't.*

Do nothing?

No—

Impossible. He had saved her life.

He had saved the ternion. And so must she—

Her hands fumbled with the bambu at her neck.

"Mistress—" the gunsmith began, shocked and hesitant.

"Stand aside," a voice said in her ear, and there was a witchery healer kneeling on the other side of Saker's body, and behind him, Perie. All her frenzy drained from her, leaving behind the coldness of desperation. She watched the healer make a fist of his hand and hit Saker hard on the breastbone, again and again, and all the while the glow of his witchery made whorls in the air around him.

She looked at Perie. "How did you know?" she whispered. She had never been so certain of anything in her life: Peregrine had brought the healer to where he was needed.

"The Way of the Oak," he whispered, and nodded at the tree that shaded them. It was an oak, an ordinary oak, its leaves dappling the sunlight.

Saker jerked and gasped. His chest rose again as breathing started. When he opened his eyes, she slumped back on her heels, shivering, aware that her own heart was thumping so hard it hurt.

"Did – did we get the sorcerer?" Saker asked. He made no attempt to rise. Every muscle in his body ached. Every joint felt battered. Even his bones pained him.

"The grenade did explode," the gunsmith said.

"He's dead," Perie said, his certainty reassuring. "So is the other one. We've done it. There are no more of them."

He shuddered. "The eagle died. We *fell*, tumbling over and over. I can't feel it anywhere." He struggled to sit up, but Sorrel pushed him down again.

When his breathing steadied and he'd composed himself, he said quietly, "I promised him this was the last thing I would ask of him. That he could go home . . ." His voice trailed away.

"I'm sorry," she said.

"It wasn't right, what I asked him to do. It wasn't right."

"No, perhaps not. But if sorcerers ruled here, would the sea eagles of Chenderawasi be safe?"

He lay still for a long while, then raised her fingers to his lips. "Thank you, Sorrel. I needed to hear that."

Gerelda staggered with fatigue as she trailed up the slope away from the battlefield. Every muscle ached. Every tendon complained. Her fingers cramped around her swordhilt. For some reason she had the weapon in her hand, rather than in its sheath, but she was no longer certain why.

When she topped the rise, someone offered her water, and she took the demijohn and drank the lot. As she handed it back, she caught a glimpse of the valley in the light of the late afternoon sun and she shuddered. It was a place of the dead, taken over now by the cut-throats and the scavengers and the corpse-pickers. Ravens and crows and rats. Human and animal. She wanted no part of it. She stumbled on to the camp.

Her thoughts were sludge and stirred only weakly, but she didn't care. She had no desire except rest. When she reached the tent she'd shared, she was barely conscious. Perie was there, and he levered the sword out of her hand and pushed her down on to her pallet. "They are dead, the sorcerers," he said. She closed her eyes as he pulled off her boots and undid her sword belt.

Dimly in the distance she heard him speak. "Saker and Sorrel and Ardhi are fine." Comforted, she tucked the words away for thinking about later; right now the information they contained melted into meaningless mush in her brain.

It was morning when she woke. Someone was shaking her and she told them to go hang themselves.

"Gerelda, no one has seen Perie since last night." Sorrel's voice.

She opened one eye and saw her sword belt lying next to her, with the sword in the scabbard. She pulled it out, glanced at the blade and shoved it back, all without getting up. "He cleaned my sword," she said, and closed her eye again.

"He's nowhere to be found," Sorrel said. "He didn't sleep here. And he left his spiker behind, on his pallet."

She sat up, both eyes snapping open. Perie never went anywhere without his spiker. He even slept wearing it. A wave of cold swept over her skin from her head to her bare feet. "No," she said, but she wasn't even sure what she was denying. "He told me last night when I came back to camp late yesterday that the last sorcerers were dead and you were all right."

She pulled her blade fully out of the sheath. It was not just clean; it had been oiled as well, although he knew better than to sharpen it. That was something she always did herself. "He knows he doesn't need the spiker any more if all the sorcerers are dead. He'll be all right. He will have gone to that oak of his to pray." She scrambled to her feet. "Um, I've got to piss."

She washed at the camp troughs on her way back to her tent, grimacing at the blood caked on to her filthy clothes. Sorrel poured her a drink and Saker handed her a plate of food. She took both gratefully and sat on the log outside to eat, not caring what she was consuming. Her last meal was already a day in the past. "We did win, didn't we?" she asked, her mouth full.

"Yes," Saker said. "Perie told us he couldn't feel a sorcerer anywhere. The Grey Lancers laid down their weapons, those who were still alive. It didn't help them. Deremer's Dire Sweepers killed them all anyway."

"I saw. That's when I left the battlefield. I couldn't stomach any more."

"No," he agreed.

She frowned, wondering at the pain in him. "We won. So what's wrong, then?"

"The eagle died," he said.

"Oh." She stared at him. "I'm so sorry, Saker. I – I can't imagine what that must be like for you."

He gave a short bark of humourless laughter. "No one can. I'm not sure I understand it myself. Anyway, right now I think we have to worry about Perie. We all know he hasn't been himself lately."

"He'll be at that oak tree. I'll look for him."

He nodded and glanced at Sorrel. "We want to leave for Vavala as soon as possible so that we can take a ship for Ardrone from there. We're anxious to get back to Piper."

"Right. I'll be with you soon. Let me see about Perie first."

She gulped down the last of the food, buckled on her sword and headed out into the woods. A ten-minute walk brought her to the oak, but there was no one there. She stood for a moment, frowning, as she glanced around. The forest was still, the oak leaves shining in the sun, leaves yellowing, some drifting lazily to the ground like golden boats floating on an invisible sea. As she walked up to the trunk, she saw clothes piled up at its foot.

His clothing.

Cold shafted her with the expectation of grief. Kneeling, she fingered the discarded tunic, so neatly folded. And there, on top of the pile, the red-tongued shoes that had belonged to his father. She laid a hand on them, tears blurring her vision.

Thoughts came to be considered and discarded, the lawyer in her assessing, rejecting, finally accepting that she would never fully understand, and that understanding didn't matter. She stood and laid her palms flat to the oak, then dipped her forehead to lean it against the bark. Overwhelmed, she stood there for a long, long while.

"Gerelda?"

She took a deep breath, released her hold on the tree, and turned to face Saker where he stood at the edge of the canopy. "I was worried . . ." he said.

The tears came in earnest as she walked towards him. "He's gone, Saker."

"There are birds in the tree," he said. "They are . . . contented. In the way birds are in a shrine-oak."

She nodded. "Yes. I think – I think it has just gained an unseen guardian."

His eyes widened. Surprise first, then shock as his gaze fell on the clothes, and finally wonderment. "By all the acorns in the oak . . ." The words were hardly more than an awed whisper. "It's become a shrine-oak?"

She reached out and took his hand. "He truly has gone where we cannot follow."

He lifted his gaze to the canopy of the oak. The leaves whispered in the breeze, soft, gentle sounds, as if to say all was well with the world.

"Let's go home," she said.

She wasn't sure where home was, except that she knew now it had to be where Saker was too.

40

Truths from the Past

Saker, Gerelda, Ardhi and Sorrel paid their respects to the Pontifect immediately on their return to Vavala by barge from the north. Fritillary was back in her workroom, as busy as ever, making use of a three-wheeled bath chair and an assistant cleric.

"A small price to pay," she said, dismissing the subject of her inability to walk. Saker thought he saw frustration in the pinched lines around her mouth, but he knew better than to offer her sympathy.

She already had the main news of the battle, as Deremer had sent a messenger a day earlier, but they filled her in on some of the details before adjourning to Proctor House to eat, bathe and sleep.

The next day, after lunch, a messenger came for Saker to tell him the Pontifect wanted to see him again.

"She's going to ask you to work for her," Gerelda said.

"Probably."

"Will you?"

He shook his head. "I'll keep my promise to Ryce. I'll be his Prime."

"Have you told Ardhi and Sorrel yet?"

"I told them I might take the post. I won't tell Sorrel why I have to, though. It would just be another burden she'd be happier not knowing." He shrugged. "I'd better go."

He found Fritillary in the Pontifect's workroom. Somehow she'd managed to resurrect the room as it'd been before Fox had taken over the palace. He could find no trace of Valerian anywhere. Still, there was something missing: Barden's touch. Fritillary's desk was a mess of papers that her secretary would never have tolerated.

"Barden knew where everything was and which should be dealt with first," she said, waving a fistful of documents in exasperation. "I still don't know what I'll do without him!"

"I'm sure there are clerics with the same intelligence and orderly mind he had. Think of it this way: there must have been a time when he was young and new to the job."

"Before my day, that was," she said, irritably. "He was already ancient when I was elected Pontifect." Her expression softened. "I loved that old man. Anyway, that's not why I wanted you to come in today. I wanted to ask you again about Peregrine. Gerelda appears to think he's become an unseen guardian for a new shrine-oak. Do you have any opinion on that?"

"Well, the oak is definitely a shrine-oak, but it has no shrine keeper as yet."

"The unseen guardian will choose its own. But Peregrine – tell me what you know."

"He was deeply troubled, driven by his need to rid the world of evil men. He became the instrument of Va-faith, or of the Shenat Ways. It made him a killer. He was *used*, in fact. That never sat well with me, or with Gerelda. Necessary perhaps, but neither of us liked the idea of what was . . . I don't know. Judicial execution?"

"Are you saying becoming an unseen guardian was his reward for being an instrument of our faith?"

"A reward?" He thought about that. "Perhaps. Or an absolution. Gerelda thinks Peregrine felt he was living on borrowed time. He ought to have died when his father did, but an unseen guardian saved him, for a purpose. That purpose has been fulfilled."

"Traditional thinking says the unseen guardians of new shrine-oaks are from ancient oaks that died. That there will never be more guardians than we already have."

"I know." He smiled slightly. "What is certain is that oak now has an unseen guardian and Gerelda said she heard the rustle of its leaves whisper words to her: 'I'll miss you, Gerelda' – and she's the least imaginative person I know."

"There has never been any indication that unseen guardians were once human."

"One manifested to me as a woman. And Perie told Gerelda that the unseen guardian who gave him his witchery was a young man." He tilted his head at her in enquiry. "What was your experience?"

"I – I turned to a shrine in a time of great despair. I had done

THE FALL OF THE DAGGER

something wrong and there were ... consequences. I had been thinking
of not continuing with my Va-faith studies. I was praying, my hand
on the oak, when I suddenly knew what I had to do in order to live
with the guilt. I had to take my final vows and serve others as a
cleric. That was the moment I received my witchery. I didn't know
what it was for a few days." She shrugged. "Some things are not ours
to understand. Let's get to one of the other reasons I wanted to see
you today. It's about the twins."

"We still have two pieces of feather. Piper is wearing her necklet.
What about the prince-regal?"

"Regala Mathilda wrote and has assured me he will wear it.
You've told me your feathers are the fallback in case the necklets
fail. I think you're wrong. You have one on you, in that pendant
you wear?"

"Yes."

"I want to hold it, to check my theory."

He had no idea what she meant, but he extracted it from the
bambu and placed it in her palm. She gazed down at it, touched it
with a finger, and then handed it back. "I think I'm right. I touched
the feather circlet too. *That* necklet was designed to stop the development of sorcery. To weaken the power."

"Yes, that's what we were told."

She held up the tiny piece of feather. "This is far more potent and
versatile. You weren't, however, told what it was for?"

"No."

"But you've used one to bring Sorrel back from certain death, and
another as part of our successful attack on Valerian, a third gave you
the connection to your sea eagle, and a fourth took you to a hidden
shrine, is that correct?"

He nodded.

"All powerful and producing very different outcomes, all of which
ended well."

He nodded again. "But we weren't told how to activate them."

"Didn't seem to matter, did it?"

"No."

"I am going to insist that you use these as soon as possible, one
on each of the twins. My power to sense the truth tells me these are

of far more use than the pretty gold-feather circlets the twins now wear. *Those* will weaken sorcery. *These* have the power to burn the sorcery out of the twins."

"Can you guarantee they won't kill them?"

"No one can guarantee that. Their power is nascent because they are so young. Their power is further diminished because they wear the necklets. Now is the time to attack that weak sorcery. I am ordering you to do it."

"You don't have the authority."

"You're still my witan. I want to make something quite clear: *we cannot risk another sorcerer*. We especially cannot risk a Lowmian Regal having that evil inside him. I want your word that you will use these tiny feather pieces as soon as possible."

"Or else?"

"Don't make me tell you what I would do. Saker, surely you understand what is at stake?"

For a third time, he nodded. He took the feather from her and placed it back in the bambu.

"Do I have your promise?"

"Yes."

She waited in silence, regarding him.

He raised his eyes to meet her gaze. "I love Piper. There is nothing I have seen in her that tells me she will grow up to be a sorcerer."

"That doesn't mean much. What I want to hear from you is that you would prefer to see her dead than to see her grow up to be one."

He winced. "Yes," he whispered finally. "I would."

"Good. Now there's one more thing. Sir Herelt Deremer has arrived from the battlefield. He wants to meet you, and I would like you to speak to him."

"I'm not much interested in talking to him."

"He owes you an apology, if nothing else."

He waved a hand in a gesture of surrender. "All right. Later. I have something more I want to talk to you about, too—"

"See Herelt first. He's in the library. Come back here afterwards."

He blinked, surprised at the abruptness of her tone, but shrugged and left the room to do as she asked.

He found the Lowmian nobleman standing at the window looking out. "Fritillary tells me you have something to say to me?"

Deremer turned, but stayed by the window. "Yes, Thank you for coming."

"I can't imagine what you have to say, unless it's that you're sorry for the death of the eagle."

Deremer blinked, taken aback. It had obviously not occurred to the man that the death of a bird could have any meaning. "No. I wanted to apologise for trying to kill you in Dortgren. And give you an explanation."

"I'm not sure I care enough to hear it. Va-faith believes in redemptive behaviour, and you certainly have done much to bring an end to the Fox family and their sorcery. I'm willing to leave the matter there. After all, I'm alive." *Pity I can't say the same for all the twin babies and Shanny Ide and Prelate Loach and all those others at the Seminary of Advanced Studies in Ustgrind . . .*

"Spoken like a witan, indeed."

He sighed inwardly. Actually, he thought he'd sounded more like a pompous rattler. A Prime should be more forgiving. "There is one thing I'm curious about. How did you know who I was that night? I was calling myself by another name, it was dark, and I didn't even know we'd met before. Yet you called me Rampion."

"We hadn't met before, no. But your face was familiar to me from your Grundorp University days, when I took a discreet interest in your career. I knew who you were the moment I clapped eyes on you again in that village. Of course, one of my spies had already told me you were in Lowmeer, working with the Seminary of Advanced Studies, so seeing you there in the midst of a Horned Plague outbreak was hardly a shock."

He frowned, puzzled. "From my university days? I know you were one of the university's benefactors, but why the sweet cankers would you remember my face? Why me?"

"I knew your mother at Oakwood University, back when I was a student there, along with Fritillary Reedling and Valerian Fox."

He knew what he was going to hear then, with ice-cold clarity. The one thing that had never crossed his mind. He wanted to turn and leave the room and never return. Instead he picked up a plain wooden chair from the corner and sat on it back to front, so that he had something to grip in front of him to stop his hands trembling. "Go on," he said and marvelled at his calm.

"The Dire Sweepers liked to keep an eye on all members of the Fox family. Valerian's father, Harrier Fox, was still alive then. At the time, we didn't know as much as we should have, but the Foxes had always been suspect. So they sent me, a young student from Grundorp, to keep a watch on Valerian when he enrolled at Oakwood. I met Fritillary there, right at the beginning of what was to be a brilliant career, but not yet possessing her witchery. She and Fox loathed each other. I don't know how or why that started, but I suspect she had the edge on him academically and he didn't like that. Especially as she was a woman, and someone from an undistinguished farming family. A nobody."

He hesitated then, as if he didn't quite know how to proceed with his tale. In spite of his antipathy towards the man, Saker was intrigued.

"I always did like strong women," Deremer said at last. "Our family is famous for women of stature and accomplishment. My mother was strong-minded, proud of her intelligence and learning, and Fritillary was like that too. And of course she had more than her fair share of ambition. I admired that. We became lovers."

Saker couldn't stop the astonishment registering on his face.

Fritillary and Deremer? A Pontifect and the head of the Dire Sweepers. Fobbing damn. When he realised his mouth was hanging open, he quickly shut it.

"You're surprised?" Deremer pulled up a chair, although he sat on it the right way around. He tapped his long thin fingers on his knees. "We were just young people, living with the intensity of the young. We told each other it meant nothing more than the satisfaction of a need, and a way of saving money. Sharing a room was cheaper, and my father kept me on a short leash financially. He thought it built character." He snorted. "Character! A Deremer!"

Saker said nothing and maintained a blank expression.

"Iris Sedge worked in the tavern. No, let's call it what it was. A student alehouse. Not nearly as respectable as a tavern. She was vivacious, pretty, bright, but not at all academic or ambitious like Fritillary." He paused, as if he was remembering. "Exact opposite, really. I'm not sure why she and Fritillary became so friendly, except that everyone liked Iris. Her Shenat parents – farmers from the hills – had wanted her to marry a clodhopping fellow called Robin Rampion. Instead, she'd run away to Oakwood. She was a free spirit, true Shenat in many ways."

He paused again, and stilled the drumming of his fingers. "Do you want to hear this? Fritillary asked me to tell you anything you want to know about your parents. But it's your choice, not mine. All I can say is this: you'll get what I think is the truth. I owe you that much."

"I want to know everything that you know." He wasn't sure he would believe it all, but he wanted to hear it.

"Fritillary said you would. Don't blame me if it's not palatable." He waited, but Saker said nothing, so he continued. "Most of the alehouse girls earned extra money by bedding the students. Iris didn't. She wasn't like that, not at all. She had a knack of charming everyone, and when she refused them they not only accepted the rejection, they loved her for it, even as they kept trying. So there we were: Fritillary and me, lovers but not in love. And Iris, tantalising Iris, flirting with everyone, and apparently unobtainable. We might have gone on like that until we went our separate ways – except we were all so young and foolish and everything spun out of control. To make the story short: Iris and I fell in love."

He sighed. "It was clay-brained. I wasn't free to marry whom I pleased! I was a Deremer, born to be a Dire Sweeper, and we could only marry people who understood what we were doing, and agreed with it. People brought up to do the unthinkable. To kill babies. We married within the Sweeper families. Always. And there I was, completely blind-sided by a deep and abiding love. I knew then that I'd never love anyone else."

Saker sat motionless, his certainty of what was coming like a stone in his gut, weighing him down. He wanted to leave the room, to say, *No! I don't want to hear this! Not now, not ever!* Instead he remained unmoving, his hands gripping the back of the chair.

"She was a remarkable woman, your mother. She made everyone around her happy. I've never met anyone else with that capacity. Of course, our feelings for one another had a bitter side. It hurt Fritillary deeply. She and Iris were close. It was a betrayal of her by both of us. There were huge arguments, bitter recriminations. Fritillary did forgive Iris in the end, but not me. Never me."

Saker still said nothing, and after a long silence Deremer took up the tale again. "Va knows how it would have ended if Iris hadn't suspected she might be pregnant. She didn't tell me, but she did tell Fritillary. It was almost the end of the university semester and we were all supposed to be heading off in different directions.

"Fox was transferring to another university. My cousin was going to take over the spying on him there. I was recalled home, unaware of Iris's condition. I looked for her to tell her I had to go, but she'd already left for her farm. I returned to my family and told my father I wanted to marry Iris. Va knows what I thought I was doing. Any wife of mine would find out about the Dire Sweepers, and that would have devastated Iris. She could never have lived with that knowledge. I never let her see that side of me."

There was another long silence before he continued.

"Iris had a pragmatic nature. She knew I came from a rich family, titled. She wanted me to be free to choose our future and she wanted me to know that it was my choice. Before I left Oakwood, she'd given a letter to Fritillary for me, telling me she was pregnant. She returned to her parents without saying goodbye and waited to hear from me. When she didn't, she married Robin Rampion. Gave birth to a boy."

"Me."

"Yes. You are my son."

"Forgive me if I don't regard that news with unalloyed joy. I can't think of anyone I would less rather call my sire."

"Can't say I blame you. Do you want the rest of the story?"

"There's more?"

"A lot."

"Go on."

"I was hurt. I never did get the letter. I didn't know about the pregnancy. I thought she'd tired of me. I told my family the affair was over and I'd do what they wanted. Life went on. I tried to get over Iris.

"Three years later, I returned to Oakwood with my father and one of my brothers on Dire Sweeper business. There had been rumours of an outbreak of the Horned Death in the Shenat Hills. After we'd dealt with that, I couldn't resist searching for Iris. I still ached for her. After finding out she'd married Robin Rampion, I sent a messenger to her with a note, asking her to meet me in Oakwood on a certain day, at the alehouse. Va knows what I hoped for: I don't. She never turned up. I waited three days and then went home. Tried again to forget her."

Saker frowned, puzzled, unable to imagine where all this was going.

"Years later," Deremer continued, "my brother was badly injured. On his deathbed and feeling guilty – which is odd, as acknowledging guilt was something that was deliberately omitted from our upbringing – he told me how he and Father had intercepted my message to Iris, read it, and sent it on its way. Afraid of what she knew, they killed her on the way to meet me."

Saker closed his eyes. He wanted to lash out, hurt someone, something. No, not anyone, just this man. His father.

His mother, murdered.

He damped down the rage. Her death was hardly Herelt Deremer's fault.

He took a deep breath, unclenched his hands from around the rungs of the chair back. "You still didn't know I was your son? When *did* you find out?"

"Fritillary told me recently."

"So, if you didn't know I was your son when I was at Grundorp University, why did you take an interest in me?"

"Your name, of course. Rampion. I realised you were Iris's son."

Rage bubbled. "Yet in Dortgren you were quite prepared to kill Iris's only child?"

Deremer looked away, unable to meet his gaze. "Yes, I was, for what I imagined to be the greater good. As I say, regret, guilt, compassion – Deremers aren't supposed to possess any of that. Would I have done it differently if I'd known you were also *my* son? Possibly. I don't have any others . . ."

He'd rarely felt so repulsed. "Va help you, Deremer, for I cannot."

Sir Herelt gave a twisted smile. "I wish Va would. But there's no help for me, except to spend the rest of my life trying to be a decent human being. I'm not sure I know how. Sometimes I even wonder – what we did: were we really always wrong? A lot of people would have died if we hadn't killed all those twins. The premise we acted on was incorrect, but the result was often beneficial. Many of them were already infected by the Foxes' 'Horned Plague.'"

"Except you also killed innocent twins who'd never had contact with a Fox. Or you persuaded others to do it for you."

Deremer inclined his head, acknowledging that truth.

Saker stood up and replaced the chair where it belonged. "The one question I'd like answered is this: why did Fritillary not give you my mother's letter at the time?"

"Ask her."

"Oh, I will." *She fobbing lied to me, the harridan!* He hid the bitter intensity of his rage beneath what he hoped was a calm exterior. "I don't know what to say. All my life, I dreamed of finding a parent who wasn't Robin Rampion. Someone who was going to swoop down and take me away from that wretched farm and care for me and about me. The nearest I ever got to that was Fritillary. I need to think about this."

"I'm sorry – sorry for everything."

Saker left the room without replying. Once out in the passage, he leaned against the wall. Thoughts hurtled through his head, colliding and coalescing. Gradually his pounding heart slowed.

His mother hadn't abandoned him. She'd been murdered. His father was a man who'd made a career out of slaughtering newborn babies, a man from a family who'd propped up the foul line of the Vollendorn Regals for generations. And Fritillary had known.

What did that make him? Beggar him speechless, if the Deremers had known of his existence, he might have been removed from Robin Rampion's care and brought up as a Dire Sweeper. He might have ended up with all the same murderous history and all the guilt of Sir Herelt.

He peeled himself away from the wall and returned to the room.

Herelt looked up in surprise.

"I'm glad I was never brought up a Deremer," Saker said. "I'm glad I never had the choices that you had to make, again and again. I feel sorry for you, and sorrier still for my mother. You apologised just then – but there was no need. You shouldn't waste any sympathy on me for the life I was left by circumstance. I had the easier road to travel, by far. Be glad of that, for I am."

Soberly, they regarded each other across the expanse of the room. Sir Herelt nodded. "Thank you," he whispered. "Go with Va, Saker."

"Va be with you." He hesitated slightly before adding, "Father."

When Saker returned to Fritillary, he thought her unnaturally still and pale.

"So," he said without preamble, "my real father is a monster from a family that has probably killed as many innocent people over generations as all the Foxes put together. And my mother was murdered by my grandfather and my uncle. That's quite a family history."

"I didn't know that last. Not until recently."

"Even so, the woman I have looked up to all my life kept the secret of my birth from me and was also at one time my father's lover."

He was used to the way she paced when agitated, so the stillness now imposed on her by her injury appeared unnatural. Her hands gripped the arms of the chair until her knuckles were white as if she strained to rise.

"What do you want me to tell you?" she asked.

"The truth. All of it. Then maybe I can just throw it away, forget it, move on." *After all, I've already sold the rest of my life to a king and agreed to do possibly dangerous magic upon a child I adore more than my own life . . .*

"What can I say? Herelt was a very charming man, once. Rich, polished, handsome – someone I would not have expected to look at me once, let alone twice. I was a novice Shenat cleric from a farming village, overly tall, with no polish, no money, no witchery, no connections, no sponsor – nothing but my intellect and my ambition. I wasn't even a cleric at heart. I took on a noviciate because the Pontificate paid my way through university. I always fully intended to refuse final ordination."

Oak and acorn, is there any end to the surprises?

"Sorry, I'm wandering off the point. Herelt did look at me – and he *desired*. That was intoxicating. I'd never had a man attracted to me, let alone one like him. There was an aura about him. He was dangerous. He was also generous, thoughtful, totally fearless. It's easy now to wonder how I couldn't see through the veneer to the darkness beneath."

"Go on."

"I was searingly jealous when he fell in love with Iris, but it also opened my eyes to what he was. Utterly ruthless. He went after what he wanted until he got it. I didn't blame her. She was a victim of his charm, just as I was. I warned her, she wouldn't listen and somehow, even after all the arguments, we remained friends. She was an easy person to love, you know.

"And then, suddenly, she left Oakwood, leaving a letter for him with me. She told me what was in it: she was expecting his baby and she was going back to her father's farm."

He raised an eyebrow.

"Yes, I lied to you when you asked about your parents."

"Why?"

"Because I needed you, and I didn't want you to walk away when you found out what I'd done. And perhaps – perhaps I didn't want you to have to deal with knowing you'd been sired by a conscience-less assassin. Better to be fatherless."

She had a point.

"Why didn't you give Herelt the letter? You didn't know about his family history then."

"You can believe what you like, Saker. That I was jealous. Or that I thought she was better off without him. Or both. It's all true."

"Do you regret what you did?" He was angry, so angry, but he controlled it. The past was gone, and anyway, he didn't have to express his anger. She knew it. With her witchery, she could read him like a book.

"I can't look at it any differently now," she said. "Yes, I took away her chance to decide her destiny, and I did it for all the wrong reasons. But if I *had* told her, if Herelt had married her, I don't think you'd be alive today. The Deremer family would have murdered her before you were born. I didn't know that then, of course. Nonetheless my decision did save your life, so I can't regret it now.

"When I heard she'd disappeared, I thought that she'd run away and left you. I was angry with her. You deserved better than that.

Still later I was told her body was found in the river near Oakwood, and I wondered if she'd committed suicide. Then I was riddled with guilt! Her child became my responsibility. I had to work, earn money to get you away from the Rampions and pay them off. That was when I received my witchery, after I made that decision."

"But you still didn't tell Herelt? You didn't know about the Dire Sweepers then, surely."

"No, but I went to my clerical mentor at the time, and asked his advice. He told me not to tell Herelt about your existence because the Pontificate was beginning to hear disquieting rumours about the Deremers. So I didn't. The years passed. Once I had my witchery, my progress upwards within Va-faith was assured, until I was in a position to send you to the university school, and later to become an undergraduate.

"Only when Herelt came here to talk about pooling our resources to fight Fox did I discover that your mother had been murdered by his family."

"Do you think she intended to leave me?"

"No. I think she meant to return."

"But we'll never know for sure."

"No. But I did know her, Saker."

"When did you tell Herelt about the letter – and that I was his son?"

"At that same meeting."

"Why?"

"To punish him for what he did to Iris? Because he had a right to know? Because I was sick of hiding the truth? Take your pick. I blurted it out when he told me how Iris had really died."

They stared at each other in silence for a moment, then he said, "I am accepting the post of Ardronese Prime, Your Reverence."

"I would prefer you worked more directly for me."

"I know, but it's not going to happen."

"I assume you are doing this not so much to punish me, but to make sure that Ardrone treats the Chenderawasi Islands with the respect and gratitude due to them?"

He inclined his head. "I hope I'm not as petty as to want to punish you for the past!"

"When do you leave?"

"Sorrel and Ardhi and I will go to Throssel as soon as we can. They will collect Piper and move on to Ustgrind. Would you inform the Regala through your normal channels to expect them in due course?"

"Certainly." She shifted uncomfortably in her chair. "No matter what happens to your feather pieces, Mathilda's twins will always need to be watched."

"Our ternion is prepared to do that for the rest of our lives. We don't know what the Regala wants with regard to her son, but the Lady Mathilda is not a ninnyhead. Surely she knows Prince-regal Karel will have to be watched."

"While I am alive, my power to detect an untruth may be handy with the twins."

"We'll bear that in mind. And I ask you to remember that we have one more safety net for the future: help from the Chenderawasi Islands – if we treat them as our equals now."

"Point taken, although I hope I don't need a reason to be equitable. I'll do my best."

For a moment they held each other's gaze in silence. Finally she said, "I will miss you, Saker. You are the closest I ever came to having a child of my own."

And that, I suppose, is the closest she'll ever come to telling me how she feels . . . He said, "It made a big difference to my life, always having you there in the background. Knowing someone cared."

"I'm glad. I did love your mother, you know. And I'm sorry I lied to you."

He nodded.

"Would you ask Gerelda to come and see me?"

"Of course."

He left her then, unsettled, one part of him glad to be gone, another part regretful. Still, when he walked away from the palace later, he felt more relief than misgiving, as if a burden had been lifted. He knew who he was, and now that he knew, his parentage mattered less, not more.

Back at Proctor House he relayed Fritillary's request to Gerelda. "I suspect she's going to offer you a job," he said.

"How do you feel about that?" she asked.

He hunted for the right words, his need to have her at his side a physical ache that he wasn't sure how to express. "I hope you'll turn it down and come with me to Ardrone. Where you could work for the Prime. Or, I imagine, for the king, if you felt so inclined."

"The Prime's lover *and* a king's lawyer. Hmmm. Tempting. Such influence!"

"As long as it wasn't the other way around."

"The other— Oh!" She started to laugh. "No. I think not." She grinned wickedly. "I've no intention of being your lawyer. I wouldn't mind checking out the first of those professional options though."

He brightened. "Right now?"

"Prime's lover, king's lawyer *and* keeping the Pontifect waiting. Be careful, Saker. All this power is going to go to my head."

He held his arms wide and she walked into them. "How long do you think we can keep her waiting?" he asked.

"Who cares?"

41

The Splitting of the Ternion

B etany.
    Sorrel looked down on the port spread out below her in the sunshine, the wharves and houses decorating the curving harbour edge liked coloured embroidery on a collar. Beyond, out of sight, was the Ardmeer Estuary, and further away still, the shores of Lowmeer.

Three years since she had been here last. No, more. She had been accompanying Princess Mathilda on her way to be married. Piper had not been born.

She looked across from the back of her mount to where Ardhi sat on his horse, face miserable. "Sore?" she asked.

He grimaced. "An inadequate description. Try 'agony', or 'tortured'." They didn't have horses in Chenderawasi, and he wasn't yet comfortable in the saddle over long distances.

Saker, who had Piper in front of him on his saddle, chuckled. The child had clung to him over the past couple of days on the ride from Throssel, as if she knew this might be the last time she saw him for a while.

His feather piece was still around his neck, and so was Sorrel's. They had discussed the question of how to use them for days and had reached no real consensus until the night they left Throssel. Sorrel, upset, had argued hard against using them at all until the twins showed signs of sorcery. Saker had countered using Fritillary's reasoning. In the end, they had both looked towards Ardhi and he was the one who made the decision.

"We should trust the *sakti*," he'd told them. "Every time we've been in trouble, it has acted to save us if we were doing the right thing at the right time."

Sorrel was dubious. "So you're saying that if we act unwisely or with bad intentions, the *sakti* won't help?"

"When I tried to steal the dagger back from Saker, it refused to come. It had to stay with him until the right moment."

"So what do you suggest?" Saker asked.

"I suggest you give your remaining piece of feather to Piper before Sorrel and I leave for Lowmeer, and we see what happens."

That was where the matter rested as they rode on down into Betany. The ternion was about to split and they had no idea how the future would unfold. Saker was with them only to say goodbye, after which he'd ride back to Throssel and Gerelda and his new post. He hadn't even asked the king for leave to go to Betany; he'd just ridden off with them again within a sennight of arriving in Throssel from Vavala.

Ryce, she thought, amused, *is going to discover that his new Prime is not as compliant as he might wish.* There was a strength in Saker now that she didn't quite recognise: a quiet resolution tinged with sadness, as if he knew where he was headed and accepted the sorrow that came with its advantages.

She was, if she was honest, hurt that he wasn't coming with them to Ustgrind. After all, they didn't know what was going to happen. Mathilda could take Piper from them for ever, and there would be nothing they could do to prevent it. She had thought Saker would put Piper first, that he would want to help them explain her situation to Mathilda. She had only to look at his face to know that the prospect of being separated from the child tore him apart.

Maybe she was being unfair. It would have been awkward for him to meet Mathilda again, given what had happened in the past, and of course he was choosing to be Prime because it gave him influence over Ryce, thereby aiding the Chenderawasi Islands. Better still, he had limited his term as Prime: ten years – which would come to an end around the time the twins were on the threshold of adulthood, and approaching the possibility of sorcerous power.

Ever since they'd left Vavala, they had been thrashing out their future paths. Saker's was already clear. Hers and Ardhi's were still muddy, but they both knew they'd have to spend time at the Lowmian court, and that it would be ideal if Ardhi found some way to influence Lowmian merchants.

Saker wasn't the only one who was making a sacrifice.

I will be placing myself in Mathilda's hands, probably for the rest of my life. I might always have to be part of court life, whether I like it or not.

Her denial of personal inclinations, though, was nothing compared to Ardhi's. His penance for the death of the Raja meant a lifetime in exile, far from his beloved islands.

As their horses ambled on their way down the slope to the port, Ardhi drew up his mount beside hers as they followed Saker. "A smile for your thoughts," he said, and gave her one of his engaging grins.

She smiled back. He could always do that for her: in a trice, turn a grim thought into a moment of joy, just with the way his face lit up and with the love she read in his glance.

"I was thinking of you and your future," she said. "Worrying about how you will manage in Ustgrind."

"Better than you think. I learned much at Javenka University, but I learned even more elsewhere. Don't forget, at fourteen I was sailing to Kotabanta with our Chenderawasi traders, watching my elders in their business transactions. On board *Spice Dragon* under Captain Lustgrader, and when I was working for Uthen Kesleer's trading company, I learned much about arrogance and ruthlessness and greed. All that time on board *Golden Petrél*, I was watching and learning better ways to achieve objectives. I know how to deal with merchants and traders and profiteers, the good and the bad. If that's my future, I won't be a helpless weevil in a rice pot on the fire, I promise you."

"But will you hate it?"

"How can I possibly hate what I do for my people and for Piper? And for you? I will miss Chenderawasi until the day I die, but that doesn't mean my life here will be miserable or unhappy! Never think that. It will be a challenge, an interesting life. Besides, I'd rather have a life with you in it than a life elsewhere without you."

She arched an eyebrow. "Should I wonder where you learned to say such beguiling things to a woman?"

"Oh, I also learned when to keep secrets . . ."

They exchanged another smile, and she rode on, more comfortable in her thoughts. Certainly, she reflected, this time she didn't have to worry about money. The last time she'd departed Ardrone, she'd had no coin at all. This time, Juster had not only insisted on making good his bet to Saker, ten per cent of the worth of the *Golden Petrel's* spice cargo, but he'd also paid an officer's cut to Ardhi for his services on board ship. More surprising was the purse handed to her by Prince Ryce, for her care of his niece. It felt astonishingly heavy. She had not yet opened it, and worried incessantly about being robbed.

Now that is a new anxiety to have, she thought. *How odd.*

Once in the port, Saker, in his role as Ardronese Prime, arranged for them to stay at the local Va-faith cloister. While the others adjourned to the portside inn to order a meal, he went to book a passage to Ustgrind for a couple and their child. Afterwards, he visited the oak shrine and had a long and troubled conversation with its shrine keeper. When he finally arrived at the inn, he was subdued.

"What's the matter?" Sorrel asked, handing him a plate of bread, cheese and pickles. "You look pale."

"I just had a serious conversation with Cob Thyme. She's the shrine keeper here." He glanced at Piper, but she wasn't paying him any attention. "We discussed ridding someone of a sorcerous contamination. I asked for permission to try it in her shrine, in case we need to tap added power from the Way of the Oak. Cob wasn't happy with the idea. In fact, she said outright that killing a sorcerer's offspring was surely safer than trying to cure her. After that she disappeared for a while into the back of the shrine – to pray about it, she said. When she came back, she said all right, we could try."

"What changed her mind?" Sorrel asked.

"I think she communicated with the unseen guardian."

They exchanged glances, wondering if that was a glimmer of hope. They all knew the shrine keeper was right. It would be safer. But how could they even consider such a solution? It was Piper's life! However, if an unseen guardian approved, then maybe . . .

"Quite apart from Piper," Saker said softly, "there's Prince Karel. Anyway, she said to come back this evening after she'd made arrangements. I'm not sure what that means."

"Did you get the boat tickets?" Ardhi asked. "When do we leave Betany?

"Yes. On the packet boat, leaving with the tide, mid-morning. By the way, I thought it was more politic to say you're a family. I think that's what you ought to do once you get to Ustgrind, too."

"I might have trouble explaining how I have a child of almost three, when I was not expecting a baby last time I was there," Sorrel pointed out. "Would you like some bread, love?"

This last was directed to Piper, who had been patting the cat over by the fire, but was now climbing up on Saker's knee. She drummed her heels against him. "Want!"

Saker cocked his head at her.

"Please, some bread, Papa Saker."

Smiling at her, he tore off a piece from the loaf for her before he turned his attention back to Sorrel. "If the subject comes up, say you met Ardhi when he was working for Uthen Kesleer and you were the Regala's handmaiden. Be vague."

"That's hardly going to work, considering Piper's age," she said.

"True," Saker conceded, "but once you've talked to Mathilda, and depending on what she wants, you might find it better to pass off Piper as a child at least nine months younger than the prince-regal. It will discourage any idea of twins, for a start, if the Regala is worried about anyone thinking of that possibility."

Yet another lie. But did it matter? "There's no reason we can't be married, is there," Sorrel said, making it a statement rather than a question.

"In fact, rather than as a fiction? No, of course not," Saker said.

"You're a cleric. Who better than the Ardronese Prime to perform a wedding ceremony?"

"I do have the Prime's seal with me."

"Do women ask men to marry them here?" Ardhi asked, interested. "In Chenderawasi, it's always the man's father who goes to the woman's mother and—"

"Oh, puddle it, Ardhi. We are getting married. We don't have parents, either of us, and if I waited for you to ask me directly, I'd die of old age still unmarried."

"Do you *really* want to wed this termagant?" Saker asked Ardhi, amused.

"Can you suggest anyone else suitable?"

Sorrel pulled a face at them. "Oh, curdle the both of you. Be serious! Let's do it, Ardhi. Now. At least we could be honest when we say we're wed, as we'll have to do in Lowmeer. They are much more persnickety about who's bedding whom there. We can marry here in the shrine, with documents supplied by the chief cleric of Betany, signed and stamped by the Prime. How much more respectable can one be?"

Ardhi glanced at Piper, and laughed.

"All right, it would be more respectable if the date preceded the birth date of our supposed daughter, but still, isn't Va-faith happy to legitimise relationships?"

"Indeed. You don't have a hope, Ardhi. Grin and bear it."

"What's marry? And what's a – a – term-grunt?" Piper asked, which left them laughing.

Respectable the procedure that afternoon may have been, elaborate it was not. Their simple vows were said, while touching the branch of the shrine-oak known as the wedding bough. The ceremony was witnessed only by Saker and an old man who happened to be praying at the shrine. The shrine keeper was nowhere to be seen.

After that, they signed the registration book at the town cleric's office – in practical terms, that was all it took: a few minutes of their time. When they stepped out into the empty street, dusk had dimmed the sky and lamps were being lit inside the portside houses, the light shining through windows to make twinkling paths across the water.

"Wedding ceremonies last at least three days in Chenderawasi," Ardhi remarked. "Are you sure we are married?"

"You have it on the best authority," Saker said. "Me. Don't try and wriggle out of it."

"I had a big wedding once," she told them, slipping her hand into Ardhi's. "Believe me, it's not the event that matters."

Saker glanced down at Piper, standing at his side, holding his hand. "I do believe it would be best if I look after you tonight, Piper, my love. Would you like to hear the story about the kitty who sailed to the Summer Seas by accident?"

"Yes!" She raised a dimpled face to his and grabbed his hand. "Yes!"

"But before that, we have something to show you," he said. "Let's go back to the oak shrine."

The underside of the tree shrine was lit by several candle lamps hanging from boughs, and the keeper greeted them unhappily when they returned. She was a tiny woman, a head shorter than Sorrel, with a tangle of grey hair in a matted mass down her back. She wrinkled her nose in distaste when she saw Piper. "This is the child?" she asked.

"Yes," Saker replied.

Ardhi lifted Piper up to sit on one of the low boughs. She'd picked up an acorn from the ground and was playing with it.

Cob Thyme tilted her head, looking at her. "There's no doubt what she is?"

"None." Saker removed the leather thong from around his neck, unstoppered the bambu and tipped the piece of Chenderawasi plume into his palm.

Piper glanced up and saw it. She reached out to seize it. "Pretty! Mine?"

As her hand closed over the piece, she went rigid with shock, then screamed. She opened her fist and the feather drifted to the ground. In the centre of her palm, a black smudge had appeared, an ugly, grimy mark. She stared at it in shock. "Don't like that! Don't want!"

"She means the smutch, not the feather," Sorrel said, as she gathered the child into her arms. "Hush, darling, everything's fine." Over the top of Piper's head, her gaze pleaded for help.

Saker picked up the feather. "Piper, sweetheart, this will take the smutch away, if you let it."

Piper had buried her head in Sorrel's shoulder, and after a moment she peeped out to look at him. "Feather's pretty. Can I have it?"

Hold out your hand like this, palm up," Ardhi said, showing her.

She did as he asked, and Saker laid the feather on top of the smutch. "The oak tree gave you an acorn for one hand," he said, "and now you have a feather from Ardhi's land in the other. Think about how beautiful they are, and that black smutch will go away and it will never come back, because you don't want it there, do you?"

She shook her head. "Don't like it." She brought her cupped hands together, enclosing the feather and the acorn tight in her grip.

Above their heads, wind swept through the tree, swaying the

branches and rustling the leaves. One of the lamps blew out and the others oscillated, sending shadows eerily dancing. Out of nowhere, biting cold swept along the boughs and spilled to the ground. Leaves fluttered down, a few at first, a patter of them, then more and more into a shower, their stalks beating against their faces, until there was a storm of whirling, curling leaves and twigs. A hail of acorns followed.

"What have you done?" Cob screamed at Saker.

Piper howled. Ardhi and Sorrel bent over her protectively, Ardhi holding his kris in his hand.

Cob shook a fist at Saker. "You've killed it! You slaughtered my tree!"

Saker pushed Piper into Sorrel's arms. "Get her out of here," he cried as acorns bounced off their heads and shoulders.

She and Ardhi ran for the open ground with the child. Behind them, Saker grasped Cob Thyme by the arm, thinking to help her out from under the oak.

She resisted, breaking away. "Don't touch me," she said, turning towards the trunk. "I die with my oak!"

He hesitated. A branch cracked like the sound of a gunshot and fell, snapping other branches as it crashed from the canopy down through the tree. When it hit the ground on the other side of the trunk, he felt the thud of it reverberate through his feet. All but one of the candle lanterns blew out.

"Cob!" he called. "Come with me." He dashed after her, but overhead another branch broke and fell, sending shards and spears of wood pouring down from above. The bulk of it fell between him and Cob, fracturing into smaller splinters as it bounced on the ground. He caught a glimpse of a figure against the trunk of the tree, but just then the last candle lantern was knocked down, more branches snapped and the shrine was plunged into darkness, full of tumult and turbulent fury.

He stumbled away, tripping and blundering until he was out in the open and Ardhi was grabbing his arm, asking if he was all right. Before he could reply, another crack of the dying tree shattered the night and the whole area lit up with light, as delicately beautiful and mellow as a witchery glow. The remaining great boughs and limbs of the shrine-oak were a skeleton against a starry sky, edges gleaming with a delicate tracery of blue. Translucent light enveloped what was left of the tree and expanded outwards until they were all bathed in the glow.

Piper stopped her crying. She held out her hand, the same one that had clasped the feather. Her palm glowed until it looked as if she was pulling the light from the tree, and indeed gradually the light did fade, limb by limb. As each branch and twig lost its colour, it disappeared, melting away into the darkness. The last vestige of glowing light was a band connecting a surface root to Piper's outstretched hand. The child, unmoving, was entranced. Finally that last beam of blue left the tree.

"Mama," she said, "I like that pretty colour!"

The light winked out into her palm and there was a moment of pitch darkness when they all saw the after-image of the glowing tree. Townsfolk arrived then, hustling from nearby houses, carrying lanterns, everyone asking in alarm what the noise had been. Had a branch fallen? They'd heard such a cracking . . . !

"The oak," Sorrel whispered to Saker and Ardhi, horrified. "*It's not there.*"

She hadn't spoken loud enough for anyone else to hear, but someone behind screamed. "Where's the oak? Where's the shrine?"

Where the tree had stood, there was just a heap of leaves and a few broken branches, the ones that had fallen first. Of the bulk of the oak, of the trunk, of Cob Thyme, there was no sign. Someone began to wail.

Sorrel turned to Saker in panic. "Did – did Piper – did sorcery—"

For a long moment, shocked beyond measure, he didn't reply. Then he said, "Piper, show me your hand, the one with the dirty mark."

Piper happily held out her closed fist. Saker unfolded her fingers. The mark was gone. Of the feather and the acorn, there was no sign.

Ardhi frowned as a larger crowd began to gather, the number of lanterns doubled and the babble and wailing around them increased. "Her sorcery didn't destroy the tree, did it?" he asked in a whisper. He was more puzzled than believing.

"No," Saker said softly. "My guess is that the unseen guardian chose to sacrifice the oak and the shrine to destroy Piper's sorcery. It was done using *sakti* and witchery." He looked around. "Take them back to our rooms, Ardhi. I'm the Prime and I have to calm people – account for this somehow. Find some lie to tell . . ." He put an arm around Sorrel. "Everything will be all right."

"But why—? Why like *that*?"

He shrugged. He had no idea.

Va only knows.

By the time Saker returned to the Va-faith cloister, it was an hour past dawn. He found Ardhi and Sorrel in the dining hall, alone.

"Where's Piper?" he asked.

"She has charmed the nuns," Sorrel said, "and they have taken her into the kitchen to eat griddle cakes. She's fine. In a much better state than we are."

"The shrine really has gone," he told them. "But there's a young sapling already shooting up where it was, amidst all the broken branches."

A tear trickled down Sorrel's cheek.

He laid a hand over hers. "In time, there'll be another tree, another shrine, probably with the same unseen guardian."

"It'll be a long while, though, won't it?"

"Fifty years perhaps, before the new oak will have gathered enough power to grant witcheries."

"And Cob Thyme?" she asked, wiping her cheek with the back of her hand.

"Her remains were there in among the debris. The shrine will have a new keeper one day."

"Oh, Va." She inhaled, eyes closed. "That blue light . . .?"

"I believe the unseen guardian converted the power of the Way of the Oak within the tree into that witchery glow, then used it to douse the sorcery in Piper."

"The guardian sacrificed the tree and the keeper? Is that what we have to look forward to in order to save Prince-regal Karel? Another shrine dying? Another shrine keeper dead?"

"We can only hope there will be a similar unseen guardian from a water shrine who will be prepared to do the same thing for Prince Karel. And seeing that we know now that unseen guardians communicate with one another, I think it likely that will happen."

"That's . . ." Grief-stricken, she groped for the right words. "That seems so . . . extreme. A whole shrine gone. A keeper killed!"

"The guardian could have murdered Piper. It was his – her? – choice to kill the shrine instead. We made that choice possible because we had the feather. They could sacrifice a child, or one of their own. Either way sorcery died."

There was a long silence as the three of them exchanged glances.

"I am so grateful," Sorrel whispered. "Such a sacrifice . . . What can I say?"

"Piper has been blessed," Ardhi said. "And so have we."

None of them gave voice to their shared thought: what if a different shrine guardian made the opposite choice when it came to the prince-regal?

They stood at the stern of the packet as it sailed out of Betany harbour bound for Ustgrind, capital of Lowmeer, watching as the figure of Saker on the wharf grew smaller and smaller. Seagulls swooped and screeched around the bay, tens of them at first, then larger numbers. Terns skimmed the water, wingtips clipping the wavelets as they crisscrossed the white foam of the ship's wake back and forth, wailing cries without end or purpose. In the sky behind the town, ravens and jackdaws and crows circled and argued in twisting, streaming flocks.

Piper clapped her hands. "Birds! Look at all the birds!"

"Sweet Va," Sorrel muttered, disturbed. "He's doing that."

"It can't be deliberate."

"No. Oh, rattle it, Ardhi – this is tearing him apart. He can't control his pain and the birds feel it. Why did he have to stay? He didn't *want* to be Prime."

"No."

She caught his unease. "You know something I don't?"

"Not really, but I've been thinking. There's only one answer that makes any sense. King Ryce wanted him to be Prime. Fritillary favoured it too, once she knew he wouldn't work directly for her. One of them forced him."

"I don't think Fritillary would have *forced* him. And how could Ryce have done so? Saker could just have said no!"

"But he didn't, did he?" He looked down at Piper. "Did King Ryce know she is Regala Mathilda's daughter—?"

"Not that I know of."

"Juster knew," he pointed out.

"And Juster and Ryce are friends – oh, we have been blind." Her eyes blurred with tears. "Of course Ryce could have forced him. 'Do what I want, or I take Piper away from you all. I'm her uncle.'"

"Could he know that Sorrel Redwing is wanted for murder in Ardrone? That would be another hold over Saker."

"I—" She paled. "It's possible."

"Saker agreed to the price. There's nothing we could have done."

"But why didn't he *tell* us?"

"He thought it better that we be upset with him than that we know the extent of his sacrifice."

She winced.

"It's not the end of the ternion," Ardhi said gently. "We'll all be together again. He limited his royal service to ten years, don't forget."

He rested a hand on Piper's head as the figure on the wharf dropped away behind. Above, the seabirds wheeled and screamed on the same wind that dried Sorrel's tears as they ran down her cheeks.

42

Guarding the Future

At Fritillary's request, backed by a letter of introduction from Prime Saker Rampion, temporary accommodation at the Lowmian Faith House was made available to Ardhi, Sorrel and Piper when the packet sailed into Ustgrind a sennight later.

Prime Mulhafen personally made them welcome. "The Regala is already expecting you," he assured them. "A letter from Pontifect Fritillary came a few days ago, asking me to arrange an audience for you when you arrived. I'll send a message today to say you are here."

"Your Eminence," Sorrel said, "we do have one more request of you. Our departure was hurried. Not so long ago, we were in hiding, and then we took part in the battle of the River Ard. We have little luggage and do not have appropriate clothing for a visit to the Lowmian court. I wonder if you could advise us—"

Before she had even finished the question, he had the answer. "Oh, we have entire rooms devoted to non-clerical clothing! You are welcome to take whatever you will, at no cost." She must have looked astonished because he explained, "All acolytes and novices have to divest themselves of their street clothing when they enter our ranks. Much of it we give to the poor, but the more elaborate clothing . . . I will arrange for you to be shown what we have."

Three days later, a sealed letter was delivered to Sorrel from the Regala, saying she would meet with her, alone, in Ustgrind Castle the following day.

"*Alone?*" Ardhi asked, glancing to where Piper napped on their bed. "I can understand that she might not want to meet me, but doesn't she want to see Piper?"

"Apparently not."

"I don't like the smell of this."

"Surely if she doesn't want to see her daughter it's a good sign for us. She will leave Piper in our care!"

"I want to come with you."

"Mathilda is not going to do anything to me, not when the Pontifect, two Primes and her brother the king all know we are here with their blessing."

"I'm coming with you, nevertheless. And so will Piper."

"Making a statement, are we? A family." She hugged him tight. "We can see how far you get, I suppose . . ."

As they threaded their way through crowded streets the following day, she was amused to notice that although people still dressed in unadorned garments, there was one change that reeked of Mathilda's influence. Colour – even bright red – had crept into the women's head-dresses. Just as astonishing was the way hair was beginning to escape from under coifs and snoods and wimples to flutter boldly at the edges of a face, or cascade in curls down a back. Men's fashion was apparently only one step behind, for they now adorned their sensible black hats with ribboned cockades of colour, and she'd seen several rich merchants with coloured lace or embroidery around their cuffs and collars.

Oh, Mathilda, how ever did you do it? Regal Vilmar Vollendorn would be glaring on the other side of his royal tombstone!

She was now clad in a dress of fine grey linen which had perhaps once belonged to a well-to-do burgher's daughter, worn with a cloak lined daringly with red silk, while Ardhi resembled a sober young man from a wealthy merchant family, with gold buckles on his shoes and a gold pin in his velvet cap. Piper was more plainly dressed in her ordinary clothes, with her circlet covered by the high neck on the bodice. They had all agreed that she continue to wear it all the time, just as an added precaution.

At the castle's main gate, and then again at the entrance to the inner bailey, they were admitted without question on the strength of the Regala's letter. At the door to the keep, however, the guard questioned Ardhi and Piper's presence and sent a messenger up to the Regal's solar. In the end, Ardhi and Piper were conducted to a waiting room on the ground floor, while Sorrel was taken upstairs to the Regal's private reception room. The footman who accompanied her, Machiel, was someone who had once known her well.

"I didn't think we'd ever see you again," he remarked. "We heard you stole something from the Regal's solar and ran away!"

She raised a sharp eyebrow. "Now does that sound at all likely? I would not repeat that calumny, if I were you. I'm here at the Regala's invitation and a rumour like that would reflect badly on the Regala's wisdom."

He paled. "Of course. Forgive me."

"Gossip – it's horrid, isn't it?" She smiled to show there were no hard feelings and chatted to him about what had happened to various servants since she'd left.

Mathilda was waiting for her. Once Machiel had gone, and the door was closed, Sorrel sank into a respectful curtsey. "Your Grace," she said. "I'm glad to see you in good health."

"Oh, don't start that," Mathilda said. "I am so sick of protocol!" She came forward to take Sorrel's hands in hers. "I have missed you, and I worried myself sick over what happened to you. I want to know everything, from the moment you left here. *Everything*. The Pontifect has been infuriatingly vague."

She's turning on the charm! "Of course. Whatever you wish to know. Piper is here with my husband. If you'd like to see her . . ."

Mathilda made a gesture of negation with a hand. "Just the story."

"It's a very long one," she said needlessly. "And I have two letters for you." She extracted them from the basket she carried. "From Pontifect Fritillary and from King Ryce. And there's a packet. That's from Lord Juster Dornbeck." She held it up. "I believe it contains fresh spices. He's the king's minister of trade and navy now, although he swears he will be back at sea in a year or two."

Mathilda waved it away impatiently. "Yes, yes, but it is the *story* I want to hear. Sit down, and tell me everything."

Almost three years had to be condensed into a coherent tale, and there were times when she had to backtrack, and parts she had to leave out. Servants came, bringing hot possets and sweetmeats, and much later to light the fire when the day grew colder. Each time, as soon as they were gone, Sorrel continued.

When speaking of the Chenderawasi, she was deliberately vague about magic plumes, and tried to give the impression – without actually lying – that the rulers were people rather than birds: people with the ability to imbue physical objects, such as the necklet and the plumes and Ardhi's kris, with magic. When relating what happened on the island, she exaggerated the powers of those people to destroy unwanted ships and sailors and factors.

And all the while she wondered why Mathilda asked only once about her daughter, wanting to know if "the child" was pretty, but her interest appeared impersonal, indifferent. She did comment that Piper was a ridiculous name, and what had she, Sorrel, been thinking of?

When a nurse brought in Prince-regal Karel to see his mother, Mathilda played with the boy for a few minutes while Sorrel watched. She didn't think he bore much of a resemblance to Piper, who was smaller framed and had dark curly locks, compared to Karel's robust build and fair, straight hair.

After a few minutes, Mathilda told him she was busy and the nurse carried him out, protesting. "It is always this way," Mathilda said with a sigh. "I don't have enough time to spend with him, poor lamb."

Sorrel had not yet related what happened at the Betany shrine when the Regala sat back in her chair, tapping her fingers on the padded arms and said, "Understand this. My hold on the Basalt Throne is tenuous. The Lowmian nobility don't like a woman having so much power. They don't like an *Ardronese* royal having so much power. I have to prove myself, again and again and again. I walk a narrow path, and on either side there are hunting dogs waiting to taste my blood."

"I can understand that," she said neutrally.

"It's strange, but do you know who helps me most? Lady Friselda! She's so scared of penury, of having to leave the comforts of court, so frightened that her granddaughter will not make a good marriage if her grandmother loses her standing here, that she will do almost anything to help me. I used to hate her so, and now she is my only reliable, albeit self-interested, ally."

Mathilda's lips twisted in a dry, humourless smile as she continued. "Deremer is on his way back to Lowmeer with the remains of his Dire Sweepers, did you know? He's another ally, afraid I'll use what I know to bring his family down. I won't, of course; I shall use him, the way I use Friselda. One word from me about him and the other Sweeper families, and their support of Bengorth's Law, and they are dead and buried. One word from them about the crime of the Vollendorns and Bengorth's Law, and Prince-regal Karel and I are dead and buried. So we do our little gavotte, each step carefully planned to prop each other up and never to let the secrets escape into other ears."

Her fingers continued their mesmerising tapping. "I keep everything inside me. I speak to no one about any of it. I have kept *your* secret. But no mistake, I am utterly ruthless when it comes to the welfare and future of my son. He *will* be Regal one day. He will be the greatest Regal this land has ever seen. Do nothing – any of you – to jeopardise that, or I'll set my Sweeper dogs on your trail. And their fear of me is such that they will obey. Do you understand that?"

"Perfectly." She kept her tone dry.

"There are some things I cannot risk," Mathilda continued. "If I acknowledge to the world that I bore twins, people will wonder what else they don't know. Perhaps they will begin to wonder if Karel really is Vilmar's son. If Piper appears at court as some unknown girl, perhaps people will see her resemblance to me or to her brother. I cannot risk that. I do not want to ever see her. The court must never see her."

"They don't look at all alike."

"I did think of asking King Ryce to raise her at his court, as his by-blow, or something similar, but I think that's too risky too."

Why couldn't the woman think of Piper's well-being for once, instead of her own? Sorrel's thought was an angry one, and she had to push it away to keep her temper. "Your Grace, she has been raised by Saker, myself and my husband. We love her and the two of us will continue to raise her – as our own, if that is your desire." Her heart was racing under her breastbone.

Dear Va, what will I do if she says no? She could take Piper, and then have her killed as soon as we turned our backs . . .

Sorrel felt sick, horrified both that the idea had occurred to her, and that she couldn't quite convince herself that it was unjust and undeserved.

Mathilda's regard was thoughtful. "This husband of yours – he's a lascar. That's a common sailor. But the Pontifect's letter said he is a royal in his own country."

"They use another word for their rulers, but yes. He was his grandfather's heir to what we would call a duchy, I suppose." If there was one thing she knew, it was that nobles and princes thought that bloodlines were important, so she had no qualms about inflating Ardhi's importance. "He's also a scholar and studied such matters as navigation and commerce at one of the world's greatest universities. He will do anything for Piper, just as you'd do anything for Prince-regal Karel."

"You can keep Piper, on the condition that she is never told who she is, nor ever allowed anywhere near the court, or her brother."

Waves of relief, followed by guilt, then sheer irritation, left Sorrel weak-kneed. "She will be well-loved and cared for, I swear. But what of the morality of her never knowing her twin brother?"

"What of it?" Mathilda shrugged. "What the two of them don't know won't worry them. Naturally, I will see to it that you are paid a stipend to cover her care. I shall tell the treasury it is a pension for your past services, as compensation for the false accusation made against you for stealing the feathers from the Regal's fan."

"Thank you, my lady." She inclined her head, her relief still unknotting the tension in her every joint even as her irritation grew. It was time to change the subject. "If I may, there is another matter that we need to discuss. More serious."

Mathilda arched her eyebrow. "Whatever could be more serious?"

Sorrel blinked. Surely Fritillary had told her that both the twins had been identified as potential sorcerers?

Of course she had!

She resisted a desire to grind her teeth. "I would think the fact that either, or both, of the twins could come into their sorcerous powers *was* more serious."

"They must have been besmirched while I was in the family way. Fox must have sent one of his sons to court to – to contaminate them before they were even born."

Sorrel resisted an urge to roll her eyes. "It doesn't matter how it happened." There was nothing to be achieved by arguing *that* point.

"The Pontifect told me, and you just confirmed it, that the Chenderawasi circlets will prevent any problems developing!"

"We *hope* so, but we are not sure how effective it will be. There are no guarantees. Necklets can be removed anyway. Once removed, no sorcerer would want to wear it again, would they?"

"What are you trying to say? You've just told me that you have a feather piece to use as well. Surely—"

"Your Grace, we have fought a long and damaging war to rid the hemisphere of the Foxes and their Grey Lancers. No one wants to see that again. The idea of a sorcerer on the Basalt Throne is unthinkable. If anyone found out that the prince-regal was—"

"By all the acorns on the oak, will you come to the point?"

"We think that the surest way to rid the prince-regal of his sorcerous stain is to use the feather piece we have, to use it *now*. But it might involve the destruction of a water shrine, and the death of its shrine keeper."

As she explained exactly what had happened at the oak shrine in Betany, Mathilda paled. By the time she'd finished, the Regala was on her feet, staring angrily out of the window. "I can't countenance the destruction of the Ustgrind shrine! Think of the scandal!"

"Think of the shrine keeper."

"If a shrine keeper knew about . . . all this, they'd have to die anyway," she snapped. "Besides, who do you think would get the blame for the disappearance of a water shrine and its spring? Your lascar would have to be there, wouldn't he? And he'd be the logical catspaw. And of course, so would I, the Ardronese usurper of power, who allowed the heir to be in the presence of wicked foreign sorcery!"

"I think you need to speak to the shrine keeper of the Ustgrind shrine."

"I can't do that! How could I trust him? What if he questioned Karel's parentage? What if he made a connection between Piper and Karel, because of what happened in Betany? He'd know about that, wouldn't he? You just told me unseen guardians talk to one another."

"Yes, but I'm not sure guardians tell their shrine keepers everything."

"The shrine keeper of the main Ustgrind spring does not like me, and I will *not* go to him. Especially as I would apparently be suggesting that he commit suicide in the interests of my son, who just happens to be a sorcerer."

Mathilda folded her arms and glared. Sorrel knew that look; there was no way the Regala would change her mind. She had to think of something else. She said carefully, "There will be a guardian and a shrine keeper somewhere who will make the sacrifice for the well-being of the Way of the Flow."

Mathilda brightened. "Our palace in the hills – that has a small waterfall shrine! Only the local staff go there. The shrine keeper adores Karel. She would do anything for him!"

Sorrel crushed a desire to judge her for her callousness. "When will you be going there next?"

"We always go in the spring, when the flowers are out. Can it wait till then?"

"The sooner the better, but yes, if that's the only way you will do this."

"It is."

"We will go with you when the time comes. But you must realise this: the prince-regal will have to be closely watched even afterwards, especially through the years just before he reaches maturity. That is when sorcery usually starts to manifest itself. We think he should continue to wear the circlet. Ardhi's Chenderawasi kris will tell us if it fails. At least, that is our hope. But the kris has to be in proximity with the wearer." Sorrel locked her gaze on Mathilda's before adding, "As often as possible."

Mathilda's eyes narrowed. "Are you saying I have to allow – on a day-to-day basis – your foreign husband around the heir to the Basalt Throne?"

"Well, not every day, but often might be a good idea," she said, almost spitting the words out, "don't you think?"

"But he's a lascar!"

"Indeed. A very handsome one. A brave one. And no fool. An asset to any court, in fact. It wouldn't have to be *every* day. Perhaps several times a month."

Mathilda glowered. "I'd forgotten how very *rude* you can be, Sorrel."

Containing her fury only with an effort, she replied, "Your Grace, if anything does go wrong with the feather's cleansing of Prince Karel, or the circlet's protection of him, something which neither the kris nor Ardhi can fix, then you will have to seek help from the Chenderawasi Islands."

"What are you trying to say? You are beginning to sound like an emissary of a nation of the Va-forsaken Hemisphere!"

"They *will* help – *if* our traders and sailors have been treating them with respect and fairness, and *if Ardhi asks them to*."

Mathilda stared at her blankly.

Sorrel said nothing.

"You mean that I have to depend on Ardhi's goodwill?"

"Yes. And also on Lowmeer having a cordial relationship with Chenderawasi. Which might be advisable anyway, considering they have incredible power which we witnessed in one of their ports. They sank one of Uthen Kesleer's newest ships and slaughtered every single member of their crew, all because they killed a bird to obtain its plumes."

Mention of Chenderawasi plumes brought a cautious look to Mathilda's face.

Yes, you remember their power, don't you?

"If it eases your mind, the other hemisphere is not Va-forsaken. Ask the Pontifect. Another point: at the moment, Ardrone has excellent relationships with Chenderawasi, while Lowmeer is anathema to them, thanks to men like Captain Lustgrader. I would suggest that you try to mend that relationship as soon as possible."

"How can I do that? Merchants hold power in Lowmeer. If they blame me for trade disasters, the Vollendorn line ends!"

"There will be disasters if you don't ask for, and follow, Ardhi's advice. Your ships will be sunk in the Summer Seas and Ardronese privateers will regard them as a legitimate target. King Ryce has already agreed to measures that will aid their relationship with Chenderawasi, the sole source of nutmeg. They are making a commitment to trade only through Kotabanta, or other agreed ports."

Mathilda stopped her drumming fingers and slumped back in her chair. Just when her long silence was beginning to be worrisome, she said quietly, "If Uthen Kesleer's ships were the guilty parties, as you say, then Lowmeer has already proven our good intentions. Kesleer is dead, executed for treason against his liege lord, Regal Vilmar, over the plumes. His trading company and his ships are now managed by a consortium in which the Basalt Throne has the largest share."

"Excellent. Then you personally have some say in how Lowmian merchants deal with the islands of the Summer Seas. As Regent for your son, the major shareholder, I imagine you can appoint board members for the trading company. You should suggest that my husband be one of them. I assure you, he has no interest in personal gain, but will strive for a fair and successful commerce in spices. His knowledge and his connections would be invaluable."

Sorrel went to her basket, saying, "I have here something that Prime Saker and King Ryce drew up." She produced several parchment sheets. "It's a code of conduct for all Ardronese ships, their captains and crews, when dealing with those lands."

"And you expect Lowmeer to follow a code drawn up by our arch rivals? Va above, Lowmeer and Ardrone have competed on the high seas from the day men learned to paddle a coracle! I can't order my merchants to act like saintly nuns, while my brother laughs at us behind our backs."

Sorrel shrugged her shoulders. "Of course, it is your choice. I suspect that without Ardhi's advice you will have more sunk ships, less spices available to you, and at a higher price – and no help if Prince-regal Karel in a fit of pique one day removes his circlet."

They stared at each other and neither would drop their gaze.

"You know I killed my husband," Sorrel said, "so you may threaten me with justice back in Ardrone, if you like, Your Grace. But remember, I know who fathered the twins."

"You are *threatening* me? How *dare* you!"

"There's too much at stake to do otherwise."

"What if people look at Piper and think she looks like Karel?"

"I don't think that's going to be a problem. They don't even look to be the same age."

"Even if I wanted you all . . . underfoot, just how do you propose that I explain your presence at court?"

"You've already begun. I left court because I was unjustly accused of stealing the Regal's feathers. With the execution of Uthen Kesleer, everyone knows he gifted sorcerous plumes to the Regal, so I am sure you can make him the villain of the piece. So, that's a start. You

411

can do whatever you like to explain my husband – it might help to say that he is a member of the Chenderawasi nobility who became a hero during the Ard River battle against the last of the Foxes. There are many who would vouch for that, including Sir Herelt Deremer."

"Even so—"

"We have a daughter, let's say nine months younger than your son, and you want the prince-regal to have a playmate of a similar age. The fact that Piper's father is foreign royalty will offer sufficient status to us all." She shrugged. "Whenever did you have a problem with manipulating the truth to suit your aims?"

There was a long silence. Then, "A pox on you, Sorrel Redwing! Sometimes I don't know whether to imprison you, or thank you. I don't know whether to bless the day I met you, or send you back to Melforn to be hanged as a murderess."

It was a capitulation of sorts, and an acknowledgement that she would do her no harm.

Sorrel smiled, suddenly happy. "We've both come a long way since that day. Look at it this way, Your Grace. Who would ever have thought you would sit on the Basalt Throne? The kind of power you once dreamed of is now yours . . ."

"I'm never going to be rid of you, am I?" Mathilda asked with a sigh. "You are going to be a stone around my neck until one of us dies of old age." She shook her head, a rueful half-smile twitching her lips. "Maybe I should be grateful. You are the one person who knows everything, so I don't have to hide a thing when I talk to you."

"Please don't tell me any more secrets. I don't want to know them."

"We have something more than secrets in common," Mathilda said, reaching out to hold her hand. For the first time Sorrel saw genuine terror in her eyes. "We both have, and love, a child who may turn on us one day. Each time we meet, we will look at each other and wonder if we will one day regret our love."

"There'll be no regret." Sorrel raised her chin. "Not ever."

"Not even if you look into those eyes of an innocent child, and you see *who* looks back at you?" She wasn't talking about herself, Sorrel knew. Mathilda was coming as close as she ever would to acknowledging who had fathered the twins.

"Not even then," she said gently. "We will raise these children with

THE FALL OF THE DAGGER

love and kindness, and *that* will make the difference. They are *your* children too. Don't forget that, Your Grace. The Royal House of Betany runs in their veins."

"I have only one child," she said, straightening her back and releasing Sorrel's hand. "Never say otherwise, Sorrel. Not ever."

When Sorrel rejoined Ardhi half an hour later, she waited until they were in the open outside the main entrance of the keep before she spoke.

"We have what we wanted," she said, clutching Piper's hand tightly as they crossed the grassed area of the inner bailey. "Mathilda has agreed to everything. We'll have a house in the city, overlooking the water, and we will bring Piper to the castle twice a sennight to play with the prince-regal. Mathilda still doesn't want to have anything whatsoever to do with Piper personally, though."

He halted in the middle of the bailey and glanced around to make sure there was no one to overhear. "Tell me everything."

"In the city, as foreign nobility and an expert on foreign trade, you will be granted a position of power in the Lowmian Spicerie Trading Company. You will also be numbered among Karel's tutors, in order to give you access to him."

"Nobility? Even though I am a disgraced member of my own family, cast out of my own land?"

"I didn't actually mention that."

He chuckled. "From a mere company language tutor to company director, that's quite a promotion! And what is the Regala Mathilda offering you?"

"Lady-in-waiting, by virtue of my marriage to said foreign noble."

He chuckled. "As if you needed marriage to be important!"

"Don't laugh. She insists that you obtain a suitable surname. Foreign or not, you have to abide by Lowmian conventions."

"You can help me make up one." He chuckled. "We'll think of something suitably pretentious! But you – a lady-in-waiting? Won't that be tedious?"

"Oh, yes, if I actually had to act as one and live at court. But it's just a title enabling me to come and go. I will find ways to amuse myself, never fear. At the moment, raising Piper will suffice!"

"She will be fine," he said, suddenly serious. "Sri Kris has never moved in her presence."

Not yet, she thought. *Maybe never.*

Only time would tell.

"And using the feather piece on the prince-regal?" he asked.

She snorted. "Her Grace has offered the small shrine at her summer palace as a sacrifice because the shrine keeper adores Karel, and not too many people would notice if it suddenly vanished."

"You don't like her much, do you?"

"Not much. I don't think she'll ever change. But then, what kind of a life did others ever extend to her? She was only ever to be a token offered to a monarch on a royal plate." Glancing down at Piper, she added, "At least her daughter will have more choices and a better life, and I think her son has every chance to be cleansed of his father's sorcery."

"A happy ending?"

"Who would have thought?" She smiled and held out her hand to him. Piper grabbed it before Ardhi could, and then the child reached for his hand too.

Together they swung Piper between them, laughing, as they walked away from the keep towards the archway to the outer bailey.

Above, from one of the windows in the Regal's solar, the prince-regal watched, his nose and hands pressed to the glass.

"Who's that, Mama?" he asked, his gaze fixed on Piper.

Mathilda turned to peer out of the window, and frowned when she saw who had caught his attention. "Oh, them," she said dismissively. "No one that matters, darling. Come, sit on my lap and I'll tell you a story about a brave little prince and the treacherous snake who came to a bad end . . ."

Acknowledgements

The first glimmer of this story was born more than twenty years ago in Malaysian kitchens, gardens and forests, while I was delving into activities as diverse as cooking with South-east Asian spices, working in the conservation of tropical birds and exploring remote rainforests and islands.

I began writing the first book of this trilogy at the beginning of 2011, and the last touches were added to this, book three, at the end of 2015. It has therefore consumed five years of my life – at a time when we were also moving house (and continents!) from Asia to Australia.

There have been many people along the way who have helped, in one way or another, too many to thank here, but I do need to mention my long-suffering husband, and my beta readers for this volume: Alena Sanusi, Karen Miller, Tehani Wessely, Donna Maree Hanson and Jo Wake. Then there's Jenni Hill, my wonderful editor at Orbit, and Joanna Kramer and all the rest of the Orbit team who had a hand in producing the three books with their magnificent covers. The maps – which I love – were done by Australian artist, Perdita Phillips.

Most importantly, though, I need to thank you, the reader.

You make it all worthwhile. Every time you buy a book, every time you rate a novel, or write a review, or mention what you are reading to someone else, you make the effort that goes into the creation of stories worth the labour. This year it was you who voted for book one, *The Lascar's Dagger*, to win two speculative fiction awards, the Tin Duck for the Best WA Professional Long Written Work, and the Australian Ditmar Award for Best Novel (which I'm honoured to say I shared with another Orbit author, Trudi Canavan!).

So thank you, dear reader.

extras

orbit

www.orbitbooks.net

about the author

Glenda Larke was born in Australia and trained as a teacher. She has taught English in Australia, Vienna, Tunisia and Malaysia. Glenda has two children and lives in Erskine, Western Australia with her husband.

Find out more about Glenda Larke and other Orbit authors by registering for the free monthly newsletter at www.orbitbooks.net.

if you enjoyed
THE FALL OF THE DAGGER

look out for

THE FALCON THRONE

book one of the Tarnished Crown

by

Karen Miller

Chapter 1

Brassy-sweet, a single wavering trumpet blast rent the cold air. The destriers reared, ears flattened, nostrils flaring, then charged each other with the ferocity of war.

"*Huzzah!*" the joust's excited onlookers shouted, throwing handfuls of barley and rye into the pale blue sky. The dry seeds fell to strike their heads and shoulders and the trampled, snow-burned grass beneath their feet. Blackbirds, bold as pirates, shrieked and squabbled over the feast as children released from the working day's drudgery shook rattles, clanged handbells, blew whistles and laughed.

Oblivious to all save sweat and fear and the thunder of hooves, the two battling nobles dropped their reins and lowered their blunted lances. A great double crash as both men found their marks. Armour buckled, bodies swayed, clods of turf flew. Their destriers charged on despite each brutal strike.

With a muffled cry, his undamaged lance falling, abandoned, Ennis of Larkwood lurched half out of his saddle, clawed for his dropped reins, lost his balance and fell. For three strides his horse dragged him, both arms and his untrapped leg flailing wildly, helmeted head bouncing on the tussocked dirt. Then the stirrup-leather broke and he was free. Squires burst from the sidelines like startled pheasants, two making for the snorting horse, three rushing to their fallen lord.

Heedless of the vanquished, the crowd cheered victorious Black Hughe, youngest son of old Lord Herewart. Hughe let slip his ruined lance, pushed up his helmet's visor and raised a clenched, triumphant fist as his roan stallion plunged and shied. The mid-afternoon sun shimmered on his black-painted breastplate, thickly chased with silver-inlaid etchings.

"Fuck," Balfre muttered, wishing he could reach beneath his own armour and scratch his ribs. "Did a more rampant coxcomb ever draw breath?"

Standing beside him, sadly plain in undecorated doublet and hose, his brother sighed. "I wish you wouldn't do this."

"Someone must," he said. "And since you refuse, Grefin, who else is there? Or are you saying our dear friend Hughe isn't ripe for a little plucking?"

Grefin frowned. "I'm saying the duke will be ripe to toss you into the dankest dungeon he can find once he hears what you've done. You know he's got no love for—"

"Aimery clap his heir in irons?" Balfre laughed. "Don't be an arse, Gref. His pride would never let him."

"And your pride will get you broken to pieces, or worse!"

Hughe had pranced his destrier to the far end of the makeshift tourney ground, so his gaggle of squires could prepare him for the next joust. Ennis was on his feet at last, battered helmet unbuckled and tugged off to reveal a wash of blood coating the left side of his face. Much of his close-cropped flaxen hair was dyed scarlet with it. He needed a squire's help to limp off the field. As the shouting for Hughe died down there came a scattering of applause for Ennis, no more than polite recognition. Harcia's rustics had little patience for defeat.

Balfre shook his head. "You know, if Hughe's a coxcomb then Ennis is a pickled dullard. Any donkey-riding peasant with a barley-stalk could push him off a horse."

"My lord!"

Turning, he looked down at the eager young squire who'd run the short distance from their rough and ready tourney-stall and halted at his elbow.

"What?"

The squire flinched. "Master Ambrose says it be time for your bout, and to come, my lord. If it please you."

"Tell Ambrose to polish my stirrups. *Fuck*. Does he think the joust will start without me?"

"No, my lord," said the squire, backing away. "I'll tell him to wait, my lord."

Balfre watched the youth scuttle to Master Armsman Ambrose. "Speaking of pickled dullards . . ." He grimaced. "I swear, Grefin, that turnip-head must've snuck into Harcia from Clemen. He's witless enough to be one of scabrous Harald's subjects. Don't you think?"

But his brother wasn't listening. Instead, Grefin was raking his troubled gaze across the nearby jostling villagers, and Ennis having his split scalp stitched by a tourney leech, and beyond him the small, untidy knot of lesser men who'd come to test their armoured mettle and now stood defeated, and the heavily hoof-scarred tilt-run with its battered wicker sheep-hurdle barrier, to at length settle on Hughe and his squires. The chuffer had climbed off his destrier and was exchanging his dented black-and-silver breastplate for one unmarked but just as gaudy. It would be a vaunted pleasure, surely, to dent that one for him too.

"Balfre—"

If this weren't such a public place, be cursed if he wouldn't hook his brother's legs out from under him and put his arse in the dirt where it belonged.

"Hold your tongue, Grefin. Or better yet, since you've no stomach for sport, trot back to the Croft and lift your lance there, instead. Plant another son in your precious wife. After all, you've only sired one so far. You must be good for at least one more."

"Balfre, don't."

"I mean it," he said, keeping harsh. Refusing to see the shadow of hurt in Grefin's eyes. "If all you can do is carp then you're no good to me. In truth, it havocs me why you came in the first place."

"To keep you from breaking your neck, I hope," said Grefin, still frowning. "What havocs me is why *you* came! Look around, Balfre. We stand in an open field, far from any great house, and those who cheer and groan your efforts are villagers, herdsmen, peddlers and potboys."

"So you'd deny the local churls an hour or two of entertainment? You're turning mean-spirited, little brother."

Grefin hissed air between his teeth. "It's a question of dignity. Aside from you, and Hughe, and Ennis, who of any note came today to break his lance? Not our cousin. Not even Waymon, and he's a man who'll wrestle two drunk wild boars in a mire."

"Come on, Gref," he said, grinning despite his temper. "Even you have to admit that was funny."

"Side-splitting, yes. And I'm sure the squires who broke themselves to save Waymon from being ripped wide from throat to cock laughed all the way to the bone-setter!"

"Grefin—"

"No, Balfre. You'll listen," his brother said, and took his elbow. "You're Harcia's heir. You owe its duke more than this joust against a gaggle of mudder knights fit only to ride the Marches."

Wrenching his arm free, Balfre looked to where Ambrose and his squires stood waiting. His stallion was there, his unbroken lances and his helmet. Catching his eye, Ambrose raised a hand and beckoned, agitated.

He looked again at his niggling brother. "Where and how I choose to romp is my concern. Not yours. Not Aimery's."

"Of course it's Aimery's concern. He has enough to fret him without you risking yourself here. Those bastard lords of the Green Isle—"

Familiar resentment pricked, sharper than any spur. "You can throw down that cudgel, Grefin. When it comes to the Green Isle, Aimery has his remedy."

"Balfre . . ." Grefin sighed. "He needs more time."

"He's had nearly two years!"

"It's been that long since Malcolm died. But Mother died in autumn, and here we are scant in spring."

"What's Mother to do with it? She wasn't his Steward!"

"No," Grefin said gently. "She was his beating heart. He still weeps for her, Balfre. And for Malcolm. Both griefs are still raw. And now you'd have him weeping for you, too?"

The chilly air stank of churned mud and horse shit. A troupe of acrobats was amusing the crowd as it waited for the last joust. Motley painted canvas balls and striped wooden clubs danced hand-to-hand and man-to-man through the air, the jonglers' skill so great they never dropped even one. From time to time they snatched a cap from a villager's head and juggled that too. The field echoed with delighted laughter.

Balfre glared at them, unamused. Aimery weep for him? That would be the fucking day. "I never knew you had such a poor opinion of my lance-skills."

"This has nothing to do with jousting," Grefin retorted. "Please, Balfre. Just . . . let it go. Who cares what a sophead like Hughe mutters under his breath?"

"I care!" Blood leaping, he shoved his brother with both hands, hard enough to mar Grefin's dark green doublet. "When what he mutters is heard by a dozen men? *I care.* And if you cared for me, *you'd* care."

"I do! But Balfre, you *can't*—"

"Oh, fuck off, Grefin! Before I forget myself and give those gaping churls reason enough to gossip for a week!"

Grefin folded his arms, mule-stubborn. "I don't want to."

"And I don't care what you want."

Holding his brother's resentful stare, unflinching, Balfre waited. Grefin would relent. He always did. There was a softness at the core of him that made sure of it. A good thing for Harcia he wasn't Aimery's heir. Such a softness would leave the duchy's throat bared to faithless men like Harald of Clemen.

At last Grefin huffed out a frustrated breath. "Fine. But never say I didn't warn you," he said, and retreated.

Still simmering, Balfre returned to Ambrose. The Master Armsman near cracked his skull in two, shoving his gold-chased helmet onto his head.

"For shame, my lord," Ambrose said in his rasping voice, come from a sword-hilt to the neck in the desperate, long-ago battle that had made Aimery duke. "Dallying like a maid. This might be a rumptiony shigshag we be at but still you should be setting of a timely example."

Balfre bore with the reprimand. The armsman had served two dukes of Harcia already, thereby earning for himself a small measure of insolence. With a nod, he held out his hands so the turnip-head squire could gauntlet him. The burnished steel slid on cleanly, cold and heavy.

Ambrose started his final armour inspection. "You been watching that rump Hughe?"

"I have," he said, twisting his torso to be certain of no sticking points in his breastplate, which was gold-chased like his helmet and worth more than Hughe's horse. "Nothing's changed since the last time we bouted. He still drops his lance a stride too soon, and sits harder on his right seatbone."

"True enough." Ambrose slapped his pupil's steel-clad shoulder. "And shame be on his tiltmaster. But for all that, he be a brutey jouster. You'll be kissing dirt, my lord, if you don't have a care."

"Then shame be on *my* tiltmaster," Balfre said, flashing Ambrose a swift smirk. "If I do kiss the dirt, I'll have to find myself a new one."

Because this was no formal tourney they lacked judges to keep time or award points and penalties. There was the lone hornblower, though, for the sake of the ragged crowd. As Hughe remounted his restive stallion, one of his squires ran to the man and gave an order. Obedient, the appointed villager blew his horn to alert the crowd to the next joust.

Balfre nodded at Ambrose, then crossed to the wooden mounting block where his destrier was held fast by two squires. As he approached, one of them was doltish enough to shift too far sideways. The stallion lashed out its foreleg and caught the man on his thigh with an iron-shod hoof. Squealing, the squire crumpled.

"Maggot-brain!" said Ambrose, hurrying to drag him clear. Then he gestured at turnip-head. "Don't stand there gawping, you peascod. Hold the cursed horse!"

The excited villagers set up another din of handbells and rattles and whistles. Stood at a distance in their second-rate armour, Ennis and the vanquished mudder knights cast envious looks at the stallion. Quivering with nerves, eager for the joust, the horse tossed its head and swished its thick black tail. As Balfre reached the mounting block it bared its teeth and snapped, strong enough to rip fingers from an unprotected hand.

"*Bah!*" he said, and punched the stallion's dish-round cheek. "Stand still!"

Walking to and fro, the hornblower sounded another rallying blast, coaxing more raucous cheers from the crowd. On the far side of the tourney ground Hughe kicked his roan destrier forward, scattering his squires like beetles. One tottered behind him, awkwardly carrying his lance.

Rolling his eyes, Balfre picked up his reins, shoved his left foot into his stirrup and swung his right leg up and over his jousting saddle's high cantle. The moment he settled on his destrier's back he felt the animal tense beneath him, its breath coming in angry grunts. Not even his heaviest gauntlets muffled its throttled energy, tingling from the curbed bit to his fingers. Through the steel protecting his thighs and lower legs he could feel his mount's barrel ribs expand and contract, and the pent-up furious power in the muscular body beneath him. This was his best horse, and they were well-matched in both temper and skill. Only for Black Hughe would he risk the beast here. But Hughe was owed a mighty drubbing, and to be sure of it he'd chance even this animal.

With a decided tug he closed his helmet's visor then held out his hand. "Lance!"

The weight of the carved, painted timber woke old bruises and strains. Stifling an oath, he couched the lance in its proper place, pricked spurs to his horse's flanks, then softened the bit's sharp bite.

The destrier leapt like a flycatcher, snorting. White foam flew from its mouth. Prisoned within his gold-chased helm, his vision narrowed to a slit and the crowd's roaring a hollow boom, Balfre laughed aloud. Aside from a writhing woman pinned on his cock, was there anything better in the world than a lance in his hand, a grand horse between his legs, and a man before him a handful of heartbeats from defeat?

No. There wasn't.

Snorting, ears pricked, the destrier settled into a stately, knee-snapping prance. He sat the dance with ease, guiding the stallion to the start of the tilt-run with nothing more than his shifting weight and the touch of his long-shanked, elaborate spurs. There he halted, and paid no heed to the crowd's wild cheering or the stallion's threatening half-rears.

"Black Hughe!" he called, loud enough to be heard through his helmet. "You stand ready?"

"I indeed stand ready, Balfre!" Hughe shouted back. "Do I have your pardon now, for the unseating of you later?"

"You'll have my pardon once you answer for your slur."

"My lord," said Hughe, defiant, then closed his own visor and demanded his lance.

As the hornblowing churl took his place midway along the rough tilt-run, horn ready at his lips, the watching villagers and mudder knights fell silent. Only the blackbirds kept up their squabbling, seeking the last grains of seed.

The horn sounded again, a single trembling note. Balfre threw his weight forward as he felt his stallion's quarters sink beneath him, felt its forehand lift, saw its noble head and great, crested neck rise towards his face. It bellowed, a roaring challenge, then stood on its strong hindlegs. Night-black forelegs raked the air. He loosened the reins, gripped the lance and spurred the stallion's flanks. The horse plunged groundwards, bellowing again . . . and charged.

Blurred, breathless speed. Pounding heart. Heaving lungs. Nothing before him but Black Hughe on his horse and the memory of his hateful taunt, dagger-sharp and unforgivable.

Seven thundering strides. Six. Five.

He tucked the lance tight to his side, closed his thighs, dropped the reins. Blinked his eyes free of sweat . . . and took aim . . . and struck.

A double shout of pain, as his lance-head impacted Hughe's armoured body and shattered, as Hughe's undamaged lance struck then glanced harmlessly aside. Pain thrummed through him like the ringing of a great bell, like the clashing of a hammer against the anvil of the world. His fingers opened, releasing the splintered remains of his lance. Then they closed again, on his dropped reins. He hauled on them, unkindly, and his destrier shuddered to a head-shaking halt. A tug and a spurring, and he was turned back to look for Hughe.

Herewart's youngest son was sprawled on the tilt-run's dirt like a starfish, his fancy breastplate dented, his helmet scratched, his brown eyes staring blindly at the sky.

"My lord! My lord!"

And that was Ambrose, the old, scarred man, running hoppy and hamstrung towards him. Turnip-head and another squire scurried at his heels. Hughe's squires were running too, the ones that weren't dashing after his ill-trained horse.

Ambrose, arriving, snatched at the destrier's reins. His pocked face, with its faded sword marks, stretched splitting-wide in a totty-tooth smile.

"A doughty strike, my lord, *doughty*! The best from you I've surely seen! Lord Grefin will bite his thumb, for certain, when he's told what he missed."

Grefin. A curse on Grefin and his milksop mimbling. Balfre shoved up his visor, then kicked his feet free of the stirrups and twisted out of his saddle. The jar in his bones as he landed on the hoof-scarred ground made him wince. Ambrose saw it, but nobody else. He held out his hands for the squires to pull off his gauntlets, and when they were free unbuckled and tugged off his helmet for himself.

"Take the horse," he commanded. "I would speak to Black Hughe."

"My lord," said Ambrose, holding stallion and helmet now. "We'll make ready to depart."

The villagers and mudder knights were still cheering, the ragtag children shaking their rattles and handbells and blowing their whistles. He waved once, since it was expected, then turned from them to consider old Herewart's son. The lingering pains in his body were as nothing, drowned in the joy of seeing his enemy thrown down.

"Lord Balfre," Hughe greeted him, his voice thin as watered wine. His squires had freed him from his helmet and thrust a folded tunic beneath his head. "Your joust, I think."

With a look, Balfre scattered the squires who hovered to render their lord aid. Then he dropped to one knee, with care, and braced an aching forearm across his thigh.

"Hughe."

Black Hughe was sweating, his face pale beneath the blood seeping from a split across the bridge of his nose. More blood trickled from one nostril, and from the corner of his mouth. He looked like a knifed hog.

"I'm not dying, Balfre," Hughe said, slowly. "I bit my tongue. That's all."

"And to think, Hughe, if you'd bitten it the sooner you'd not be lying here now in a welter of your gore, unhorsed and roundly defeated," he said kindly, and smiled.

Hughe coughed, then gasped in pain. "My lord—"

"Hughe, Hughe . . ." Leaning forward, Balfre patted Black Hughe's bruised cheek. Mingled sweat and blood stained his fingers. He didn't mind. They were his prize. "I'm going now. Without your horse and armour. I didn't joust you for them."

"My lord," said Hughe, and swallowed painfully. "Thank you."

"Not at all. And Hughe, for your sake, heed me now. Remember this moment. Engrave it on your heart. So the next time you think to slight my prowess with my lance? You think again – and stay silent."

Hughe stared at him, struck dumb. Balfre smiled again, not kindly. Pushed to his feet, spurning assistance, gave Hughe his armoured back and walked away.

* * *

Temper sour as pickled lemon after his fractious dealings on the Green Isle, Aimery of Harcia disembarked his light galley in no mood for delay. Not waiting to see if his high steward and the others were ready, he made his way down the timber gang-plank, booted heels sharply rapping, and leapt the last few steps with the ease of a man half his age. The surety of steady ground beneath his feet at once lifted his spirits. Ah! Blessed Harcia! Never mind it was little more than a stone's throw from the mainland to the Green Isle. He'd stick a sword through his own gizzards before confessing to a soul how much he hated sailing.

"'Tis good to be home, Your Grace," said his high steward, joining him.

Staring at the busy harbour village of Piper's Wade crowded before them, Aimery breathed in the mingled scents of fresh salt air, old fish guts, people and beasts. Some might call the air tainted, a stench, but never him. It was the smell of Harcia, his duchy, sweeter than any fresh bloom.

"We're not home yet, Curteis. Not quite." He smiled. "But this'll do. Now, let's be off. I can hear the Croft calling."

His party's horses had been stabled against their return at nearby Piper's Inn. With their baggage to be off-loaded from the galley and transported by ox-cart, he led his people to the inn with purposeful haste, greeting the villagers who greeted him with a nod and a friendly word in passing, making sure they knew he was pleased to see them but alas, could not stop . . . only to be halted in the Piper's empty, sunlit forecourt by a wildly bearded man in embroidered rags.

"My lord! Duke Aimery!" Skinny arms waving, the man shuffled into his path. A soothsayer from the old religion, half his wits wandered off entirely. Lost, along with most of his teeth. Twig-tangled grey hair, lank past his shoulders, framed a seamed and sun-spoiled lean face. His pale grey eyes were yellowed with ill health, and sunken. "A word, my lord! Your pardon! A word!"

It was held bad luck to spurn a soothsayer. Aimery raised a warning hand to his four men-at-arms. "Keep yourselves. There's no harm here. See to the horses and you, Curteis, settle our account with the innkeeper."

They knew better than to argue. As he was obeyed, and his scribe and body squire hastily took themselves out of the way, Aimery turned to the ragged man.

"You know me then, soothsayer?"

The soothsayer cackled on a gust of foul breath. "Not I, my lord. The stars. The little frogs. The wind. The spirits in the deep woods know you, my lord. But they whisper to me."

"And what do they whisper?"

Those sunken, yellow-tinged eyes narrowed. "I could tell you. I should tell you. But will I be believed? Do you honour the spirits? Or . . ." The soothsayer spat. Blackish-green phlegm smeared his lips. "Are you seduced by the grey men, my lord?"

The grey men. The Exarch's monks, harbingers of a new religion. It had barely scratched the surface of Harcia, though its roots grew deep in other lands. The soothsayer stared at him, hungrily, as though his reply must be a feast.

"I'm seduced by no one," he said. "Every philosophy has its truth. Speak to me, or don't speak. The choice is yours. But I'll not stand here till sunset, waiting."

The soothsayer cocked his head, as though listening. Then another gusting cackle. "Yes, yes. I hear him. A needle-wit, this Aimery. Prick, prick, prick and see the blood flow." A gnarled finger pointed to the early morning sky, eggshell-blue wreathed in lazy cloud. "Three nights past, my lord. As the moon set. A long-tailed comet. The sign of chaos. Were you witness? It made the black sky bleed."

Three nights past at moonset he'd only just crawled into his borrowed bed on the Green Isle, head aching with arguments. "No. I didn't see it. I was asleep."

"Asleep then, asleep now." Eyes stretching wide, the soothsayer shuffled close. "Time to wake, my lord duke, and see the trouble festering under your roof."

A clutch at his heart. "What trouble?"

"There was a man who had three sons. Lost one. Kept one. Threw the third away. The fool."

"What do you mean? What—"

"Be warned, my lord duke," the old man wheezed. "Unless you open your eyes you will sleep the cold sleep of death." A rattle in the scrawny throat, a sound like the last breath of a dying wife. A dying son. "And no right to say you were not told. You have to know it, Aimery. A long-tailed comet cannot lie."

But a man could. A mad man, his wits scattered like chaff on the wind. Aimery stepped back. "Be on your way, soothsayer. You've spoken and I've listened."

"Yes, but have you heard?" The soothsayer shook his head, sorrowful. Or perhaps merely acting sorrow. Who could tell, with a mad man? "Ah well. In time we'll know."

It was nonsense, of course. He had little time for religion, old or new. But the soothsayer looked in a bad way, so he pulled a plain gold ring from his finger.

"Take this, old man. Buy yourself a warm bed and hot food. And when next the spirits whisper, whisper to them from me that a faithful servant should be better served."

The soothsayer's eyes glittered as he stared at the ring. Then he snatched it, and with much muttering and arm-waving hobbled out of the forecourt.

"Your Grace," Curteis murmured, arriving on soft feet that barely disturbed the raked gravel. "Is aught amiss?"

Aimery frowned after the soothsayer, an indistinct bundle of rags vanishing into the high street's bustle. Mad old men and their ramblings. Throw a stone into any crowd and you'd likely strike at least three.

"No. Can we go?"

Curteis nodded. "Yes, Your Grace. As it please you."

They rode knee-to-knee out of the inn's stable yard in a clattering of hooves, with his body squire and his scribe and his men-at-arms close at heel.

"Be warned, Curteis," he said, as they scattered pie-sellers and cobblers and fishwives before them along Piper's Wade high street, "and share the warning with them that ride behind. I wish to sleep in my own bed under my own roof sooner rather than later. Therefore we shall travel swiftly, with few halts, and should I hear a tongue clapping complaint I swear I'll kick the culprit's arse seven shades of black and blue."

"Yes, Your Grace," said Curteis, smiling. He was well used to his duke.

With the past two weeks fresh in mind, Aimery scowled. "I tell you plain, man, I've heard enough clapping tongues lately to last me till my funeral."

"The lords of the Green Isle were indeed fretsome, Your Grace."

"Fretsome?" He snorted. "Snaggle-brained, you should call them. Vexatious. Full of wind. Especially that cross-grained fuck Terriel."

"Your Grace," agreed Curteis. "Lord Terriel and his noble brothers farted many noisome words. But you set them well straight."

Yes, he did. And woe betide a one of them who again dared defy his judgement. That man, be he ever so lordly, even the great and grasping Terriel, would find himself so handily chastised there'd be scars on his great-grandson's arse.

Bleakly satisfied, still impatient, Aimery urged his iron-dappled palfrey into a canter, then swung left off the high street onto Hook Way, which would lead them eventually to his ducal forest of Burnt Wood. If the rain held off and no mischance befell them, with the horses well rested they'd be in and out of the forest by day's end. Spend the night in Sparrowholt on its far side, leave at dawn on the morrow, ride hard with little dallying and with fortune they'd reach the Croft before sunset.

And so it proved. But when he did at last trot beneath the arching stone gateway of his favourite castle's inner bailey, feeling every one of his fifty-four years, he found himself ridden into yet another storm. For standing in the Croft's torchlit keep, clad head to toe in unrelieved black velvet, was old Herewart of nearby Bann Crossing. He trembled in the dusk's chill, tears swiftly slicking his withered cheeks. Waiting with him, stood at a wary distance, Balfre and Grefin.

"What is this, Balfre?" Aimery demanded of his accidental heir, even as his gaze lingered on his youngest son. His favourite, now that Malcolm was dead. "Why am I greeted with such confusion?"

He'd sent a man ahead, to warn of his arrival and stir the castle's servants to duty. As they hurried to take the horses and relieve Curteis and the scribe of their note-filled satchels, and the men-at-arms waited with their hands ready on their swords, he saw Balfre and Grefin exchange disquieting looks. But before his heir could answer, Herewart let out a cry cracked-full of grief and approached without leave or invitation.

"Your Grace, you must hear me! As a father, and my duke, only you can grant me the justice I seek!"

"Hold," he said to the men-at-arms who were moving to protect him. Then he looked to his steward. "Curteis, escort Lord Herewart within the castle. See him comforted, and kept company in the Rose chamber until I come."

Very proper, though he was also weary, Curteis bowed. "Yes, Your Grace."

"Your Grace!" Herewart protested. "Do not abandon me to an underling. My years of loyalty should purchase more consideration than that. I demand—"

"*Demand?*" Summoning a lifetime's worth of discipline, Aimery swung off his horse to land lightly on his feet. "My lord, be mindful. Not even a lifetime of loyalty will purchase a demand."

Herewart's colour was high, his wet eyes red-rimmed and lit with a burning fervour. "A single *day* of loyalty should purchase the justice I am owed. And be warned, Aimery. Justice I'll have, as I see fit, and from your hand – or there will be a reckoning. This is not cursed Clemen, where *in*justice wears a crown!"

Silence, save for Herewart's ragged breathing and the scrape of shod hooves on the flagstones as the horses hinted at their stables. Aimery looked to his sons. Grefin stood pale, arms folded, lower lip caught between his teeth. There was grief for Herewart there, and fear for his brother. As for Balfre, he stood defiant. He knew no other way to stand.

Belly tight, Aimery looked again at Herewart. "What has happened, my lord?"

"My son is dead, Your Grace," said Herewart, his voice raw. "My youngest. Hughe."

The blunt words tore wide his own monstrous, unhealed wound. "I'm sorry to hear it, Herewart. To lose a son untimely is—"

"You must know he was murdered," Herewart said, bludgeoning. "By your son and heir, Balfre."

"*Liar!*" Balfre shouted, and would have leapt at the old man but for Grefin's restraining hand. "It was ill chance, not murder, and he'd still be alive had you taught him how he should speak of Harcia's heir! The fault is yours, Herewart, not mine, that your son's bed tonight is a coffin!"

Aimery closed his eyes, briefly. Oil and water, they were, he and this son. Oil and flame. *Balfre, you shit. When will you cease burning me?* "What ill chance?"

"None," said Herewart, glowering. "Hughe's death was purposed. Your son challenged mine to a duel and killed him."

"*Duel?*" Balfre laughed, incredulous. "It was a joust! I unhorsed him by the rules, and when I left him he was barely more than winded. How can you—"

"No, my lord, how can *you*!" said Herewart, a shaking fist raised at Balfre. "My son made a ribald jest, harmless, and *you*, being so tender-skinned and pig-fat full of self love, you couldn't laugh and let it go by. You had to answer him with your lance, you had to goad him into unwise confrontation in the company of churls and mudder knights and take your revenge by taking his life! He breathed his last this morning; his body broken, your name upon his blood-stained lips."

Pulling free of his brother's holding hand, Balfre took a step forward. "Your Grace, Hughe's death isn't my—"

Aimery silenced him with a look, then turned. "My lord Herewart, as a father I grieve with you. And as your duke I promise justice. But for now, go with Curteis. He'll see you to warmth and wine while I have words with my son."

Herewart hesitated, then nodded. As Curteis ushered him within the castle, and the inner bailey emptied of servants, squires, men-at-arms and horses, Grefin tried to counsel his brother but was roughly pushed aside.

"Balfre," Aimery said, when they were alone. "What was Hughe's jest?"

His face dark with temper, Balfre swung round. "It was an insult, not a jest. And public, made with intent. I couldn't let it go by."

"Grefin?"

Grefin glanced at his brother, then nodded. "It's true. Hughe was offensive. But—"

"But *nothing*!" Balfre insisted. "For Herewart's son to say my lance is riddled with wormwood, with no more strength to it than a pipe of soft cheese, and by lance mean my cock, never mind we talked of jousting, he questioned my ability to sire a son. He as good as said

I wasn't fit to rule Harcia after Aimery. And that's treason, Grefin, whether you like it or not."

Grefin was shaking his head. "Hughe was wine-soaked when he spoke. So deep in his cup he couldn't see over its rim. He was a fool, not a traitor."

"And now he's a dead fool," said Balfre, brutally unregretful. "And a lesson worth learning. My lord—" He took another step forward, so sure of his welcome. "You can see I had no choice. I—"

"Balfre," Aimery said heavily, "what I see is a man possessed of no more wit and judgement at the age of three-and-twenty than were his when he was *five*."

Balfre stared. "My lord?"

"You killed a man for no better reason than he had less wit than you!"

"But Father – I was wronged. You can't take Herewart's part in this!"

Oh Malcolm, Malcolm. A curse on you for dying.

Aimery swallowed, rage and disappointment turning his blood to bile. "Since last you saw me I have done nothing but ride the Green Isle, hearing complaints and chastising faithless lords who count their own petty needs higher than what is best for this duchy. And now *you*, Balfre, you encourage men to defy my decree against personal combat. What—"

"It was a *joust*!" Balfre shouted. "You've not banned jousting. I was obedient to all your rules. I made sure of a tilt barrier, my lance was well-blunted, and I—"

"And you killed a man, regardless," he said, fists clenched. "Much good your obedience has done you, Balfre. Or me."

Balfre's hands were fisted too. "That's not fair. Father—"

"*Do not call me Father! On your knees, miscreant, and address me as Your Grace!*"

Sickly pale, Balfre dropped to the damp ground. "Your Grace, it's plain you're weary. You shouldn't be plagued with the Green Isle. Appoint me its Steward and I'll—"

"Appoint *you*?" Aimery ached to slap his son's face. "Balfre, if I let you loose on the Green Isle there'd be war within a week."

"Your Grace, you misjudge me."

"Do I?" He laughed, near to choking on bitterness. "And if I were to break my neck hunting tomorrow and the day after I was buried you learned that Harald of Clemen had yet again interfered with Harcian justice in the Marches? Tell me, would you tread with care or would you challenge *him* to a joust?"

"Harald is a cur-dog who sits upon a stolen throne," said Balfre, his lip curled. "Thieves and cur-dogs should be beaten, not cosseted. If Harald feared us he'd not dare flout your authority, or entice Harcia's men-at-arms to break your decrees, or demand unlawful taxes from our merchants and—"

"So you'd challenge him with a naked sword, and slaughter two hundred years of peace." Aimery shook his head, stung with despair. "Never once doubting the wisdom of your choice."

"Your Grace, there's no greater wisdom than overwhelming strength and the willingness to use it."

And so the decision he'd been avoiding for so long, like a coward, was made for him. He sighed. "I know you think so, Balfre. Grefin—"

Grefin looked up. "Your Grace?"

"The Green Isle has been left to its own devices for too long. Therefore I appoint you its Steward and—"

Forgetting himself, Balfre leapt to his feet. "*No!*"

"Your Grace—" Alarmed, Grefin was staring. "I'm honoured, truly, but—"

"Enough, Grefin. It's decided."

"No, it isn't!" said Balfre. "You can't do this. Like it or not I'm your heir. By right the Green Isle's stewardship is mine. You *can't*—"

Aimery seized his oldest son's shoulders and shook him. "I must, Balfre. For your sake, for Harcia's sake, I have no other choice."

"You're a duke," said Balfre, coldly. "You have nothing but choices."

"Ah, Balfre . . ." Run through with pain, he tightened his fingers. "The day you understand that isn't true is the day you will be ready for a crown."

Balfre wrenched free. "Fuck you, Your Grace," he said, and walked away.